John Case is also the author of the novel *The Murder Artist*. He lives in Charlottesville, Virginia.

DANCE OF DEATH

Photojournalist Mike Burke has risked his life in every war zone on earth. But when his helicopter crashes in Africa, he loses his heart to the woman who saves him. That's when he decides it's time to stop dancing with the devil. However, a twist of fate dashes his dreams, leaving him adrift in Dublin with bittersweet memories. But the devil isn't done with him yet . . . An ocean away, Jack Wilson leaves prison burning for revenge, with a dream of his own — only Wilson's dream is the world's nightmare. Driven by his obsession with a Native American visionary, and guided by the secret notebooks of the man said to have 'invented the twentieth century', Wilson dreams of Apocalypse — and plans to make it happen . . .

Books by John Case
Published by The House of Ulverscroft:

THE MURDER ARTIST

JOHN CASE

DANCE OF DEATH

Complete and Unabridged

CHARNWOOD
Leicester

First published in Great Britain in 2006 by
William Heinemann
The Random House Group Limited
London

First Charnwood Edition
published 2007
by arrangement with
William Heinemann
The Random House Group Limited
London

British Library CIP Data

Case, John
  Dance of death.—Large print ed.—
Charnwood library series
  1. Indian dance—Fiction 2. Suspense fiction
  3. Large type books
  I. Title
  813.5′4 [F]

ISBN 978–1–84617–801–6

Published by
F. A. Thorpe (Publishing)
Anstey, Leicestershire
Set by Words & Graphics Ltd.
Anstey, Leicestershire
Printed and bound in Great Britain by
T. J. International Ltd., Padstow, Cornwall

This book is printed on acid-free paper

For Paco Ignacio Taibo, Justo Vasco,
and the Semana Negra crew

PROLOGUE

LIBERIA SEPTEMBER 2003

There was this . . . *ping*.

A single, solitary noise that announced itself in the key of C — *ping!* — and that was that. The noise came from somewhere in the back, at the rear of the fuselage, and for a moment it reminded Mike Burke of his brother's wedding. It was the sound his father made at the rehearsal dinner, announcing a toast by tapping his glass with a spoon.

Ping!

It was funny, if you thought about it.

But that wasn't it. Though the helicopter was French (in fact, a single-rotor Ecureuil B2), it was not equipped with champagne flutes. The sound signaled something else, like the noise a tail rotor makes when one of its blades is struck with a 9mm round — and snaps in half and flies away. Or so Burke imagined. *Ping!*

Frowning, he turned to the pilot, a Kiwi named Rubini. 'Did you — ?'

The handsome New Zealander grinned. 'No worries, bugalugs!' Suddenly, the chopper yawed violently to starboard, roaring into a slide and twisting down. Rubini's face went white and he lunged at the controls. Burke gasped, grabbing the armrests on his seat.

1

In an instant, his life — his *whole* life — passed before his eyes against a veering background of forest and sky. One by one, a thousand scenes played out as the helicopter tobogganed down an invisible staircase toward a wall of trees.

In the few seconds it took to fall five hundred feet, Burke remembered every pet he'd ever had, every girl he'd kissed, every house apartment teacher friend and landscape he'd ever seen. Candyland and Monopoly. Christmas lights and incense, Chet Baker and the stalls along the Seine. His past washed over him in a wave, and kept on coming. As the helicopter sawed through the air, he remembered the dawn coming up behind Adam's Peak, and the three-point shot he'd taken against Park High, the way it rattled the rim with two seconds left on the clock — and the celebration that followed. A shit-shot, yes, but . . . *thank you*, Jesus!

His mother's face appeared like a curtain of rain between his seat and the altimeter, while lines of long-forgotten poetry ran through his head and the smell of gardenias — gardenias? — filled the cockpit.

The pilot yelling. Or not quite yelling . . . screaming. *The pilot is screaming*, Burke thought.

Not that there was anything Burke could do about it. They were going down fast — plummeting really — and only a miracle could save them. Burke didn't believe in miracles, so he sat where he was, listening spellbound as a voice in

2

the back of his head recited notes for an obituary:

Michael Lee Burke . . .
27-year-old Virginia native . . .
award-winning photographer . . .

As the helicopter's undercarriage scraped the tops of the trees, Burke saw his future telescope from fifty years to five seconds. Still, the memories came — only now, he was almost up to date.

Last night, he'd gone out drinking with Rubini. And they'd ended up singing karaoke at the Mamba Point Hotel. Burke sang 'California Stars' to the hoots of some UNMIL types, but he must have done all right because he went home with a Slav agronomist named Ursula who was reliably said to be the last natural blonde in Monrovia. She was probably still asleep in his room, just as he'd left her, arm crooked above her head on the pillow, like a movie star swooning for the cameras.

As a blizzard of vegetation slammed into the windshield, Burke had an epiphany. A 9mm round wasn't going to kill him. What was going to kill him was a tidal wave of bad karma brought on by years of photographing people *in extremis*. Whatever his intentions, however benign they might have been — to expose, to explain — the simple reality was that he'd made his living on other people's despair.

The more painful the images in the photographs he took, the better they sold. That fact did something to a person. The favelas in Rio, the orphanage in Bucharest, the red-light district in Calcutta — he thought he'd been doing a public service when in reality it had all been a kind of well-intended voyeurism.

And now today, barely a week before his twenty-eighth birthday, he was on his way to take pictures at a refugee camp for children who'd suffered amputations in the diamond wars.

Except . . . he wasn't going to make it. He wasn't going anywhere but *down*.

The helicopter dug deeper into the canopy of the forest and Burke wordlessly realized he'd never again take another photograph. One way or another, he was done with that.

Jesus!

Something came through the windshield with a crash and Rubini's forehead exploded, sending a spray of blood and brains through the cockpit. Burke caught a mouthful as the chopper meteored through the trees, bucking, plunging, falling like a box of tools, slamming finally into the waterlogged earth of a swamp.

So this, Burke thought, *is what it's like to be dead* . . . But that didn't make much sense. If you were dead, you didn't *feel* dead. So maybe he was dying. That made more sense because he felt as if every bone in his body was broken. He tasted blood in his mouth. He was shaking. And the world was turning, slowly, round and round.

His eyes flew open and he realized what was happening. The helicopter was revolving on its axis like a bluebottle fly in its death throes. The overhead rotor slashed at the water, the earth,

4

and the trees, then flew apart like a grenade, sending shrapnel in every direction.

The engine coughed, spluttered, and whined, showering sparks through the cockpit.

With great difficulty, Burke fumbled with his seat belt. Even the smallest movement was painful. His body was a bag of broken glass and thorns. And he was covered with blood. It ran down the side of his face, and his shoulders were soaked.

But that wasn't right. It wasn't just blood. He took a deep breath, and choked on it.

Aviation fuel!

His fingers tore at the seat belt, but even as it popped open, he realized it was too late. A soft *whump* announced the fuel's ignition and, in an instant, the cockpit was engulfed. His shirt went off like a flare and, for a moment, it seemed as if the side of his *head* was on fire. Stumbling and falling, he erupted out of the cockpit, tearing the shirt off his chest, staggering blindly until a fallen log caught his foot and spilled him into a pool of shallow water.

Where he lay for hours or days, delirious and suppurating. Incredibly, his burns attracted the attention of bees, who fed on the clear liquid oozing from his skin. Occasionally, he rose to consciousness, only to faint dead away. It was the pain, of course. That and the sight of the apiary embedded in his chest.

Bad karma? Oh, yeah . . .

1

WEST BEIRUT TWO YEARS LATER

They sat on revolving stools at a small plastic table under the proprietary gaze of Colonel Sanders. Sunlight poured through the oversized windows. Behind the Corniche, the beach curled away like a ribbon of gold, and the Mediterranean sparkled.

Hakim, the older man, sat with his hands folded in front of him, like a schoolchild waiting for class to begin. They were beautiful hands, with long and elegant fingers, and they were carefully manicured. 'Too much!' he said, nodding toward the windows.

The younger man, whose name was Bobojon Simoni, screwed his face into a squint, and nodded. 'I know. It's too bright.'

The older man shook his head. 'I meant the glass. If there was a car bomb . . . '

Bobojon nibbled on a chunk of popcorn chicken, then wiped his hands with a paper napkin. 'That was a long time ago. No one's fighting now. It's different.' He balled up the napkin and dropped it on the tray.

His uncle grunted. 'It's always *different*,' he said, 'until something goes off.'

Bo chuckled. He would like to have said something clever, but that wasn't his way and, besides, there was too much noise. A baby wailed in the center of the restaurant. Behind the counter, the manager berated a teary-eyed cashier, while a mix tape of Tony Bennett and Oum Kalthoum floated above the tables.

The older man lifted his chin toward a poster of the KFC colonel, plastered against the window. 'You think he's a Jew?'

Bo glanced around. 'Who?'

His uncle nodded at the poster. 'The owner. He has the lips of a Jew.'

Bo shrugged. He was dressed in a black T-shirt and a pair of carefully ironed Lucky Brand jeans. Mephisto loafers and a Patek-Philippe watch completed the ensemble, all of which had been bought the week before at a shopping mall a few blocks from his new apartment in Berlin.

'If he's a Jew,' his uncle continued, 'the meat's probably halal.'

Like he cares, Bo thought. But what he said was: 'Right.' In fact, Bo didn't know a whole lot about Jews. He'd heard there were a couple in Allenwood, but . . .

'Let's walk,' his uncle said, suddenly disgusted.

Outside, Zero and Khalid sat in the BMW, smoking cigarettes. Seeing Aamm Hakim leave the restaurant with his nephew, they scrambled out of the car to fall in step behind. Nineteen years old, they dressed alike in short-sleeved shirts, running shoes, and jeans. Zero carried a brown paper bag with a grease stain on its side. Khalid swaggered beside him, a Diadora gym bag hanging from a strap over his shoulder.

Since they'd already eaten and weren't going to a soccer match, Bo was pretty sure that the bags held something heavier than sandwiches and a jockstrap.

It was a beautiful day. But then, it was always a beautiful day in Beirut. Just down the coast, near the Summerland resort, he could see windsurfers zipping back and forth under a cloudless sky.

He and his uncle walked arm in arm, heads bent in conversation, moving toward the city's improbable Ferris wheel, past vendors of coconuts and corn on the cob. It was Sunday, and the Corniche was mobbed. There were kids on Rollerblades, lovers and joggers. Girls in abbayas, girls in miniskirts. Syrian commandos lounged against the seawall, preening in their tiger stripes.

'Berlin, it's okay for you?'

Bo nodded. 'Yeah.'

His uncle smiled. 'What do you like best about it?'

'The work.'

'Of course you like the work,' his uncle said. 'I mean, besides the work.'

Bo shrugged. Finally, he said: 'The architecture.'

'Really?'

'Yes. I like it. It's new.'

His uncle walked with his eyes on the ground, his brow furrowed in thought. 'And the pussy?'

Bo nearly choked.

His uncle smiled. 'In Berlin,' he said, 'it's *crazy* pussy!' He took Bo by the arm. 'I am told this.'

Bo couldn't believe it. The color rose in his

9

cheeks. He looked away, mumbling something that even he didn't understand.

His uncle laughed and pulled him closer. Suddenly, he was serious. 'Find a girlfriend,' he ordered. 'German, Dutch — whatever. Take her out. Be seen with her. And get rid of the beard.'

Bo was astonished. 'But . . . it's *haram*!'

His uncle shook his head. 'Do what I tell you. And stay away from the mosques. They're filled with informants.'

It took him a second, but then he understood. And smiled. 'Okay,' he said.

'Your friend — Wilson — he's a *kaffir*?'

'Well . . . ' Bo let the sentence die. There were nicer ways to say that Wilson wasn't a Muslim.

His uncle threw him an impatient look. 'You trust him?'

'Yes.'

Hakim looked skeptical. 'A Christian?'

'He's not a Christian. He's not anything at all.'

His uncle scowled. 'Everyone is something.'

Bo shook his head a second time. 'With him, it's different. He's not religious.'

'Which makes Mr. Wilson . . . what?'

Bo thought about it. Finally, he said, 'A bomb.'

Hakim smiled. He liked melodrama. 'What kind of bomb?'

'A 'smart' bomb.'

The answer seemed to please his uncle, because he stopped at an icecream cart to buy each of them a Dove Bar. When they resumed walking, Hakim asked, 'But this bomb of yours, why does he want to help us?'

'Because he's angry.'

Hakim scoffed. 'Everyone's angry.'

'I know, but . . . Wilson is angry in the right way. We want the same thing.'

A dismissive puff of air fell from his uncle's lips, as he looked down and shook his head. 'I can't believe you'd trust an American.'

'He's not an American. I mean, he is, but he isn't. Wilson's people, they're like us.'

'You mean they're poor.'

Bo shook his head. 'Not just poor . . . ' They paused to watch an Israeli jet slide across the sky, beyond the reach of the anti-aircraft guns hidden in the slums. Nearby, a cloud of pigeons fell upon an old woman with a small bag of corn. 'They're like we used to be. Desert people.'

His uncle scoffed.

'They lived in tents!' Bo insisted.

'You see too many films.'

His nephew shrugged. 'It was a long time ago. But they remember. Just as we do.' Bo was not a man with a large vocabulary, or he might have added 'figuratively speaking.' Because, of course, no one in his family had ever lived in a tent, unless you counted refugee tents set up by the Red Cross. Bo's father was a Cairene laborer who'd emigrated to Albania after the Sixty-seven War. He'd grown up in a two-room flat in a slum on the outskirts of Cairo. So he was an Arab, yes, but not the kind who rode horses or hunted with falcons. As for his mother, well . . . she was the fifth daughter of an Albanian farmer. Muslim, yes. Arab, no.

Still, he *remembered*.

Aamm Hakim sunk his teeth into the Dove Bar's chocolate plating, and resumed walking. 'This Wilson — tell me again how long you've known him.'

There was no hesitation: 'Four years, eight months, three days.'

'Not so long, then.'

Bo chuckled. Bitterly. 'It *seemed* like a long time. Anyway, it was 24/7. We might as well have been married.'

It was his uncle's turn to shrug. 'He'll have to be tested. I won't work with a crazy man!'

'He's not crazy.'

Hakim gave his nephew a skeptical look. 'Not even a little?'

Bo grinned. 'Well, maybe a little.'

His uncle grunted an I-told-you-so. 'In what way?'

'It's just a small thing,' Bo explained, 'but — '

'What?'

'Sometimes, he thinks he's a character in a novel.'

Hakim stared at him, nonplussed. He wasn't quite sure just what it was that his nephew was saying. 'A novel?' he asked.

Bo nodded.

'You mean, like this man, Mahfouz? A novel like one of his?'

Bo bit into his Dove Bar, savoring the interplay of chocolate on vanilla. 'No, Uncle. Nothing as good as that.'

2

The first thing Jack Wilson did when he got to Washington was take a bath. Which was strange. Because baths had never been his thing, not at all. But after nine years of showering under surveillance, the prospect of a long hot soak by himself was irresistible.

So he lay in the water with his eyes half-closed, listening to the faucet drip, transfixed by the silence, mesmerized by the steam. Slowly, the days and nights in prison began to fall away, like blocks of ice calving from a glacier.

One of these days, he thought, *I'll go to a hot spring. Like the ones they have in Wyoming. Just me and the rocks and the water, the trees and the stream. Pine needles. They say it's a whole other world. A world like . . . Then.*

The day replayed itself at its own speed. First, the fingerprinting at the prison in Pennsylvania, then the paperwork, then the dressing out. This last, a joke. Because nothing fit. Just his shoes and his watch. And the watch was dead.

Not that it mattered. Everything that happened in Allenwood, or in any prison for that matter, happened early, and went downhill. There was nothing to do except time, and the badges got you up at dawn to make sure you did

13

every second of it. So you didn't need a watch — you needed a timer. Something that counted backward in years, months, and days.

That morning, when the last gate rolled back, it was about an hour after daybreak. A federal Bureau of Prisons van waited outside the fence, fuming under an iron sky. The driver took him and another guy to a bus stop outside a country store on the outskirts of White Deer. It couldn't have been more than twenty degrees out, and all Wilson had for a coat was the suit jacket he'd gone to prison in.

He'd hurried inside, but he didn't stay long. There was a 'No Loitering' sign on the register, and the cashier had a look on his face that said 'This means you.'

So he and the other guy stood in the cold like a couple of temple dogs, wary of one another, stamping their feet at the entrance to Buddy's Pik 'n Pak. The locals, cannon fodder to a man, wouldn't even look at them.

Was it — were *they* — so obvious?

Well, yeah. There was the van, for one thing, with 'B.O.P.' stenciled on the side. (*That* was a clue.) And the running shoes. No one on the outside wore running shoes in winter — not when there was snow on the ground. And then there was the 'luggage' each of them carried: a cardboard box with duct tape along the seams. No wonder people looked the other way. (Not that looking away would save them. Nothing would save them. Nothing could.)

Eventually, the bus showed up. In a blast of wit, the other guy said something like, 'Well, if it

14

ain't the Long Dog!' (*Get it? Like the bus is a Greyhound?*) They each bought tickets to the Port Authority in New York, which turned out to be as hivelike as any federal prison he'd been in. But it was exciting, too, because it was the first time in years that Wilson could spend money — real money — in a store. So there was a hot dog at Nathan's, and a newspaper at Smith's. After that, he got on a second bus, heading down to Washington.

He rolled in a little after four o'clock, and took a cab to the Monarch Hotel, where there was a room waiting for him, courtesy of Bo. (And a good thing, too. He had less than fifty dollars on him.)

'Everything's taken care of. Room service, minibar, Nintendo . . . ' The clerk smiled at his little joke, then slid a registration card across the desk. 'If you'll just fill this out . . . '

Wilson printed his name, then hesitated when he came to the space for an address. There was a chance, if not a likelihood, that the desk clerk would recognize a phony zip code. But the only zip code he could think of was the P.O. Box at Allenwood, which wouldn't do at all. So he changed the last number to six and made up the rest. *12 Pine St., Loogan, PA 17886.* The clerk didn't blink an eye, which probably meant that he'd never been in prison. If he had, he'd have smiled, because a 'loogan' was slang for an inmate who'd gone nuts.

'Will you need any help with your luggage?'

Wilson looked up. Was this guy dissing him? The cardboard box that held his belongings rested on the floor beside him. 'That's okay,' Wilson said. 'I can carry it myself.'

The clerk cocked his head deferentially, then slipped a Ving Card into the registration folder. Jotting down a room number on the outside, he pushed the folder across the counter, and paused. Looked thoughtful. Frowned. 'I think we may be holding something for you,' he said. Turning away from the counter, he disappeared through a doorway, then reemerged a few seconds later, offering a FedEx Pak as if it were a coronation pillow. 'Welcome to the Monarch . . . '

★ ★ ★

Wilson lay in the tub for half an hour, topping off the hot water with little twists of his left foot. At some point, the temperature of the bath was almost the same as his own so that, with his eyes closed, he couldn't be sure where the water began and he ended. It was as if he'd dissolved.

Asleep, awake, he floated between two worlds and multiple identities. Copworld and Washington. Inmate and guest. Light danced on the back of his eyelids.

A voice in the back of his head whispered, *You can't let go like this. You float, you dream — you end up like Marat.*

He was thinking of the painting, the one by Jacques-Louis David with the revolutionary dead in the tub. Supine. Bled out. At Stanford, Wilson's art history professor had joked about the picture, saying it gave new meaning to the word 'bloodbath.' (Which reminded him: He had work to do.)

A wall of water surged to the end of the tub as Wilson got to his feet, climbed out, and went to the sink. Standing in front of the mirror, sleek and flushed and glistening, he felt like a snake that had just crawled out of its skin.

But the tats on his chest gave the lie to that. With a broken needle and a ballpoint pen, his cellmate had scratched a ghost shirt into his flesh. A crescent moon on one shoulder, stars on the other. Birds and a bear, a dragonfly and a rough sketch of the man whose name he shared, copied from a daguerreotype in a book. And just below all that, a dipsydoodle of dots and slashes that, translated from the Paiute, read:

When the earth trembles,
Do not be afraid.

He was the Ghost Dancer.

Drawing a razor across his cheek, it occurred to him — not for the first time — that the ink might have been a mistake. It was the kind of macho bullshit that was everywhere in prison, as unavoidable as the smell of Lysol.

If anything, he was inconveniently memorable, even without the ink. For one thing, he was six-four — and he'd been working out for years, living clean in the cage they'd built for him. His face was the color of copper, flat and broad. His nose was a hook between his eyes, which were, like his hair, Jim Jones black.

He had the light beard of his people, so he

didn't need to lather. Just a few scrapes and he was done. Tossing the razor into the wastebasket, Wilson reached for the white robe on the back of the door. Putting it on was like stepping into a cloud.

The FedEx Pak lay on the bed, just past the bathroom door. Stripping the package open, he found a videocassette box inside and, with it, the winter issue of *Documenta Mathematica*. With a faint smile, he opened the journal, and turned to the title page:

J. WILSON:
ISOTROPY AND FACTORIZATION IN PHASE-CONJUGATE SCALAR PAIRS

A soft snort of satisfaction propelled him over to the minibar, where he found a chilled split of Veuve Clicquot. Working out the cork with a soft pop, he took a long pull from the bottle. *How many federal prisoners*, he asked himself, *had published articles in mathematics journals over the past year? Had there been another? Almost certainly not.* And it wasn't a fluke, either. This was his third publication in the last four years, which would have been good enough for tenure at a lot of universities. And his degree wasn't even in mathematics!

Tossing the journal onto the bed, he turned his attention to the video box. Prying it open, he found a stack of hundred-dollar bills held together by a metal clip, and a blue passport with copper-colored lettering: *República de Chile*. Even without opening it, he knew what he'd find inside: a picture of himself and, if he was lucky, the name he'd requested of Bobojon. He opened the passport with a mixture of hope and trepidation.

And there it was. The name: *d'Anconia. Francisco d'Anconia*. A plume of adrenaline shot through his heart as the realization hit him: *It's on. It's actually on.* Vertigo whirled in his chest and it seemed, almost, as if he were looking into an abyss. His heart kicked. The room turned and there it was, just as Nietzsche said: The abyss was looking into *him*.

Maybe, he thought, *maybe this isn't such a good idea. Maybe the thing to do is start all over. Just take the money and run.* He could set up shop in Mexico, and go to work on his own. Just take it apart, brick by brick, all by himself. He didn't need Bo for that. He didn't need anybody.

But he definitely needed money. More money than this, actually. Which is why he had Bo, Bo and his partners.

Swigging champagne, he sat down on the bed and stripped the tape from the box that he'd brought with him from Allenwood. Inside were a sheaf of old patents, a battered Sony Walkman, and copies of motions his lawyers had filed. There were also a couple of cassette tapes (Colloquial Serbian, I & II) and a small collection of well-thumbed books: *Hari Poter i kamen mud rosti, Atlas je zadrhtao*, and *Plato's Dialogues*.

Stacking the books on the table beside the bed, he slipped cassette #2 into the Walkman.

He'd listen to it later.

But first, he decided to hit the stores. There were a couple of things he ought to get, just to look respectable. A coat, for one thing, and a decent pair of shoes. A sportswatch.

As he dressed, his eyes strayed to the VHS box. Its cover depicted a busty blonde, eyes wide with terror, fleeing a tidal wave of unimaginable proportions. Between the blonde and the wave was a doomed, if futuristic, metropolis on which the film's title was stamped in bloodred letters: *Atlantis — Pop. O!*

Wilson wondered if the box was supposed to be a joke, but decided that it wasn't. In all likelihood, it was Bo's idea of 'research.' And why not? Even if the drowned civilization was a myth, its relevance was clear.

Lying awake in their cell at night, they had talked about a lot of things, including the books they were reading. Wilson introduced Bo to Nietzsche, and Bo repaid him with the words of an Arab revolutionary named Qutb. Atlantis came up in the context of a television show they'd watched and the two of them had talked about it often. Since Plato was the source of the Atlantis myth, Bo insisted that the tale must be true. Wilson was skeptical, but the myth had a certain utility: It reinforced the notion that civilization was a fragile enterprise.

★ ★ ★

It was dark when Wilson left the hotel, but it wasn't late. He took a taxi across the Potomac to the Pentagon City mall, where he went Christmas shopping for himself, using some of the cash Bo had sent. He found a pair of shoes he liked at Allan Edmonds, a cashmere overcoat and a change of clothes at Nordstrom's. A jeweler replaced the battery in his watch, and he bought the few toiletries he needed at the local Rite Aid. By then, it was too late to get a haircut, but not to buy a laptop. He found a cheap one at Circuit City Express, right there in the mall. Incredibly, it cost half as much as his old computer, the one the government had seized, and this one came with ten times the power and fifty times the memory.

The ride back to the hotel was bumper to bumper, but Wilson didn't care. Sitting in the back of a taxi with a pile of presents for himself reminded him of the glory days when Goldman Sachs was calling twice a day with updates on . . . what did they call it? The 'impending financial event.'

So it was great to be out again, out on his own, cruising the political theme park that was Washington. The Pentagon on one side, Arlington on the other. River and bridge. The shrine to Lincoln. The setting made him feel like he was starring in his own movie.

Then he was back at the Monarch, and he had to hand it to Bo. The place was a palace, a tower of glass with an eight-story atrium filled with fountains and tropical plants, marble walkways and Persian rugs. Women in expensive suits sipped martinis on white couches in the lobby, while businessmen and

21

bureaucrats huddled over little bowls of nuts, talking quietly.

There was a time when he'd have taken all of this for granted. But that was then, when he was flying around the country looking for venture capital. Now, he took nothing for granted. Not even the little bowls of nuts.

Even the elevator was a marvel, a dimly lighted sanctum of inlaid woods, with a Cole Porter melody piped in over the soft whir of the cables. In the air, a hint of perfume. Quite a change, in other words, from the dead white light and pale green cinder block, the incessant clamor and general stink of the last few years.

When he got to his room, Wilson unpacked the laptop and plugged it into a jack beside the phone. It took about ten minutes to get everything up and running, and then he was on the Internet for the first time in a long while.

Going to my.yahoo.com, he logged on with the user ID ('wovoka') and the password they'd agreed upon ('tunguska'). The home page loaded slowly, at first, then all in a rush. Clicking on Mail, he selected the Draft folder, where he found a single message waiting:

To:
Subject: thursday
Message: just wait in room. dont go out

Wilson erased the message, and replaced it with 'That's what I'll do.' Then he saved the new draft and signed out.

The protocol was his idea. Yahoo!'s e-mail accounts were free, and they were accessible to anyone with an Internet connection and the right password. As easy to abandon as they were to open, the accounts contained a feature that allowed the user to store messages in a Draft folder until they were ready to be sent, which, in the case of Wilson's communications with Bo, would be never. For them, the folder served as a bulletin board, a password-protected message center that was, to all intents and purposes, invisible. Since the messages were 'drafts,' and the drafts were never sent, they wouldn't show up on anyone else's radar screen.

That was the idea, at least.

just wait in room. dont go out

In other words: *I'm on my way.*

Good, Wilson thought. *The sooner we get started, the better.* Meanwhile, he had the Internet. Wilson hadn't surfed the Net for years, and the prospect excited him. This Google thing . . . it was like nothing he'd ever seen. He put his own name in the box, surrounded by quotes, then hit Return and watched as nearly 200,000 hits were generated. Most were not about him. He shared his name with lots of other people, including a shortstop for the Pittsburgh Pirates, a Florida car dealership, and the president of the University of Massachusetts — not to mention his namesake. So he added 'prison' to the search, hit Return a second time, and watched as the number of hits fell to 1,408. He might have narrowed it down even further, adding words like 'patent' and 'conspiracy,' but there was something else that Jack Wilson wanted to do even more.

Backspacing through the Google data field, he erased the earlier entry, and inserted what he really wanted to know about: 'russian brides.' In an instant, he had a million hits. Clicking on a website called ukrainebrides.org, he trawled through the pictures and the pitch: *Marina . . . Olga . . . The Russian woman is a feminine gal . . . Lydmila . . . It is in her expectation to be a lady. Tatyana . . . The Russian woman has no interest in women's lib. She works for husband first! Career is second!*

This thing with the brides was Bo's idea. Their last year together in Allenwood, the two of them had sometimes lain awake, talking quietly about what it was going to be like *After*. For Bo, *After* would take care of itself, *inshallah*. Not so for Wilson, who wasn't a Muslim. For Wilson, *After* was going to take a lot of work. And unlike Bobojon, he expected to survive it.

Wilson's cellmate saw himself as a dead man, so his interest in Paradise was predictable. Listening to Bo talk about it, Wilson got the impression that 'Paradise' was a lot like a spa, except that the spa was up in the clouds, where wine was served by transparent virgins who were desperate to go at it for the first time.

Still, it was Bo who told him about the Russian brides. But now, Wilson saw, it wasn't just Russians. You could pick from different countries: Colombia, the Philippines, Thailand. You could have any kind of girl you wanted. Just click on the little box that read *Add to Cart*, and

24

the woman's e-mail address was yours. After that, it was up to you to woo her, meet her, marry her.

The page that Wilson was looking at contained a dozen photographs of attractive, if heavily made-up, women with long hair and coy smiles. There was a brief résumé next to each, listing their particulars.

Lydmila, for instance, tipped the scales at 57 kilos and 168 centimeters. She was twenty-four years old. Blond hair, blue eyes. A 'technologist' by profession. 'Warmhearted.' Enjoyed the occasional drink. Smoking? No. Hobbies? Yes! Sewing, knitting, and decorating cakes. 'Is seeking respectable Western gentleman with kind heart.'

Well, Wilson thought, *that lets* me *out*.

Sitting back in his chair, Wilson remembered that he had an appointment with a social worker on Thursday, a person charged with 'assisting' him in his adjustment to life on the outside. There would be job and housing leads, earnest advice, etc. For the smallest part of a moment, he toyed with the idea of going through with the meeting. If nothing else, it would be interesting to see if the Pentagon was paying attention. Did they know he'd been released? Would they restrict his employment? His travel? Maybe.

But only if they knew he was out. Only if they were paying attention.

In the end, it didn't really matter. There was a war on, and not just the war in Iraq. As Wilson saw it, the real war had not started until that very morning. It began the second he walked out of

Allenwood a free man.

But there was another way to look at it, too. In a sense, the war was as old as the Ghost Dance — older, even.

So there wasn't any point in meeting with the government to talk about Jack Wilson's future. He didn't have one.

And neither did it.

3

He couldn't sleep.

The thing was, he didn't know what they'd ask him to do. All he knew was that a lot of people were going to get wet. Otherwise, what was the point? Still . . .

The night slowly drained toward dawn. At some point, he fell into a light, fitful sleep, the kind that leaves you tired. When he woke up, it seemed to Wilson that he'd just dozed off — and that it was now morning. But a glance at the clock told him it was noon.

He took a quick shower, called room service, and dressed quickly, putting on the clothes he'd bought the night before. Breakfast arrived on a trolley, looking like an African village on wheels, its chafing dishes gleaming like so many silvered huts. Bacon and eggs, toast and hash browns. Orange juice and coffee.

wait in room dont go out

He nibbled on a slice of raisin toast. It was all he could stomach. Except for the coffee. He drank a pot of it, slowly pacing from one end of the room to the other, saucer in one hand, cup in the other. Seeing the remote, he picked it up and, without thinking, touched the On button, then just as quickly snapped it off as a wave of applause hit him in the face.

Regis and Kelly. (*Twelve to one.*) He might as well have been looking at his watch.

In China, people could smell the time of day. There were coils of incense made with spices and herbs, and as the incense burned, the fragrance changed. Sandalwood, frankincense, lavender, patchouli. A procession of scents marked the hours.

The same thing was true in prison, except that instead of incense, there was television. A cascade of laugh tracks, sound tracks, and quiz shows created a background hum of ambient noise. After a while, you didn't need a watch to tell the time. You could hear it.

Except in Supermax.

Supermax was different. He'd spent four years in the Feds' Administrative Maximum Prison in Colorado, locked down twenty-three hours a day the first two years. And it was like doing Supertime. He lay on a concrete bunk in a concrete cage, watching a twelve-inch black-and-white monitor. The monitor was embedded in the wall, and permanently tuned to 'spiritual programming' and lectures on anger management. High up on the wall, a four-by-forty-eight slit of a window offered a view of the sky. Fluorescent lights burned day and night.

Most days, the guards took you in shackles to a bigger cell that had a chin-up bar. This was the exercise room, and it was yours alone for an hour a day. The strange thing was, he looked forward to going there because, every so often, he'd cross paths with another prisoner. That crazy-looking English guy, the one with the bombs in his shoes, was one. And the Unabomber — Ted Kaczynski — he was another.

Seeing Kaczynski gave him hope that when they moved him from Level 1 to Level 2, there'd be someone to talk to. But it took him two years to make that trip and, in the end, Wilson never saw him again. Too bad. Because the two of them — they thought alike in a lot of ways.

wait in room don't go out

With a growl, Wilson dropped into a chair beside a bank of windows overlooking the atrium. Eight stories below, the lobby was steeped in the false twilight that bad weather brings.

He waited. Watched. Dozed, thinking, *What if it's a setup? What then? What if —* A soft knock rattled the door.

It took him by surprise because he hadn't seen Bo enter the hotel, hadn't seen him cross the lobby floor. Lifting himself from the chair, Wilson went to the door and pulled it open, only to be surprised a second time. No Bo. No friends of Bo. Just a young Latino guy standing beside a luggage trolley. On the trolley: a pair of suitcases, cocooned in shrink-wrap.

'I guess you've been waiting for these,' the bellman said.

Wilson blinked, did his best to conceal his surprise. Said, 'Yeah. Yeah, I have!'

'Okay if I put them in the corner?'

'Yeah, sure. Wherever.'

The kid lifted the bags by their straps and, one at a time, stacked them on the luggage caddy next to the armoire with the TV and minibar. Wilson fumbled in his pockets for change, found a ten-dollar bill, and handed it to him.

'Hey, thanks!' the kid said. 'You need something, you ask for Roberto, okay?'

When the door closed, Wilson sat down on the edge of the bed and stared at the suitcases. They were carry-ons — black Travelpros with retractable handles and in-line wheels. Nice suitcases. And not particularly light. You could tell by the way the kid carried them, shoulders hunched and elbows tight against his sides. They probably weighed twenty pounds each.

He took a deep breath. *This is it*, he thought. *The rest of my life. Shrink-wrapped.* Crossing the room to the computer, he logged on to the Yahoo! address that he'd visited the night before, and clicked on the Draft folder. The connection was slow. It seemed as if the page would never load, but when it did, he found a single message with the Subject and To lines left blank.

Good meeting with contacs. You and me, we show good faith, they get it together for us. Okay? This means (you ready? here goes)

Remove shrinkwrap.
Do NOT pull out handels. Do not!
Take to terminel at Dulles.
Now, pull out handels.
Walk away.
You have 10 minutes.
I am in hourly parking lot 6 to 6:30.
Look for Jeep in Row 15.
No show? I go. But then you have a problem.
Hope not.

Wilson parsed the words with a deepening frown. No question, the message was authentic. Draft mode was exquisitely private, and even though the words were unenciphered, he and Bo had agreed on a convention to authenticate the messages between them. The first sentence of every communiqué would contain four words. No more, no less. It was prehistorically simple, but it worked well enough.

Falling back in the chair, he raised his eyes to the ceiling. *One target ought to be enough,* he told himself. *One person ought to be plenty. An undersecretary of something or other, or just a derelict. In fact, a derelict would be perfect because there wouldn't be any publicity — and it would still make the point. Anything bigger was stupid. Anything bigger was overkill.*

The more he thought about it, the more upset he became. How would he get away? Not just from the airport, but . . . all the way away? The feds would be looking all over the place. Unless . . . unless it was 'a suicide bombing.'

Wilson thought about that. *You have 10 minutes.* Would he? Would he really? And what about Bo? *Look for Jeep in Row 15.* Okay. He'd look. But what if there *was* no Jeep?

The room felt uncomfortably warm. A bead of sweat zigzagged down his spine. His heart was revving like a motorcycle at a stoplight.

Get a grip.

The words fell from his lips in a whisper. 'You have to make this work,' he said. Then he took a deep breath and, leaning forward, erased the

31

message from Bo, letter by letter. When the box
was empty, he typed

Please don't be late.

and sat back, thinking, *I'm gonna need things.*
Gloves. And a hat . . .
He thought a while longer.
And a sling . . .

4

It's one sad story after another, Wilson thought, riding in a cab out to the airport. *And you have to get past that because, after a while, the stories no longer matter. The faces no longer matter. All that's left is the event. It's like . . .*

The Arizona! No one thinks about the sailors, burning, drowning, dying in their bunks. Or the good *volk* of Dresden, incinerated from the air. The streets of Hiroshima, the trading desk at Cantor Fitzgerald — the dead are everywhere. So you can call it whatever you want. You can call it an atrocity. But in the end it always comes down to the same thing. It's History.

And as for the dead, no one remembers their names. But Manson and Mohammed Atta — they're a part of us now, as familiar as the dark. The truth is, after a while the shock fades and even a massacre artist like Cortéz is celebrated as a hero. A bringer of culture, a great explorer. Prometheus, drenched in blood.

The past softens. What begins as a massacre is packaged as news and consumed as 'infotainment.' Eventually, it turns into a television mini-series.

But not this time. This time, there won't be any reenactments. Or any news, for that matter. Just the event. Then nothing. The idea made him smile.

No one remembers the yellow ribbons and

teddy bears, he told himself. The snapshots and handwritten notes — artifacts that appear out of nowhere, like mushrooms after a soaking rain. All forgotten. In the end, the walls and floors are washed down with hoses. The abattoir turns into a memorial. Tourists gawk.

Like when that English princess died in France. He was in Colorado at the time, locked down as a Level 1 prisoner in Supermax. But there was a program about it on one of the godsquad shows. People stood in the rain for hours, waiting to sign some kind of 'book of remembrance,' at her funeral. He wondered about it for a long time. What did they get out of it? Eventually, he decided they wanted a piece of her death, a piece of her celebrity.

'You need a receipt?' the cabdriver asked.

Wilson snapped out of it. 'No, that's okay.' He took a deep breath. *Put on the hat.*

He had to remind himself, because he almost never wore a hat. But this was different. This was *it*, and there were cameras all over the place. So he clapped the Borsalino on his head, pushed open the door to the cab, and stepped out into the slush.

A light snow whirled through the air.

Flight crews and passengers were coming and going with suitcases, carry-ons, and kids. *Good,* Wilson thought. *It's busy. 'Busy' is good. 'Busy' is what they want. 'Busy' is the whole point.*

Moving quickly around to the back of the car, Wilson waited as the driver popped the trunk, then he stepped forward. 'I'll get them,' he said.

Seeing his passenger's arm in a sling, the

driver looked surprised, but figured what-the-hell.

Wilson reached into the trunk and, using his 'good' arm, hauled the suitcases out by their carrying straps.

'You want a skycap?'

Wilson shook his head. 'That's okay,' he said, handing the driver a couple of twenties and a ten.

He was standing by the curb with his overcoat draped across his shoulders like a cape. A chenille scarf hung from his neck, which served also as a fulcrum for the silk sling in which his left arm was hung. Taxis, cars, and vans pulled in and out around him, disgorging passengers under the 'Departures' sign. A few yards away, a young white cop strolled along the middle of the road, slapping the roofs of idling cars, chiding everyone to 'Keep it moving! Let's go!'

The temperature was just below freezing. Wilson could see his breath tumbling in the air as he stood in the slush, staring at the suitcases. *Pull them out. Pull the handles out. But . . .*

The cop was looking at him.

What the fuck, Wilson thought and, reaching down, jerked the handle up from the suitcase, half expecting a thunderclap of light and fire. Nothing. He pulled out the second handle. Nothing again! With a sigh of relief, he shot the cuff on his right arm and checked the watch he'd bought for the occasion.

This was not the kind of watch that complements a cashmere overcoat. It was, instead, an inexpensive digital sportswatch with a plastic band the color of graphite. Set to TIMER, it read 10:00:00. Pressing the button at the base of the watch, the one marked START, Wilson watched the numbers begin to morph, forming and re-forming. 9 minutes, 54 seconds . . . 9 minutes, 51 seconds . . . 9 minutes —

Looking up, Wilson swung his head from left to right, and caught the eye of a skycap. The man hurried over.

'Where to?'

'B-A.'

'You got it!'

A thin black man with flashing eyes and perfect teeth, the skycap bent to his task, depressing the handles into the suitcases. Then he swung each of the bags onto a cart and turned to go. 'First class, right?'

Wilson faked a chuckle, but his heart wasn't in it. 'I wish,' he said. His voice sounded hollow, even to himself. A soft guffaw from the skycap as the man leaned into his cart, and pushed off toward the automatic doors. Then a *whoosh* of air, a burst of noise, and they were in the terminal, engulfed by the chaos of the place. The skycap nodded toward a line of passengers that serpentined inside a maze of ropes, curling back and forth in front of the ticket agents' counter.

'You could be here awhile.'

Wilson shrugged.

'I'll put these up front,' the skycap told him. 'That way you won't have to kick 'em through the line.'

Wilson fumbled a five-dollar bill from his pocket, thanked the man for his help, and joined the winding queue in front of the British Airways counter. There were fifty or sixty people ahead of him, bored and impatient, tired even before their trip began. With their luggage and carry-ons, they looked like refugees. Wilson watched as the skycap made his way to the front of the line, where he stopped and dragged the suitcases from the cart, using both hands. Then he called out something to one of the ticket agents, and nodded in Wilson's direction. The agent looked up, saw the sling, and nodded.

Wilson's shirt was damp with sweat, which gave him a chill, but his face was flushed and hot. His stomach was waltzing in his gut and, worst of all, a moiré pattern was beginning to form in the corner of his right eye, a silver flutter that amounted to a hole in his peripheral vision. Soon, he knew, the glitter would spread from one eye to the other, and then he'd be blind. Or almost blind. Bedazzled, in any case.

Like a dance troupe, the people in front of him lifted their suitcases. Stepped forward. Stopped. Set their bags down, and fell back in conversation.

The first time it happened, when he was nineteen or twenty, Wilson didn't know what it was, or what to do. He'd been scared to death. Thought he had a brain tumor. Thought he was going blind for real. But no. They gave him a CAT scan at the hospital, and the results were normal. The doctor called it an ophthalmic migraine, a rare condition that seemed to be stress-related. There wasn't much in the literature about it, but they thought it had something to do with intelligence, because the only people who 'expressed' a migraine in quite that way were 'off the charts.'

So the eye thing wasn't a problem, really. Just an inconvenience. And the trade-off was that, while he ended up with a migraine, it didn't hurt. And it wouldn't last long. Half an hour at most, and only a couple of times a year. Often enough that by now Wilson knew what to do: Ride it out.

Which wasn't so easy, really. Because the only time he ever got these things was when he was under a lot of stress.

Not that he couldn't handle it. In high school, his senior year, he caught three passes in a game with a herringbone pattern undulating in the air between him and the ball. Years later, in a meeting with the government's lawyers — when they told him they were fucking him — he had one then, too. And no one noticed. No one saw what he'd seen: the gleam in the air, dancing between them. So he sat there, blind as a bat and surrounded by lawyers, listening as the guy from the Pentagon explained what he called 'the facts of life.' 35 USC 131. Eminent domain as it applies to intellectual property.

The next time it happened was . . . when? At his sentencing! And, after that, on the Con Air flight out to Colorado. Where they buried him alive for what amounted to wishful thinking. (Or as the court put it, for 'solicitation of murder.')

But no one knew about his eyes, no one ever guessed. Not the guards, and not the other prisoners. So, really, it was just one of those things, one of those 'Here we go again' kind of things.

Still, it wasn't something you could ignore. And now it was taking over, glazing everything in the corners of his eyes. His peripheral vision was almost gone. People and things were beginning to disappear. Soon —

' — time?'

Wilson blinked. 'Sorry?' The woman in front of him, a girl, really, was asking him the time.

'I just asked, 'Is this your first time?''

He tried to focus, to see around the aura or through it, but of course he couldn't. Even so, he could tell she was young, maybe twelve or thirteen, with henna-colored hair, cut short. And a backpack. Green earrings, which snapped into focus for a moment. *Gumbys*. 'First time for what?'

'Flying.'

The question was so naïve, so very much out of left field, that he almost laughed. 'No,' he said. 'I've been up a couple of times.'

She nodded thoughtfully. After a bit, she asked, 'Is it scary? I've never actually flown before.'

'No kidding!'

He glanced at his watch. *5:48 . . . 5:45 . . . 5:43.* 'It's a lot more dangerous on the ground,' he said. 'Planes are pretty safe.' The line edged forward a couple of steps, and he saw that she moved awkwardly, leaning on a cane and dragging her left leg.

'Looks like you've been skiing.'

A soft, regretful chuckle. 'No, I've never been skiing.'

He thought she was going to say something else, but the moment passed. Then the line inched ahead again, and so did she. No cast. Just the cane. *Something congenital, then.*

'What about you?'

At first, he didn't know what she meant. Then he remembered the sling, and — 'Oh, you mean *this*! Yeah, I was at . . . Killington.' He could see Gumby's awkward smile floating behind the moiré pattern. In five or six minutes, the girl would be gone. Almost all of them would be.

He could almost see it: the blood and the glass, bodies wet and smoking on the marble floor. People staggering through the rubble, shell-shocked, deaf and bleeding. And the silence — like after a car crash. Everything would be silent, if only for a couple of seconds. Then the quiet would give way to a wail of recognition. The air would fizz and the cries would go up, filling the vacuum with noise until it exploded into a long, collective scream.

Restraining the impulse to glance at his watch, Wilson lowered his head toward the girl, and said, 'Excuse me?'

She turned and looked up at him.

'Would you mind holding my place?'

'No,' she said. 'I mean, *sure*! I'd be happy to.'

' 'Cause I'll just be a minute.' A hint of embarrassment in his tone.

'No problem!'

'Thanks.'

With a wince that was meant to be a smile,

Wilson set off in the direction of the newsstand, leaving the queue, the girl, and the suitcases in his wake. It took all the willpower he had not to look over his shoulder and not to break into a run, but to walk slowly toward the restrooms —

And keep going.

An escalator delivered him, sweating and out of breath, to the baggage area below. He looked at his watch, but the glitter in his eyes made it impossible to read. *2:40? 2:10? 39 seconds?* He couldn't be sure.

Walking faster now, he went through a passageway to the outside, then quickly crossed the road to the short-term parking lot. *Row 15.*

The Jeep wasn't there. Wilson's stomach did a backflip, and a sizzle of panic shot through his chest. They'd fucked him.

He was looking around — there was nowhere to go — waiting for the world to explode, when he heard a horn and, turning, saw the Jeep, one row behind him. And there in the Jeep, Bo was laughing, waving him over. Wilson dashed between a phalanx of parked cars, yanked open the door to the passenger seat, and dove in.

As the car began to roll, Wilson realized that they weren't alone. There was a guy in the backseat who looked like an Arab — an older guy he'd never seen before. And he was smiling. Nodding approval.

Likewise Bobojon, who was good to go, with the parking chit in his lap and dollar bills at the ready. Even so, it was taking a long time to get out of the lot. A BMW sat in front of them at the parking attendant's booth, while the woman

41

behind the wheel rummaged through her purse, babbling apologies. So they sat there in the Jeep, waiting for the terminal to blow, waiting for all hell to break loose, while this crazy bitch rooted around for her Platinum card.

The guy in the backseat leaned forward, a pack of cigarettes in his hand. Wilson took one and, doing his best to conceal the trembling in his hand, accepted a light.

Blowing a stream of smoke at the windshield, he squinted at his watch. *1:12 . . . 1:08 . . . 1:04*

The woman continued to paw through her purse.

He wanted to kill her. He wanted to scream. He wanted to kill her and scream.

Not Bo. He looked from Wilson to the woman, and back again. Said something to the other guy in Arabic. And laughed.

A moment later, so did the woman. She threw back her head with an exclamation they couldn't hear, and pulled a wedge of plastic from her purse. *Voilà!* The bored attendant swiped the card through the long slot in his credit-card machine and waited for the receipt to print. It only took about thirty seconds, but every one of them seemed like a long, torturous minute. Finally, the woman grabbed the chit and sped off, wiggling her fingers out the window. *Toodle ooh.*

Thirty seconds later, Wilson and his friends were behind her on the Dulles Toll Road, heading into Washington. Bo was so loose he was practically whistling, but Wilson was hardwired to the watch on his wrist — as if *he* was the one who was going to blow. *0:04 . . . 03 . . . 02 . . .* The hair on his arms was standing on end, and the muscles in his back began to spasm.

Bo threw him a glance, then looked away, eyes on the road. Wilson's heart was crashing against his chest when the watch beeped and, out of nowhere, Bo lunged at him with a shout: **'BAMMM!'**

The guy in the backseat chuckled.

5

It was things like this that worried Ray Kovalenko. Not the scimitar-rattling on al-Jazeera or the nonstop threats on Al Faroq. It was the stuff he couldn't explain. Like the tall guy with the sling and the suitcases.

The FBI agent sat in the darkened room, nibbling on one of the stems of his sunglasses. At the far end of the conference table, a black-and-white video played in silence on a nineteen-inch Provideo monitor. A time-and-date stamp glowed at the bottom of the screen:

12−18−04 17:51

The resolution was decent, Kovalenko thought, but the contrast was lousy. A slurry of grays, and not much more. You'd think TSA could do better than that.

The tape had been made at Dulles. A passenger agent for British Airways noticed a pair of suitcases sitting in front of the ticket counter 'for half an hour, maybe more,' and called Transportation Security. When no one claimed the bags, TSA cordoned off the area and alerted the airport police. A Special Response Team was dispatched, and the terminal evacuated.

The 'first responders' (that's what they were, and that's how they thought of themselves) were leery of the situation and wanted an EOD unit sent out, so the suitcases could be destroyed in situ. Wiser heads prevailed.

A skycap remembered wheeling the luggage up to the counter. 'Guy had his arm in a sling, so I put the bags up front. No big thing. We do it all the time.'

The rep from 2-TIC — the Terrorist Threat Integration Center — coughed, then coughed again. Kovalenko glanced at her, his brow curdling into a frown.

Andrea Cabot was something of a legend, a bright and attractive CIA officer who might, or might not, have been forty. It was said that she had 'her own money' — and lots of it. Having grown up in Morocco (her father ran the Port Authority in Casablanca), she liked to joke that English was her 'third language.' French and Arabic were the first two, Chinese the fourth.

Now, she wore a dark suit and a string of pearls, three-inch heels, and contact lenses that were unnaturally blue — a pure indigo color that you saw only at Disney World. Like Kovalenko, she was on her way to somewhere else. In her case, to Kuala Lumpur — 'KL' to the cognoscenti — where she was soon to be chief of station.

Interesting woman, Kovalenko thought. And not shy. Someone said she'd once sung the 'Star-Spangled Banner' in front of forty thousand people at a soccer match at RFK Stadium. So she had guts. Too many, perhaps. One of the guys he played poker with, a counter-intelligence drone at the Agency, said she'd gotten her tit in a wringer over a rendition she'd set up in eastern Turkey. The snatch went off without a hitch. They slammed the subject into the back of a refrigeration van and drove him three hundred miles to a plane that was waiting to take him to Gitmo. Imagine everyone's surprise when they opened the door and the raghead fell out, dead. Some kind of air-handling problem.

There were a couple of stories like that — or not *stories*, really. More like innuendos. A bird colonel who'd worked with her in Turkey frowned when Kovalenko asked about her. But all he said was, 'Interesting woman . . . ' What do you mean? Kovalenko asked. 'Well,' the colonel said, looking uncomfortable, 'she can be pretty aggressive in an interrogation setting. Not that that's necessarily bad,' he hastened to add. 'It's just . . . kind of surprising when you see it.'

None of this bothered Kovalenko. As far as he was concerned, Andrea Cabot was just about perfect. Her only drawback — the only reason he didn't give her a tumble, really — was the Mandarin Chinese thing. That's what worried him. That's why he frowned. Because if Andrea spoke Chinese, she was probably speaking *to* Chinese. So while the cough could be anything, a cold or the flu, it might also be something else. Something Chinese. Like SARS or the bird flu.

As Kovalenko turned this thought over in his mind, he saw Andrea lean toward the monitor and squint. 'Freeze that,' she whispered.

Kovalenko did. In the picture, a man stood near the end of a serpentine line in front of the British Airways counter. He wore a long dark overcoat, and a hat. You could almost make out his face.

'That's the guy?' Andrea asked.

Kovalenko grunted. The man in the frame had his arm in a sling, as if it were broken. And maybe it was. But Kovalenko didn't think so. The sling was probably just a ploy, a way of getting his bags up to the counter without having to carry them, without having to stand with them. It was the kind of thing Ted Bundy did before they put him to sleep.

'Okay,' Andrea said. The monitor sprung back to life. Another cough.

That's all I need, Kovalenko thought. *To drown in my own sputum.*

He'd been running on empty ever since 9/11, hopscotching from Washington to Hamburg, Hamburg to Dubai. Dubai to Manila. Djakarta, Islamabad. Except for Hamburg, it was one shithole after another. By now, his resistance was nil, his circadian rhythms so out of whack, his body felt like a Pharoah Sanders solo. And this building, squirreled away in the Navy Yard, was a big part of the problem.

'A secure facility,' its windows had been bricked up since the early seventies, when the NRO had taken it over to study satellite imagery. It was, literally, a place 'where the sun don't shine.' Sometimes, it seemed as if everyone who worked there was sick or coming down with something. *Like me,* Kovalenko thought. *I've been coming down with something for a long, long time.*

On the monitor, the man with the sling spoke to someone in the line ahead of him.

'Who's that girl?' Andrea asked, peering at the monitor. 'Do we know who she is?'

A laconic voice with a British accent drifted down the table in the darkness. 'Nohhhhhh.' The way he said it, the word seemed to go on and on. 'I'm afraid we don't.'

'Why not?' Kovalenko asked. 'It's your plane. You've got a flight manifest. How hard can it be?'

The Brit sucked in a lungful of positive ions, and sighed. A spook named Freddie, he was one of the liaisons from MI-6. 'Well, it can be very difficult, indeed!' he said, leaning forward. 'There were a hundred and thirty-one females aboard that flight, and they were listed by name. Not by age, weight, or position in line. We don't have the manpower to track them all down,' Freddie insisted. 'Especially when nothing has actually *happened*.' He looked at Kovalenko. 'Perhaps when you get to London — '

'London?' Andrea asked.

Kovalenko shrugged.

'We're in the presence of the new Legat,' Freddie explained. 'Hasn't he told you?'

'No.' Andrea looked impressed.

'It isn't official,' Kovalenko mumbled.

On the monitor, the man with the sling turned away from the girl, and strolled out of the picture.

'That's it,' Kovalenko announced. 'Let there

be light.' It was the ninth time he'd watched the tape, and there was nothing more to be learned from it.

Above them, fluorescent lights flickered to life with a staticky hum. Kovalenko got to his feet and crossed the room to a library table, where a pair of Travelpro suitcases lay open. In each of the suitcases was a bundle of newspapers. The newspapers were tied together with twine, and there were no fingerprints. Anywhere.

'Twenty-two pounds,' Kovalenko said. 'Each.'

'Ten kilos,' Freddie observed.

'My point, exactly,' Kovalenko said.

Andrea smiled, idly rolling a pearl between her thumb and forefinger. After a moment, she said, 'Twenty-two pounds is not what you'd call an American number. Whoever packed the bags was thinking metric.'

The Brit thought about it for a moment, and chuckled. 'Well, now we're getting somewhere. Not only has nothing happened, *but . . .* ' He narrowed his eyes, and with a furtive look, glanced left and right. 'There's reason to believe a 'furriner' may have been behind it.'

Even Kovalenko laughed. But only for a second. 'Actually,' he said, 'something *has* happened.'

Freddie's voice was thick with skepticism: 'Oh? And what was that?'

'There was a test.'

The Brit considered the possibility.

'That's what this is all about,' Kovalenko announced.

'Possibly,' Freddie said. 'Or perhaps it was just a prank.'

'Well, if it was a prank, it was an expensive one. Those carry-ons are new,' Kovalenko told him, 'and they don't come cheap.'

'You're right, of course, but . . . why bother? If you want to kill a lot of people at the airport, what's the point in practicing? Why not just . . . *go in* and be done with it?'

'Exactly,' Kovalenko replied.

The MI-6 man made a face. 'For that matter, why bother with the airport? The train station is a softer target. Restaurants, theaters . . . '

Kovalenko turned to his left. 'Andrea?'

A little *zzzip* of nylon as the CIA officer crossed and uncrossed her legs. For a moment, she pursed her lips, and mused. Finally, Andrea said, 'I think what Ray's suggesting is, this isn't about the airport. It's about the man with the sling. Someone was testing *him*,' she decided. 'Not the airport's security.'

Freddie considered the possibility. After a moment, he asked, 'And why would they do that?'

Andrea shrugged. 'I guess they wanted to find out how far he'd go.'

Kovalenko nodded. 'Well, now they know. He goes all the way.'

6

DUBLIN JANUARY 24, 2005

Soft.

That's what the Irish called it when the weather was like this, more mist than rain. Mike Burke stood by the window next to his desk, idly watching the street below. Every so often, a gust of rain rattled the glass, and his focus would shift to the pane itself, where beads of water spattered and ran.

His office was a large room with high ceilings in a rose-brick building at the edge of Temple Bar, a famous maze of narrow streets and alleyways near the River Liffey. From where he sat, Burke could see the roof of Merchants' Arch, the covered byway in which a fictional character named Leopold Bloom had once stopped to buy a book — a pornographic novel, as it happened — for his wife, Molly.

As cold and wet as it was, Burke wanted to go running. There was a gym bag under the desk with everything he needed — except the chance to use it. He had an appointment with a client, a man named d'Anconia, and d'Anconia was late. The man had telephoned that very morning to ask about forming a company. On the quick, as it were.

Fair play, Burke thought. That's what we do.

But his mind wasn't on it. He was thinking about Kate's father, aka 'the Old Man,' whose name was engraved on the brass plaque beside the heavy oak doors that gave entrance to the office:

THOMAS AHERNE & ASSOCIATES

Bit of a lie, that. Other than Burke, there *were* no associates. Nor had there been for months. Not since . . . well, not since Kate died.

Even now, the words took his breath away. Stuttering senselessly in the back of his mind, they suggested a sentence that had no end, an idea so impossible it could only be stillborn. *When Kate died . . .*

Where do you go with a thought like that — a *fact* like that? Her death was an avalanche. One minute, he was standing in her light, dreaming of the years ahead of them . . . then the earth fell away from his feet. Blindsided, he was buried alive in his grief. Eventually, the cold found its way to his heart, and slowly took hold. Grief drained to numbness and then he felt nothing at all.

The old man was even worse off. One day he was there, holding forth behind his desk, and then he wasn't. For years, everyone had said, 'The firm is his life. You take the firm away, and Tommy's a goner.' Not true, as it turned out. The firm was the old man's way of life, a hobby, and a fascination, but Kate . . . Kate had been life itself.

He'd raised her from a sprog (his word).

Taught her to build sand castles, ride horses, read the Greats, and be wary of boys. Tommy had watched in delight as she took on more and more of her mother's beauty, the ginger hair and emerald eyes, her skin like an empty sheet of paper — had swelled with pride when she breezed through Cambridge with a first, and came to Dublin for her residency. Then she did the unimaginable, turning her back on the genteel comforts of a surgeon's life in Ireland to cast her lot with a doctors' charity that packed her off to a godforsaken clinic on the malarial edge of a never-ending war.

Enter, Mike Burke.

Not right away, of course, but soon enough and quite dramatically. Two years after Kate arrived in Liberia, Burke fell out of the air a few miles from her clinic. And lay there, smoking.

A rebel army recon unit, led by the self-anointed 'Colonel Homicide,' found him. They may, in fact, have shot him down. He lay in a ditch at the edge of the forest, one leg broken and half an ear torn off. His chest and shoulders were flayed with burns. The burns were infested with bees, and he was flickering in and out of consciousness.

According to the dreadlocked colonel, Burke looked as if he'd been there for days. 'I seen his ride, and the ride's junk, burned out, it's *cold*! And this white boy, he's layin' in the muck like a bad sign, like a signal from Jesus, swimming in bees. Hieronymus, he wants to take the man's main machine. You know — just reach in and pull it out, like we do sometimes. That way, we sendin' a message. Like a Hallmark card. Only *this* man, his passport says 'America'! Land of the free! So now, we all humanitarian. Show the positive side of the struggle.' Hoping for a reward, the dreadlocked colonel and his men dragged Burke over to the pickup they were driving (a 4 × 4 technical with a .50-caliber machine gun mounted in the back), and tossed him onto a pile of ammunition belts. Then they drove him to the Irish lady doctor's clinic in Porkpa.

A moldering shantytown of huts on the flanks of a dirt road, Porkpa was proud of its infirmary. With a dozen beds, a tiny lab, and its own ambulance, the clinic — a concrete box with a rusting tin roof, its walls painted ocher, pink, and teal — was the only 'infrastructure' for miles around. In her first year at the clinic, most of Kate's time had been taken up with pediatric care and midwifery, health education and vaccination. When the war heated up, the clinic's priorities changed. By the time Burke's helicopter crashed, killing the pilot, the clinic was a round-the-clock trauma unit, with gunshot and machete wounds at the top of its To Do list.

With his broken leg and second- and third-degree burns over ten percent of his body, Burke remained at the clinic for seven weeks. There wasn't any reason to keep him that long, but neither was there anywhere for him to go. Four days after Burke's ill-fated helicopter ride, the capital underwent a paroxysm of violence. Even if you could get there, nothing worked. Its

54

ports were closed, embassies shuttered. Redemption Hospital was in ruins, pounded by mortars and looted by gunmen. Burke was better off in Porkpa.

Though 'better off' wasn't what you'd call ideal. The clinic was a makeshift operation at best, and infections were a constant threat. Medical supplies were scarce, and the staff — never large — wandered off as the war drew nearer. A month after Burke's arrival, Kate found herself with a single nurse's aide, nine patients who couldn't be moved, and a security guard who could not have been more than twelve years old. There was nothing for Burke to do but get well or die.

When he was able to move around, he did what he could to make himself useful, sitting up nights in the doorway with a shotgun in his lap. Before long, he was changing bandages and helping out in the kitchen. His biggest coup was the generator. Everyone said it was dead — 'Black smoke is death-smoke!' — but Burke didn't buy it. He'd grown up on a farm, and on a farm you fixed things. The generator at the clinic was a John Deere. It was bigger than the one his father had in Nellysford, but it worked the same way and had the same problems. After tinkering with it for an hour, Burke saw that the intake port was plugged. Ten minutes later, it was purring like a cat.

In his spare time — and he had nothing but spare time — he made a chess set out of shotgun shells, plumbing supplies, and empty medicine bottles. It was ugly, but it worked. Kate was too tired in the evenings to take the game seriously, but since it was the only game in town — literally — they played nearly every night.

And as they played, they talked. He learned about her childhood in Ireland, her boyfriends at Cambridge, and her love of medicine. As for Africa? 'Where else can I deliver babies one day, and the next, treat guinea worm, gunshot wounds, and AIDS — not to mention the likes of you!'

He admired her clarity. His own situation was more ambiguous, and even embarrassing. Though only thirty, he'd spent most of his adult life traveling around the world, 'taking pictures in all the wrong places.' That was the only way to get published if you weren't known: You went where others wouldn't go. To cities like Grozny and Algiers, Monrovia and Port-au-Prince. The kinds of places where the best hotel in town was the one with the most sandbags.

He was working with the F-Stop Cooperative in New York, and most of the time he loved it. The life. The people. The pictures. Flying in and out of places. *Just being there.* You get off a plane in a city like Algiers, and everything snaps into focus. Just like that — right there, right then! Be here now. It was a great way to get 'centered,' because if you didn't, you wound up in an orange jumpsuit with a knife at your throat.

So it's like being one of those divers, she teased.

What divers?

The ones in Acapulco who jump off the cliffs.

He shook his head. *I'm not a cowboy,* he told

her. *It's not just the bang-bang.*

Ri-iighhht.

No, really! He'd worked as a reporter, and writing just wasn't the same. Whatever you wrote, it was never quite right. There was always someone you hadn't interviewed, or something you didn't quite grasp. Photography wasn't like that. A picture was a fact in a way that words on a page could never be.

Burke told Kate how he'd gotten started on a weekly newspaper in Virginia. The paper wasn't unionized, so he'd worn a lot of hats: writing articles and editorials, taking pictures and doing page layouts. There was a police scanner in a corner of the office, buzzing and crackling, diodes gleaming. Word of a fire, a shooting, a crash, and he was out the door with his cameras.

How exciting, she yawned. *A crash.*

Well, yeah, it was! A lot of the time, Burke told her, he rode shotgun with the newspaper's main photographer, an older guy named Sal, who said things like, 'Never go anywhere unless you're strapped.' He meant with a camera.

So you're always ready to take a picture.

Well, yeah, Burke said, but it's not just that. The real point is that having a camera with you — even a small camera — changes you.

Changes you?

He nodded. *Makes you braver*, he said.

How?

If you have a camera, you want to get the picture. So you stand your ground. Most people won't do that. They see people running, screaming, they head the other way — it's

57

instinct — but a good photographer stays where he is. He waits for the image.

And if 'the image' is a tidal wave?

Burke laughed. *It helps to be a good swimmer.* But he'd always had second thoughts about photography. Though he'd won a boxful of awards, and covered everything from a gypsy wedding in Siberia to the dragon-boat races in Macao, most of his work revolved around mayhem. An earthquake in Turkey, a mass grave in Kosovo, a beheading in Chop Square. After a while, you got used to havoc. It began to seem almost normal.

And that couldn't be good for your soul, Burke thought. It was one thing to be an accidental witness, someone who just happened upon a scene, and quite another to stick a camera in a dying man's face — as he had done on more than one occasion. There was something shameful about taking a picture like that. It made you complicit in the mayhem.

Sounds like bad karma, Kate told him.

Burke smiled. 'Yeah,' he said, 'something like that.'

★   ★   ★

Chess wasn't their only diversion. There was an alfresco theater, of sorts, in the ruins and weeds of what used to be the post office. Each Friday night, a dozen metal chairs were unfolded and deployed before a badly damaged wall of whitewashed cinder blocks. An antique 8mm film projector sputtered to life, casting its spell

58

along a beam of light, flickering with the vectors of moths and flying beetles. In the second month of Burke's sojourn in Porkpa, he and Kate paid half a euro each to see Richard Burton in *The Robe*, John Wayne in *Hatari!*, and Michael Rennie in *The Day the Earth Stood Still*.

Where the films came from was a mystery.

What was not a mystery was the attraction that he and Kate began to feel for each other. Maybe it was inevitable. They were young. It was Africa. After the Michael Rennie movie, they made out like a couple of kids, sitting on a couch at the clinic. It only lasted a minute or two, then Kate pushed him away and, with a sly smile, suggested they go to bed.

But not with each other. She needed time to think, she said, then kissed him on the cheek, and left the room, slyly humming. It took him a while to recognize the song. 'Just One of Those Things.'

Which was funny, but inaccurate. Whatever it was between them — love, lust, or loneliness — it wasn't 'one of those things.' It was a different 'thing' entirely. He was going to tell her that when the unthinkable happened.

They were 'rescued.'

Or *he* was. Kate was upriver delivering a baby when a UN convoy rolled into Porkpa, escorting a truck with a red crescent on its side. Pulling up to the clinic in an armored personnel carrier, a Nigerian captain jumped to the ground, and promptly announced that everyone was being evacuated.

'Everyone?' Burke eyed the little truck.

'Yes,' the captain insisted. 'All the white people. Everyone!'

Burke thanked him for his trouble, but declined the invitation, only to be told that it wasn't an invitation. It was an order. An argument ensued. Burke stood his ground. He wasn't going anywhere. Not without the doctor.

He woke up half an hour later on the floor of the truck, his wrists bound with FlexiCuffs. Driven to the airstrip at Belle Yella, he was put aboard a UN helicopter with other evacuees, and flown to an American naval ship that was standing off the coast. Two days later, he was in Washington.

His apartment was a one-bedroom co-op on Connecticut Avenue, a couple of blocks north of the zoo. There was nothing special about it except that, in the morning, he could hear the gibbons singing above the traffic. It was never a place in which he'd spent a lot of time, but it was an address, at least, and it was where he kept his books and clothes.

He tried to get in touch with Kate, but there wasn't any way. The shortwave was down, and her e-mail came back as undeliverable. There didn't seem to be an Irish embassy in Monrovia. She might as well have been on the moon.

What did she think had happened to him? Did anyone tell her? Did she think he'd caught the first ride out, leaving without a word? That's the way it must have seemed . . .

There was a number for Doctors Without Borders in New York, and he called it. They referred him to the Paris headquarters of

Médecins Sans Frontières. In his best high school French, he asked about the clinic in Porkpa.

C'est fermé.

Et la directeur?

His accent must have been execrable, because the person at the other end of the line sounded pained: *It is okay to speak English, please?*

Absolutely! You were saying: The clinic's closed.

Yes, it is closed.

And I was asking about the director. Dr. Aherne.

She is no longer with us.

Burke froze. *What?*

Yes! I am afraid it is no longer possible to work in Liberia. It is too dangerous.

Oh . . . he began to breathe again. *Do you have a phone number for her?*

Yes, but I am afraid it is confidential. Perhaps, if you like, we could forward a letter?

He wrote the letter that same afternoon, and tore it up that evening. In the morning, he sat down with it for a second time. But there was so much to say, so much to explain. Not about his disappearance. That was the easy part. The hard part was talking about them. The two of them.

What *about* them? When he thought about Africa, and all the things that happened there, the memories were like hallucinations. The helicopter yawing as its rotors came apart. The ground rushing toward him. The little blanket of bees on his chest. Kate.

In the end, the letter was as much to himself

as it was to her. It went on for pages and days as he came to grips, not only with his feelings for Kate but with the uncertainties of his own identity. Who was he? Who did he want to be? What was important? What was not? The more he thought about it, the more he realized that the answers rested with Kate.

By then, he'd cold-called all the hospitals in Dublin. Did they have a Dr. Aherne working for them? Indeed, they did. They had Ahernes and Ahearns. Orthopedics, pediatrics, and family medicine. Mary, Rory, and Declan. Which one did he have in mind?

It was at Meath Street Hospital that he found her. The hospital's new directory listed Katherine Aherne as a physician in the Casualty Ward. But she wasn't to start for a week or two, and when she did, the receptionist said, she'd probably work nights and weekends. 'That's how we break them in,' she confided.

In a way, he was relieved not to be able to reach her. There was too much to say, and what if she hung up on him? At least, with the letter, he could say what he felt. And he would, just as soon as he got it right.

In the meantime, he had plastic surgery at Sibley Hospital. There wasn't anything to be done about the splashes of scar tissue on his chest and shoulders, but the doctors were able to make his ear, or what was left of it, 'cosmetically acceptable.'

It was a strange time. He began to work out at the Y, lifting weights and playing basketball in the

62

mornings. Most afternoons, he read the paper over coffee at a sidewalk table outside Foster Brothers, or wandered through the city's museums. There was a poker game on Thursday nights at James McLeod's place, but that was all the 'socializing' that he did.

By now, word had gotten out that he was back, and editors were calling. F-Stop had a commercial assignment for the Patagonia catalog: a three-day trek through Chile's Torres del Paine. Was he interested? He thought it over for about an hour. Then he caught a plane.

That night, he lay awake in a window seat, gazing into the darkness of the Atlantic, miles below. In the morning, he changed planes at Heathrow, and flew on to Dublin in the afternoon. Reeling with jet lag, he took a room at an expensive hotel on Grafton Street, and dropped into bed. When he awoke five hours later, he went to Meath Street Hospital and took a seat in the waiting room on the Casualty Ward.

The next night, he did the same. And the next. And the next. Eventually, one of the nurses took pity on him, and let drop the information that Dr. Aherne lived in Dalkey. 'Like Bono,' she said.

It was easy to find her after that, but it took a weekend to sort things out, and another week to court her. Two weeks after that, they were married.

The old man gave her away. He liked Americans in general and Burke in particular, not least of all because Burke was content to stay in Dublin for as long as Kate wanted to be there. Soon, Burke was working at 'the Firm,' helping the old man with incorporations. Within a year, Kate was running the Casualty Ward at the hospital, and life was grand. They began to talk about a baby.

Then the sepsis.

7

When Kate died . . .

The old man just stopped coming in. After a while, the bookkeeper left to take a job with a software start-up in Rathmines. Then Fiona, the nineteen-year-old Goth receptionist, drifted off in the direction of Ibiza, leaving Burke by himself in a suite of offices that the old man no longer visited or cared about.

It can't go on like this, Burke told himself. Not with the old man drinking the way he is, sitting alone in that haunted house with too many stairs and too many memories. Not with the firm making so little money. And not, Burke thought, not with me treading the days as if they were water.

The truth was: Kate was gone, and she wouldn't be coming back. That was a fact.

But it wasn't *just* a fact. It was a circumstance so massive as to constitute its own dimension. For Burke and the old man, Kate's absence was their longitude and latitude, intangible as space, but just as real — and just as empty. And maybe, for the old man, it was something more. A black hole, pulling him in.

A puff of rain hit the window.

Burke blinked. His reverie dissolved. In the street below, a taxi pulled away from the curb, leaving a man on the corner, stranded in the drizzle. The man was looking around, as if to get his bearings. *D'Anconia*, Burke thought. *Must be him*.

Leaving the window, he sat down at the antique wooden desk that, technically, was the old man's. The necessary forms were in an envelope on the blotter. At the edge of the desk was a silver-framed photograph of Kate. Dressed in her surgical scrubs, she stood in a puddle of mud, smoking a cigarette at the entrance to the clinic in Porkpa.

Burke listened for d'Anconia's footsteps on the stairs, but he heard none. Then a soft knock trembled the doors.

'Come in.' Burke got to his feet, half expecting Peter Lorre.

But his visitor was nothing like that. Only a few years older than Burke himself, d'Anconia was handsome enough to be someone's leading man. His hair was long and black, swept back in a way that seemed artfully disarranged. Square jaw, white teeth, strong nose, olive complexion, and just enough stubble on his cheeks to make it seem as if he didn't care about appearances. But the Borsalino hat gave the lie to that, as did the cashmere coat and bright scarf.

'Francisco d'Anconia,' his visitor announced, and closed the door behind him.

They shook hands. 'Mike Burke. Can I get you something?'

D'Anconia dropped into a wing chair beside the desk, brushed the rain from his hat, and laid it in his lap. 'No, thanks,' he said. He glanced around, then nodded to a cluster of photographs on the wall. 'Nice pictures.'

'Thanks.'

'You take them?'

Burke nodded.

D'Anconia cocked his head. 'What about that one?' he asked, pointing to a photograph of a spectacular ravine whose mist-ridden slopes converged in a jumble of boulders to form a channel through which a wild river ran.

Burke answered without having to look. 'Tsangpo Gorge.'

'Where's that?'

'Tibet.'

D'Anconia removed a packet of cigarettes from the pocket of his coat, and tapped it against his wrist. 'One of the things I like about Europe,' he said. 'A guy can smoke.' He paused. Lit up. Exhaled. And frowned. 'I was expecting what's-his-name. The guy on the plaque. Aherne.'

A wince of regret from Burke. 'Tommy's not well,' he said. 'He's not what you'd call 'a young man.''

D'Anconia's brow sunk into a V. 'So you're . . . what?'

Burke pushed a business card across the desk. 'An 'associate.''

'I don't mean that,' d'Anconia said. 'I mean, you sound American.'

'I am. Dual citizenship.'

'And how does that work?'

'My grandfather was a Connemara man.'

'And that makes you Irish?' d'Anconia asked.

Burke shrugged. 'You have to apply, but it's pretty much automatic. And my wife was Irish, so . . . ' He changed the subject, 'And what

67

about you? Have you been here long?'

'No. Just got in.'

'Ah, but you'll be here for a while! You've business in Dublin.'

D'Anconia shook his head. 'Not really. It's just a connecting flight. I'm out of here in the morning.'

'Then I guess we'd better get to work.' Reaching for the envelope and forms, Burke unwound a length of string that bound the flap of the envelope to a paper disk on the back. 'Y'know, I never asked how you found us. The old man will want to know.'

'The old man?'

'Mr. Aherne.'

D'Anconia grunted. 'I saw an ad. The Aer Lingus magazine. It was in one of the classifieds.'

'Oh, ri-iight! The classifieds! Well, I'm glad to know something's come of that,' Burke confessed. 'Because they're damned expensive.' Removing the forms from the envelope on his desk, he laid them out between them.

'What happened to your ear?'

Coming out of nowhere, so unexpectedly, the question made Burke smile. It was like a child's question. 'I was in a crash,' he said.

'What kind of crash?'

'Helicopter. There was a lot of fuel flying around.' He made a gesture with his right hand, tossing it out as if he were sowing seeds. 'I got burned.'

'You must have had a good surgeon,' d'Anconia said. 'You have to look twice to notice anything.'

Burke again changed the subject. 'When we spoke on the phone, I think you said confidentiality was key.'

D'Anconia nodded.

'In that case,' Burke said, 'a limited liability corporation is what you want. With an Isle of Man venue.'

'Isle of Man?' d'Anconia asked.

'It's in the Irish Sea. Oldest legislature in the world. Pretty place. Very historical.'

'But it's *English*, right?'

Burke tilted his head from side to side. 'It's a sovereign state, but the U.K. handles its defense and foreign affairs.'

A ripple of suspicion flickered in d'Anconia's eyes. 'I thought the idea was to form an Irish corporation. When we talked on the phone, I assumed — '

'If that's what you want, that's what we'll do,' Burke told him. 'But if it's confidentiality that you're after, then it's the Isle of Man you want. Not Ireland.'

'Why?'

'Because,' Burke explained, 'unlike the Irish, the Manx don't require disclosure of a corporation's 'beneficial owner.' Which is about as discreet as it gets, because people can't disclose what they don't know.'

D'Anconia thought about it. 'What about a Panamanian corporation?'

Burke smiled. 'Well, there's always Panama. And Vanuatu! In fact, there are a couple of dozen funky venues that will happily take your money, open a bank account, whatever. But they don't

69

inspire confidence — and they *do* attract attention. On the other hand, the Isle of Man is a part of Europe. And even though it isn't actually British, it's British-*ish*. If you see what I mean.'

D'Anconia chewed it over for a moment. 'Okay. Let's do it.'

Burke picked up a pen, and leaned forward. 'I'll need a little information — and a check for thirteen hundred euros.'

'Cash all right?'

'Cash is fine.'

'And what do I get for that?'

'You get a limited liability corporation, registered on the Isle of Man, with all its firewalls intact. You get a registered agent in Dublin — that's us — and a checking account with five hundred euros on deposit.'

D'Anconia looked pleased. 'Which bank?'

'Cadogan.' He pronounced it the British way: *Cuh-duggin*.

'Which is . . . where?'

'Channel Islands,' Burke explained.

'And they're what? British?'

Burke shrugged. 'Emphasis on the '-*ish*.''

D'Anconia grinned.

'There's a bit of paperwork to get through,' Burke said. 'Certificates of shares, articles of incorporation, the nominees' declarations — '

'Nominees?'

'Names on paper,' Burke explained. 'When the corporation is formed, they act as its directors.'

'I understand, but in real life — who *are* they?'

No one had ever asked him that question before. 'You mean, what do they do when they're

70

not being 'names'?'

D'Anconia nodded.

'Well, lots of things. Being a name is a kind of sideline. It's like a perk that comes with being Manx.' He gestured at one of the papers on his desk. 'Amanda Greene, for instance. She's actually pretty interesting. Bright woman. Lost her husband — '

D'Anconia waved him off. 'I'm sure it's a very interesting story,' he said, 'but the point is, she gets paid to let you use her name?'

For a moment, Burke didn't say anything. D'Anconia's bluntness was a surprise, like finding an occlusion in a gemstone. 'That's right,' he said. 'She acts as a director, and the corporation pays her one hundred euros for her trouble.'

'Each year?'

'No,' Burke replied. 'It's a onetime fee.'

D'Anconia nodded thoughtfully. 'And how much does she know about the corporation?'

'Just its name. Which reminds me, you're going to need one. I may not be able to get what you want, but I can try.'

D'Anconia looked thoughtful. 'I was thinking . . . what about the Twentieth-Century Motor Company? Could you get that?'

'I can try,' Burke promised, writing the name on a Post-it. Then he paused. 'You said 'the *Twentieth*-Century Motor Company'?'

'Right.'

'Kind of archaic, isn't it?'

D'Anconia shrugged.

'Well,' Burke said, 'it doesn't matter, really.

Half the companies we form are generics like the Two-One-Two Corporation or ABX.'

D'Anconia thought some more. 'You said there was some kind of declaration?'

'Right. The declaration says that the company is brand-new, and that the directors don't have any claim against its assets. Nor will they, if they're dismissed. And they always are. The package you get includes their resignations — signed, but undated.'

'What about the bank account? Can the nominees — '

Burke shook his head. 'No. You're the only signatory. Which reminds me, I'll need your passport.'

'My passport?'

'For the bank.'

'What's the bank got to do with it?'

'They need to know who you are,' Burke explained. 'Someone walks in off the street, says he's you . . . the bank has to be sure. Trust me, you *want* the bank to be sure.'

D'Anconia extracted a passport from his overcoat, and pushed it across the desk.

The colors were a surprise. Blue and gold. *He's Chilean?* 'I'll just be a minute.' Burke crossed the room to a copying machine in the corner. The machine came to life. After a moment, a light flared. He turned to the emergency contact page, where an address in Santiago had been penciled in. The copying machine flared a second time.

'Is that it, then?' d'Anconia asked. 'We're all set?'

'Almost,' Burke replied. Returning to the desk, he handed the passport back to his client, and sat down. '*Diga me, es su primer viaje a Irlanda?*'

For a moment, d'Anconia didn't move. Then he cocked his head to the side, and held Burke's gaze for what seemed like a long time. Finally, he said, '*Si, vale. Primer tiempo.*'

Burke smiled. The guy's accent was about as Spanish as a California roll. 'Well,' he said, 'it's a great country.'

'So let's do it then,' d'Anconia said. Reaching into his coat, he pulled out a leather wallet, fat with bills. Counting out thirteen one-hundred-euro notes, he laid them on the desk in a sort of fan.

Burke gathered the bills together, and put them in a lockbox in the bottom drawer. Then he wrote out a receipt, and handed it to d'Anconia. 'So I can forward everything to the address in your passport? To Santiago?'

D'Anconia looked thoughtful for a moment, then shook his head. 'I'm not going to be there for a while. But I'm going to need the bank details — wire-transfer codes and all — as soon as possible. I think the best thing to do would be to send it all to my hotel.'

Burke winced, and shook his head. 'A hotel — '

' — is all I can give you. I'll be in Belgrade, at the Esplanade, for a couple of weeks.'

With a sigh, Burke made a note. 'The thing is, there's going to be correspondence.'

D'Anconia frowned.

'It's unavoidable. But I can put you on the Hold Mail list,' Burke told him. This was a roster of clients who should never be contacted by the firm. Any communications should originate with the client himself. The concern of people on the Hold Mail list, almost universally, was the concealment of assets — from wives, creditors, and governments.

'Excellent,' d'Anconia said.

'But you'll have to check in with us from time to time. There's an annual tax. If it isn't paid, the corporation will lose its standing.' Burke could see that d'Anconia wasn't listening. Maybe he didn't care what happened to the company. Maybe he'd use it for a single transaction, and walk away. If so, it was no skin off Burke's nose. With a smile, he got to his feet, signaling an end to the meeting. The two men shook hands, and d'Anconia let himself out the way he'd come in.

Burke shook his head, and smiled ruefully. Moving to the window, he watched as his client left the building, shoulders hunched against the rain.

He's either avoiding taxes, or evading them, Burke decided. Either way, it wasn't any of his business. Let the IRS do its job, and he'd do his.

Even so, there was something about d'Anconia that bothered him, and it wasn't his nationality. No, the thing that bothered Burke about d'Anconia was his name. It was somehow familiar, like the name of a second- or third-string celebrity.

Maybe that's it, Burke thought. Maybe he's an actor.

He could imagine him playing a doctor on TV — a brilliant young surgeon who, just for the fun of it, killed the occasional patient.

8

BAALBEK, LEBANON FEBRUARY 18, 2005

Wilson stood with his back to the wall, watching the ragheads dip the cans, one by one, in buckets of gasoline. He'd been in the warehouse all day, so the gas was in his clothes, in his hair, in his pores. He could taste it. Which was frustrating, because he desperately wanted a cigarette. But even if he went outside, he couldn't just light up. If he did, he'd go off like a flare.

The other thing about going outside was his babysitters: Zero and Khalid. Around twenty years old, they wore boots and jeans and American T-shirts ('Give a Hoot, Don't Pollute!'), and carried Heckler & Koch submachine guns as casually as umbrellas. They went with him everywhere, thanks to Hakim, and it was getting on his nerves. The one guy's English was almost nonexistent, but the other one spoke it well. The real problem was: They wanted to be his *friends*. They wanted to go to America! So they were constantly mugging in his direction, bobbing their heads and smiling insanely, as if to say, *Death to America, but not to you, my friend! For you — falafel! For us, green cards!*

He told Hakim: *I don't need a bodyguard, much less two — much less the Fukwitz twins!* The Arab insisted, and maybe he was right.

Beneath its veneer of Gallic and Arab civility, Lebanon was a tinderbox. Always had been, always would be. And Baalbek was just . . . so much kindling.

A flyblown crossroads in the Bekaa Valley, the city lay at the foot of a long, bare hill, crowned by the Sheikh Abdullah barracks. This was the fort where American hostages had been kept, chained to radiators and pipes, during the 1980s. Hakim wanted to show him the cells, but there hadn't been time and, anyway, Hakim didn't trust the Syrian intel people who were headquartered there. Which was too bad, because Wilson knew something about prisons, was interested in prisons — and he wondered about the cells. Had the hostages been able to see the ruins across the road? It would have made a difference — because the ruins were as spectacular as they were unexpected.

From an engineering standpoint, they were mind-boggling. There was a brochure at the hotel. It said they were the remains of a Roman sanctuary. The centerpiece was the Temple of Jupiter, a colossus assembled on a foundation so broad and deep that it contained more stone than the Great Pyramid at Giza.

It was a wreck now. Fifty columns lying in the grass, tumbled this way and that, as if a forest of stone had been felled.

To the Romans, it was 'Heliopolis,' City of the Sun. The brochure said that it was here, on the trade route between Damascus and Tyre, that the apostle Paul saw the Light. You'd think there'd be a plaque or something, but there was nothing.

77

Just a flyer on a telephone pole, advertising the summer music festival that took place each year amid the ruins. This year: Björk and Sting.

The warehouse in which Wilson stood, wishing he could smoke, was a prefab hulk with broken windows and rusting joints. Set back from the road on an acre of hardpan, it was cold inside — except where the welders worked.

There was a ton of hash in place — quality smoke, grown locally under the supervision of Hakim's contacts in the Ministry of Defense. Even with an assembly line, getting the product ready to ship took time. Each 'hand' weighed half a kilo and had to be packaged so that it would be undetectable as it moved across borders. This meant putting the product into small plastic bags, a pound at a time, then wiping down the bags with sponges soaked in gasoline.

When the bags were clean, a different set of workers would drag them on carts to the other end of the warehouse, where they would be put, one by one, in five-by-seven tins about an inch thick. The tins would then be taken to a separate room, where they'd be sponged down with gasoline, then placed in somewhat larger tins. The larger tin would then be filled with melted wax and soldered shut. After one last dip in a bucket of gas, the tins would be laid in the bottom of fifty-five-gallon drums. Then, a forklift hauled the drums to a large room at the far end of the warehouse, where each barrel was fitted with a metal plate, creating a false bottom, just above the hash. The drums were then filled with about fifty gallons of pomegranate molasses, and sealed. Finally, each drum was spray-painted with the words MELASSE DE LIBAN.

By Wilson's reckoning, it was going to take upwards of two hundred drums to package it all. But when they were done, there wasn't a sniffer-dog in the world who'd bark at it.

★　★　★

That night, he had dinner with Hakim. Though Wilson had been in Lebanon for nearly a week, he had yet to speak to the Arab for more than five minutes at a time. They'd come to Baalbek in separate cars, following the Bekaa Valley as it curved north, arid and blond, between opposing mountain ranges. Once in Baalbek, Wilson was left to himself (and his minders), while Hakim made arrangements about the hash.

The hashish was a recent development, and it was an unpleasant surprise. During their time in Allenwood, Bo had assured him that finding money for Wilson's project would not be a problem — money was never a problem. At the time, Hakim's military operations had been subsidized by a prince who occupied a high position in the Ministry of the Interior in Riyadh. In return for the prince's financial assistance, Hakim had promised to restrict his operations to targets outside the Happy Kingdom. And so he had.

But all that changed after 9/11. The prince was killed in an automobile accident (or so the Saudis claimed), and Hakim's money supply dried up almost overnight. By the time Wilson was released from prison, operations were being funded with cloned and stolen credit cards, bank robberies, kidnappings, and drugs.

Just as Hakim had once worked with a prince in the Saudi Ministry of the Interior, he now worked with a general in Lebanon's Ministry of Defense.

The Bekaa Valley was quilted with fields of marijuana grown on large and modern farms. Harvested with tractors and dried in barns, the plants were hand-rubbed through sieves of cloth, creating a resinous dust that was easily compressed into blocks of hashish.

It was up to Hakim to package the product and move it — that's where Wilson came in. He would have preferred to be given a suitcase full of cash, and sent on his way to carry out his operation. Instead, he found himself having to earn the money the hard way, plunging into a Triangle Trade of drugs and guns and diamonds.

Moral issues didn't bother him. He was beyond that. What worried Wilson was the fact that he was putting his life in the hands of a man who hated Americans. All he really knew about Hakim was what Bo told him. And Bo was insistent that the less Wilson and Hakim knew about each other, the better it would be for both of them. Still, he'd learned a few things about his dinner companion.

According to Bo, 'Aamm Hakim' was a Jordanian. An Islamist, he'd attended universities in Iran and the United States. In the 1980s, he'd fought with the Taliban against the Russians in

Afghanistan, and with Hezbollah against the Americans in Beirut. When the Lebanese civil war wound down, he formed his own organization to carry out operations under contract to foreign intelligence agencies and others requiring deniability.

Were Hakim and his group a part of al-Qaeda? Wilson asked. Bo turned the question aside. Al-Qaeda isn't like that, he told him. There's a big al-Qaeda, and a little al-Qaeda. The big al-Qaeda is more of a network than an organization. It's like the Internet, he said, a cloud of constantly changing connections, with no central command, a loose association of people with shared affinities. Some know each other, most don't.

Does your uncle know bin-Laden? Wilson asked.

Uncomfortable with the question, Bo replied with a non sequitur: 'They don't call him bin-Laden. They call him the Contractor.'

The FBI's 'Most Wanted' website had its own version of Aamm Hakim. According to the Bureau, Wilson's dinner companion was an Egyptian, né Hakim Abdul-Bakr Mussawi, aka Ali Hussein Musalaam, Ahmed Izz-al-Din, and half a dozen other names.

He had a degree in accounting and was 'the alleged military operations chief of the Coalition of the Oppressed of the Earth.'

Wilson had clicked on the FBI link that explicated the ideology of various al-Qaeda splinter groups. The Coalition was composed of Salafi jihadists 'who believe that ridding the

81

world of modernity will result in an Islamic Revival, returning Muslim peoples worldwide to Islam's most righteous path. While not rejecting technology as such, Salafi jihadists do reject Western (and especially U.S.) cultural hegemony. Orbiting the true believers at the center of the Coalition,' Wilson read, 'is the usual assortment of mercenaries and foot soldiers.' According to the website, the Coalition was responsible for 'attacks on American facilities in West Africa and the Far East.'

★　★　★

Wilson and Hakim sat in the dining room of the Hotel Dumas, a dilapidated relic with high ceilings and dusty chandeliers. If anything, the guest rooms were even more decrepit, with wooden beds little better than pallets. In its heyday, the place had been a destination of considerable glamour, hosting the likes of Josephine Baker and Charles de Gaulle. But that was then; now the Bekaa's dust had taken hold. Pipes clanked. Doors creaked. Towels and rugs were threadbare.

But the food was delicious.

With the exception of Zero and Khalid, sipping tea at a table near the door, Wilson and Hakim were alone. Their party seemed to be the hotel's only guests, though whether this was by accident or design was uncertain.

By now Wilson was not shocked by the arrival of the bottle of wine or the pleasure Hakim took in the ritual. Despite the Islamic ban on alcohol, the Arab liked to peruse the label, take a careful sniff of the cork when the waiter presented it, and judiciously taste the small splash of wine poured into his glass.

Hakim smacked his lips, nodded, and dismissed the waiter. He poured a glass for himself, then Wilson.

It was as if Hakim had read Wilson's mind. Holding his glass up to the light, he sent the liquid into a slow, centrifugal spin. Finally, he took a sip. 'I'm Takfiri,' he explained, his voice low and matter-of-fact. 'You know this word?'

Wilson shook his head.

'It means that for us, the rules don't matter. Wine, a girl, even pork — everything is allowed. Nothing is *haram*.'

'Sweet,' Wilson remarked.

Hakim ignored the sarcasm. 'It's not 'sweet.' Everything is different for us. It has to be.'

'Why?'

'Because we're in a war,' he said, 'and because we're 'behind the lines.'' Hakim said this as if he were explaining the obvious. 'For us, sin is a kind of disguise.'

Wilson nodded.

'It makes me invisible,' Hakim said.

Wilson got it, but he didn't buy it. After a week in Lebanon, it was obvious that the Arab knew how to enjoy himself, whatever the Koran might say about it. Their second night in Beirut, Hakim had gotten drunk in the bar of the St. Georges Hotel, eventually wandering off with an expensive-looking girl young enough to be his granddaughter. Was that an exercise in cover?

Either way, there was no denying Hakim's commitment to 'the cause,' and even to the plan at hand. However skeptical he may have been of working with an American, however doubtful he may have been that Wilson's project would work, Hakim had come through on every promise. And why shouldn't he? Wilson wondered. It wasn't as if the Arab was doing it for shits and giggles. Once the two of them hooked up in Antwerp, Hakim would walk off with seventy percent of the take. So even if Wilson's own operation went nowhere, the Arab would make a great deal of money. And Wilson would be taking all the risks.

Hakim drained his glass, then poured another. The waiter came and went in a blaze of smiles, distributing a mezze of small dishes around the table. Hakim swirled his wine, somehow managing to do so without ever seeming to move his hand.

'You haven't said anything about Belgrade,' Hakim remarked.

Wilson shrugged. 'Not much to tell. I did what I went to do. It snowed.'

'And then you came here.' It didn't sound like a question, but it was.

'No,' Wilson told him, wondering how much the Arab knew. 'First, I went to Lake Bled. *Then* I came here.'

'Lake Bled?'

'Slovenia.'

Nodding to himself, Hakim tore a chunk of pita in half and, using it as a scoop, slid a mound of baba ghanoush into his mouth. 'And what's in Slovenia?'

'A notebook.'

'Oh, yes, the famous 'notebook'! Bo told me about it. You found it!?'

Wilson nodded. 'I did. Many notebooks.'

Hakim smiled encouragingly, humoring the man across from him. He didn't really understand what the American was up to. Bobojon had explained it to him months before, but none of it made much sense. The operation had something to do with this crazy scientist, Tesla, who'd been dead fifty years. Some lost books. A bomb that wasn't a bomb. The way his nephew told it, the American was going to 'stop the motor of the world.' Hakim laughed. *The motor of the world!*

'What's so funny?' Wilson asked.

The Arab shook his head. 'I was thinking of something else,' he lied. There was no point in insulting Wilson. Even if he was crazy, he'd been tested — and he'd passed. So he was a serious man and the important thing was to humor him, as a favor to Bobojon. Bobojon was doing serious work. And besides, Hakim needed help moving the hash. He paused. 'I have good news for you!'

'What's that?' Wilson asked, trying not to sound suspicious.

'Tomorrow you're going to Tripoli.'

Wilson was puzzled. 'Libya?'

Hakim shook his head. 'Not that Tripoli,' he said. 'This one's in Lebanon, fifty miles north of Beirut. It's the main port. Everything goes through there. Molasses, too.'

Wilson's annoyance vanished.

'I've arranged a car. You'll leave in the morning.'

'What about them?' Wilson lifted his chin in the direction of his babysitters.

Hakim turned in his seat and waved to the boys, whose faces lit up in smiles. 'They go where the cans go.'

'And after the cans?'

'They go everywhere.'

Pushing a wedge of pita into a soft dune of hummus, Wilson brought it up to his mouth. 'And once I'm in Tripoli, how do I find the ship?'

'No problem,' Hakim told him. 'It's in the port. Turkish flag. More rust than paint. The *Marmara Queen*.'

'And they're expecting me?'

Hakim shrugged. 'They're expecting 'the shipping agent' for Aswan Exports. That's you. It's your molasses.'

'What about visas?'

'You won't need any. Belov will meet you on the docks in Odessa. It's all arranged. He'll walk you through.'

Wilson frowned.

'What?' Hakim asked.

'I was thinking about Belov,' Wilson said. 'Why doesn't he rip me off? Just take the product, and walk away?'

'He won't do that,' Hakim told him.

'Why not? Who's going to stop him, Zero and Khalid?'

'Maybe not, but . . . I wouldn't underestimate them,' Hakim said. 'They're good boys.'

Wilson chuckled ruefully. 'You realize I don't

know shit about guns, right?'

Hakim shrugged. 'So what? We do a lot of business with Belov,' Hakim said. 'He won't try to cheat us. It wouldn't be smart. And Belov's *very* smart. He's Russian, but he works out of Sharjah. So we have a little influence. His planes are there, and he has a couple of warehouses. It's a good place for him. He won't risk that. Not for something like this.' He brought the tips of his thumb and forefinger almost together. 'Anyway, if I'm wrong, you'll be the first to know.'

'That's what worries me.'

Hakim smiled, then popped an olive into his mouth, worked it around, and spat the pit onto the floor. 'I'm going out of town for a few days,' he announced. 'So maybe you'll get to Antwerp first. Either way, get a room at De Witte Lelie Hotel. Can you remember that? 'The white lily.' Like the flower.'

Wilson nodded. 'Then what?'

'When I get there, we'll go to the diamond exchange. You and me. There's a Jew we do business with.' He closed his eyes and shook his head, then opened his eyes again. 'He'll take the diamonds, arrange the wire transfers. As we discussed: It's seventy-thirty. You get the thirty. After that? You're on your own.'

Wilson forked a chunk of lamb kebab into his mouth, and savored it on his tongue. 'What about Bo?'

Hakim looked puzzled. 'What about him?'

'Will he be there?'

'Of course not.'

'Why not?' Wilson asked.

'He does special work. Even I don't see him.'

Wilson dipped a chunk of pita into a dish of gray puree, and brought it up to his mouth. 'What *is* this stuff?'

'Lamb tartare.'

Wilson set the bread aside. 'What does 'special work' mean?'

Hakim considered the question. Finally, he smiled and said, 'My nephew, he's good with computers. So he helps us with communications.'

'How?'

The Arab sipped his wine, then carefully set the glass on the table. Folding his hands in his lap, he said, 'Let me give you a bit of advice.'

Wilson raised his chin.

'We're in business together,' Hakim told him. 'You and me and Bobojon. Which is good. But you're not one of us. And the way things work, it's better if you're not too curious. People get nervous. *I* get nervous. And that could be bad for you.' When Wilson said nothing, the Arab sat back in his seat and frowned. 'Tell me something. Why are you doing this?'

Wilson rolled his eyes in a way that said, *It's complicated.*

Hakim wagged a finger at him. 'You know what I think? I think you're an intellectual.'

Wilson grinned. 'I'm an engineer,' he said. 'It's not the same.'

'Of course, but . . . when you were in prison, my nephew says that you were reading — always, you were reading. He says you read Qutb. Is that true?'

'Yeah.'

'Which book?'

'*Milestones.*'

The Arab nodded to himself. 'What did you think?'

Wilson pursed his lips. Until he was hanged by Egypt's Nasser, Sayyid Qutb was a revolutionary who preached a return to Islamic purity and the overthrow of corrupt Arab regimes. More than anyone else, his views had shaped the thinking of people like Osama bin-Laden. 'I think Qutb is fine,' Wilson told him, 'if you're an Arab.'

'And if you're not?'

'If you're not, you need to look for someone else.'

'I couldn't agree more,' Hakim exclaimed. 'To each his own! So what about you? If not Qutb, who?'

Wilson shrugged.

'Bobojon said you have Indian blood,' Hakim persisted.

Wilson said nothing.

'Forgive me,' Hakim said. 'I know nothing about Indians. Just the old movies.' He paused. 'But tell me, does your tribe have anyone like Qutb?'

'My 'tribe'?' Wilson repeated. 'No, 'my tribe' doesn't have anyone like Qutb. No tracts, no pamphlets, no Fiery Flying Rolls.'

Hakim laughed. 'Then what? What do you have?'

'Laments.'

'Laments?'

Wilson nodded. 'Yeah, there's a lot of sad songs.'

'That's *it*?'

'No,' he said. 'We have the Ghost Dance.'

Hakim laughed, and poured each of them another glass of wine. 'Sad songs and dances! What a people!'

The Arab's sarcasm struck a nerve. But even as the adrenaline curled through Wilson's chest, his features remained as neutral as a sundial. After a moment, he said, 'I didn't know my parents. I grew up in foster homes. So I didn't have any history — none that I knew, anyway. Someone said I was Indian, and I *looked* Indian. But it never meant anything. The first time I heard about the Ghost Dance, I was just a kid. I was in the dentist's office, and there was an article in a magazine.'

'Yes?' Hakim looked confused, perhaps a little drunk.

'It was just an article. And pictures of a man they called Wovoka. He was all tricked out in a ghost shirt, with stars and moons on it.'

Hakim frowned. He had no idea what the American was talking about. *Ghosts?*

Wilson continued: 'It turned out, we had the same name. Not 'Wovoka,' but the same *real* name. I guess I kind of forgot about it, you know? Until later, when I went to prison. My second year in Supermax' — he laughed at the memory — 'I'm sitting in my cell, watching the wall. And it hits me! This thing with the name — it's no coincidence. It's who I am. Literally! So it's my past, my future. Everything.'

Hakim nodded absently. Wilson could see his confusion draining to boredom, the boredom to irritation. 'What are you talking about?' Hakim glanced around for the waiter.

Wilson cocked his head. The Arab didn't have a clue. And then he realized why. Hakim didn't know his real name, or if he did, he'd forgotten it. To Hakim, he was 'Frank d'Anconia' — and that was that. So there was no point in telling him about the other Jack Wilson. For Hakim, the coincidence didn't exist.

Finally, Wilson said, 'I'm talking about the Ghost Dance,' he said. 'It's what we have instead of Qutb.'

Hakim frowned. 'But you haven't told me what it is.'

Wilson leaned forward. 'Wovoka . . . he had a vision. He saw the Indians begin to dance. By themselves, at first, and then with their ancestors. After a while, the earth shook and the dancers . . . well, in the vision, the dancers went into the sky. Just floated up. Then the earth swallowed everyone who was left. Which was the whites. All the Indians' enemies. After that, the world began to heal.'

'To heal.'

'Yes. It went back to the way it was, the way it had been,' Wilson explained.

Hakim stared at him, blinking dully. Finally, he said, 'I think you've had too much alcohol.'

Wilson took a deep breath. The fat bastard in front of him would never understand.

Then the Arab did something unexpected. With a wave of his hand, he brushed the conversation aside, and reached into the shoulder bag on the floor beside his seat. Removing a small black jewel box, he set it down upon the table, and pushed it toward Wilson. 'This is for you,' he said, and lowering his head, touched his fingertips to his chest.

Wilson eyed the box. It was one of those velvet-covered cases used for wedding rings. 'I didn't know you cared.'

Hakim smiled. *Open it*, his eyes said.

For a moment, Wilson hesitated. Then he reached for the box and, prying it open, found a bloodred capsule in the silk niche that was meant for a ring. It wasn't a vitamin.

Hakim chuckled. 'Till death do us part.' Lifting the left side of his shirt collar, he offered a glimpse of an identical capsule taped to the collar's underside, where a collar stay might have been.

Wilson stared at the capsule. 'You think I'd take this?'

Hakim shrugged. 'That's up to you,' he said. 'But if you're caught, they'll hurt you.'

Wilson closed the box, and put it in his pocket. 'It's painful?'

Hakim shook his head. 'No. You see pictures from Jonestown? Afterward? Everybody's smiling.'

Wilson leaned forward. 'That was rictus. It's different.'

9

The car nosed around a rotary out of Jounieh and angled off in the direction of a sign that pointed the way to Tripoli.

The driver was stern-faced and silent. Zero and Khalid, on the other hand, sat in the backseat talking animatedly and nonstop in Arabic. The language washed over Wilson like white noise, with only the occasional word or phrase in English to claim his attention. *Okay! Fifty Cent! Viagra . . . them Knicks.*

Zero and Khalid were there for his protection. Or so Hakim claimed. But Wilson knew better. Yes, they would protect him if someone tried to rip him off, but their main purpose was to make sure that he didn't walk off with Hakim's cut.

After a couple of hours jouncing up a decrepit highway, they entered the dusty outskirts of the port. They passed a derelict orchard, the weeds high between the evenly spaced trees, then a squatter's village of brightly colored tents.

'Syrians.' Khalid sneered. 'They take all the jobs.'

The Syrian encampment gave way to apartment blocks that looked like mausoleums. The ground and buildings were the same dun color.

Kids chased a soccer ball, kicking up clouds of dust. A woman in white robes swept with a broom.

From the backseat Zero spoke in a voice suddenly louder than it had been. Khalid laughed, a soft scoffing sound. He said, 'No way.'

At the checkpoint leading to the docks, the driver flipped open a worn wallet and extracted a folded piece of paper, which he handed over for inspection. The guard perused it, carefully refolded it, and handed it back, giving some instructions.

They passed a couple of small freighters being unloaded by gantry cranes, then skirted a large structure that looked to be a drydock. And then, there it was: The *Marmara Queen*. The links that made up the anchor chain were as thick as Wilson's wrists. It flew the Turkish flag, crescent and star bright white against the crimson background. As the driver pulled up in the shadow of its enormous bow, a mammoth crane swung out over the deck and began to lower a bright blue container.

'Look at the size of this thing,' Khalid said. 'It's bigger than a football pitch.' He nodded toward the blue container. 'You think that's ours?'

Wilson shrugged. He knew one thing for certain. Hakim had a lot of juice, so barring some major catastrophe, the container *would* be on board before they sailed.

Wilson's job was to accompany the hash to Odessa, where he would exchange it for a consignment of arms. Wilson would then escort the shipment of arms to Africa where it would be traded for diamonds — which he would deliver to Hakim at the De Witte Lelie Hotel in Antwerp.

Which meant that he was a glorified mule. Just like the girls who ferried coke up from Colombia, he would be earning his fee by putting himself at risk. Each leg of the journey would be dangerous and the peril would escalate as the trip continued. Wilson understood that there were dozens of things that could go wrong, with the greatest exposure at the points of transaction. Until he turned over the diamonds to Hakim, his ass was on the line.

It was quite a résumé to compile in a short stretch of time: drug trafficker, arms dealer, gem smuggler. But the rewards were commensurate with the risks. It wasn't the safest way for someone with no funds to make a lot of money, but it was the fastest.

The ship was an odd sight, the huge deck holding as many as a hundred or more containers, different in color but each the size of a small cottage. About two thirds of the way between the prow and stern, the clean, white, many-windowed bridge hove into view, like a castle looking down on a shantytown.

The driver dismissed them with a curt nod, their signal to get out.

Zero and Khalid carried their well-worn backpacks, as well as the Diadora bags that held their weapons. Wilson's wheeled suitcase seemed conspicuous as they crossed the ship's gangway.

He pushed in the handle and carried it by the strap.

It was six flights of metal steps up to the bridge. Khalid, a heavy smoker, gasped.

They found the first officer on the bridge, drinking coffee and tapping away at a computer. Shaking Wilson's hand with a firm grip, he wore a big smile, showing large white teeth. Struggling to find enough English, the officer explained that he was in charge of the cargo, of which they were technically a part.

Zero asked a question in Arabic.

The first officer looked at Zero as if he hadn't noticed him before and now that he'd focused, didn't like what he saw. A fleeting expression of distaste came and went, followed by a dismissive shake of the head. 'Maybe two hours,' he said in English.

* * *

Wilson's bodyguards were placed in Spare Officer Cabin #3; Wilson in Spare Officer Cabin #4.

'Not bad,' Khalid said, as the seaman opened the door on a utilitarian space. 'Look, TV.'

'Only Turkish videos,' said the seaman who'd escorted them. 'Facilities down hall. You need, you go now, then you stay here until someone get you.' He held forth an admonishing finger. He ushered Wilson down the hall toward his cabin and repeated the advice with exactly the same intonation.

Wilson surveyed the space — bed, sink,

mirror, built-in wardrobe and chest of drawers, TV, CD player — then stretched out on the bunk. There was something cell-like about it, although it did have a window.

When a container settled onto the deck, there was not much noise, but he felt it. The ship shuddered beneath the thin mattress, reminding him of similar moments in prison when gates slammed shut, or thick electronically controlled doors thudded to a close.

Because he had never been on a ship before, Wilson would have liked to watch the mechanics of its departure. He would also have enjoyed exploring the vessel itself. And then, too, he wanted a cigarette.

Instead, he was required to wait, but that was something he was good at. Whatever normal impatience he might once have had, prison had obliterated. In an interval such as this, in the absence of any real tension, he was free of yearning.

He pulled from his wallet the computer-printed photograph of Irina and looked at her for a moment. It was small, just a little larger than a postage stamp, small enough that it did not need to be folded. It fit easily into one of the slots in his wallet intended for credit cards. He knew from experience how destructive repeated folding could be — even to a letter, let alone an image.

And this image was not even of good quality, printed out as it was from a Kinko's computer onto ordinary paper. He had cut Irina's picture from a gallery of Ukrainian girls (thirty-two to the page) all looking for an American suitor, all smiling.

The women were not looking for love. He knew that. They were looking for a ticket. A ticket out.

He had selected Irina on the basis of a thumb-sized image of mediocre quality, and yet, as he looked at her face, some generosity of spirit shone through. He had e-mailed her twice through the auspices of ukrainebrides.org, which acted as a broker and an intermediary. It solicited memberships, the cost calibrated to the number of women you could contact. It published pictures and biographical notes on the available girls. It outlined and enforced the proper steps of courtship, from the exchange of letters, to the delivery of chocolates and flowers, all of which might one day culminate in a 'romantic visit.' Ukrainebrides would also arrange temporary visas for prenuptial visits and, eventually, marriage ceremonies.

Or one might follow a more direct route, signing on for a 'romance tour,' during which an interested man might attend, in locales from Yalta to Kiev, parties at which fifteen to twenty 'suitors' would roam a crowd of a hundred available women.

Wilson was following the traditional 'court-ship' route, starting with the exchange of letters. His first e-mail contained a brief description of himself as the well-off thirty-year-old business-man Francisco d'Anconia, currently in the import/export trade. Her reply, demure and hesitant, told him she worked as a waitress in a coffee shop in Odessa. She lived with her parents and two sisters. Although he reminded himself that her halting language was due to the linguistic inadequacy of the translator, and not childlike innocence, it still charmed him.

His second message was more of a love letter, praising her beauty, setting forth his own desire for 'someone to share my life with.' This was true. *After*, he did not want to be alone. He'd spent enough time alone. *After*, he wanted to share his life with a woman. He wanted a family. Her reply was an outpouring of poetic longing made all the more touching by the fractured syntax.

He returned the photograph to his wallet. The chance of meeting a worthy lifemate through a commercial matchmaker called ukrainebrides-.org would be the equivalent of hitting the lottery. He knew that.

On the other hand, he didn't believe in coincidence. Was it only chance that placed him on the *Marmara Queen* — which was taking him and his drums of molasses to within a few miles of Irina's home?

As he punched up the pillows and kicked off his shoes and let his eyes fall closed, Irina's smiling face remained in his field of vision. He fell asleep in the soft envelope of imagined domestic bliss.

★   ★   ★

The vibration woke him, a powerful thrum. For a moment, he was alarmed. The sensation seemed to be coming from within him, a destructive resonance. When he realized what it was — the ship's engines had started — he laughed at himself. A few minutes later, he heard the clanking of the anchor chains as they were winched aboard.

They were under way.

It wasn't long before a chirpy little guy rapped on the door. The man had been sent by the first officer to give the promised tour. He was the third officer, he told them, and his name was Hasan. He smiled, disarmingly, showing two gold teeth front and center. 'This is a very fine ship. Hasan is happy to show you around.'

First, the lifeboats. Khalid scratched his head and frowned, eyeing the distance from the boats to the water. 'Hasan can promise you these will not be necessary.'

Zero was selected to model the life jacket, giggling as Hasan tightened the straps.

They reviewed the location of fire extinguishers and Hasan demonstrated how to use one.

Safety issues dispensed with, they were shown around the galley, the dining room, and then the game room. Khalid's eyes lit up at this spartan area — boasting dartboard, chess set, football, and Ping-Pong table.

All the time, the officer peppered them with details about the ship. He showed them the bridge, with its view to the horizon above a deck crowded with containers, then took them down to the engine room, a vast and immaculate space, with huge brass pistons pumping away. It smelled heavily of oil.

Back on deck, Hasan led them to a kind of alleyway between the containers, where it was possible to walk to the bow. If they wanted to do this, they must first inform him and report back when they returned.

At the rail, they looked down at the chop and churn of the water. It was a cold, damp day and the sight of the roiling sea made Wilson uneasy. Under them, the ship moved as if it were alive.

'It require more than one kilometer to stop the ship,' Hasan said, 'so don't falling overboard.' Zero instinctively shrank away from the rail, as Khalid translated.

'Is two days to Istanbul, one day in port there, and then another three days to Odessa. You don't get off in Istanbul?'

Wilson nodded. 'We don't have visas for that.'

'Hasan regrets. A great city.'

Wilson nodded again.

'Is it possible to check e-mail?' Wilson asked.

'Oh yes. Hasan gives you half hour per day, this is okay?'

Wilson smiled and raised his arms at this unexpected generosity and Hasan volleyed back his golden smile.

'The best time you come after dinner, yes? But,' he cautioned, 'computer work from satellite. Sometimes signal good, sometimes not so good.' He shrugged. 'Hasan cannot guarantee.'

★ ★ ★

Zero and Khalid were soon bored and spent almost all of their time in the game room playing

101

football. For Wilson, after all those years in Supermax, boredom did not exist. He easily fell into the rhythm of being at sea: the air, the gulls, the vast expanse of water, the regular meals, his daily walk to the bow in the canyon amid the containers.

He liked the bow, where it was quiet. If he looked over the edge of the deck, he could just see the bulbous front of the ship where it met the water. For centuries, the bows of ships had been like knives. But not any longer. Wilson pondered the change until he understood. A bulbous prow would raise the bow. This would make the ship more efficient by reducing the impact of the bow-wave. He wondered about the man whose insight it was, and if he'd gotten credit for it.

★   ★   ★

Zero and Khalid.

Wilson had little real interest in his companions, but during his long years in captivity, he'd become quite skilled at extracting information from those whose lives intersected with his. He was a good listener. That's what made people think they liked him. He was willing to endure orgies of self-pity and jailhouse rationalizations with what seemed to be an empathetic ear.

The truth was, it was a defensive skill. He paid attention to the other inmates — as well as to the guards — because it gave him an edge.

So it was that without consciously drawing them out, he'd learned quite a bit about his sidekicks. Zero was twenty-two, Khalid twenty-four. They had both grown up in the Shatila refugee camp in Beirut. Khalid, the English-speaker, had a bit of a mean streak. Zero was a happy-go-lucky kid with a signature high-pitched giggle. It interested Wilson that neither were zealots. They worked for 'the cause' because they had virtually no marketable skills. One thing they *could* handle was trouble. Neither would hesitate to pull the trigger. Khalid had few illusions about where his life was headed. 'I'll die in some checkpoint fuckup, something stupid like that.'

It wasn't the lure of the martyr's afterlife — the renewable virgins, the wine, and the honey — that made them soldiers in a dangerous cause. It was, instead, a reaction to the squalor and boredom of Shatila, and a recognition that soldiering was the only work available for young men with little education and fewer prospects.

If, God forbid, they should be killed in the struggle, they'd be martyrs. This, at least, would earn them the respect of everyone who mattered. Their families would be compensated, and their pictures would be posted on the walls of streets in West Beirut. For a week or two, they'd be celebrities. Until it rained, or until someone else was killed.

Meanwhile, they dreamed of emigrating to Canada or America, the very places to whose destruction they were dedicated (if only in word). A likable kid, Zero had a crush on Jennifer Aniston, and insisted that if he could just get to Hollywood, she would be his. Khalid was more complex. His father was an engineer, his mother a pharmacist. Neither had worked at their professions in years. Khalid's own education had been hit-and-run, at best. Prior to casting his lot with the Coalition, he'd worked as a baggage handler at the airport. Since then, he'd fought in Chechnya, where a barber had removed his appendix in the back of an abandoned bus. When Wilson asked him why he worked for the Coalition, Khalid shrugged and said, 'It's a job. And Abu Hakim is good to us.'

★ ★ ★

Three nights after departure, the ship sat at anchor in the Sea of Marmara, Istanbul twinkling on every side. Two dozen ships strung with lights gave a festive look to the scene, although they were all freighters, waiting to make their way east or west, to the Black Sea or the Aegean.

It was almost funny how much Wilson missed the thrum of the engines. The city, with its smoky fog, mosques, and minarets was spectacular, and he was sorry he could not go ashore.

As they did every morning, the muezzin called the faithful to prayer over loudspeakers crackling with static and howling with feedback. The effect was at once industrial and strangely romantic.

After breakfast, Hasan tapped on Wilson's cabin door. He looked unhappy. 'Dock strike in Istanbul.'

'Dock strike?'

'Hasan can report that many voyages, dock strike. Dock strike Piraeus. Dock strike Naples.

Dock strike — this time — Istanbul.'

'How long will we be here?' Wilson was alarmed.

'No way to know. Maybe . . . few days. Hasan regrets.'

Wilson asked if he could use the computer to get a message to his 'business contacts in Odessa.' Then he went to tell Zero and Khalid the bad news. They shrugged and turned back to the television. They had the TV tuned to al-Jazeera and Wilson realized he was watching some kind of bust: A man with a hood over his head was being shoved into the backseat of a black Hummer.

'What's this?' Wilson asked.

'Malaysia,' Khalid replied. 'They say he's al-Qaeda.'

On the screen, the Hummer was moving slowly through a crowd of cops and soldiers. They parted slowly, as if reluctant to let the man go.

Khalid turned away from the TV. 'Anybody they bust, he's *always* 'Qaeda.' Look at how many cops they have.'

A few minutes later, Hasan returned and told Wilson it was okay to use the computer. Wilson immediately walked to the bridge to do so.

He maneuvered into the Yahoo! account that he and Bo used to communicate, and tapped in the password. There were a few e-mail messages, all of them spam. Wilson deleted a couple, then went into the Draft folder. No messages waited. He typed his own:

It's very quiet here. Dock strike will delay arrival. Don't know for how many days. Please advise party waiting for me that I will be late.

He left the message in the Draft folder, signed out, then walked to the bow. Everything was fine, he told himself. Nothing was wrong, it was just a delay. But what if the man in Odessa could not accommodate the change in schedule? What would Wilson then do with his 'molasses'? Hakim was on some kind of trip; if he was unavailable, who would reorganize the transaction in Odessa?

And beyond Odessa, Wilson had his own deadlines. He had to be back in the States with the money by April. Even then, it would take some luck and a lot of hard work if he was to have the device ready by June 22, the day of the Sun Dance.

He told himself there was nothing he could do to alter the situation. Worrying about it was like turbulence in a physics equation, a dissipation of energy. Still, he felt the uneasiness as a kind of physical discomfort.

Wilson stared down into the water. He watched the choppy waves form and re-form. It seemed like chaos, and yet, it was anything but. Like everything else, the swell and crash of the sea was amenable to rational analysis. The movements of the water were a function of the wind's force and direction, the sinuous shoreline and undersea currents, the temperature of water and air, the moon's pull and the flux of the ships, lolling at anchor . . . in *just . . . that . . . way.*

Not chaos, then, but God, or something like it.

10

KUALA LUMPUR FEBRUARY 27, 2005

They were spectacular, in their way.

Lying on the floor, doing her yoga exercises, Andrea Cabot could see the Petronas Towers gleaming in the distance. Monumentally modern, the buildings were the city's erectile glory, proof positive in Malaysian eyes that the future belonged to Islam. A Westerner could not be in KL for more than an hour, if that, without being told that these were 'the tallest freestanding twin towers in the world.' Left unsaid now was that the Towers were taller, even, than the World Trade Center.

Sorry about that.

To Andrea, who'd taken the bungalow in spite of the view rather than because of it, the Towers were a constant admonition. Built on the site of what had once been a racetrack, the steel-and-glass structures paid homage to Islam in both large and small details. The buildings' footprint consisted of two squares superimposed upon each other at an angle, so that they formed an eight-pointed star. Within the confines of that footprint were a six-story shopping center; a mosque for six thousand worshippers; offices for the likes of Microsoft, IBM, and Bloomberg; and a Mandarin Oriental Hotel. In a peculiar gesture of architectural piety, care had been taken to ensure that the urinals were oriented in the general direction of Japan, so that when the buildings' occupants peed, they did so with their backs toward Mecca.

At the embassy, which gave Andrea her thin veneer of diplomatic cover, the consensus seemed to be that the Towers' most important architectural feature was the sky-bridge, a gimballed contraption connecting the buildings near their midsection, forty-two floors above the street. This was, by all accounts, a safety feature. Should some lunatic fly a plane into one of the buildings, office workers could escape from one tower to the next.

Which was neat, but did little to mitigate the fact that in this sexually repressed society, the Towers, when seen from a distance, resembled nothing so much as gigantic vibrators aimed at the heavens.

Andrea's bungalow was situated in the center of a gated and well-guarded compound on the edge of the luxe Ampang district. Built by CIA contractors in the late 1980s to house the chief of station, it had a palmy garden, a lighted swimming pool, and a luxurious safe-room that did double duty as a bath.

It wasn't just that the safe-room was 'safe.' It more or less *was* a safe. Linen wallpaper concealed a hardened steel lattice, sandwiched around bullet-resistant Kevlar. The ceiling and floor were reinforced concrete, the door capable of stopping anything less than a round from an RPG. There was a closed-circuit television monitor tuned to cameras throughout the house and grounds, and a radio transmitter hardwired directly to a hidden antenna across the street. Like the open telephone line in the living room, the transmitter was monitored twenty-four/seven by the communications duty officer at the U.S. embassy.

So it was as safe as any place could be in a city that served as a convention center for jihadists from all over the world. Not for Andrea the fate of William Buckley, the chief of station kidnapped in Beirut during the 1980s.

She kept Buckley's picture in a silver frame on the dresser in her bedroom. It was there among pictures of her family: mom and dad, her sister, niece, and . . . Bill. Anyone who saw the picture would assume that the man in the frame was a relative, a husband, or a boyfriend. But the truth was, they'd never met. He was there on the dresser as a daily reminder, an object lesson in what not to do.

In the short time that she'd been chief of station in Kuala Lumpur, Andrea had given a lot of thought to Buckley. A patriot who built miniature dioramas of Revolutionary War battles, he'd spent much of his life abroad, moving from one flyblown Muslim capital to another, fighting a precocious and dirty war against what the Arabs were beginning to call 'al-Qaeda' — The Base.

A grim and secretive man, he owned neither house nor apartment. Home was a suite in an executive hotel in downtown Washington.

And he was obviously his own worst enemy.

109

Reading the reports, it was clear to Andrea that Buckley was as much a victim of his own hubris as he was of the terrorists who'd kidnapped him. His sense of immunity was as profound as it was mistaken. Living in the midst of an urban guerrilla war, in a city where mortar attacks were commonplace, Buckley chose to live in a penthouse. In West Beirut! To say it was the wrong side of town was to understate the matter.

Beirut was cleft in two by the Green Line, a bombed-out-no-man's-land that divided the city into East and West, Christian and Muslim. In East Beirut, people prayed to Jesus. In West Beirut, they prayed to Allah.

What was he thinking? Andrea wondered. A penthouse in West Beirut? He might as well have put up a tent on a firing range.

Andrea moved from one asana to another. With glacial grace, she performed the Sun Salutation, raising her face toward the Petronas Towers. *Buckley!* she thought. *How macho!* The most important spook in the Middle East didn't even have a chase car to follow him to work.

In the end, his abduction took less than a minute. Buckley's car, a beige Honda, was parked outside his apartment building on the Rue Tanoukhi. As he pulled away from the curb, a white Renault cut in front of him, blocking the way. Two men jumped from the Renault, waving guns and shouting. One of the kidnappers pulled Buckley from his car. Another grabbed his briefcase.

Pushed onto the floor of the Renault, the CIA

110

man was covered with a blanket and told to keep his mouth shut. The Renault took off, turned a corner, and headed for the Corniche. Within minutes, it was stopped at a checkpoint run by an Islamic militia. Gunmen waved the gunmen on. From the checkpoint, it was a short drive to the slums. There, the chief of station was taken to a windowless basement, where he was blindfolded and chained to an eyebolt in the floor.

A report from an agent in Hezbollah stated that Buckley's interrogation lasted months. The source reported that the American had been tortured with the help of a Palestinian doctor, who administered drugs and monitored the prisoner's vital signs.

The interrogation was said to focus on CIA operations in Lebanon, including kidnappings and assassinations that the Agency had 'outsourced' to allies in the Lebanese armed forces and Christian militias.

From there, the area of inquiry expanded to include Buckley's earlier assignments. He'd worked in Egypt and Syria, and served on the CIA review board that evaluates agents in the Middle East. That in itself should have disqualified him from serving in the area, because once he was kidnapped, it ensured that the cover of every agent in the Middle East was blown.

They got him back in a coffin. Whether Buckley had been tortured to death or died of malignant neglect was uncertain. Neither was it known where he'd been kept during his long months of imprisonment or how often he'd been moved.

Andrea had read the accounts of other hostages who told of being moved from one dungeon to another in the cruelest of possible ways. Bound and gagged, the prisoners were wedged into boxes attached to the undersides of trucks. The only air available to them was a mixture of diesel fumes and dust.

Catch a cold, and you could be dead.

The only way to get through something like that was to zombie out. Andrea had trained for precisely that contingency. Like every other CIA officer sent to a danger post, she'd been subjected to mock interrogations at the Farm, the Agency's training facility near Williamsburg, Virginia. As a part of that training, she'd been 'encrated.' That's what they called it when they stuffed you into a box and left you to think about it for a couple of hours. Or a couple of days.

And that was why she did yoga exercises every morning. It wasn't so much the stretching as the breathing. After years of practice, she found that she could lower her resting heartbeat to fewer than thirty beats a minute. Any lower, and she'd have been hibernating or dead. Which was more or less what you wanted to be if you woke up in a box.

A quavering beep floated up from the watch on her wrist, reminding her that it was time to get going. She had an appointment at the regional interrogation center that morning, and she didn't want to be late. A man was being tortured on her behalf. The least she could do was watch.

11

As the embassy's Mercedes wound its way through the hills outside the city, Andrea sat in the backseat, crossing and uncrossing her legs, reading a report. The report was four days old, and this was the third time she'd gone over it.

In the front seat, Marine sergeant Nilthon Alvarado adjusted the rearview mirror, ostensibly to see if they were being followed, in fact to admire the chief of station's legs.

The report was from the MSB, the Special Branch of the Royal Malaysia Police. It concerned a CIA-MSB operation targeting a thug named Nik Awad, who was known to be a liaison between the Kumpulan Militan Malaysia (KMM) and Jemaah Islamiyah (JI). These were terrorist networks hell-bent on making Malaysia part of an Islamic republic whose borders would stretch from northern Thailand to the farthest island in the Philippines. The CIA's interest was parochial. Awad was thought to be planning an attack on the American military base in Sumatra.

Recently, telephone surveillance had generated an interesting lead. In a call from Berlin, Awad was asked to facilitate the visit of 'a friend from Beirut.' The friend was identified only as 'Aamm Hakim,' and Awad was to meet him at Subang Airport.

Since Awad was going to be detained anyway, the Special Branch decided to wait for the

113

friend's arrival. A day or two would make no difference, and Subang Airport was as good a place as any to take Awad down. When the time came, plainclothes MSB officers fell in step behind Awad as he waded into the crowd in the Arrivals terminal. When he exchanged *abrazos* with a man coming out of Customs, they swooped.

Which is when it got interesting. 'Aamm Hakim' was traveling on a Syrian passport issued to a man named 'Badr Faris.' The passport appeared to be valid, and Mr. Faris was not on any of the lookout lists. From an intelligence standpoint, he was cherry. And having just entered the country, he'd done nothing wrong, so there were no real grounds for holding him. Not even under the Internal Security Act.

Special Branch was disappointed. With hopes of netting a big fish, instead, they had a businessman who claimed to be looking for a site on which to build a condom factory. They were skeptical, but there was nothing they could do. The man's political views were unknown, and he didn't seem particularly religious. On the contrary, 'Faris' was a clean-shaven businessman who obviously enjoyed himself. His suitcase contained a bottle of Jack Daniel's, a photo-magazine called *Beaver Hunt*, and a business card for an erotic massage and escort service in Beirut.

As to the call from Berlin, Faris claimed he knew nothing about it. 'A friend in Beirut offered to put me in touch with Mr. Awad. Said he could be helpful. I thought, okay, why not? I assumed my friend placed the call himself, but . . . apparently not. As to who he called in Berlin, I have no idea. I've never been there.'

So how had Awad recognized him?

Oh, you know how it is . . . I was looking for him, he was looking for me. We saw each other looking around . . .

Andrea looked up from the report. So why did they call him 'Aamm Hakim'? she wondered. 'Aamm' was an Arab honorific, referring to an uncle on the paternal side. If Faris was the uncle, who was the nephew? Was it the guy in Berlin who'd placed the call? Or was it Awad himself? It had to be one or the other, and yet, according to Faris, he didn't know either of them. Obviously, Faris was lying.

Andrea's eyes returned to the report.

After an hour of questioning, the MSB agents were about to let Faris go, when one of the detectives noticed something about his shirt collar. 'What *is* that?' he asked, reaching for the collar.

All hell broke loose. Coming out of his chair, Faris drop-kicked the detective in the balls, and bolted for the door. That was as far as he got. One cop dragged him to the floor, while another pinned him by the arms. He had something in his hand that he wouldn't let go of — until the detective with the sore balls stomped on his elbow, snapping the ulna.

A pill rolled onto the linoleum and, suddenly, it was clear that Mr. Faris was no ordinary businessman.

Since then, Andrea had visited the interrogation center on two occasions. Each time, she sat outside Room 11, listening through headphones to what the Malaysians called a 'disciplinary interrogation.' If she had a question, she would ask it of Jim Benerjee, MSB's liaison to the Agency, and Benerjee would put the question to the interrogators in the room. In this way, Andrea could truthfully say that she had not participated in Mr. Faris's questioning (or 'so-called torture').

By then, 'Faris' was more subdued than he'd been at the airport. No more shouts of 'God is great!' Instead, there was a lot of heavy breathing, punctuated by questions posed in a voice that was alternately angry and cajoling. The answers came with a quaver, sometimes followed by a crackle of electricity as Mr. Faris's inquisitors lit him up with a stun gun.

So far, they'd learned almost nothing. However, the fingerprint check had come back positive. The detainee's real name was Hakim Abdul-Bakr Mussawi. Special Branch files identified Mussawi as a fifty-four-year-old Egyptian who'd been expelled from the Muslim Brotherhood twenty years earlier for excessive militance. Since then, he had been implicated in the activities of the KMM, Jemaah Islamiyah, and the Baalbek-based Coalition of the Oppressed of the Earth. There were warrants for him in his homeland and five other countries. Both the Ministry of the Interior in Oman and the FBI were offering rewards.

But if Andrea had anything to say about the matter, it would be a while before they'd learn about Hakim. There was no point in making a splash — it would just send Hakim's friends packing. Better to keep him under wraps. Maybe she could leverage him.

★   ★   ★

The interrogation center was a complex of modern buildings about twenty miles from Kuala Lumpur. Built with U.S. funds in the aftermath of 9/11, it lay at the end of a two-lane access road, behind a juggernaut of concrete barriers and electrified fences topped with concertina wire.

Banerjee was waiting for her at the registration desk on the mezzanine. He was a tall, ethnic Indian with a pockmarked face and a razor scar under his chin, where a thief had tried to kill him. Andrea had met him in the States two years earlier, when he'd attended an anti-terrorist training module at the Farm. A Special Branch lieutenant in his early thirties, Banerjee liked to skydive on weekends, jumping out of the plane with his pet python, Roosevelt, draped over his shoulders.

He handed Andrea a visitor's pass. 'You signing in?'

She answered with a Mona Lisa smile and a little shake of her head.

Banerjee shrugged, and swiped his pass through a slot in one of the turnstiles. 'After you.'

'What about Dr. Najib?'

'He's waiting for us,' Banerjee told her.

'Good. There's something I'd like to try.'

'And you need a doctor for it?'

Andrea shrugged. 'It's just a precaution. I don't want to kill the guy.' She paused. 'How is he, anyway?'

Banerjee rolled his eyes. 'Same as yesterday. I think he's still in capture shock.'

The interrogation rooms were in the subbasement. Stepping into the elevator, Banerjee pressed the button for B-2. As the doors closed, Muzak played quietly from a speaker above their heads . . . *We all live in a yellow submarine* . . .

'I meant to ask . . . ' Andrea said. 'Have you talked to the FBI?'

'Not yet.'

Andrea was pleased. 'So they aren't in the picture.'

'Well, they know about Awad. We're sending them dailies of his interviews. But I don't think anyone's said anything about Faris.'

'Faris?'

'That's the name on his passport,' Banerjee told her.

'I know, but — What about the fingerprints?'

'Oh, that! Yeah, that's . . . that's a real contradiction. We're looking into it.'

Andrea gave him her searchlight smile. 'So . . . '

'So, he's just another detainee. For now, anyway.'

Her smile became even wider. Banerjee thought she had the whitest and most even teeth

118

he'd ever seen. 'How long can you keep it like that?'

The lieutenant looked doubtful. 'Not long.'

'Well . . . '

They both knew that the longer Hakim Mussawi remained in Malaysian custody, the more they would get out of him. While the CIA and the military had taken off the gloves after 9/11, they'd put them back on more recently. For a while, torture had been defined in terms of 'organ failure.' No organ failure, no torture. Then Abu Ghraib hit the fan and suddenly, hostile interrogation techniques required legal reviews and special permissions that were not granted often enough — to Andrea's way of thinking.

No one wanted his or her name on a piece of paper saying yes, it was okay to beat the crap out of a prisoner, or, if the spirit moved you, to immerse him in a tub of lye. It could screw up your whole career path.

After the recreational torture at Abu Ghraib was exposed, new protocols went into effect. It was still okay to torture people but you couldn't actually *hurt* them. You could terrorize them, but you couldn't flay them.

Discomfort, even 'intense discomfort,' was okay, but only for a while. Prisoners might be placed in stress positions, but there were limits. Only one hour at a time, and no more than four hours in a day.

This would not break a hard man. Better, then, to humiliate him, or bring him to tears by threats to a loved one. That took time, though, and if you were in a hurry, you wanted an ally like Malaysia, which had yet to ratify the Optional Protocol to the United Nations Convention Against Torture. If the MSB wanted to play by the old rules, sliding splinters of glass and bamboo under the fingernails of the people they detained, that was an internal matter. So long as Andrea didn't enter the room or ask a direct question, the CIA could take the position that it had nothing to do with the interrogation.

The funny thing, Andrea reflected, was all the crap about whether torture actually *worked*. Senator McCain insisted that it didn't, but Andrea could show him a lot of Vietnamese video that gave the lie to that. In her experience, torture worked a treat. Liberals denied it, but that was because they didn't want to deal with it.

If torture didn't work, why did the Agency fight so hard to be exempted from prohibitions of the practice? If torture was ineffective, why was it so widely practiced? The fact was, if you tore someone's fingernails out, that person would probably answer your questions — and truthfully, too, so long as the person was led to believe that things would go harder if the information was found to be false.

Of course, there were limits. Torture stopped working when the person being questioned ran out of secrets. At that point, the subject would begin to make things up to avoid further punishment. But a skilled interrogator would usually know when that point was reached. It was the point at which the subject agreed that, yes, he'd shot John F. Kennedy and set fire to the Reichstag.

'After you . . . ' Banerjee stepped aside as the elevator doors slid open. They entered a vestibule at the end of a long, wide corridor. Fluorescent lights, tiled walls. In some ways, the center resembled a hospital, except that people went in healthy and came out sick — if they came out at all.

A security officer looked up from behind a gray metal desk.

'I'll sign,' Banerjee said.

The guard handed him a pen. Banerjee scribbled in the Vistor's Log, checked his watch, and noted the time. Under 'Detainee,' he printed the name 'Faris.'

The guard glanced at the book, then jerked his head toward the corridor. 'Number Eleven,' he said. 'I'll tell Dr. Najib.' He picked up the phone and dialed an extension.

Banerjee led the way. Ahead of them, a man in camouflage fatigues was trying to maneuver a wheelchair through the doorway to one of the rooms. Banerjee gave him a hand with the door, and Andrea saw that it was a woman in the chair, and that she was cuffed to the frame. Her chin was on her chest, and she seemed to be praying.

Then the door closed, and they continued walking toward Room 11. Andrea was struck by how wide the corridor was, as wide almost as the ones in Langley. And like the corridors at home, this one had a color-coded stripe running horizontally along one wall, all the way down to the end. It was a yellow stripe, about six inches wide, but its purpose was the same as the ones at headquarters. Basically, they let people know at a glance if you were somewhere you didn't belong. Red pass, yellow stripe — you wouldn't get far.

Arriving at the door to Room 11, Andrea hesitated. Once she entered the room, she was crossing a line. She would no longer be an observer, but a participant.

It's worth it, she thought.

Still, she hesitated. The room would stink. Places like this always did. Fear and anger soured the sweat of everyone in the room. And if it got rough, there would be other smells as well. Reaching into her hand-bag, Andrea removed a small jar of Vicks VapoRub. Unscrewing the cap, she dipped a pinky into the grease, then dabbed a bit at each of her nostrils. It was a trick she'd learned in college, working part-time on the weekends at the city morgue. As always, the mentholated scent delivered a rush of half-remembered sensations. For an instant, she was ten again, lying in bed with a cold, the humidifier puffing away at her bed-side.

This is so fucked up, she thought. Banerjee knocked. They entered.

★ ★ ★

The room was a clean, well-lighted place that smelled bad. In the center of the room, Hakim Mussawi was strapped to a stainless-steel table under a buzzing fluorescent light. A nurse was at his side inserting an intravenous feed into his left arm. Hearing Andrea and Banerjee enter,

122

Mussawi raised his head, then fell back in exhaustion.

An elderly doctor in a white coat came over, smiling. 'I'm Dr. Najib,' he whispered. The name bar on his coat was covered with a piece of white tape. A sensible precaution, Andrea thought.

'How's our patient?' Banerjee asked.

'Oh, he's been a bad boy,' Dr. Najib reported. 'He admits nothing!'

'Well, perhaps we can change that,' Andrea said.

'I'm sure we can,' Dr. Najib replied. 'But it may take a while. He's a tough nut.'

'Maybe not,' Andrea said. Reaching into her purse, she removed an ampoule of glass, and handed it to the doctor. 'Have you used Anectine before?'

Dr. Najib held the ampoule up to the light. 'Not as such. What's the generic?'

'Succinylcholine chloride,' Andrea told him.

Dr. Najib made a face. 'In that case, yes, of course. At the hospital. We use it all the time for tracheotomies when we intubate. Makes it easier for the tube to go in.'

'So what are you going to do?' Banerjee asked. 'Relax him to death?'

'Pretty much,' Andrea said. 'The thing is, when they use it in a hospital, the patient is unconscious. I'd like Dr. Najib to administer it while our friend is awake.'

Najib stared at Andrea. 'Really!' he said. 'But how can you question him? I mean, you can ask him whatever you want, but how do you expect him to answer you?'

'Well, you're right, of course. He won't be able to speak. But that doesn't matter, because I'm not going to ask him anything. I'm just going to talk to him for a couple of minutes and then, when the drug's worn off, there may be one or two things that he'll want to get off his chest.'

Banerjee gave her a look that said, *Are you nuts?* Then he shook his head, as if to clear it. Finally, he said, 'So, it's painful?'

'Not exactly,' Andrea told him.

'What does *that* mean?' Banerjee asked.

'It means it's disturbing, but it isn't painful.' She turned to Najib. 'It might be a good idea to have a cardiac-assist pump on hand — just in case.'

The doctor nodded in agreement, and left the room.

Andrea turned to Banerjee. Speaking quietly, so that the man on the table couldn't hear, she said, 'Dr. Najib's going to give him a shot of Anectine. It's fast-acting, so — '

'What does it *do*?'

'Well,' Andrea said, 'it causes paralysis. Progressively. After thirty seconds, the muscles in the face begin to go numb. Then the numbness spreads to the throat and down to the chest. The diaphragm slows, and after a minute or two, it stops pumping.'

Banerjee thought about it. 'So . . . '

'It's like turning to wood. You can feel the muscles dying, the flesh going dead. You can't breathe, but your system's flooded with adrenaline. So you're in a panic, but you can't move. It's like a bad dream. A nightmare, only real.'

Banerjee blanched.

Andrea smiled that wonderful smile of hers. 'Aversive conditioning. I've been dying to try it out in an interrogation setting.'

'Well, I'm sure it will be interesting.' Banerjee looked unnerved.

Andrea crossed the room. The subject was lying on his back with his eyes closed, and she could see that he'd had a hard time of it. His right arm was in an air cast, and his lower lip was split, where a tooth had gone through it. His left cheek twitched uncontrollably, and there was something wrong with the fingers of his left hand.

Lifting his hand, she looked at it closely. His thumb was perfectly manicured, and completely intact. But his second and third fingers were missing the nails, and the two other fingers were black with blood. Someone — Banerjee or Najib — had driven something under the nails.

She let go of his hand, which fell to the table with a soft thud. Hakim Mussawi looked at her, then just as quickly looked away.

'We need to talk,' Andrea told him. 'Do you understand English?'

He kept his head turned to the side, and said nothing.

She repeated the question in Arabic.

Banerjee came over to the table. 'His English is actually quite good,' the detective said. 'He went to college in California. Chico State. I looked it up. That makes Mr. Mussawi a Wildcat. Isn't that right, Mr. Mussawi?' Banerjee gave the

125

man's broken arm a squeeze, and watched him gasp.

Andrea shook her head. and Banerjee let up. In a soft voice, she said, 'Hakim, I want you to look at me.'

No way.

The door to the room opened and closed behind her. Dr. Najib wheeled an apparatus to the side of the table.

'How much would you say he weighs?' the doctor asked.

'Ninety kilos,' Banerjee guessed. 'He's got a gut.'

The doctor produced a syringe. 'Sixty milligrams, then.'

While Najib readied the injection, Andrea spoke in a quiet voice. 'Hakim, I want you to listen carefully. I'm an American intelligence officer. And you're in some really deep shit. But I can get you out of here. I can make this stop. But you have to give me something.' She paused. 'Do you understand what I'm saying?'

Nothing.

'I'm ready,' Najib announced, holding the syringe like a handgun, with the barrel pointed toward the ceiling.

With a sigh, Andrea made room for him at the table. 'We didn't have to do this,' she said. 'And I hope we won't have to do it again. And again. And again.'

Mussawi began to stir.

Banerjee laid a hand on his arm. 'Stay!' The needle went in.

Andrea looked at her Rolex. She had six

minutes. One for the drug to take effect. Two for the muscles to die. Another two to suffocate. And a minute to come out of it.

Timing was everything.

Her watch was a Lady's Oyster Perpetual Date, eighteen-carat gold. She'd given it to herself as a present when she made chief of station. She admired it now as the second hand swept through its first quarter turn, then another and another. When she finally looked up from the watch, she saw that Hakim's jaws had begun to slacken. The tic in his cheek was gone, and the puzzlement in his eyes was turning to alarm.

She said his name in an admiring and regretful way. 'Hakim, Hakim . . . I can't imagine how you've held out so long. You've been *so* brave. But no one holds out forever. No one can.'

His head lolled on the table.

'I want to make a deal with you, Hakim.' *Three minutes.* 'But I don't know if I can. The thing is, I can't do *anything* for you . . . unless you do something *for me.*'

The Anectine was roaring through his bloodstream now, crashing down a chain of neurotransmitters, wreaking havoc on his nervous system. Andrea reached down, and turned his head to face her, so that he was staring into her eyes.

It was strange. He didn't look as if he had a care in the world. On the contrary, he had the bland look of a man who'd died in his sleep.

She searched his eyes, and saw that they were the color of mud, glassy, and bloodshot. The opposite of her own.

It didn't take a mind reader to guess what he was thinking, to guess what he was going through. Paralysis, suffocation, and panic. He was dying from the inside out.

'I know you've acted against the United States in the past. So, of course, the FBI will want to talk to you. But that's not the point.' She kept her voice steady and low, patient and slow, so that he'd hang on every word, desperate to end the moment. 'That won't get you out of here,' she said. 'What gets you out of here is me. Nothing else. No one else. And it's just like I said, I'm an intelligence officer. Not a cop. So I'm not interested in yesterday's news. I need to know what's going to happen tomorrow. I need to know *who's* going to happen tomorrow.' *Five minutes, fifteen seconds.* 'If you can help me with that, we can walk out of here in half an hour. And if you can't, well, Hakim, in that case, *this* goes on forever.'

She took a step back from the table, and waited. Patiently, expectantly.

But there was nothing. No movement at all.

She'd killed him.

Then a tremor rolled through his chest, and she realized that she'd been holding her breath, waiting for him to breathe.

She glanced at her watch, and saw that she'd timed her speech perfectly, coming to the end just as his muscles began to relax.

Suddenly, his body jerked on the table. A snarl curled from his throat, and he gasped. '*There's an American!*' he said. 'He's building a machine.'

128

He hacked up the words, and spat them out. 'He says . . . '

    'What?'

    'He says he's going to stop it.'

    'Stop what?'

    'The motor.'

    'What *motor*?'

    'The motor of the world.'

12

ISTANBUL FEBRUARY 28, 2005

The dock strike lasted seven days, seven *hard* days given that Istanbul, with all its glories, was right there, almost close enough to touch. The smells of grilled fish and lamb wafted toward them from the ferryboat stop at Karakoy, where vendors clustered to serve the crowds of commuters. Khalid joked that they could swim from the ship to the shore. And they probably could have. But no. Without transit visas for Turkey, they were confined to the *Marmara Queen*.

So Wilson worked. Day after day, he sat at the desk in his room, plugging variables into the equations he'd worked out in prison, consulting the notes he'd made while studying Yuri Ceplak's journals at Lake Bled.

The one problem he hadn't been able to solve concerned the photon flux that takes place when a standing gravitational wave interacts with its electromagnetic counterpart in a static magnetic field. After the Tunguska disaster, Tesla had been nearly obsessed with the problem. And there, in Ceplak's notebooks, was a marginal notation in Tesla's own hand, one that turned the conundrum into an epiphany. Tesla had solved it! Wilson was now confident that he could focus the beam with astonishing precision, once he factored in the target's harmonic.

But first the weapon had to be miniaturized so that the focusing mechanism could be tested in the field. Among other things, this meant identifying targets that were relatively 'soft' and easily accessible. Not the White House, but Hoover Dam. Not the Cheyenne Mountain Operations Center, where NORAD was head-quartered, but the Golden Gate Bridge. Not the Pentagon, but . . . Culpeper.

Wilson smiled, contemplating the damage he was going to do. It would be massive and clever, and come out of nowhere — like dry lightning on a clear day.

He was still immersed in his equations when he heard shouting on the docks. A few minutes later, a knock on his door confirmed his suspicions. 'Hasan is pleased to inform you dock strike is over!' In four hours, they were under way.

★　★　★

He was asleep when the ship, having carved its way through the swell and chop of the Black Sea, hove into sight of Odessa. It was the slowing of the engines that woke him up. His heartbeat was synchronized to their vibrations, so that, when the engines slowed, it hit him like a heart attack, and jerked him wide awake.

He dressed quickly and went out on the deck, which was slick with rain. The city was barely visible behind a curtain of fog. Sea and sky bled into each other, producing a gray wash, a sort of maritime white-out. Which was disappointing, because Odessa promised to be an interesting city. According to the captain, at whose table Wilson had sometimes dined, Odessa had once been the Soviet Union's largest port. 'This is so,' the captain told him, 'because the water is warm year-round. Everywhere else, it's locked in ice.'

Without the push of the engines, the ship seemed almost to be still. But that was an illusion. Styrofoam cups and cigarette butts trailed in their wake.

Wilson shifted from foot to foot.

Bo had left a reassuring message in the Draft folder of their Yahoo! account. Their friend in Odessa was aware of the dock strike in Istanbul, and would adjust his schedule accordingly. *Relax*, Bo wrote. *Everything's cool.*

That's what Wilson told himself, but he couldn't shrug off his unease. He fingered the red capsule Hakim had given him in Baalbek, a capsule he kept taped under his shirt collar. It worked by chemical suffocation, denying oxygen to each of the body's cells. It was a fast and violent way to die, but it wasn't Wilson's way.

Almost idly, he stripped the capsule from under his collar, and dropped it over the side.

He could see Odessa clearly now. The docks were right in the middle of the city, with the port authority headquartered in a huge ugly concrete structure, and obscuring 'the Potemkin steps' beside it.

Wilson had read about the famous staircase in his guidebook and was anxious to see it. A broad

132

flight of 192 steps cascading down the hillside to the Black Sea, the stairs were an architectural marvel, constructed to exaggerate normal perspective. From the base they were said to appear unimaginably steep, an effect achieved by their gradual narrowing from a width of sixty-eight feet at the bottom to forty feet at the top.

The steps were made famous in a scene in Eisenstein's *Battleship Potemkin*. In the film, czarist troops open fire on the civilians of Odessa. A mother falls. A baby carriage careens down the steps, bouncing past one body after another, its innocent occupant bound for destruction. Blood is everywhere.

Good movie, Wilson thought. He looked forward to seeing the real thing.

★ ★ ★

Transit visas had been arranged, the sheets of paper already attached to their passports.

Wilson and his bodyguards were met at the foot of the gangway by a skinny guy with a bad complexion who introduced himself as Sergei. 'Mr. Belov sends his apologies. He regrets that he cannot be here until tomorrow. His daughter performs in a — ' He frowned, then moved his fingers as if playing a piano.

'Recital,' Wilson said.

'Yes!' Sergei agreed with enthusiasm. 'Permit me,' he said, grabbing Wilson's suitcase. 'This way.' Within ten minutes, they were through Customs, submachine guns and all. 'Express line,' Khalid said. Zero giggled.

Half an hour later, they were checking into the first-class Hotel Konstantin.

Zero and Khalid were elated by the idea of a day at such a hotel, especially once they checked in and learned that their room had a Playstation 2 and a copy of *Grand Theft Auto*.

Wilson was glad, too, because he would spend a day in the same city as Irina. Despite his fantasies about her, he was pragmatic. He knew that the women on the website were glammed up for their photos and would look, in real life, rather different. Some looked like prostitutes to him, heavily made up and showing plenty of cleavage, although that might be a cultural difference. In contrast, Irina seemed demure, like a housewife in an old sitcom. Someone who would serve tea and grow flowers.

Wilson did not intend to call her or speak to her, but he was desperate to have a look.

★ ★ ★

At three o'clock, he sat at a tiny table in the Cafe Mayakovsky on Deribasovskaya Street. It was a large and busy room with perhaps a dozen waitresses — his own a heavyset pink-faced brunette. He ordered tea and while he waited, fixed his eyes on the double swinging doors through which the waitresses came and went from the kitchen, trays aloft. Each wore a lacy frill pinned to her hair, and a green-checked uniform with white apron. They moved with grace and efficiency, even the older and fatter

134

ones, gliding between the crowded tables, avoiding one another with a kind of intuitive radar, bending the knee to serve the hot drinks and dainty pastries. To Wilson, whose brain sought order and pattern everywhere, it seemed almost choreographed in its rhythm and balance, and he watched it with pleasure.

Then he saw her.

She came through the swinging doors, heavy tray aloft, walking with the posture of a dancer. Wilson felt a spark of pure joy at the sight of her, probably, he thought, no more than the low-voltage shock of recognition. It was akin to the satisfaction of finding the pivotal equation, or fitting the last bolt into a construction.

She was more petite than he'd imagined, yet her body was curvaceous. He was glad to see that. Scientific studies proved a connection between the proportion of waist-to-hip size and fertility, a biological explanation of why men were attracted to such women. Unlike in her smiling photograph, her face was set in an expression of earnest concentration as she gracefully made her way through the crowded room to a table at the window.

He drank a second tea, watching Irina come and go from the kitchen.

Now she was clearing a table, hoisting her tray to her shoulder and then taking a moment to survey the area — for a customer wanting a check, for a new customer, for whatever waitresses look for — when her eyes caught his.

There was, of course, no sign of recognition on her part — he had not sent his own photograph. But he felt a quick sexual spark that took him by surprise. He held her gaze until she looked away. She was flustered and tripped on the leg of a table. Some silverware slid off her tray onto the floor and she knelt to pick it up.

He was tempted to help her.

Instead, he signaled his waitress and paid the bill, leaving a generous tip. Irina looked back his way once more, just before heading into the kitchen with her tray. This time, she smiled, and he returned the smile, and there was a band of sensation between them that was almost electric.

It occurred to him that he could wait outside the restaurant. Follow her home. Find a way.

But no, it wasn't time. Not yet . . .

13

Bobojon Simoni stood by the curb, looking up and down Yorkstrasse for a cab. Behind him, like a page from the comics, a wall of graffiti showed George Bush hanging from a streetlight, while New York burned on the bricks behind him.

In lights above the bank across the street, a sign blinked the time and temperature: 4:03 0°. Twilight and freezing. At least officially. In reality, it was raining one minute and snowing the next. Then it would turn into something in between, a sort of flying slush. Whatever it was, it stung his eyes as he gazed into the wind, screwing his face against the ice, blinking hard.

It was his own fault. He'd forgotten to bring the book, and now he was paying for it. He could see it, almost as if it were right in front of him, sitting on the table in the kitchen: a solid rectangle, neatly wrapped in brown butcher's paper, taped, and tied with string. Addressed to the shop in Boston, all the book needed was a couple of stamps and a Customs form, and it could go on its way. Only now, because he'd forgotten it, he'd have to go back to the apartment and pick it up.

He'd left about forty-five minutes ago, with a list of errands in his head: *uskadar post office*

137

toilet paper prayers. The idea was to have a cup of coffee at the Uskadar, a small cafe on a side street not far from the mosque. Like most of the cafe's customers, the coffee was Turkish, and it wasn't very good. But the owner was a 'Bosniak,' and like Bobojon, he loved football. So there was always a match on the TV, high up on the wall behind the counter, and workmen watching.

The cafe itself was less than a mile from his apartment, but if he walked back home to get the book, the post office would be closed by the time he returned. Finding a cab could be difficult, though, especially since it was raining. Taxis were never plentiful in 'SO36' — the down-at-heels neighborhood that Bobojon shared with nearly two hundred thousand 'guest workers,' mostly Turks and Kurds. It was the old postal code for the eastern half of the Kreuzberg district, where Checkpoint Charlie was a tourist attraction.

He might as well go back to the cafe. He could mail the book in the morning and no one would care. The decision made, he was turning to leave when, out of nowhere, a taxi sluiced up to the curb, windshield wipers thudding back and forth. The driver leaned across the seat to the window, and looked up at him. '*Wo zu?*'

★ ★ ★

Jurgen preferred to work alone, and he usually did. But today was different. Today, he needed a partner.

They had been waiting outside Simoni's building for twenty minutes, sitting half a block

138

away in a black BMW with a broken defroster, windows dribbling with steam. They did what they could to keep the windshield clear, wiping away the fog with the front page of *Bild*, a tabloid newspaper. The headline read 'Turbo Orgasms' and came with the picture of a brunette who appeared to be having one.

It was all a little embarrassing. And that was unfortunate, because Jurgen wanted to impress the woman in the seat beside him. Clara was new to the BfV. What must she think? First the defroster and then this turbo person! Of course, she pretended not to notice, but . . . *mein Gott!*

In the end, they just rolled down the windows, pulled their coats close, and froze.

The thing about today was, they didn't know what the target looked like. All they had was a name (Bobojon Simoni), an address, and a telephone number. For all they knew, Herr Simoni was twenty years old. Or forty. Or sixty. He might be tall or short, fat or thin. Well dressed and bearded. Tie-dyed and clean-shaven. But a Bosnian — or someone traveling on a Bosnian passport.

Jurgen couldn't work it alone — there was just no way to be sure the flat was empty. Sometimes people didn't answer their phones. Sometimes they sat in the dark or napped on the couch. So he'd use the *Wachtturm* ploy. Go up to the door, and knock three times. If someone opened the door, he'd give him a handful of tracts and a copy of the *der Wachtturm*. Then Jurgen would launch into his spiel about Jehovah's Witnesses and the end-times. Most of the time, the door would slam shut in their faces, and that would be the end of it. But not always. Wind him up with a couple of beers, and Jurgen would tell you how he'd converted a member of the Red Brigades to Jesus.

He checked his watch. Five after four. It would be dark soon. He dialed the flat for the third time. Again, no answer. He turned to Clara. 'Shall we?'

She made a face.

'C'mon,' he said. They got out of the car.

She was a pretty woman, maybe ten years younger than Jurgen himself, and he wanted her to think well of him — and of the BfV. The Office for the Protection of the Constitution was an elite intelligence service whose main responsibility was tracking extremists — left, right, and religious. Clara's former employer, the BKA, was the criminal police. The BfV was different. Sexier, somehow.

As they crossed the street to Simoni's building, heads down against the weather, it occurred to Jurgen that most people would take them for social workers, what with their battered briefcases and woolen overcoats. And that was good, because nothing could be more ordinary. Social workers were to Kreuzberg as steelworkers were to the Ruhr.

She would install the bug while he searched for a computer. If he found one, he'd clone the hard drive to the laptop in his briefcase. The whole business shouldn't take more than ten minutes, but of course, it would seem like hours. It always did.

The only question mark was Simoni himself. They had no idea where he was or when he'd return. Two days earlier BfV had received a query from Malaysia, a flash cable from the CIA station chief in Kuala Lumpur. During a recent debriefing, a foreign national detained under Malaysia's Internal Security Act indicated that an attack on U.S. property and personnel was imminent. Simoni was implicated in a communications capacity.

The BfV got to work immediately. Within twenty-four hours, they were able to establish that Herr Simoni had entered Germany on a Bosnian passport. He'd come to Berlin from Beirut about six months earlier, and rented a two-room apartment at Oranienstrasse 54. Soon afterward, he opened a passbook account at a local branch of the Dresdner Bank, where his monthly balance averaged 936 euros. Though he did not appear to have a job, neither was he receiving public assistance. None of the informants at the Mevlana mosque were familiar with a person of that name. Inquiries were continuing.

The flat turned out to be a walk-up on the third floor. Jurgen was puffing when they got to the door, so it took him a second to catch his breath. When he was ready, he opened the briefcase he was carrying and took out a handful of religious tracts. He gave a couple to Clara, then broke into as bright a smile as his tobacco-stained teeth would allow, and rapped smartly on the door. As far as they knew, Simoni was living alone, but you could never be certain.

Maybe he got lucky the night before. Maybe he had a dog. Maybe . . . nothing.

The flat was quiet as a stone. Jurgen gestured for Clara to step aside, and when she did, he got out his kit and picked expertly at the lock. A few seconds later, and they were in.

★   ★   ★

'I'm right back!' Bobojon declared. 'I get package, we go post office!' The driver shrugged. Bobojon climbed out of the cab and bounded up the steps to Oranienstrasse 54.

Inside, the smell of cabbage hung in the stairwell, buoyed by an updraft of Arab music flowing from the janitor's apartment in the basement. Bobojon didn't mind the smell. If anything, it reminded him of home.

He took the first three flights of stairs two steps at a time, then paused to catch his breath. He was in okay shape. Not like when he'd just gotten out of prison, but not bad, either. He walked everywhere in Berlin, even in the winter, and worked out at a kickboxing studio four nights a week. So it only took him a moment to get to his door.

He fumbled for the key in the pocket of his coat, came up with it, and turned it in the lock. To his surprise, the door didn't open. So he turned the key again, the other way, and then it did. For a moment, he stood where he was with a frown on his face, thinking he must be losing it. How could he go out without locking the door? And then the answer came to him: He

142

couldn't. He wouldn't. So he pulled out the little gun that he carried, a Makarov, and stepped inside.

A young woman — maybe twenty-six, nice-looking, short brown hair, net stockings — was standing frozen at the kitchen table with a look of horror on her face. The telephone was on the table in front of her, disassembled, the speaker and earpiece next to the handset. Beside the phone was his package. He didn't stop to think about it. His gun came up and, almost as a reflex, he shot her in the face, tearing a hole in her cheek, then fired again as she fell, blowing a chunk out of her neck. She did a sort of pirouette before she fell. Suddenly, blood was everywhere — on the walls and the floor, on the side of the sink. Clawing at the linoleum, dying to get away, she was at the epicenter of it all. And Bo felt sorry for her, he really did. But he shot her again, this time in the back. Finally, she lay still. By then, his heart was a jackhammer, so loud in his ears that he almost didn't hear the gasp that came from his left. Turning toward the noise, he saw what looked like Christian religious tracts falling to the feet of a man with a Glock. There was no time to react. Bobojon could almost feel the man pull the trigger. It didn't even take a second, but the moment lasted forever and, in it, Bobojon realized where he'd seen the tracts before — in Allenwood. Then the Witness pulled the trigger a second time. Bobojon felt the side of his face explode as the bullet spun him around and sent him staggering. For a moment, he was bright with pain. Then his legs gave way and he sank toward the floor. The Witness kept firing, tearing new holes in him, but by then, Bobojon could feel his body shutting down. The gunshots sounded farther and farther away as a red mist fell like a curtain behind his eyes. *Oh shit*, he thought, *I'm dying . . .*

14

ODESSA, UKRAINE MARCH 3, 2005

Wilson sat by himself in the hotel's lobby,
drinking tea while he waited for Belov. It was
midafternoon, and the lobby was suffused with a
wintry light. Zero and Khalid were playing
backgammon at a table near the door,
occasionally looking up in annoyance at a tour
group of Orthodox Jews, who were arguing with
the desk clerk in a language Wilson didn't
understand. Nearby, a couple of businessmen sat
on the edge of a white leather couch, reading
newspapers.

It was three o'clock when Maxim Pavelovich
Belov arrived, brushing the snow from his
shoulders. Seeing him, it occurred to Wilson that
he looked like a million bucks — or about two
percent of his net worth. (Wilson had Googled
him the night before.)

A former KGB major, Belov wore a Savile
Row suit under a black vicuna overcoat, and a
sable hat of Soviet army design. Snowflakes
sparkled in the fur. According to a report by a
UN investigating team, he was forty-three
years old and held an economics degree from
the Institute of Social Relations in Moscow.
He was also one of the largest small-arms
dealers in the world, having gotten his start

145

flying South African gladiolas to Dubai, where the flowers sold for ten times what he paid for them.

Striding directly over to Wilson, Belov pulled off his gloves, clicked his heels with a look of bemusement, and held out his hand. 'Welcome to Evil Empire!' he said, his voice filled with gravel. 'Or what's left of it. Did you enjoy yourself last night?'

Wilson got to his feet and shook the Russian's hand. A low-pitched buzzing sound emanated from an improbably pink pair of earphones dangling from Belov's neck. White Stripes. 'I was surprised when you didn't meet the ship,' Wilson told him.

Belov laughed. 'I *never* 'meet ship.' Maybe you smuggle drugs. Viagra, even!' He laughed again. 'That's all we need. You ready?'

Wilson nodded. With a heads-up to Zero and Khalid, he followed Belov out to the street, where a pair of Cadillac Escalades idled in the snow, their windows gray with steam. A small flag flew from a plastic standard on the passenger-side fender of each car. The flags consisted of a black field, emblazoned with a silver sheriff's badge — the kind with a six-pointed star.

It was odd, Wilson thought, but so was the way the Russian came and went without bodyguards. Then he saw that this wasn't actually true. As he got into the back of the second Escalade, he saw the 'businessmen' from the lobby, the ones who'd been sitting on the white couch, climb into the car ahead of

146

him. Apparently, they'd been watching him for more than an hour before Belov himself appeared at the hotel.

One by one, each of the car doors slammed shut against the sleet. Belov slapped the top of the seat in front of them — two quick raps with the palm of his hand — and the cars pulled away from the curb.

'First time in Odessa?'

Wilson nodded. The car was soundproofed or armored, or both. He couldn't tell. Either way, it had the feeling of a cocoon.

'You see Steps?'

'Yeah.'

Belov sat back in his seat. 'First time I see steps, I cried. Not like baby. But . . . I'm wet in face. Maybe you feel same way when you see Statue of Liberty. No?'

'No.'

Belov laughed.

The SUVs gathered speed as the city petered out into farmland, the earth fallow under a blanket of snow and litter. They were heading away from the sea, moving inland over a road that needed repairs. 'So how do we do this?' Wilson asked.

Belov shrugged. 'Easy. First, we go nowhere.'

Wilson shot him a look.

'No joke. Place we're going . . . this place doesn't exist.' He cocked an eye at Wilson. 'You know Transniestria?'

Wilson shook his head.

'I rest case,' Belov said. 'Ten, fifteen miles. Like being on moon.'

'Why is that?'

Belov thought about it. Finally, he said, 'Perestroika! Remember? Means, 'restructure,' I think.'

Wilson nodded.

'First thing, big cutbacks for army. Then Wall comes down. Soon, everything comes down. No more Evil Empire, okay?'

Wilson nodded a second time.

'Okay. So, soldiers come home. Cuba, Germany, everywhere — it's *hasta la vista!* But now, we have big surpluses. Tanks and APCs. Artillery! Choppers, rockets. Mortars, missiles. Antiaircraft guns. They have to put surplus somewhere, right? So where do you think?' Belov raised his chin toward the windshield. 'Transniestria.'

As they neared their first checkpoint, the Russian explained that Transniestria had been a part of Moldova, which, in turn, had been a part of Romania until the end of the Second World War. Annexed by the Soviet Union, Moldova declared its independence when the USSR dissolved. Russian troops remained where they were, however, on Moldovan territory east of the Dniester River. That was fine with the locals, who liked the idea of an independent state allied with Moscow. And so Transniestria became what diplomats like to call 'a fact on the ground.'

The only problem (other than the country's extreme poverty) was that almost no one recognized it. This meant that its citizens were effectively stateless. As far as the rest of the

148

world is concerned, Transniestria doesn't exist.

'Transniestria, he is No-Man's-Land,' Belov said. 'Big problem. No country, no trade. No trade, no money. So everyone is poor. Not good. Someplace else, normal poor country, poor is okay. Look at Argentina. Africa! People get in line to give money. IMF, World Bank, Soros. Morgan Stanley! Here? No! No country? No help! All you can do is leave. Except you can't leave, because to leave, you need passport. And Transniestrian passport, this is like cartoon.'

'So what do they do?'

'They get passport somewhere else. In Russia, maybe, or Ukraine. Third best is Internet. You'd be surprised how many Knights of Malta living in Tiraspol.'

'What's Tiraspol?' Wilson asked.

Belov did a double take. 'This is capital of Nowhere,' he explained. 'Maybe twenty miles now. But first, airport. I show what you're buying!' Belov told him. 'You see with eyes!'

Wilson's shoulders heaved. 'If you tell me it's all there, I'm sure it's fine.'

Belov slapped Wilson on the knee, and guffawed. 'I never do business this way! First time! So tell me, what happens? You land in Congo. Client opens crate. And — uh-oh! Is grapefruits! What then?'

'Well,' Wilson said, 'then I'd have a problem.'

'No shit!'

'But that won't happen,' Wilson told him, 'because then *you'd* have a problem.'

Belov looked surprised. 'With *you*?' he asked.

149

The question was almost cheerful.

'Of course not. I'd be dead by then.'

'Is true! You'd have red hole.' The Russian tapped his forefinger, three times in rapid succession, against his forehead. 'Right here.'

'I know.'

'So . . . for me? I don't see problem.'

'You'd have a really *basic* problem,' Wilson said, punning on the only Arabic he knew.

Belov looked puzzled for a moment, and then he chuckled. 'Is good joke. 'Basic.' You mean al-Qaeda.'

'Well, Hakim and his friends.'

Belov nodded. 'True.' The Russian pursed his lips. After a moment, he said, 'So! We go to airport. Maybe you don't know guns, but you know grapefruits from grenades, right?'

Wilson laughed. 'Yeah,' he said. 'Grapefruits are pink inside.'

'Okay, so you see crates, and later, maybe you talk to Hakim. And you tell him: 'No pink.' '

★   ★   ★

The Tiraspol airport was nothing like Wilson expected. He'd imagined the kind of airstrip you find in the Caribbean: a ribbon of asphalt running past a cinder-block terminal. But what he found, instead, was a military base with barracks and hangars, and runways capable of handling the biggest cargo planes.

Chain-link fences, four feet apart, circled the base. Each was topped with razor wire. The Escalades came to a stop in front of a

150

guardhouse, and cut their engines. A soldier appeared beside the car, and ordered the driver to roll down the window. As he did, a second soldier examined the undersides of the Escalades, using a mirror attached to the end of an aluminum racing jack.

Belov and the soldier chatted in Russian for a bit, then the soldier saluted and waved them on. Leaving the road, they followed a dirt track that ran beside the fence for half a mile until it came to an end at a hangar on the far side of the airfield. Belov motioned for Wilson to follow, then put up a hand when Zero and Khalid began to follow.

'Just you,' the Russian said, his breath like smoke in the freezing air.

Wilson hesitated, then gestured for his bodyguards to wait. They looked disappointed. And thoroughly chilled. Other than a sweater that Zero had acquired on the ship, they were wearing the same clothes they'd worn in Baalbek. T-shirts and jeans. Cheap jackets.

Sucks to be them, Wilson thought, and kept walking. A gust of wind brought tears to his eyes.

Inside the hangar, a medium-size cargo plane, more than a hundred feet long and almost as wide, occupied the entire space. It was painted a gray-blue color that Wilson guessed would make it hard to see from the ground.

'Golden oldie!' Belov exclaimed. 'Like me!' He laughed. 'Antonov-seventy-two. I get from Aeroflot, ten years now. Very good plane.'

'How much does it carry?' Wilson asked.

'Ten tons, metric.'

'Nonstop?'

Belov scoffed. 'No way. Not even close. Not even with extra tanks.'

'So we have to refuel.'

Belov nodded.

'Where?'

The Russian smiled. 'Sharjah.'

Wilson thought about it. 'That's kinda out of the way, isn't it?'

The Russian looked surprised. 'You know Sharjah?'

'I know where it is,' Wilson told him. Hakim had mentioned the place at dinner, and Wilson looked for it on a map in the lounge aboard the *Marmara Queen*. One of seven sheikhdoms in the Emirates, it was a patch of sand on the Persian Gulf, just across from Iran. Which put it about two thousand miles southeast of the hangar they were standing in.

The Congo, on the other hand, was south*west*. And that's where they were going.

Belov smiled. 'We're in Sharjah two hours, maybe three. Not to worry.'

The Russian cocked his head for Wilson to follow him around to the rear of the plane, where a hinged cargo-loading ramp disappeared into the fuselage. Nearby, a pair of battered forklifts sat amid a dozen containers, some sealed, some open. The Russian handed him a typewritten list on a single sheet of onionskin paper. There was no letterhead, just the word CEKPET stamped in ink at the top of the page.

36 type-69 40mm (man-portable) RPGs (w/4X telescopic sight)	$124,200
90 rockets (40 mm)	35,050
200 assault rifles: AK-47 7.62mm (30-round magazines, side-folding)	84,460
1,000 boxes, 20 each cartridges 7.62mm	10,100
50 Franchi SPAS-12 combat shotguns	55,000
500 boxes, 10 shells (00 gauge)	8,320
10 flamethrowers (Brianchi)	1,460
4 vests (Kevlar)	1,220
12 stabiscopes (Fujinon, 3rd generation)	201,550
100 Rigel 3100 tactical night-vision goggles	505,200
300 combat boots	25,075
1 Meillor 37mm dual antiaircraft gun	188,256
100 antiaircraft shells (37 mm)	9,500
10 mortars 60mm	17,600
100 60mm shells	14,300
400 pounds liquid explosive (Triex)	80,500
200 pounds RDX plastic booster	32,040
400 time delays, electronic (solid- state programmable, one hour to 90 days)	83,600
1 special kit	33,500
30 man-portable air defense systems: Russian Strela-2 (SA-7a) 1968	54,000
15 1.17 kg infrared seeker, 5 feet long, 30–40 lbs	105,260

TOTAL: $ 1,670,191
(1,429,992 euros)

Wilson studied the list, curious about just what it was he was delivering to Africa. ' 'Cekpet'?'

' 'Secret,' ' Belov explained. 'I don't have English stamp.'

'And this?' Wilson asked, pointing to an entry.

'Stabiscope? Special binoculars, with gyroscope! On vibrating platform, is stable like rock. Good for helicopter, APC. Tank, too. Come! I show you.' He grabbed a crowbar that was leaning against the wall, and led Wilson up the ramp and into the plane.

The fuselage was cavernous, with belt-loader tracks running along the floor under wooden palettes held down by tensioning buckles and cargo nets.

Wilson glanced at the list. 'What's this?' He pointed to the entry for thirty Strela-2s.

'Manpads.'

'Which are what?' Wilson asked.

'Missile. Like Stinger.' To illustrate, he rested the crowbar on his shoulder. Aiming at an imaginary plane, he squeezed off an imaginary shot. 'Hold like bazooka,' he said. 'Pull trigger, and . . . *boom*!'

'And this . . . 'special kit'? What's that?'

'Poison kit,' Belov said. 'Four kinds, all by mouth or DMSO. So watch what you eat, and don't touch!' He chuckled, then grew serious again. 'ECC: tastes like shit, but no one ever complains. One taste, convulsions. Number two: THL. Forty-eight hours, mouth to morgue. So, have time to leave. Then heart stops. Number three is CYD: liver dies, kidney dies. Four hours, maybe six. Last one? MCR. Ugly way to die! Organs decompose. Totally. They open you up, inside looks like soup, so obvious foul play.'

'And the DMSO . . . '

'Is solvent. Mix with poison, put on keyboard,

154

doorknob, rifle, whatever. One touch, right to bloodstream — tits up.'

Wilson glanced around. 'When do they finish loading?'

'Tonight. When pilot get in. Very important he get balance right.'

'And this is everything?'

It seemed to Wilson that Belov hesitated before he nodded.

'What?' Wilson asked.

'Is small thing . . . '

'In a deal like this?'

'Yes, yes! Is small thing. I show you!'

The Russian went from pallet to pallet until he found what he was looking for. Using the crowbar, he pried up the lid on one of the boxes. 'Look!' he said. 'These African guys, they want Russian RPGs, but . . . no way, José. Impossible, even for me! So, I substitute Type Sixty-nines. Chinese made. Not bad. And cheaper.'

Wilson stared at the gunmetal-gray cylinders. 'What if they don't want them?'

'If they don't, I take them back. Is five percent off bottom line. No problem. Customer always right.'

'Actually, it's seven point one percent,' Wilson told him.

Belov frowned. 'How you figure?'

'It's arithmetic. You need a pencil?'

Belov looked at him for a moment. And blinked.

★　★　★

They came to the first in a series of checkpoints about two miles from the airport. Soldiers in olive-drab camouflage were dragging a striped wooden barrier back and forth across the two-lane road, questioning drivers, waving them on. Nearby, a concrete blockhouse stood by the side of the road, its foundations soaked in mud, its walls filigreed by gunfire. Smoke curled from a rusty stovepipe in the roof.

There were a dozen trucks and cars waiting in line, up ahead of them. Wilson felt the Escalade slow as one of Belov's bodyguards leaned out the window, shouting angrily and waving a gun. For the first time, Wilson saw that the car's windows were about an inch thick.

From a wooden hut on the other side of the barrier, an officer emerged. Seeing them, he straightened almost to attention, and saluted.

Belov saw that Wilson was impressed. 'Fender flags.'

Wilson nodded. 'I meant to ask; where are they from?'

Belov chuckled. 'From here. Nowhere. They're company flags.'

Wilson gave him a questioning look.

'Is bullshit government here,' Belov said. 'Like Wild West. So Sheriff Corporation steps in. Makes law. Owns things.'

'Like what?'

'Airport. Hotel. Kentucky Fried. *Mercado*. Telephones. Electricity. Everything that works.'

'And you're, what? The president?'

Belov scoffed, and shook his head. 'Small fish.'

Wilson thought about it. 'So where are the big fish?'

The arms dealer shrugged. 'Deep water. Red Square.'

Wilson nodded, then turned his eyes to the landscape outside. The sleet was changing to snow. Flakes the size of quarters floated toward them.

'Lagos,' Belov added, seemingly to himself. Then he flashed a wolfish grin. 'Geneva . . . Dubai.' He laughed.

'I get the picture,' Wilson told him.

'Virginia Beach . . . '

★   ★   ★

Tiraspol turned out to be a forlorn anachronism of the Soviet era. Whatever charms it might once have had, had long since disappeared, bulldozed into oblivion by communist urban planners. In their place stood block after block of soulicidal apartment buildings, concrete warrens ablaze with graffiti.

'So, what you think?'

'I think it looks like shit,' Wilson replied.

'Looks like? Is!' Belov chuckled.

They entered a roundabout with an enormous statue of Lenin at its center. Nearby, a couple of soldiers stood in the cold, smoking cigarettes beside a tank. They eyed the Cadillacs warily, then looked away.

'Hotel just ahead,' Belov said. 'Not bad. Like fucked-up Intercon. But one night only, so . . . no big deal. In morning?' He answered his

157

own question by cupping the palm of his hand, then flattening it out in what looked like a Hitlerian salute. 'Flaps up.'

Wilson felt his stomach growl. 'You know someplace to eat?'

'Hotel. Chinese restaurant. Not so bad.'

'I was thinking I'd get something to eat, maybe take a walk.'

Belov shook his head and chuckled. 'Maybe not,' he said. 'You get lost, Hakim kills me.'

'You could draw me a map.'

Belov rolled his eyes. 'Map is problem.'

'Why?'

'Is crime!' Belov declared.

'What is?'

'Map! In Transniestria, having map is crime.'

'You're kidding,' Wilson said.

'No. Map is big security issue. Anyway, you don't have visa. So, is better you stay off streets.'

'I could get one, couldn't I? How hard could that be?'

'Impossible!' Belov told him.

'Why?'

'Because you're here,' Belov told him. 'Without visa. So — '

' — is crime.'

Belov grinned. 'Exactly. Cops ask questions. Anyway, Transniestrian visa is only good for eight hours. Day-trip for Ukrainians.'

'That's *it*?'

Belov nodded. 'Yes, 'it'! Better you stay off street.' Wilson started to object, but Belov cut him off. 'I know. This is pain in your ass, but . . . ' The arms-dealer raised his hands, as if

158

he were surrendering. 'So much I can do only.' By way of ending the conversation, he donned the pink earphones, lay back in his seat and closed his eyes.

★ ★ ★

The manager was waiting for them in the lobby of the Red Star Hotel, a concrete cube with mouse-gray carpeting. Behind the front desk, a heroic haute-relief of Elena Ceauşescu hung from the wall.

To Wilson's eyes, the hotel had the ambience of a Day's Inn, but the manager was impressive. Snapping his fingers like castanets, he summoned a posse of elderly bellboys, who hurried over to stand at attention beside each of their bags.

Greeting Belov with a warm handshake and a quiet joke in Russian, the manager waived the formalities of registration. Going over to the desk, he picked half a dozen keys from a rack on the wall, and began handing them out. One to Zero, another to Khalid. A third to Wilson.

On Belov's advice, they avoided the elevator (which was subject to electrical outages) and followed the bellboys up the stairs to the second floor.

To Wilson's surprise, the room was fine. Large and comfortably furnished, it had cable TV and a small desk next to the window. Atop the desk was a neatly printed card with instructions on how to access the hotel's high-speed Internet connection for 'only' thirty euros an hour.

He was about to do just that when a wave of fatigue washed over him. Sitting down on the bed, he ran a hand through his hair and thought about taking a shower. That would wake him up. But the mattress was as soft as goosedown could make it, and the hotel quiet as a stone. Lying back on the pillows, he closed his eyes, and listened. The wind was like a bellows, gusting hard, then dying. It threw bits of ice at the windows, making a ticking sound that was barely audible. And then, nothing.

When he awoke, the room was dark. But it wasn't late. Not really. Rolling out of bed, he crossed the room to the minibar and broke the seal on the door. Inside, he found a couple of bottles of Slavutych Pyvo, which looked like beer.

And was.

Picking up the remote, Wilson snapped on the TV, then flicked through the channels until he found one in English. It was a live feed from Iraq. Half a dozen kids were kicking the shit out of a dead soldier, lying next to a burning Humvee while a mob danced in what looked like a pool of blood. In a voice-over, President Bush counseled the world that democracy was 'hard work.'

Wilson snorted.

Meanwhile, images flashed upon the screen. More smoke, this time from a suicide bombing in Kabul. Men running with stretchers. Women and sirens wailing. Nervous soldiers looking on through identical pairs of polarized Oakleys, M-16s at the ready, guns pointing at heaven.

160

Then a trauma ward. A man on the floor, looking as if he were bleeding out, a woman thrashing in pain —

This is nothing, Wilson thought. *This is bullshit. If they think this is bad, wait'll they get a load of me.*

The idea made him smile. *It's like an orchestra*, he told himself. The mayhem on the tube was the visual equivalent of the noise that an orchestra makes as it gets ready to play, with each of the images corresponding to an instrument being tuned. The cacophony was massive and uncoordinated, a traffic jam of noise and violence. But then — soon — the conductor would tap the podium with his baton, and the first note of every symphony would descend: silence.

Then the storm.

Wilson took a long swig of Slavutych. Duty called. He hadn't checked his messages since he'd left the ship. He plugged his laptop into the telephone, and waited for the computer to boot up, musing all the while on the idea of himself as a kind of conductor. An artiste! If you listened hard enough, you could almost hear the applause, people shouting *Maestro! Maestro!*

He clicked on the Internet Explorer icon, went to my.yahoo.com and signed in. Clicked on Mail, clicked on Draft — and there it was, a single note dated two days earlier, the address line left blank:

I can't find Hakim.

15

TIRASPOL-SHARJAH

The Antonov rumbled down the tarmac, flaps at attention, the plane shaking and shuddering, roaring toward liftoff. A wall of pine trees loomed behind the fences, growing taller and taller and then they were gone. The plane's vibrations faded to a pulsed thrum as Tiraspol dwindled beneath the wings, a toy slum in a wintry landscape.

Sitting in the cockpit with Belov, the pilot, and the engineer, Wilson relaxed as the plane banked to the south. The Russian lighted a cigar, puffed mightily, and cocked his head toward the engine on the port wing. 'Exhaust! You see?'

Wilson glanced out the window, where a stream of turbulence poured over the wing. 'What about it?'

Belov made a graceful gesture with his hand, creating a sine wave in the air. 'Russian genius puts engine on top, not under wing — so makes possible short takeoffs. Also, landings! Crappy fields, this is no problem. In Africa, I'm using grass airstrips, always. So . . . is big deal. Normal plane, no way.'

'What's the trade-off?' Wilson asked.

Belov shrugged. 'Not-so-big plane. If I have Antonov-twelve, I haul twenty tons — not ten!'

He waggled a finger in the air. 'But then I need good runway, mile long, plus.'

Wilson looked out the window. As the plane climbed, he could see the engine on the left side of the plane. It was sitting on the leading edge of the wing, and he could see the exhaust flowing over the ailerons.

'Okay if I go back — check out my friends?'

'Sure! Is okay!' Belov said. 'But no cooking!'

Wilson stared at him. 'What?'

'No cooking! What you don't understand?'

'You're kidding.'

Belov shook his head. 'Look at floor! Sometimes Arab peoples, they think because it's metal, no problem! I'm telling you, they don't know shit. So you tell them: no cooking.'

'I will.'

'Good.'

Unbuckling his seat belt, Wilson got to his feet. Through the window, he could see the Black Sea stretching toward the horizon. 'How long to Sharjah?' he asked.

'Five hours,' Belov told him. 'Maybe six.'

The pilot turned to him. 'Sometimes, we have problems in Iraqi air-space.'

'What kind of problems?' Wilson asked.

'F-16s.'

Leaving the cockpit, Wilson walked back to where Zero and Khalid were seated on folding metal chairs, bolted into the side of the fuselage. They were smoking cigarettes, and each of them had a Diadora bag in his lap. On the floor in front of them was a dull black scar where someone had tried to cook dinner.

Wilson glanced around.

'Everything okay?'

Khalid chuckled. 'He's scared shitless,' he said, nodding at Zero.

'Well . . . ' Wilson paused. 'Lemme ask you something.'

Khalid's eyebrows shot up, as if to say, *Shoot*.

'You make any calls last night?'

Khalid frowned. 'No,' he said. 'I call no one. Him, too! No calls.'

'What about the Internet?' Wilson asked.

The plane hit an air pocket, and Zero turned white.

Khalid's frown deepened, then softened into embarrassment. He was thinking that Wilson was upset about the hotel bill. So he blamed his friend. 'Yeah,' he said, confessing on Zero's behalf. 'He goes on pussy dot com, when I'm in the shower, y'know? Five minutes, maybe ten, I'm in the shower. When I get out, I see what he does, I make him get off.'

'No problem.'

'Maybe fifteen minutes — '

'Don't worry about it,' Wilson told him. 'What I wanted to know was, you hear from Hakim? You get any e-mail from him?'

Khalid shook his head, looking relieved. 'No,' he said. 'We don't get nothing from Hakim.'

★ ★ ★

They touched down in Sharjah a little after three.

Exiting the plane was like leaving a theater in

164

midafternoon. A wall of heat fell on them, and the sky went off like a flare. Wilson fumbled for his sunglasses, squinting so tightly he might as well have been blind. Pools of oil, real or imagined, glittered on the tarmac. In the distance, a cluster of bone-white buildings shimmered in the molten air.

'Dubai,' Belov said, raising his chin toward the horizon. Behind them, a small truck began to tow the plane, heading for a hangar at the end of the runway.

'How long are we here?' Wilson asked.

'We leave tonight. You hungry?'

'I could eat,' Wilson said.

'Good. Come. I get you dinner jacket.'

'Where we going?'

'Dubai. Couple miles.'

'What for?'

'Tea,' Belov replied.

'Tea?'

'With sandwiches!' Sensing Wilson's skepticism, the Russian gave an apologetic shrug and said, 'In Moscow, I am taking you to whore-house. Have ashes hauled, no problem. Here? In Arab country? Is tea.'

*　*　*

Wilson had never ridden in a Bentley before. It was nice.

As was Burj Al Arab. Built to resemble the sail of the world's biggest dhow, it stood about a thousand feet offshore at the end of a concrete causeway that linked it to Jumeirah Beach. Belov

165

bragged that it had the tallest atrium in the world, the highest tennis court, the most expensive rooms —

'And . . . Underwater restaurant! What you think?'

'Sounds uncomfortable,' Wilson told him. 'Sounds like a fuckup.'

Belov frowned, then got the joke and laughed. As they entered the atrium, a maître d' caught their eye and led them to a linen-covered table near the fountain. Palm trees rustled in a fake breeze as a column of water shot into the air, a hundred feet or more, and then fell back — only to erupt again and again. Children ran shrieking among the tables, shattering the decorum. The temperature was about sixty-five degrees. Despite the jacket he was wearing, Wilson shivered.

'Hey!' Belov exclaimed, pointing across the room, where an entourage of gangsta wannabes followed a muscular black man to the elevators. 'Fifty Cent! I know! You want shake hand?'

'Maybe another time,' Wilson told him.

The Russian shrugged, then beckoned a waiter to their table. 'Having tea for two.' The waiter closed his eyes, inclined his head, and backed away with a practiced smile.

Belov sat back in his chair, and regarded Wilson with a wry smile. 'Halfway there,' he said.

'A little less.'

'Few miles, maybe. Who's counting?'

'I hope someone is. I'd hate to come up short.' Wilson looked around. 'Max . . . '

'What?'

'Why are we here?'

Belov shrugged. 'I said! Refueling. Is long way, Congo.'

'I mean, *here*. In the Magic Kingdom, or whatever you call it.'

'Burj Al Arab. Everyone knows this place. Is famous!'

'So we're, like . . . tourists?'

'Not tourist! Smelling roses. Is good.'

Wilson gave his head a little shake, as if to clear it. 'How long does it take to refuel?'

'Half hour.'

Wilson looked at his watch.

Belov leaned in, and lowered his voice. 'We don't just take fuel.'

'No?'

The Russian shook his head.

'Then what?' Wilson asked.

'We paint.'

'Paint?'

Belov put his thumb and forefinger together. 'Little bit. On tail. Where numbers are.' His voice dropped twenty decibels and an octave. 'I tell you something confidential.'

'Okay . . . '

'Is two Antonovs in hangar.'

Wilson thought about it.

Belov continued: 'So we paint. Then we change transponders. Number Two Antonov takes off for Almaty. You know Almaty?'

Wilson shook his head.

'Shit town. Not important,' Belov said. 'But good decoy. Now comes dark, and Number One Antonov is flaps up.' He sat back with a worried glow, as if he'd just explained the general theory

167

of relativity to the guy behind him in a supermarket line. 'You understand?'

Before Wilson could reply, the waiter returned, wheeling a cart crowded with pots of hot water and plates of tiny sandwiches. A tea-caddy was produced, and they selected their teas — English Breakfast for Wilson, and an infusion of echinacea, palmetto berries, and nettle root for Belov. 'For chakras,' he explained, looking a bit embarrassed.

'Excellent choice,' the waiter said, and slipped away.

Belov leaned in. 'How much you know about Congo?'

Wilson shook his head. 'AIDS and diamonds. Used to be Belgian. Lots of resources, lots of poverty.' He paused. Thought for a moment. 'And they're killing each other.'

Belov nodded. 'Three million dead in five years.'

Wilson sampled one of the sandwiches, a mixture of cream cheese, apricot, and salmon on an equilateral triangle of Wonder Bread whose crusts had gone missing. Not bad, but it would take about ten of them to have an impact. He tried another: buttered pumpernickel with thinly sliced radishes. Even better.

'There's gold,' Belov confided. 'Also copper and . . . you name it. This place we're going, Ituri province — it's next to Uganda, okay? Beautiful, beautiful mountains . . . ' He closed his eyes for a moment, then just as suddenly opened them. 'But! This place, it's death. Ten years, now, they're fighting. I think it goes on forever.'

'Who's behind it?' Wilson asked.

168

'You! Me! Them! Everybody!' Then he rattled off a string of acronyms.

Wilson wolfed down another sandwich. Tried to figure out what it was. Dijon mustard and cranberry sauce. Bits of turkey. 'This guy we're in business with — '

'Commander Ibrahim. He's Ugandan, so . . . he's having good English!'

Wilson looked puzzled. 'What's he doing in the Congo if he's Ugandan?'

'Diamond mines,' Belov said. 'Near Bafwasende.'

'Which is where?'

'Lindi River. Maybe thirty klicks from airstrip.' Belov grinned. 'This is pygmy place. My advice: Don't fuck with them.'

Wilson sat back in his chair. He was thinking, *It's going to happen.* He glanced around, and tried to imagine it. A place like this, multiplied by a million . . . The systems break down, and it's lights out! The fountain dies, the heat builds up. But, wait a second, what's that? The generators! *We're saved!* The lights flicker back to life, and everyone sighs in relief. There's a rush of laughter and small talk, and then — uh-oh! — the generators die. Food begins to spoil, and the place begins to stink. And maybe, just maybe, they can't get out. The doors are automatic, and they look like they weigh a ton. If you couldn't get out — if you were locked in — after a couple of days, it would be like a George Romero film. The idea made him laugh. Talk about 'cannon fodder'! All these people, the waiters and sheiks, businessmen and brats, sweltering in this bell jar of a hotel — entertained, perhaps, by 50 Cent. (We can only hope.)

'What is funny?' Belov asked.

Wilson shook his head. 'Nothing, I was just . . . So what's the drill, once we get there?'

Belov shrugged. 'Drive to Bafwasende. Meet Commander Ibrahim, so we have chitchat. If hunky-dory, you get paid. Then, I think, you go to Kampala next day.'

'What's in Kampala?' Wilson asked.

'Airport. Is gateway to world.'

'And you're where?'

'I'm back to Sharjah.'

Wilson sipped his tea. It occurred to him that once Belov left, he'd be on his own — except for Zero and Khalid — and he'd be carrying four million dollars in diamonds. 'Tell me something,' he said.

'What?'

'This guy, Ibrahim, he's pretty tight with Hakim, right?'

Belov nodded.

'So what happens if I go missing?'

Belov frowned. After a moment, he said, 'Depends.'

'On what?'

'Diamonds. If you go missing, is sad! We have tears in Sharjah, Beirut, but . . . we move on. Unless diamonds go missing, too. Then, I think, we have big problem. For everybody. Colonel Ibrahim, too.' With a grin, the Russian tapped his temple with his forefinger. 'I see wheels turning, but . . . don't worry. Many times, Hakim sends people to Congo. We don't lose no one yet!'

Wilson nodded, but he didn't look happy. He was thinking about Bobojon's e-mail from the night before. 'What about Hakim? What happens if he goes missing?'

Belov's cheeks swelled up like a blowfish. He sat like that for a few seconds, then slowly exhaled. Finally, he said, 'Is end of world.'

16

CONGO MARCH 5, 2005

Higher was safer. Higher was smoother.

Leaving Sharjah just after midnight, they'd climbed to thirty-five thousand feet over the Empty Quarter, and stayed at that altitude until Ethiopia was behind them. Somewhere over the southern Sudan, they began their descent, dropping lower and lower as they approached Uganda's border with the Congo. As the plane sank gently into a sea of clouds, the moon winked out and the wings began to shiver, and then they began to bounce.

'Seat belt,' Belov said.

The cockpit was quiet and dark, the instrument panel glowing softly, the fuselage creaking. Belov and the navigator talked softly in Russian, while the pilot made adjustments to the controls.

Wilson buckled up. A flash of lightning, and everything went nova — the sky, the cockpit, the men's faces. And then it was night again. Through the window, Wilson saw a wall of thunderheads flickering in the dark.

The plane yawed.

'Better get down quick,' Belov said.

'Yeah, that lightning — '

'Fuck lightning! Is bad neighborhood. Stingers, Strelas — a real mess!'

Wilson looked at the arms dealer. 'Whose fault is that?' he asked, as the plane fell through a hole in the night, eliciting a yelp from the passenger cabin.

Belov chuckled.

The altimeter was turning counterclockwise and the fuselage was rattling, hard, when a dinner service crashed to the floor in the galley behind them. Wilson kicked a cup away and searched the ground for lights, an airport — anything.

'Weather like this, I think: Dag Hammarskjold,' Belov confessed. 'You know? Big UN guy. Went down over Katanga. Long time ago.'

'Missile?'

Belov shook his head. 'No! Was shit weather, so . . . they're flying on instruments, okay? Bad guys hijacked beam — sent plane into mountain. No more Hammarskjold!'

Wilson shuddered, his eyes straining in their sockets. He could imagine what it would be like, roaring out of the clouds into a wall of rocks and trees. At least it would be quick. A glimpse of the end, and then The End. But if a bomb went off inside the plane, or if a missile hit them . . . Maybe the fuel tanks would explode, and it would be over in an instant. But what if the plane broke up slowly, piece by piece? What if the passengers fell through the air like birds with a virus, like suicides — or like those people who stepped off the World Trade Center's roof?

Lights flickered under the wings as the Antonov shredded the clouds at twelve hundred feet. The pilot leveled off in the direction of what

173

had to be the airstrip, a rectangle of lights embedded in the darkness ahead.

They were all business now, jabbering in Russian as the plane sank toward the runway. The landing gear dropped with a terrifying thump, and for a moment, Wilson was sure they'd been hit — though by what or by whom he had no idea. Pressing his forehead against the window, he could see the exhaust pouring over the wing, the ailerons fluttering, and, up ahead, a handful of trucks and military vehicles standing in a field, headlights beaming the way.

★　★　★

The plane could not have been at rest for more than thirty seconds when the cargo door began to lower. By then, Zero and Khalid were at the ready, duffel bags in one hand, H.K.'s in the other. The Diadora bags were left where they were, on the floor of the plane. They wouldn't be needed in Africa, and the guns could not be taken to Antwerp.

Belov led them down the ramp, where they were blinded by the lights of trucks and military vehicles parked on the verge of the airstrip. Wilson took a deep breath, inhaling Africa for the first time.

'Max!' A giant loomed in the headlights, came forward and embraced the Russian with a rumbling chuckle. By Wilson's estimate, he would not have been out of place in the forecourt of the San Antonio Spurs, and looked to be about Wilson's own age. He had ritual scars on each of his cheeks and a large diamond in the lobe of his left ear. Dressed in combat boots and taupe fatigues, he wore a double-barreled shoulder rig with a Glock hanging, half-cocked, in each of his armpits. One step behind him, and on either side, was a cherubic-looking twelve-year-old with a Kalashnikov.

'Commander Ibrahim, permit me, I introduce Mr. Frank,' Belov announced.

Commander Ibrahim crushed Wilson's hand in his own, all smiles, then stepped back with a look of exaggerated suspicion. 'American?'

Wilson nodded.

Belov, looking nervous, said, 'Mr. Frank is Mr. Hakim's good friend. We do good business together.'

Commander Ibrahim nodded thoughtfully. Finally, he said, 'Takoma Park.'

The African's voice was deep, with a British accent. But Wilson had no idea what he was talking about. 'Excuse me?'

'Takoma Park! Do? You? Know it!'

Wilson glanced at Belov, but the Russian looked away, as if to say, *You're on your own.* 'You mean, the suburb — the one in Maryland?'

'And D.C. — part of it's in Dee Cee.'

Wilson nodded. 'Yeah,' he said. 'I've been there once or twice.'

Commander Ibrahim thumped his chest with his fist, then pointed a finger at Wilson. 'Well, I was there two fucking years!'

Wilson didn't know what to say. Said: 'Hunh!'

175

Commander Ibrahim turned to the boy-soldier on his right. 'That's my homey,' he declared.

The kid laughed.

★ ★ ★

The drive to the mining camp near Bafwasende was about fifty kilometers along a dirt track that, to Wilson's surprise, was in decent condition. They rode in a sleek Mercedes sedan, with Commander Ibrahim in the front beside the driver, smoking a spliff. Wilson availed himself of the foldaway wet bar to nurse a tumbler of Glenmorangie, neat, and Belov did the same. For Wilson, it was a narcissistic moment, but for Belov, it was just another day at the office.

Their escorts, front to back, were an armored personnel carrier and a 'technical.' The latter was a Jeep Grand Cherokee whose roof had been sawn off to accommodate a light machine gun where the rear seat had been. Flat-black with primer, the defrocked SUV had improvised armor, as well as a constellation of bullet holes in the front left fender. An effort to putty them over with epoxy had been unsuccessful, and cosmetically insane.

The APC was a BTR-70, according to Belov (who'd sold it to Commander Ibrahim). It had coaxial machine guns and was totally amphibious. 'Nice Russian car!' Belov bragged. 'They make in Arzamas plant — in Nizhny Novgorod. But heavy! Ten tons, I think!'

'Eleven,' Ibrahim corrected.

176

Belov was about to disagree when their conversation was cut short by a burst of machine-gun fire from the technical.

Wilson saw a group of men scatter from the side of the road, scrambling into the bush.

Belov and Commander Ibrahim laughed.

'What the fuck was that?' Wilson asked.

Ibrahim chuckled. 'Local people,' he said. 'No worries.'

'Did we hit 'em?'

Ibrahim shrugged. 'I don't know.' The way he said it, he might as well have added, *Like it matters?*

Wilson glanced out the back window, saw the sky brightening in the east. 'So where did they go?'

Belov snorted. 'Nowhere! They're back in five minutes. Like roaches!'

Ibrahim turned to Wilson. 'You saw the rope?'

Wilson shook his head. He hadn't seen anything but half a dozen men running for their lives.

'There was a rope across the road,' Ibrahim told him. 'They tie it to a tree.'

'So?'

'When cars come, they raise the rope. This means you're supposed to stop.'

'*You* didn't stop,' Wilson said.

'I have an armored personnel carrier. Why the fuck would *I* stop?'

Belov chuckled. Ibrahim laughed.

'They call themselves 'tax collectors,' ' the commander said, his smile fading to black. 'So I guess they think they're the government. But I

177

don't think so. You ever see a tax collector sitting beside the road with a rope?'

Wilson shook his head.

'Well,' Ibrahim said, 'I see it every day. And it pisses me off.'

They continued on their way for nearly an hour, until they arrived at a compound of prefabricated buildings, huddled together behind a concrete wall topped with razor wire and broken glass. Half a mile from the mining camp, the compound was Commander Ibrahim's 'executive offices and military headquarters.'

'You might as well get some sleep,' Ibrahim said, 'while my friend and I go over the cargo. I'll show you around this afternoon.'

This was fine with Wilson, who was tired from the long flight. Trailed by Zero and Khalid, he followed a bare-chested pygmy up a staircase to the building's second floor, where half a dozen rooms were set aside for visitors. The rooms were simple but well kept. Wilson's came with an air conditioner that sounded like a truck with a thrown rod. Even so, it brought the temperature down to the eighties, and wrung a steady stream of moisture from the air.

Wilson kicked his shoes off, and lay down on the bed. As tired as he was, sleep was hard to come by. He felt a mosquito land on the hairs of his arm and, opening his eyes, watched as it began to feed. When it seemed to Wilson that the bug was engorged, he closed his fingers into a fist, and tightened the muscles in his arm. The mosquito was trapped, its proboscis pinned beneath the skin. Wilson's veins stood out in low relief. His arm trembled. The insect popped.

It was one of the games he'd played in Supermax.

He closed his eyes again, then just as quickly opened them when he heard a quarrel in the hallway outside his room. Getting to his feet, Wilson stepped into his shoes, went to the door, and pulled it open.

Zero and Khalid were arguing with a pygmy who, fierce and terrified, was threatening them with a knife. A Ugandan soldier came pounding up the stairs, yelling at everyone to 'Knock it off!'

Wilson pulled his bodyguards away, while the soldier did his best to calm the pygmy.

'What's going on?' Wilson asked.

The soldier looked up. 'He says your friends insulted him.'

Khalid scoffed.

The soldier turned to Khalid. 'You're lucky he didn't kill you.'

Khalid hefted his Heckler and Koch, as if to say, *Not likely*.

It was the soldier's turn to scoff. 'He would have filleted you.'

'Fuck that,' Wilson said. 'What's he talking about? How did they insult him?'

'He's supposed to guard your room,' the soldier replied.

'So?'

'Your friends wouldn't let him.'

'It's our job,' Khalid insisted. 'We sit outside — in a chair — with the H.K.'s. We take turns, you know?'

179

'So what's the problem?' Wilson asked.

'He wants the chair. So he pulls a knife.'

The pygmy started to say something, but Wilson waved him off. 'Tell him we're sorry,' Wilson told the soldier. 'Tell him he can guard my room.' As the soldier translated, Wilson turned to Khalid. 'Why don't you just get another chair?'

Khalid shrugged. 'We could do that.'

'There's one downstairs,' the soldier said.

Wilson nodded. 'I'll go with you.'

As they walked down the corridor, the soldier laughed. 'Your boys are pretty good!' he said. 'Or pretty dumb.'

'Why do you say that?' Wilson asked.

The soldier laughed again. 'This pygmy, he'll kill you in a heartbeat. Everybody knows that. So your boys took a big chance for you!'

As they went down the stairs to the main offices, a wave of laughter and shouting rolled toward them. The source of the noise turned out to be a clutch of boys, none of them more than thirteen years old, hovering over a laptop computer in an empty office. At first, Wilson thought they were playing a video game, but then he saw they were online and at a porn site.

The soldier screamed 'Out! Get out!' and threw a head-fake at them. They ran.

Wilson turned to the soldier, who was laughing. 'You have a satellite connection out here?'

The soldier nodded.

'All right if I use it?'

The soldier shrugged. 'Sure,' he said, and went

off in search of a chair.

Wilson sat down before the monitor, cracked his knuckles, and typed: *www.yahoo.com*.

He was hoping for news of Hakim.

Clicked on Check Mail. Clicked on Draft. The page appeared. And to his surprise, he found not one message, but two. *I can't find Hakim* had yet to be deleted — which pissed him off. It was a small thing, but an irritating one. Now was not the time to get sloppy about security. God knows, the protocols were simple enough. Wilson checked the deletion box, and went on to the more recent message which, like its predecessor, was addressed to no one and had a Subject line that read 'None.'

> Found Hakim. No problem.
> He was meeting with friends.
> Wants you to get in touch.

Wilson stared at the message. He felt as if he'd been punched in the stomach. 'Found Hakim'? The words — or more accurately, the number of words in the first sentence — pushed him back in his chair.

He tried to rationalize it. Maybe Bo had forgotten . . . But no. How do you forget a protocol as simple as theirs? You don't. Which meant that Bobojon hadn't written the message. Someone else had. Someone who knew enough about Bobojon's e-mail to know that he was using Draft mode to communicate. But how could that be?

Wilson flashed back to the *Marmara Queen*,

181

when the ship had been at anchor off Istanbul, waiting for the dock strike to end. Zero and Khalid had been watching television — some Arab channel — and someone was getting busted on camera. There was a man with a hood over his head. Men with guns. Wilson said: *What's this?* And Khalid said: *Malaysia.* Not Berlin. *Malaysia.*

Wilson's ass tightened. He thought hard. *I can't find Hakim.* That was Bobojon, no question. Four words. And then this phony message about getting in touch. Who was *that?* Wilson thought about it for all of about fifteen seconds, and began to put it together. There weren't a lot of possibilities. *I can't find Hakim.* Obviously, Hakim had gone missing, and Bobojon had worried about it. Now, *Bobojon* was missing, or if not missing, no longer in control of his own communications. So Hakim must have given him up. And now the police were looking for Wilson.

Or someone.

Did they know who he was? Did they know his name — where he was — what he was doing? Maybe.

Or maybe not. If Bobojon talked (and everyone talked if you tortured them enough), they would know everything. And that would be the end of it.

But they didn't know everything. For example, they didn't know about the protocol he and Bobojon had used, so maybe Bo had gotten away. Or maybe he'd been killed.

Hakim was a different story. To Hakim, Wilson

182

was a sideshow — a guy named 'Frank d'Anconia,' one of Bobojon's projects. An American with crazy ideas. How much could Hakim actually tell them? How much did he actually know?

Well, Wilson thought, *he knows everything about the hash, the guns, and the diamonds. He can tell them where I am and what I'm doing, and he can tell them where I'm going. He can tell them what I look like, but he can't tell them who I am — not exactly. The most he could say was that I'd been in prison with Bobojon. But that could be a lot of guys. Bo had done a lot of time.*

So he was safe for now. The CIA, or whoever they were, might be waiting for him in Antwerp. But they wouldn't come after him in the Congo. Not in a war zone, not with the government five hundred miles away.

Of course, if Ibrahim found out about Hakim, all bets were off. The diamonds would disappear. And so, in all likelihood, would Wilson. He'd end up at the bottom of the mine, or on a spit.

Found Hakim . . . get in touch.

I don't think so.

He went to the mine in the afternoon. It was nothing like he'd imagined.

If he'd thought about it at all, he'd have expected to find a tunnel with narrow-gauge tracks leading into the earth — a sort of coal mine. Or else a mountain stripped into tiers,

183

with massive machines clawing at the ground. Instead, he found something stranger. A landscape with the pox.

The mine was a gigantic pit, maybe two hundred yards across, dug to a depth of about thirty-five feet. This enormous hole was criss-crossed with berms of yellow earth that framed a score of smaller pits in which teams of emaciated miners stood up to their knees in stagnant groundwater, sweating under the watchful eyes of armed foremen.

In each pit was a wooden trough with a wire mesh at the bottom. Gasoline engines pumped a steady stream of water into the troughs, while diggers fed them with shovel after shovel of excavated stones, pebbles, and soil. The rushing water washed and tumbled the rocks, making the smaller stones fall through the mesh at the bottom. At the end of each trough, a boy shoveled the finer gravel into piles.

Stripped to their shorts and slaked with mud, the 'shake-shake men' scooped this finer gravel into the circular wooden sieves that gave them their name. Stooping to the surface of the water, they whirled the sieves in such a way that the muck and clay sluiced to the edges, while the much heavier, diamondiferous gravel coagulated in the middle.

Somehow the shake-shake men could spot a quarter-carat diamond in the rough without fail. And when they did, they froze in place, and whistled to the foreman, who'd come running.

'How much do you pay them?' Wilson asked.

His guide laughed. He was the same man

184

who'd driven them from the airstrip in the Mercedes. 'Well,' he said, 'the ones we pay get sixty cents a day, American. And food. The others just get food.'

'The others?' Wilson asked.

The driver grinned. 'There are some we don't pay.'

'Why not?'

A shrug. 'Bad boys. Lugbara people. Prisoners of war.'

'But you feed them.'

The driver nodded. 'Of course. They have to eat. So, two cups of rice a day. Cassava, sometimes. I'm telling you, man, that's Easy Street you're looking at.'

★   ★   ★

An hour later, Commander Ibrahim was seated at a card table outside a concrete hut in a compound at the mine. It was here that the diggers and shake-shake men received their pay and rations, and it was here that punishments and rewards were meted out.

Wilson and the Mercedes driver entered the compound as Ibrahim was lecturing what looked like a family. There was an older man, who might have been in his forties; his wife, who seemed about the same age; and a young mother with three children: two boys, about ten, and a girl who couldn't have been more than five. The family looked terrified.

Belov was nearby, leaning against the compound's wall.

185

Wilson joined him. 'I thought you'd be gone by now,' he said. 'I thought you'd be heading back to Sharjah.'

Belov shook his head, and nodded toward Ibrahim. 'Commander Ibrahim isn't happy, so . . . I'm still here.'

'What's the problem?'

'Problem is bullshit!' Belov said in a low voice. 'He makes argument over RPGs.'

'Why?' Wilson asked.

'He wants Russian RPGs. But I don't have. So I give him Chinese. Is perfect copy! No difference. Good weapon.'

'So?'

'So it's up to Hakim,' Belov told him.

Wilson looked skeptical. 'And how does *that* work?'

'Easy. He calls him on phone.'

Wilson felt his heart lurch. He glanced around. 'Hakim?'

'Yeah.'

'He can do that?' Wilson asked.

'Why not?'

'From here?'

Belov shrugged. 'With satellite phone? Yeah!' Belov looked at him. 'What's the matter? Is there problem?'

'No, I — ' Before Wilson could could finish the sentence, a militiaman came into the compound, dragging a boy by the hair. The boy was naked, and he'd been badly beaten.

Seeing him, the family cringed. The little girl moved toward the boy with open arms outstretched, but was quickly captured by the

186

older man, who clutched her to his chest. The mother burst into tears, and soon, the whole family was keening.

'What's *this*?' Wilson asked. The boy couldn't have been more than thirteen.

Belov shook his head. 'Bad shit,' he muttered. 'They say he steals diamond, so . . . he's fucked.'

The grandfather — if that's who he was — appealed to Commander Ibrahim. Wilson couldn't make out a word of what he was saying — he was speaking Swahili, or something like it. But he was pleading hard in a low, tremulous voice.

Ibrahim adopted a judicious pose, frowning thoughtfully as the grandfather spoke. Occasionally, he looked at the others in the compound — at Wilson and Belov, at the soldiers, at the boy — and nodded, as if to say, *Good point*. It seemed, almost, as if he'd been persuaded by the older man's speech, but then he grew bored with the charade, shook his head, and clapped his hands twice, in rapid succession.

Turning to the soldier at his side, he said, 'Get on with it.'

With a grin, the soldier went into the pink building, and emerged, a few seconds later, with a jerry can of gasoline in one hand and a tire in the other.

Seeing this, the family let out a wail, the mother screamed, and the boy staggered where he stood. It seemed to Wilson that his knees buckled. But they didn't give way. The boy just stood there, swaying in the courtyard. It was almost as if he was listening to music that no one else could hear.

Moving quickly to his side, the soldier slipped the tire over the boy's head, then dragged his right arm through the hole at its center. Finally, he lashed the boy's wrists together behind his back, using a plastic ziptie. Then he filled the tire's hollow core with gasoline, splashing it liberally over the boy himself, who was quaking to his family's screams and pleas.

Wilson couldn't believe what he was seeing.

Ibrahim patted the air with his hands, and made a *shhh*-shing sound. 'Nothing is decided,' he said. Then he turned to Wilson. 'Did Belov tell you?'

'Tell me what?' The air was heavy with the smell of gasoline. It felt like the compound might explode.

'About the cargo,' Ibrahim said.

Wilson did a double take. Was this supposed to be a threat? The boy who'd taken the diamond was standing ten feet away, quivering, his hands cuffed to a tire drenched in gasoline. The kid was about to go off like a Roman candle and Ibrahim picks this very moment to bitch about the cargo? 'Yeah,' Wilson said. 'He told me. You've got a problem with the RPGs.'

'No! *You've* got a problem with the RPGs.' He stared hard at Wilson.

'So why don't you call Hakim?' Belov asked.

'I did!' Ibrahim said.

Wilson felt his jaw drop.

'*And?!*' Belov demanded.

'He wasn't there.'

Wilson realized that he wasn't breathing. So he took a deep breath. Let it out.

Commander Ibrahim reached into a bag that was lying on the ground at his feet, and retrieved a satellite phone. 'They said he'd be back in an hour.' He consulted a scrap of paper, and punched a series of numbers into the phone.

'I don't think this is such a good idea,' Wilson said.

Ibrahim looked puzzled. So did Belov. Nearby, the family was kneeling in the dirt, holding hands and praying.

'Why not?' Belov asked.

Wilson didn't know what to say. 'It's late.'

Ibrahim gave him a look that questioned his sanity.

The boy with the tire around his shoulders sank to his knees.

The telephone must have rung six or seven times before anyone answered. Wilson's heart was crashing against his ribs, while threads of silver began to wiggle and curl in the corner of his left eye.

Commander Ibrahim jumped to his feet, shouting into the phone. 'Hallo? Hallo? Who is this?' He listened for a moment, then growled with impatience: 'Speak English, for God's sake! Where's Hakim?' He listened for a while longer. 'Then get him! Who the fuck do you think I'm calling? It's his phone, isn't it?' He kept his ear to the satellite phone, but turned to Wilson and Belov. In a quiet voice, he asked, 'So what should I do with the boy?'

189

'Let him go,' Belov said. 'You've made your point.'

Ibrahim nodded. 'I suppose . . . What do *you* think?' he asked, raising his chin to Wilson.

Wilson didn't know what to say. The vision in his right eye was beginning to go, and his thoughts were elsewhere. 'I've got my own problems,' he muttered. If Hakim didn't come to the phone (and why would he, how could he?), Ibrahim would begin to wonder. And that could not be a good thing in this place, under these circumstances.

Ibrahim frowned. 'We all have — Hallo? Hakim! Where the fuck have you been? Speak up, man! I can barely hear! Look, we've got a problem with the glass samples that you sent. Yes, 'the glass samples'!' A long pause. 'Well, some of the glass was made in China. What the fuck am I supposed to do with . . . what? No, it's not a lot of money. Maybe ten percent.'

'Maybe six percent,' Belov mumbled.

Commander Ibrahim was smiling now. 'Okay, my brother! Now, you're talking! I'll tell him what you said . . . What? Yes, of course, he's standing right next to me. Okay, okay, but . . . all right, no problem.' Commander Ibrahim handed the phone to Wilson. 'He wants to talk to you.'

Belov was smirking.

Wilson was nearly blind, his eyes spangled with neural fireworks that only he could see. He laid the phone against his cheek, and said, 'Hello?'

Ten seconds passed before Hakim said a word, and when he did, his voice was weak and

190

tired-sounding. 'Frank?'

Stupidly, Wilson nodded. Then he caught himself, and said, 'Yes?'

'It's Hakim . . . '

'I know.'

'So . . . everything's okay? At your end, it's okay?'

'Yeah,' Wilson said. 'It's fine.' *How many people are listening,* Wilson wondered. *And where are they keeping him?*

'Then I'll see you in Antwerp in a couple of days.'

'Right,' Wilson said.

'At the De Witte Lelie Hotel. As discussed.'

'Right.'

A moment later, the phone went dead.

Wilson took a deep breath, then tossed the phone to Commander Ibrahim.

Who was smiling. 'Sorry, Charley! He says you get ten percent less.'

Belov took a step toward him, looking outraged, but Wilson put a hand on his sleeve. 'It's okay,' he said. 'We'll make it back the next time around.'

Commander Ibrahim turned his attention to the boy with the Firestone necklace. 'I've decided,' he said. Then he paused, savoring the moment as everyone's eyes turned to him. 'He's just a boy . . . from a poor family . . . and it was a small diamond.'

The family was nodding in agreement. The boy, too.

'But . . . ' Ibrahim paused for a second time.

Wilson could see it coming.

191

'I have a mine to run,' Ibrahim said. 'So here's what we're going to do.' Ibrahim reached into his pocket, and pulled out a lighter. Moving around the table, he went to the family clustered on the ground, and gave the lighter to the mother. 'Light him up, Mother . . . '

She wailed.

Seeing what was happening, her son scrambled to his feet. But with the tire around his neck, and his hands behind his back, it was impossible to get anywhere. One of the soldiers grabbed him by the tire, spun him around, and shoved him back the way he'd come.

The mother was hysterical.

'Well, if you won't do as I ask,' Ibrahim said, 'we have an even bigger problem.' Still looking at the mother, he raised his hand and snapped his fingers. On cue, three soldiers came out of the little pink building, carrying five tires and a can of gas. The family gasped, and one of the younger boys swooned dead away.

But Ibrahim was having a grand old time, and so were his men. Some of them were laughing, and all of them were bright with excitement. 'Light him up, and that's the end of it! I promise you, Mother, once the boy toasts up, you can go home!' He waited for her to say something, but she didn't. She was shaking her head so hard, it seemed almost as if it might fly off. 'You understand, don't you? You're as responsible as the boy is! More! You brought him into the world. So now, I think, it's up to you to take him out. If you don't want to do that, if you can't do that, I'll quite understand. But then, I'm afraid, there's a tire for each of you!'

Ibrahim sank to his haunches, a few feet in front of the mother, and looked her in the eye. 'What's it to be, then? You're in charge, Mother! You decide! The boy — or the family? C'mon!' He spun the lighter's little wheel, and a flame flickered.

'Let her alone,' Wilson said.

Commander Ibrahim turned, and stared.

Wilson stepped forward with his hand out, palm up. 'Let me do it.'

17

It was a test.

If, like Nietzsche's superman, Wilson was (as he believed) 'beyond good and evil,' then any remnants of 'conscience' he might have were artifacts — the detritus of his own evolution. *Static*.

If he thought about it, he could probably work out an equation for it. A formula for the moral equivalent of the signal-to-noise ratio.

The idea, of course, was to shed his conscience as if it were a snakeskin. Just walk right out of it and keep on going. If anyone came after him, they'd see it in the grass, a ribbon of scales — and they'd wonder: Was *Wilson* nearby? Was he *hunting*?

It was important to Wilson — essential, really — that he should be comfortable with the violence inside him. And so, the boy . . .

His eyes rolled back as Wilson approached, cigarette lighter in hand. He stood in front of the kid for what seemed like a long time, waiting for him to look up from the ground. That was a part of it — having the strength to look his victim in the eye, embracing his fear, while accepting the injustice that was about to take place.

The boy must have sensed this as well, because he kept his eyes on the ground for what seemed like a long time. When, finally, he shook himself from what seemed like a waking swoon, and looked up, Wilson met his gaze for an instant, then spun the lighter's little wheel and lit him up.

The kid came alive in a rush, darting this way and that, engulfed in flames and trailing a veil of acrid black smoke. Militiamen leaped out of his way, laughing, as if they were playing a game of blind-man's bluff. Every so often one of the soldiers would spin him around with a kick in the ass or a tug on the tire. But the game didn't last long. It was over in thirty seconds. Though Wilson couldn't be sure, it seemed to him that the boy had a heart attack. One minute he was running around, making noises, and the next . . .

There was a sort of clumsy pirouette that ended with the boy sinking to his knees, clawing at the tread. Then he stiffened, and that was that. Like a tree, he toppled sideways, and lay in the dirt, smoking.

By then, Wilson himself was breathing hard, as if he were the one who'd been running around. Which was funny, because he hadn't actually done anything. Just spun a little wheel, and pressed it to the boy's chest.

He searched his heart for what he felt and, to his surprise, found that there was nothing there. The kid was dead, that's all.

Shit happens.

★ ★ ★

But that was yesterday, and now Wilson had his own problems.

Commander Ibrahim had arranged for a

technical to take him to the Ugandan border, near Fort Portal. There, an armored car would be waiting to drive him to Kampala. From the Ugandan capital, he could catch a plane to London, and before he knew it, he'd be in Antwerp.

Wilson declined the offer. Entering Uganda from the Congo in an armored car would attract too much attention, he said. He told the militiaman that he and Hakim had discussed it in Baalbek. And they'd decided that he should go to Bunia. Hakim's friends would arrange for a boat. He'd cross Lake Albert at night, avoiding the Customs' police and soldiers. In Uganda, Wilson and his party would travel by motorcycle along bush roads to the main highway, and from there to Kampala. Zero and Khalid would be with him all the way, providing a measure of security.

Ibrahim was skeptical, but in the end, it wasn't his problem. He had his guns. Wilson could do what he pleased.

'Is there a bank in Bunia?' Wilson asked.

'Of course,' Ibrahim replied.

Wilson thanked him. 'I'll need a safe-deposit box until the boat leaves.'

'No problem.'

In reality, of course, there was no boat, nor were there any 'friends.' Bunia was simply Plan B, a way for Wilson to rid himself of Ibrahim while finding a buyer for the diamonds he could no longer sell in Antwerp.

Because whoever was sending messages from Bobojon's computer was undoubtedly holding

196

Hakim as well. If Wilson showed up at De Witte Lelie Hotel, he'd probably be 'renditioned.' The moment he walked in, the CIA, FBI — whoever it was — would take him down. They'd stab him with a needle and that would be that. He'd wake up with a hood on his head, chained to a seat in Terrorist Class on his way to a prison that didn't exist.

Thus, Plan B.

The capital of the Congo's most dangerous province, Bunia was the African equivalent of Deadwood. A swarming dystopia, ripe with garbage, sewage, and disease, the city was a crumbling slum of three hundred thousand people — many of whom were starving, sick, and desperate. Not far from Lake Albert, it was a little piece of hell in an otherwise heavenly setting.

The diamonds Commander Ibrahim had turned over in exchange for the arms — more than three pounds of preselected 'rough,' ranging in size from three to five carats — were concealed in a beautifully carved ironwood head, hollowed out for the purpose. There were 7,263 carats, and every one of them was of gemstone quality. Commander Ibrahim guaranteed it, and Wilson took the militiaman at his word. And why not? Ibrahim and Hakim were in business together, while Belov and Wilson were merely their agents. The business was as bloody as it was lucrative, and it was built on trust. If you asked either man why he trusted the other, he would talk about Allah, and the cause they shared. He would invoke the Umma of Muslim solidarity,

197

and allude to a decade of secret operations in which the two of them had been engaged. But in the end, both men knew that their trust was held together by something even stronger than Islam. It was held together by one man's gun and the other man's knife, and by each man's certain knowledge that the other could reach out and touch him, wherever he might be.

So if Ibrahim said the diamonds were good, the diamonds were good.

Even so, Wilson had done a bit of reading, and he'd learned that the diamond industry was an interesting one. Among other things, it was the quintessential cartel.

For more than a century, the price of gem-grade diamonds has been controlled by the South African DeBeers company and its partners. The firm accomplished this by creating a vertically integrated monopoly that enabled it to limit the supply of diamonds. It was able to do this because DeBeers owned all or part of nearly every diamond mine in the world. Those gems that it did not produce it bought through a subsidiary, the so-called Diamond Corporation.

In this way, the market was cornered.

Each year, some 250 'sight-Holders' were invited to London by the Central Selling Organization, or CSO. This, too, was a DeBeers creation, candidly referred to by Israeli diamond buyers as 'The Syndicate.'

In London, sight-Holders were permitted to buy presorted parcels of diamonds at fixed prices, usually $42,500 each. The parcels could not be examined until after they were purchased, and so were something of a pig in a poke. If a sight-Holder didn't like what he got, he was free to reject a parcel. But if he did that, he'd soon be out of business. No further invitations would be forthcoming from the CSO.

So the sight-Holders accepted what they'd been given, trusting DeBeers in much the same way that Wilson trusted Commander Ibrahim.

After buying their parcels, sight-Holders would resell them to wholesalers on the diamond exchanges of Antwerp, Amsterdam, New York, and Ramat Gan (Israel). Meanwhile, an artificial scarcity was maintained by the Diamond Corporation, which bought surplus diamonds wherever they might be found. These diamonds were stored by the kilo in London vaults, or left in the ground to be mined at a later date (if ever).

Conflict diamonds were the wild cards in the game. These were gems mined by the supernaturally violent rebel militias in Sierra Leone, Angola, and the Congo. Wrested from jungle riverbeds by de facto slaves earning sixty cents a day, 'blood diamonds' made their way to the world's exchanges by irregular routes, without the intervention of the Syndicate.

Because these conflict diamonds fueled wars throughout West Africa, while undermining the price of diamonds sold by the CSO, DeBeers worked to establish protocols that would ensure that 'legitimate diamonds' came with a certificate of origin.

There was an ironic symmetry in this, Wilson thought. End-user certificates were forged or

199

bought to enable the sale of arms to third parties like Commander Ibrahim, whose militia presided over a slave colony charged with mining diamonds in the jungle. Why, then, shouldn't the diamonds require a certificate of their own, one that rinsed the blood from the stones by creating a phony paper trail all the way from Africa to the bride's ring finger?

Though blood diamonds were no different from others, except in the violence of their provenance, they were sold at a discount to their counterparts from South Africa, Australia, and Siberia. According to Hakim, Wilson's diamonds would fetch about four million dollars, about half of what they'd bring if DeBeers was marketing them.

The only problem, now that Hakim was hanging upside down in the hold of an aircraft carrier, was finding a buyer. With June 22 looming closer and closer, Wilson had no time to lose.

★ ★ ★

They got into Bunia a little after noon, pulling up in front of the heavily sandbagged Banque Zaïroise du Commerce Extérieur. While Zero and Khalid waited outside, Wilson went in to meet the manager.

Mr. Bizwa was an East Indian gentleman in his late forties. He sat behind an ornately carved Empire desk, beneath a portrait of the president, Joseph Kabila. Greeting Wilson with a firm handshake, he gestured to a chair and asked how he could be of help.

'I need a safe-deposit box,' Wilson told him. 'For this!' He produced the ironwood head, swaddled in cloth, and set it on the desk.

'May I look?' Bizwa asked. Wilson nodded, and the bank manager unwrapped the sculpture.

'I think it's probably pretty valuable,' Wilson said.

Bizwa frowned. 'Well,' he said, 'it's certainly . . . very nice.'

'I bought it in Uganda,' Wilson told him. 'Helluva good deal.'

There was a weak smile from Bizwa as he folded his hands, and tried to look helpful.

'I figured, since I'm in the neighborhood, I'd come over here. See what I can see.' He winked.

Bizwa looked puzzled. 'You mean, diamonds?'

'Bingo!'

'Well, you've come to the right place.'

'That's what I'm told.'

'But you're not in the diamond business yourself?' Bizwa asked.

Wilson shook his head. 'No, I'm a coffee buyer.'

Bizwa snorted with laughter. 'You came to Bunia to buy coffee?'

'No, no,' Wilson said. 'Like I said, this is just a side trip.'

'I see,' Bizwa replied, though he clearly didn't.

Wilson glanced over his shoulder, then leaned forward. In a whispery voice, he confided, 'I was hoping you could help me out. I'll want to buy a diamond. On account of I'm getting married,' Wilson explained.

201

'How nice!'

'So I was thinking . . . three, maybe four carats, rough. They say the rough diamonds, when they're cut, lose half their size. So that would be, what? One and a half to two carats.'

'Mmmmnnn.'

'You think it's doable?'

Bizwa nodded. 'Yes. Quite doable.'

'But illegal, *n'est-ce pas?*'

The banker smiled. 'Well, I don't think you'll have any difficulties. To begin with, there aren't any police. Just traffic people who haven't been paid for a long time.'

'What about the UN? I saw — '

'Uruguayans, Bangladeshis . . . they have a pretty full plate. And then, of course, what you're suggesting . . . it's what people *do* here.'

'Is it? Tell me about that. What do they do?'

'They buy and sell diamonds. It's the entire economy.'

'Ah!' Wilson pretended to think about that. Then, he said, 'So you could recommend someone! A diamond salesman?'

Bizwa gave him a hapless look. 'Well, of course, but . . . they're everywhere. Every taxi driver has a diamond to sell, or knows someone who does. Every militiaman, every — The thing is, it can be a bit dangerous. They could take advantage of you.'

'That's what I'm afraid of,' Wilson told him. 'I could be taken to the cleaners!'

'My best advice would be to stick with the dealers who have shops. They're Lebanese, mostly. And having a shop means they'll be there the next day. The cabdriver might not.'

'And they're Lebanese, you said?'

Bizwa shrugged. 'Almost all of them. There's a Chinese gentleman, but I wouldn't recommend that you do business with him.'

'Why not?'

Bizwa looked uncomfortable. 'Well, he's more of a *wholesaler*, and . . . ' Bizwa made a face.

'What?' Wilson insisted.

'He has a reputation,' Bizwa said.

'I see.'

They sat without speaking for a moment, listening to the whir and click of the ceiling fan.

'Well, I'm sure you'll find something,' Bizwa told him.

'Thanks. And one more thing . . . can you recommend a hotel?'

Bizwa winced. 'The only real hotels are closed, I'm afraid. But I'm sure there's room at the Château.'

'Château?'

'Lubumbashi House. It was the governor's mansion, once, I wouldn't call it a 'mansion,' really. It's more of a bungalow. A large bungalow.'

'What happened to the governor?'

Bizwa frowned. 'Passed away.'

'I'm sorry. Must have gotten sick, huh?'

Bizwa shook his head. 'No, I wouldn't say he was sick. Healthy as an ox, actually.'

Wilson nodded thoughtfully. 'But this hotel . . . it's safe, right? I mean, for someone like me?'

Bizwa pursed his lips. 'Yes, I think so. Journalists seem to like it. Visiting NGOs, government people — there's quite a bar scene.' He smiled. 'A safe-deposit box might be a good idea.'

★   ★   ★

Lubumbashi House was a rambling bungalow whose stucco walls were filigreed by not-so-long-ago gun battles. A graceful shambles, the villa sat in ruined gardens, surrounded by an eight-foot wall whose gray surface danced with lizards. At the side of the house was an empty swimming pool with a crater in the deep end.

'What happened to the pool?' Wilson asked as he filled out a registration form for himself and his companions, paying for the first night in cash.

The manager, a tired-looking Belgian with alcohol on his breath, shrugged. 'Mortar attack. Two years ago.'

'Anyone killed?'

The manager shook his head. 'Not in the pool,' he said, and handed Wilson a pair of keys. 'No sheets or towels, I'm afraid. Maybe tomorrow. If you'd like a complimentary drink . . . ?' He gestured to an adjacent room.

Wilson thanked him. Zero and Khalid demurred. They wanted to see their room.

The 'bar' was actually a sort of living room, with couches and easy chairs scattered across polished wood floors. Ceiling fans turned slowly overhead, driven by a generator rattling in the garden. Besides himself and the waiter, who doubled as a bartender, Wilson was alone in the

204

room with a burly Portuguese who might have been sixty years old.

'Frank d'Anconia.'

'Da Rosa. Jair da Rosa.'

Wilson dropped into a leather club chair, and signaled the waiter. 'Gin and tonic,' he said. 'And whatever my friend's drinking.'

Da Rosa smiled. 'Merci.'

'And what do you do, Mr. da Rosa?' Wilson asked.

'Me? I organize. I am an organizer of outcomes.'

Wilson looked puzzled. 'What sort of outcomes?'

'Military ones.'

Wilson laughed. 'And how's business?'

'Good! It's always good in Africa, though I think, maybe not so good as last year or the year before.'

'I'm sorry.'

The mercenary made a gesture, as if to say, *C'est la vie*. 'I have hopes. These things turn around. They always turn around.'

The waiter arrived with a tray, holding two gin and tonics. The Portuguese raised his glass in a silent toast, revealing a small tattoo between the thumb and forefinger of his right hand. Three blue dots that formed a triangle. 'Chin-chin!'

Wilson took a sip. 'So, business was better . . . before?'

Da Rosa's cheeks inflated for a moment. He blew a little puff of air across the coffee table between them. 'Business was great,' da Rosa replied. 'There was an African World War.'

205

The expression was new to Wilson, and he must have shown it.

'Nine nations, twenty militias, four million dead,' da Rosa explained.

'Four million?!'

Da Rosa made a rocking motion with his right hand. 'A hundred thousand, this way or that.'

'I had no idea.'

'Blacks,' he said, as if that explained everything. 'And it wasn't all at once. It took four or five years, so I think, perhaps, you missed it. But yes, four million. It was really *something*.'

Wilson didn't know what to say. Sipped his drink.

'And you?' da Rosa asked. 'What about you? You're a tourist? An opera singer? What?'

Wilson chuckled. He was unsure how much to say, and decided to stick to the story he'd given at the bank. 'I'm a coffee buyer.'

Da Rosa pursed his lips, and nodded. 'Interesting business. Arabica or robusta?'

Wilson blinked.

Da Rosa laughed. 'Diamonds, then.'

Wilson shrugged.

'Buying or selling?' da Rosa asked.

He thought about it. 'I guess that depends. Are you in the market?'

Da Rosa snorted. 'No! Too dangerous. But you should visit Lahoud — Elie Lahoud. He'll give you a good price and, if you mention my name, maybe there's something in it for me. Who knows?'

'Lahoud . . . he's Lebanese?'

'They're all Lebanese,' da Rosa assured him.

Wilson frowned. He wanted to avoid the Lebanese, some of whom might have crossed paths with Hakim and his friends. The last thing he needed was Zero and Khalid chatting with their countrymen. The less they knew, the better. In fact . . . 'Someone said there's a Chinaman.'

Da Rosa grimaced. 'Yes, of course — Big Ping! Has a shop on the Rue de Gaulle. Wear Kevlar.'

Wilson laughed. 'That bad?'

Da Rosa shook his head. Drained his drink, and rattled the ice. 'No, he's okay. But you don't go to Big Ping for a couple of diamonds. He's more of a wholesaler.'

'I thought they were all wholesalers,' Wilson said.

'Well, they are. Only Ping, he's dealing directly with the militias, so he's comfortable with big loads.'

'Sounds dangerous.'

'Not for him.'

'Why not?' Wilson asked.

'Because he's a triad,' da Rosa told him. 'Sun Yee On.'

Wilson frowned. 'Which is what?'

Da Rosa pursed his lips. 'Fifty thousand gangsters, working as a team. Like Wal-Mart, but with guns.'

★   ★   ★

Wilson went looking for Big Ping's shop the next morning, following a crudely drawn map that the hotel's manager had given him. Even with the map, it wasn't easy. Most of the streets were unmarked, and the buildings were unnumbered. He could have asked someone on the street, *How do I get to Big Ping's?* But if da Rosa was right, that would be like asking the way to Al Capone's.

So they walked. And walked some more.

Zero and Khalid did their best to look mean. That was what they did — that was their whole thing — and they glowered with the best of them. But Wilson could tell they were scared. There were lots of AKs on the street, and everywhere you looked, there were people with handguns in the backs of their jeans. Walking a step behind Wilson, Khalid grumbled, 'I thought we'd be in Europe now. Hakim said — '

'I thought so, too,' Wilson lied. 'But there's special business.'

Khalid was silent for a while, peering at the signage, and eyeing a gang of nine-year-olds that trailed behind them. 'Hakim never said anything about 'special business.''

Wilson glanced over his shoulder. 'That's why it's special.'

Suddenly, Zero let out a bark, and pointed to a sheet-metal sign hanging above a heavily carved wooden door at the end of a narrow alley.

777 EX-IM 777
PING LI ON, PROP.

An Asian man sat on a stool beside the door, a shotgun resting across his knees. The moment Wilson entered the alley, the man got to his feet and waved his forefinger from side to side.

Wilson hesitated, and then he understood. He turned to Zero and Khalid. 'Wait here.'

$$\star \quad \star \quad \star$$

Big Ping's office was cool and dimly lighted, with a couple of small glass cases holding a modest display of cut and uncut diamonds. Overhead, a bank of fluorescent lights buzzed noisily, while a table fan turned left and right atop a painted Chinese chest. A heavily carved ivory screen stood by itself in the far corner of the room.

An elderly Chinaman waited behind one of the counters, his face blank. Nearby, a handsome young Asian in a white linen suit sat on a folding chair with his elbows on his thighs, flipping through a tattered copy of *Hustler*.

Wilson looked into the old man's watery eyes. 'Mr. Ping?'

The old man's face twisted into a frown. 'No Ping!' He hesitated for a long moment. Eventually, a smile flickered under a tangle of nostril hairs. 'You want buy diamond?'

Wilson shook his head.

The smile vanished as the old man snorted in contempt. 'So! You sell diamond!'

Wilson gave him an incredulous look. 'That's amazing! You should be a private eye.'

The old man wasn't laughing, but the guy in the white linen suit cracked a smile. Dropping the magazine, he got to his feet. 'I'm Ping.'

Wilson turned to him. Offered his hand. 'Frank d'Anconia.'

'I know.'

'You do?'

'Yeah. You're the one who set the kid on fire . . . ' With a gesture of his hand, he led Wilson behind the ivory screen, where a massive iron door was bolted into the wall. Beside the door was a nickel plate with the outline of a hand engraved on its surface. Ping pressed his own hand into the engraving. A diode flared, and the door sprung open on its hinges. 'In here . . . '

The doorway led to a windowless room — a vault, of sorts, where the air was heavy with cigarette smoke. Two men sat at a heavy wooden table that was covered in green baize. The men were drinking tea.

One of them looked like an oversized Buddha with beige teeth. The other man was da Rosa, who glanced over his shoulder with a laugh and said, 'What took you so long?'

Wilson frowned. He didn't like being played.

The fat man chuckled, and lighted a foul-smelling Gitane. As a gesture of goodwill, he made an effort at English: 'Good night!'

Da Rosa laughed. 'I see you've met Little Ping.'

Wilson glanced at the young man in the white suit.

The young man smiled. 'My father's English isn't very good. But, please, have a seat.' He gestured to a chair. Wilson took it.

The fat man — Big Ping — leaned forward: 'American?'

Wilson nodded.

'We don't see a lot of Americans here,' da Rosa said. 'You're like a celebrity.'

Big Ping's eyes widened. His great head nodded, as if to confirm some astonishing insight. 'You CIA?!'

Wilson shook his head. 'No.'

Big Ping looked disappointed. Said something to his son in Chinese.

Little Ping translated. 'He says, if you're CIA, we could do some good business.'

'I'll bet we could. Only . . . I'm not.'

'Too bad. You want some tea?' Little Ping asked.

Wilson shook his head.

Big Ping's brows collapsed into a chevron. Leaning toward Wilson, he demanded, '*Qui vous-êtes? Que voulez-vous?*'

Wilson turned to Little Ping. 'Tell your father that I don't speak French.'

Little Ping shrugged. 'He wants to know who you are, what you want.'

Wilson sat back in his chair. Then he glanced from Big Ping to da Rosa, and back again. The silence began to peal. Somewhere in the room, a clock ticked.

Finally, Big Ping smiled, as if he'd just had another realization. With a look of great contentment, he placed his hands palms-down, fingers spread, on the baize-covered table. Little Ping remained where he was, hands crossed in front of his crotch.

It took Wilson a moment, and then he saw it. All three of them had the same tattoo: a triangle of little blue dots between the thumb and forefinger. Wilson glanced at da Rosa.

The mercenary smiled. 'I was born in Macau.'

Big Ping nodded.

Little Ping said, 'Mr. da Rosa's a good friend. We don't have secrets from him.'

Wilson thought about it some more, and decided he didn't have much choice. With a sigh, he said, 'Okay, I've got a couple of diamonds to sell. Quite a few, actually.'

To Wilson's surprise, da Rosa said something in Chinese. Big Ping replied, and da Rosa laughed. Turning to Wilson, he said, 'He says he doesn't see any diamonds. He wants to know if you've stuck them up your ass.'

Wilson acknowledged the *bon mot* with a weak grimace. 'No,' he said. 'I decided to use the bank. It seemed more professional, somehow.'

Little Ping laughed as da Rosa translated.

Wilson complimented him. 'You speak Chinese. I'm impressed!'

Da Rosa shook his head. 'It's not Chinese. It's Fuzhou.'

When da Rosa failed to elaborate, Wilson turned to Little Ping.

'My family's from Fujian,' the younger Ping explained, 'so the Fuzhou dialect comes naturally. Most Chinese don't understand it, so it's like talking in code. Good for business.'

Big Ping looked uncomprehendingly from Wilson to da Rosa to his son. Then he stubbed his cigarette out, and cut loose with a burst of incomprehensible lingo.

Little Ping nodded, and turned to Wilson. 'My father says you should go to the bank, and bring the diamonds here, so he can evaluate them.

He's a good appraiser, and he'll give you an excellent price.'

Wilson dismissed the idea with a bored nod. 'Right! But you know what? I don't think we'll do that. Because it occurs to me that maybe — just maybe — something might go wrong, and, well, I could be robbed. So we'll do something else. But *before* we do anything, there's a couple of things I need to know.'

Little Ping translated for his father. Finally, he said, 'Yes?'

'If we agree that four million dollars is a fair price, can you handle it?'

Suddenly, Big Ping gave up the pretense of not speaking English. With a wave of his hand, he interrupted his son's translation, and said, 'Of course.'

Wilson turned to him. 'Good. And if we do business, you can wire the money to my bank?'

'*Oui*,' Big Ping replied. 'If everything is in order, we can make the transfer through the HongShang Bank.'

'Great! So we'll do it like this: We'll go to the Banque Zaïroise, and take a look at the diamonds. They have a private room available for box holders, and you can bring any equipment you need.'

'Then what?' Big Ping asked.

'If we're in agreement, you ask your bank to make the wire transfer to my bank. Not the one in Bunia, but a British bank. Isle of Man. I'll wait with you until my bank confirms the funds are in the right account. Then we'll go to the Banque Zaïroise a second time. I'll give you the

213

diamonds, and . . . bye-bye.'

'Bye-bye,' Big Ping repeated.

'And there's one other thing,' Wilson said.

'There's always 'one other thing,'' da Rosa observed.

'I've got two friends outside . . . ' Wilson told them. Big Ping raised his eyebrows in a way that was meant to be a question. 'I want to make sure they're taken care of.'

Big Ping cocked his head, and frowned. Little Ping looked bewildered. After a moment, he said, 'I think it's better — you pay your own people.'

Wilson shook his head. 'That's not what I mean,' he said. 'What I mean is, I want you to *take care of them.* Can you do that?'

Silence. Da Rosa looked puzzled. Big Ping stroked his chin. After a moment, he turned to da Rosa with a grin and said, 'Flyswattah! He means: flyswattah!'

★ ★ ★

It went down exactly as Wilson expected.

In the morning, he went to the bank with the Pings, who brought along a kit with a felt cloth, a small microscope, and an array of loupes. The three of them sat at a small iron table in a glorified broom closet for nearly three hours, looking at the diamonds, one by one. Eventually, Big Ping got to his feet, and announced they had a deal. There would be no bargaining. He would pay four million dollars, as Wilson suggested.

Less a finder's fee for da Rosa, he added. Plus

214

a second fee for the wire transfer, and a third fee for what he called 'the other business.' Wilson agreed with a hurried 'Okay, okay!,' sealing the deal before the Chinaman tacked on a value added tax and cab fare.

In the end, Wilson would receive $3.6 million by wire transfer from Hong Kong to St. Helier.

He handed the Chinaman a piece of paper with the transfer codes he needed, and promised to meet him at his office the next day. Zero and Khalid would accompany him. In the meantime, it was decided that he would stay in his hotel, where Ping and his friends could keep an eye on him. Once the wire transfer came through, he would accompany Ping to the bank and give him the diamonds.

That night, Wilson treated the boys to a dinner of elephant steaks, washed down with a bottle of what was alleged to be Dom Pérignon, but which tasted suspiciously like Asti Spumante.

He told the two of them that he'd spoken to Hakim by satellite phone from Big Ping's office, and that the old man was delighted with the way things had gone. He had reservations for each of them on a flight from Kampala to Antwerp in two days' time. Big Ping's people would take them to Kampala, and Hakim would meet them at the airport in Antwerp. And there was one other thing, Wilson said. He had a surprise.

Khalid's eyes widened. 'What?' He looked like a kid, coming downstairs to a Christmas tree.

'You're getting a bonus,' Wilson told him.

'A bonus?'

Wilson nodded. 'Ten thousand dollars.' He

paused for a second, and added, 'Each.'

Khalid gasped.

Zero looked from one man to the other, then tugged at his friend's galabia, demanding that he translate. Khalid spoke softly in Arabic, and a look of ecstasy came over them both. For a moment, Wilson was afraid Zero might burst into tears.

So he slapped him on the back with a laugh, and basked in his bodyguards' delight. They were good kids, and it was nice to see them happy.

Da Rosa sat by himself at a separate table, nursing a gin and tonic. As he watched the celebration unfold in front of him, he shook his head in disbelief. This guy, d'Anconia, was a piece of work.

★ ★ ★

Little Ping was notified of the wire transfer by e-mail at eleven a.m. the next morning. Wilson confirmed the transaction in a call to the St. Helier bank twenty minutes later. At noon, he met the Pings at the Banque du Zaïroise du Commerce Extérieur. Together, the three of them went into the bank, leaving their bodyguards outside, warily eyeing one another. It was, Wilson reflected, quite a crowd. Zero and Khalid on one side, and on the Pings' behalf, their counterparts: four young gunmen in T-shirts and sunglasses, none of whom was old enough to drink in California.

Inside the bank, the older Ping examined the

216

diamonds for a second time. When he'd confirmed that this was the same batch that he'd seen the day before, he moved the diamonds, head and all, to a second safe-deposit box — one that he'd rented for the purpose. With a satisfied look, he shook Wilson's hand. 'That's that,' he said.

Wilson cocked his head. 'Except for that other thing . . . '

Big Ping nodded. 'Of course,' he said, and beckoned Wilson to follow him. 'We take care of that now.' Together, they walked back to the Chinaman's office.

Wilson didn't know what to expect. He had very mixed feelings about what was going to happen. He liked the boys, he really did. But their loyalties were to Hakim, not to him, so they were a danger to him now. Hakim's associates would soon come looking for their money, and when they did, it would be a whole lot safer for Wilson if Zero and Khalid weren't around to help them.

Which was too bad. Terrible, really, but that's the way it was. Great men did terrible things. How else were they to accomplish their dreams? That was the tragedy of the world-historical man. He sacrificed his humanity to the greatness of his vision and, in doing so, condemned himself to a kind of solitary confinement, sealed off from the rest of the human race by the impenetrable barrier of his own greatness.

You don't blame a lion for killing a gazelle. It's what the lion does.

When they arrived at the door to the office, Little Ping took Wilson by the arm, and nodded toward Zero and Khalid. 'Tell them to wait here.'

Khalid heard and understood.

Little Ping had sodas and chairs brought to them. Zero thanked him effusively, and the boys sat down outside the heavily carved wooden door, just under the sign with the lucky numbers.

Going up the stairs to the second floor, not knowing what to expect, Wilson stood before a window, watching the alley with Little Ping. Soon, Big Ping huffed up the stairs, talking quietly on a cell phone.

Zero and Khalid were talking and laughing when a dusty pickup truck with improvised armor appeared at the end of the alley. Zero got to his feet, shooing the truck with his hand. The driver ignored the gesture, and began to back into the alley, ever so slowly. As he did, the truck began to emit a slow beep, warning people out of the way. *Beep beep beep.*

Khalid jumped to his feet with a shout, yelling angrily at the driver to get out of the alley. *Beep beep* — Khalid fired a warning shot into the air. And then the truck accelerated.

There was nowhere for them to go. The truck was almost as wide as the alley. In a panic, the boys fumbled with their guns, finally getting off a burst of shots, as they staggered backward into the concrete wall of Big Ping's emporium.

There was a shriek of panic, and one of them

(Wilson thought it was Khalid) screamed '*Mr. Frank!*' Then the truck slammed into them, cutting Zero in half and mangling Khalid from the hips down.

The building shook, but Wilson couldn't take his eyes away. Watching the scene in the alley was like watching an anaconda devour a pony. It was horrible and mesmerizing all at once. The truck rolled slowly forward a couple of feet, its tailgate dripping. Khalid lay writhing on the ground, his right arm thrashing uncontrollably, as the driver shifted into reverse. *Beep beep* — The truck rolled over them, and the building shivered a second time.

The warning signal stopped as the truck rolled back the way it had come out, and stopped. The driver's window rolled down, and da Rosa stuck his head out from behind the steering wheel. Seeing the mess at the end of the alley — his handiwork — he gave the men on the second floor a thumbs-up.

Big Ping nudged Wilson with his elbow and, grinning, said, 'Like . . . fly*swattah*!'

18

BERLIN MARCH 16, 2005

Just the sight of her irritated Pete Spagnola. Which was not good, since she was his deputy and Spagnola saw her three or four times a day. A Smith graduate, she was arrogant, ambitious, and, though still nominally young, fat enough to seem almost matronly. Even her gender-bending name pissed him off. Madison Logan. It sounded like an airport.

Because of something powerful and armored in her physique, he had, in a moment of inspiration, dubbed her 'Humvee.' The name was so apt that it prompted guilty laughter the one time he'd let it slip. But it had gotten back to her, of course. (That was one of the problems: *Everything* got back to her.)

He was himself, by his very nature, a risk taker. That's what had driven him to join the Central Intelligence Agency — his love of adventure. It was an irony of fate, then, that a guy who might have prospered as a NASCAR driver or a jungle guide had ended up mired in such a stolid bureaucracy. The Agency, once proud of its nimble and bold spies, had long ago adopted a don't-rock-the-boat mentality so profound that even the collapse of the Soviet Union had gone unremarked upon until after the fact. (To have mentioned it earlier would have encouraged budget cuts.)

To make matters worse, Spagnola worked under embassy cover. He spent his days laboring among the worker bees of the State Department, a bureaucracy even more constipated than the Agency's own.

Eighteen years of keeping his head down, and more or less going through the motions, had nearly extinguished his ability to pay attention to his work, except in the most superficial way.

So when Humvee tapped on his office door, and Spagnola gestured her in, he wasn't really listening to what she said. Not at first, anyway. She was talking a mile a minute, like his daughter did, Bugs-Bunny-fast, a veritable burst-transmission.

He was wondering if he could wangle an extra day's leave so he could take the family skiing. And he was thinking about the recent volatility of one of his investments, a Canadian natural gas play in Kazakhstan.

But some intensity of focus on Humvee's part got through to him, or maybe it was the name she dropped: Bobojon Simoni.

Simoni was the al-Qaeda operative who'd gotten himself killed two weeks earlier, when the BfV raided his Berlin apartment. 'What?'

'I *said* we made a mirror image of Simoni's computer, and when we took a look at it, we found an application called Stegorama.'

Spagnola frowned. 'Stegorama?'

'It's a steganography program. In this case, freeware — you can download it from the Net.

You know what steganography is?'

'What's the difference? You're going to tell me anyway, right?'

A patient sigh. 'It means 'hidden writing,' ' she said. 'That's what it means in the Greek, literally.'

'Okay . . . '

'But in this case it means information that's concealed in pictures. Or music files.'

'And how do you hide a message in a picture — or a song?'

The Smithie in her smirked. 'Digital information is just digital information,' she revealed. 'A graphic file or an audio file is still composed of bits and bytes, just like a text file. With a program like Stegorama — and there are dozens of them — you can embed information in the image. You could put two photographs of the same thing, taken from the same angle, side by side, and they'd look identical. But the one containing encrypted data is actually a compressed version of the original. You just can't see the difference without a microscope.'

Spagnola was interested now. 'Realllly!'

'Yes,' Humvee said. 'Really. The Steg programs decide which parts of the image are least important to its visual integrity, and that's where the cipher is embedded. It's hidden in the boring bits, so to speak. In the background, or whatever.'

'And Simoni was doing this?'

She shrugged. 'He had the program. So we sent his computer to the States. They were working their way through the graphic files. He

222

had a couple of hundred JPEG files in the Pictures folder. So the search was glacial. But they found what they were looking for — '

'Messages?'

'Statistical deviations in the byte counts. They could tell there were too many bytes in the files, which is a dead giveaway.' She paused. 'But, yes,' she said in a grudging voice, 'there were 'messages' in the pictures. *Encrypted* messages. NSA's working on the decrypts now.'

Spagnola frowned in thought. 'So . . . I don't get it. Where were the pictures going?'

Humvee pursed her lips. Finally, she said, 'Remember the book they found?'

'In Simoni's apartment.'

'Exactly.'

Spagnola nodded. 'Yeah, it was a Koran or something. He had it wrapped up like it was a bomb.'

'And he was mailing it to a bookstore in Boston,' Humvee reminded him.

'Right.' Suddenly, his eyes widened as if a lightbulb had gone off inside his head. 'So he was communicating with someone in the bookstore!'

Humvee shook her head. 'No, the bookstore owner didn't know squat. The Bureau sent a couple of agents to interview him — and the guy is exactly what he seems to be: someone who buys old books.'

'Then what's the point?' Spagnola asked, frustrated that he had to tease the information out of this great block of feminine pulchritude.

'The Bureau asked him how he came to buy

223

this particular book, and guess what he tells them? He tells them he found it on eBay.' She waited for Spagnola to connect the dots.

'You mean — '

She nodded. 'Simoni was posting his pictures on eBay auctions, so anyone could access them. If you had the Steg program and knew where to look, you could find the messages, no problem.'

'And the books?'

'Forget the books,' Humvee told him. 'The only reason Simoni delivered the books was to back up his cover. Otherwise, eBay would have bounced him.'

Spagnola blinked a couple of times. Finally, he said, 'I see.' And he did. It was brilliant. Simoni was using eBay as if it were a dead-drop. It was al-Qaeda 2.0.

'So the agent,' he said, 'the guy Simoni was talking to, he didn't have to do bupkes.'

Humvee shook her head. 'EBay was just a bulletin board. All the agent needed to do was to plug 'Akmed's Books' into the Search bar, and wait for the page to pop up. If he had Stegorama on his computer, and remembered the password, extracting the message was a cinch. Of course, if it was encrypted, he'd have to decode it. And, unfortunately, that seems to be the case with the messages they've found. They're all enciphered.'

'So we don't know what they say.'

'Not yet.'

'How long before they crack it?'

Humvee shrugged. 'It's al-Qaeda, so they put us at the front of the queue, but who knows? Maybe tomorrow. Maybe next week, maybe — '

224

'What about tracking the people who went to the website?'

'*EBay?!*'

'Not *all* of eBay. Just the pages with Simoni's pictures.'

Humvee stared at him as if he had pencils in his nostrils.

'You go to a website,' Spagnola insisted, 'you leave footprints. I know that much.'

Humvee patronized him with a smile. 'You mean, cookies?'

'Yeah. Cookies.'

Humvee shook her head. 'The website might leave a cookie on your computer, but your computer wouldn't leave a cookie on the website.' She paused to let this sink in. 'If we had a suspect, we could look at his computer to see if he'd gone to a particular site . . . maybe. But I don't think eBay's servers keep track of everyone who accesses it.'

'How do you know?' Spagnola asked.

'I don't. But even if they did, they wouldn't keep track of everyone who visits every auction, especially if they don't bid. And why would Simoni's people bid? They probably have their own Korans already.'

'But you'll check,' Spagnola insisted.

Humvee shrugged. 'Sure,' she said. 'I'll check.'

Spagnola crumpled the can of Coke Light and tossed it into his wastebasket. He was just beginning to realize that Humvee had screwed him. This was a high-profile operation and she hadn't bothered to tell him anything until they hit a dead end, and sent the computer to NSA.

225

Of course, there would be a copy of her brief on the desk of the chief of station, and the old man would know that this was all Humvee's work and initiative, not Spagnola's. Anger rose in his chest. He could feel his face burning.

'Why didn't you tell me about this?'

'You mean — '

'The steganography! The fact that Simoni was using eBay.' His hands flew up. 'Everything.'

'I'm sorry,' she said, without a hint of regret. 'It just didn't seem like your kind of thing.'

'My kind of thing?'

He chewed her out for two minutes. Who did she think she was? He was her boss! He couldn't believe she'd taken it on herself to contact NSA! What was she thinking?

She flushed, but she couldn't hide a look of triumph.

Now he'd have to stay in town, Spagnola thought, waiting for the decrypts. Visions of his escape to the slopes with his wife and daughter faded.

'So,' he said, 'we're on hold.'

'More or less.'

'I was hoping to get away for the weekend.'

A soft *tsk* fell from her lips. 'Well,' she said, 'it's only Wednesday. And let's face it, NSA has its own fish to fry. I'd be very surprised if we hear anything at all before next week.'

Spagnola looked hopeful. 'Really?'

'Probably the end of next week.'

'Okay,' Spagnola decided, feeling better about it all. 'Just make sure you keep me in the loop, okay?'

'Absolutely.'

⋆ ⋆ ⋆

The NSA decrypts were hand-delivered to Madison Logan's office on Friday afternoon, about an hour after lunch. Her first instinct was to take them directly to Spagnola's, but then she remembered what he'd said about getting away for the weekend. So she put the packet, unopened, in her personal safe, and grabbed her coat. On her way out, she asked the third-floor receptionist to let Mr. Spagnola know that she'd left for a dental appointment — a root canal — and would probably not be back until Monday.

In fact, she went shopping in the Uhland Passage, where there was an upscale boutique that specialized in couture for 'plus-size' women. At four o'clock, she called the office to see if there were any messages.

'Mr. Spagnola was asking for you,' the receptionist told her, 'but then he left. He said it wasn't urgent.'

Hurrying back to the office, she went to her safe and retrieved the package of decrypts. A quick glance told her they were dynamite. Picking up the phone, she dialed Spagnola's office. After the fifth ring, she left a message. 'This is Madison,' she said. 'The decrypts we were talking about just came in. I think they're important. If you'll get back to me, I'll bring them right over. Otherwise . . . I'm not quite sure what to do.'

Her ass covered, she took the elevator to the chief of station's office, knocked, and entered.

'What do you have?' he asked, looking up from his desk.

'Lots,' she told him, laying the envelope in front of him. 'But the best part is a list.'

'What kind of list?'

'A list of accounts in half a dozen offshore banks, and deposits made to those accounts by Herr Simoni.'

'You mean the mook with the Korans? The eBay guy our friends blew away?'

She smiled brightly, and nodded.

The COS opened the packet, and looked at the top page.

'That's sort of an executive summary,' Madison Logan told him. 'Eyes Only. Just the good parts.'

The COS grunted, his brow furrowed.

Deposit $8,400
Account #98765A4
Bank Hapoalim
Tel Aviv
10-05-04

Deposit CH72,900
Account #87612342
CBC Bank & Trust, Ltd.
Cayman Islands
9-02-04

Deposit €2,342
Account #3498703
HSBC Bank
Jebil Ali Free Zone
9-22-04

Deposit $25,000
Account #3698321W
Cadogan Bank
St. Helier, Jersey
12-20-04

Deposit £31,825
Account #0000432189
Single Bank Privat
Geneva
1-27-05

There had been a lot of second-guessing after the fuckup at Simoni's apartment. The yahoos from the BfV had managed to kill a man whose capture would have been invaluable.

But that was then, the COS thought, and this was now. The list in his hands was gold. He looked up with a satisfied smile. 'This is excellent work, Madison. Really, excellent! What does Spagnola think?'

A hapless look came over her. 'I'm afraid he hasn't seen it yet, sir.'

'What?'

'No. He, uhhh, well, I think he left early. A ski trip or something.'

19

BUNIA-ZURICH MARCH 20, 2005

The sooner Wilson got out of town, the safer he'd be. It had taken only a day for the wire transfer to clear between Hong Kong and St. Helier. He would have paid almost any amount for transportation to Kampala. But this was Bunia. A failure to bargain would seem suspicious. So he negotiated for five minutes with the man offering a ride in his beat-up Renault.

They got to Entebbe in the evening, too late to fly anywhere Wilson wanted to go. There was, however, a Kenya Airlines flight at five thirty in the morning, connecting to Zurich via Nairobi and Amsterdam.

At the driver's suggestion, he spent the night at the Speke Hotel, an old-world relic with comfortable beds, good security, and a wireless Internet connection. The driver spent the night in the courtyard of the hotel, sleeping in the backseat of his car.

Wilson ate dinner in his room, then trawled the Internet for news of Bobojon and Hakim. Using different search engines, he looked for February or March news reports from Kuala Lumpur and Berlin, mentioning anyone named Bobojon or Hakim. Nothing. So he tried it again, omitting the names, and looking instead for reports from the same cities using the words 'terrorist' and 'arrest.' There were dozens of stories, but only two could be considered 'hits.'

The first was a short article in *Dawn*, Malaysia's biggest English-language newspaper. The story was dated February 24, and recounted the recent arrest of two men at Kuala Lumpur's Subang Airport.

Sources identified one of the arrested men as Nik Awad, an alleged liaison between Kumpulan Militan Malaysia (KMM) and Jemaah Islamiyah (JI). The second man, traveling on a Syrian passport, was not further identified. Police said the second man attempted to commit suicide at the airport, but was prevented from swallowing a poison capsule.

Both men were detained under provisions of the Internal Security Act. Police are said to be investigating a terrorist plot to attack an American military base in Sumatra.

Wilson read the story three times. The salient facts were three: the time frame, the venue, and the suicide attempt. Late February was about the time he'd dined with Hakim, just before he set sail for Odessa; Hakim had been on the way to Kuala Lumpur; and the suicide attempt, well, it could only be him.

The second story was on the CNN website. It was a March 1 report, datelined Berlin. An antiterrorist investigation had ended in a shootout at the suspect's apartment. An agent of the Office for the Protection of the Constitution (BfV), Clara Deisler, thirty-one, had been killed. The suspect, killed in an exchange of gunfire, was a 'guest worker' with links to Islamist groups in Bosnia and Lebanon. The investigation was continuing.

Wilson searched for a follow-up, using Deisler's name, but all he found were German newspaper articles with the same date as the CNN report. There was no follow-up. Which was strange. Two people had been killed in a gun battle in downtown Berlin. One was a terrorist; the other — a woman, no less — was a government agent. And then . . . nothing.

So the story was being suppressed.

But was it Bobojon? Wilson couldn't be sure, but it seemed likely. Among other things, it would explain the phony message left for him in Draft mode. The Germans had Bobojon's computer. Which probably meant that the CIA did, too. How long, then, before they found out about the Cadogan Bank?

The answer was anyone's guess. For all Wilson knew, the feds could be watching the bank already. But he doubted that. The FBI and the CIA were bureaucracies like any other, except they were secret. This enabled them to conceal a lot of their blundering. But 9/11 made their modus operandi obvious: They moved slowly, fucked things up, and demanded more 'resources.'

Still, they *had* a lot of resources, so it wasn't as if you could ignore them.

So the question was: What would *he* do if he

were in their shoes? He thought about it for a moment, and decided that the first thing he'd do was block wire transfers out of the Cadogan account. With so much at stake, 'Francisco d'Anconia' would then be expected to contact the bank. At that point, his whereabouts might be traced, or the feds would try to lure him to Jersey.

Before they could do that, though, they'd need to know about the Cadogan Bank, and then they'd have to get the bank's cooperation.

Did they? Had they? Wilson couldn't be sure.

★　★　★

He got into Zurich a little after eight the next evening, after traveling nearly fifteen hours. Grimy and exhausted, he contented himself with a snack at a gyro joint in an alley off the Nieder-hof, where the city's tourist traps were concentrated. This done, he walked along the quay beside the river, his eyes on the swans, then crossed a foot-bridge into the old town, where he found a room at the wildly expensive Hotel Zum Storchen.

The next morning, he wandered the streets until he found the vast Jelmoli department store, just off the elegant Bahnhofstrasse. There, he bought new clothes and a leather suitcase. Returning to the hotel, he took a long, hot shower that amounted to a kind of exfoliation. The fire and stink of Bafwasende, the chaos and grime that was Bunia, washed from him until all that was left was the ghost shirt that was his skin, and the injunction:

When the earth trembles,
Do not be afraid

When he checked out, half an hour later, the girl at the reception desk didn't recognize him — and then, when she did, she giggled. Clad in Armani, Bragano, and Zegna, he seemed, almost, to have stepped off the cover of *GQ*. Walking to the Bahnhof, he took the first train to the airport, and rented a car.

It was a jet-black Alfa-Romeo convertible. If the weather had cooperated, he'd have driven with the top down all the way to Lake Constance. But the weather had turned, and the sky was spitting at him as he headed east, skirting the edge of the Zurichsee.

There was only one way to find out if anyone was on to him. Move the money. Or try to. If the wire transfer went through, he was still a step ahead of them. If it didn't . . . he wasn't.

Either way, there were problems. If the Cadogan Bank dragged its heels or raised objections, it meant that someone was on to him. And he'd have to run.

If, on the other hand, the bank made no objection to a wire transfer, he still had a problem: What was he going to do with $3.6 million in cash? He'd done the math, and even if it was all in hundred-dollar bills, that much cash would fill a couple of suitcases, at least. And it would weigh a ton. How was he supposed to get the money into the States? Just walk it through Customs? That would be like playing Russian roulette with a derringer. And even if he got the money through Customs, then what? He couldn't just put it in a bank. The DEA would be all over him.

And there was another problem, as well. Even if the wire transfer went through and he found a way to get the money into the States, there were people who would be looking for him. Not just the FBI and the CIA, but Hakim's partners in the Lebanese Ministry of Defense. They'd fronted the hash, and they'd expect to be paid for it. This had been Hakim's responsibility, but now that Hakim was missing, it was up to Wilson.

Of course, the Lebanese didn't know his name. But they almost certainly knew about Belov (not to mention Zero and Khalid). It wouldn't take long for the Lebanese to find out that the deal had gone through in Bafwasende, and that Wilson's bodyguards were killed in Bunia soon afterward. They might even learn that he'd fenced the diamonds through Big Ping. And they would no doubt suspect that he'd decided to keep both his share and theirs.

Not that there was anything they could do about it. Not unless they found him.

Wilson mused about each of these problems as he drove through the rolling Swiss countryside on the way to tiny Liechtenstein. At three o'clock in the afternoon, he crossed the unmanned border that separates the two countries. Immediately, the road began to climb, cutting back and forth across the mountainside, straightening out when the Alfa rolled into Vaduz, Liechtenstein's manicured capital. He parked on the street in

235

front of the Banque Privée de Stern, and went inside.

The manager, Herr Eggli, had the look of a young Einstein, with a nimbus of blond hair exploding in every direction. Everything else about him was orderly and precise. His skin was as clear and smooth as a sheet of paper, colorless but for the blush of health in his cheeks. He wore a dark suit and gold-rimmed granny glasses, and spoke English with a British accent. Behind him, floor-to-ceiling windows looked out upon the snowcapped mountains that defined the Rhine Valley, even as they hulked above it.

Wilson took the leather wing chair that was offered, crossed his legs, and explained that he wanted to arrange a wire transfer.

'I'm afraid that facility is only available to our clients,' Herr Eggli explained.

'I understand that,' Wilson said. 'I was hoping to become one.'

Eggli's face dissolved in regret. 'We don't actually do much retail banking.'

'Of course not, but, well, it's quite a bit of money that's involved,' Wilson said.

Eggli gave him a curious look. 'Oh? May I ask how much?'

'About three million euros,' Wilson told him.

The banker paused, then nodded thoughtfully. 'Well,' he said, 'I don't see any obstacles, really. We can open an account straight away, if you'd like.'

'I would.'

'There's very little paperwork. I'll just need to see your passport. And then, of course, I'll need

236

the banking codes for the wire.'

Wilson slid the d'Anconia passport across the polished wooden desk.

'I've always thought it's a bit like checking into a hotel,' Eggli joked. 'Except, of course, the guests are money.'

Wilson chuckled politely.

'If you'd like, I can arrange the wire transfer this afternoon.'

'Terrific.'

The banker pinched a couple of forms from the top drawer of his desk, and began to fill them in, relying on Wilson's open passport and asking a couple of questions about the Cadogan account. After a moment, he looked up with a smile. 'Your English is very good.'

Wilson smiled. 'I grew up in the States.'

'I thought as much.' The banker completed the paperwork, then handed it to his new client. 'If you'll just sign at the bottom . . . '

Wilson signed d'Anconia's name, and gave Eggli his account number and password at the Cadogan Bank.

The banker got to his feet, and crossed the room to the door. 'I'll just be a minute.'

Wilson made a gesture, as if to suggest that he had all the time in the world. In reality, he felt as if he were about to implode. It had just occurred to him that the feds might not be as stupid as he'd supposed. If they were on to him, if they were watching the Cadogan Bank, they might very well let the wire transfer go through — after alerting the authorities in Vaduz.

A minute later, the door swept open, and Eggli

swept in. 'No worries.' He resumed his seat behind the desk. 'The wire should clear overnight, so the money will be available in the morning. Ten-ish, I'd guess.'

'That's great. You're very efficient.'

'We try. Even if, technically speaking, we're not Swiss, we try. And now, is there anything else I can do?'

'There is,' Wilson said. 'If you could recommend a hotel — '

'Of course!' Eggli exclaimed.

'And a stock.'

'Excuse me?' The banker seemed befuddled.

'The bank invests its client's monies, does it not?'

'Absolutely,' Eggli said.

'Well, then, I'd like you to invest mine.'

Herr Eggli was delighted. 'Yes, well, we have quite an array of instruments. Bonds, shares, mutual funds. May I ask your objective?' He sat with pen poised above a clean sheet of paper.

'My objective,' Wilson told him, 'is to walk out of here with three and a half million dollars in stock.'

The banker chuckled nervously. When he saw that his client wasn't laughing, he said, 'You're speaking figuratively, of course.'

Wilson shook his head, slowly. 'Not at all. I want you to buy shares in . . . whatever. Nestlé. Roche. I don't care, really, as long as they're publicly traded. When you've made the trades, I'd like the shares couriered, on an expedited basis, to my hotel.'

Eggli winced through the explanation. '*Typically*,' he said, 'we act as a repository for our clients' shares. It's safer that way. We're a bank, after all. And we have a vault. If you'd like to see it — '

'I'm sure it's sturdy, but . . . can I be candid?'

The banker looked surprised, but said, 'Of course.'

'I'm in the midst of a very unpleasant divorce — '

'I'm sorry.'

Wilson shrugged. 'It happens. And when it does, I can promise you it's a lot better to be liquid than not. So I'd feel more comfortable if I held the shares directly.'

Eggli nodded understandingly, but he wasn't buying it.

'Let me ask you a question,' Wilson said.

'Of course.' Eggli put the pen down, and folded his hands on the desk.

'How much is the bank's commission?'

The banker blinked. 'Excuse me?'

'Your commission! For executing trades. How much do you charge?'

Eggli pursed his lips. 'Three-fourths of one percent.'

Wilson did the math. 'So that's . . . twenty-seven grand.'

'I'm sorry?'

'Your commission on the trade will be twenty-seven thousand U.S. dollars.'

Eggli's expression never changed. He sat where he was, as he was. And then, with a shrug of surrender, he got to his feet and shook hands.

'I think you mentioned Nestlé, Roche?'

'Whatever,' Wilson told him. 'They're all good.'

★ ★ ★

Standing in the Immigration Control line at JFK, passport in hand, Wilson felt tense, though he told himself there was nothing to worry about. He'd left the United States a couple of months before, using his Jack Wilson passport to enter Ireland. After that, he'd used the d'Anconia passport. Anyone looking at Wilson's real passport would assume that he'd flown to Ireland and stayed there for the past two months.

But there was a problem, nevertheless. When the immigration officer swiped Wilson's passport through a magnetic reader, something popped up on her computer screen. Wilson couldn't see what it was, but it was enough to generate a phone call.

'If you'll just take a seat over there . . . ?' It wasn't a question, really.

Soon, a good-looking Homeland Security agent arrived on the scene. She spoke with the immigration officer for a moment, then beckoned for Wilson to follow her to a cubicle.

When the door closed behind them, she gestured for Wilson to sit down at a small table. Wilson read her name tag: Carolyn Amirpashaie. *What kind of name is that?* he wondered, unable to guess her ethnicity. 'Is there a problem?'

She leafed through his passport with a frown. Finally, she said, 'I don't know.' Looking up, she

240

said, 'Is this your real name?'

Wilson acted as if the question took him aback. Finally, he said, 'Yeah . . . Jack Wilson.'

'Is that a nickname? 'Jack' for 'John'?'

Wilson shook his head. 'No, it's 'Jack' on my birth certificate.' He smiled. 'My mother was a big fan of the Kennedys.'

'How nice . . . ' She leafed through the passport again, but this time much more quickly. 'So, what countries did you visit, Jack?'

'It's on the form,' he told her. 'I was in Ireland for a couple of months, and then a couple of days in Switzerland.'

'Right.' She glanced at his Customs & Immigration form, which showed his arrival on a flight from Zurich. 'And what were you doing there?'

'Nothing, really. Saw some friends. 'Explored my Celtic roots.' ' He chuckled good-naturedly, but his hands were clammy, and the peripheral vision in his left eye was beginning to flutter.

'In Switzerland?' she asked.

Wilson's laughter sounded forced, even to himself. 'No,' he said. 'In Ireland.'

'But then you went to Switzerland?'

'At the end of my trip, yeah. I was only there for two or three days.' He watched as she picked up his passport, and leafed through its empty pages a second time.

'They didn't stamp it,' she said.

'Who?' he asked.

'The Swiss.'

'No, they just waved me through.'

She nodded. 'They're like that,' she said. Then

241

she cocked her head. 'You don't look Irish.'

Wilson took a deep breath. It suddenly occurred to him that whatever this was about, it couldn't have anything to do with Bobojon or Hakim. If it did, Homeland Security wouldn't leave him alone with someone named Jill. Which meant, what? Why had they stopped him? There was no way for Wilson to know, but it might have been as simple as the fact that he'd paid cash for his ticket. Either that, or they'd integrated some of their databases, making data from the Bureau of Prisons accessible to customs and immigration officers. If so, it was no skin off his nose. He'd done his time, and he'd gone to Ireland. So what?

Relaxing, he turned on the charm. 'Actually,' he said, 'I do . . . look Irish, I mean.' Leaning over the table, he lapsed into a playful brogue. 'As a matter of fact, darlin', you're looking at the map of Ireland.'

She tried not to smile. 'I don't think so,' she said.

'You're not sayin' you never heard of the 'black Irish,' are you?' Certainly, Wilson had. His college girlfriend had written a master's thesis on the Celtic diaspora.

The Amirpashaie woman shrugged. 'Well, I've heard the phrase, but — '

'You're looking at a direct descendant of some poor castaway whose ship went down with the Spanish Armada. Some of the Spaniards washed up on the Emerald Isle. Married the local colleens. And why not? They were all Catholics. And this is the result: my smiling mug. Dark hair, dark eyes. Mediterranean skin. Y'know,' he said, 'some people think the Melungeons are

242

descendants of that same Iberian blood.'

'The Melungeons?'

'In Appalachia. Which is fascinating when you think about it,' Wilson said, 'because they've done mitochondrial DNA studies and — '

'Mr. Wilson?'

'Yes?'

'This sounds like a lot of blarney.'

'Oh,' he said, faking a look of deep disappointment.

She smiled, and handed him his passport.

The hassle continued at Customs, but it was no big deal. An agent went through his suitcase with great deliberation, but there was nothing to find. Wilson had burned the d'Anconia passport in Zurich, and FedExed his stock certificates to Vegas, where he would pick them up in a day or two.

Once he had the shares in hand, he'd open a bank account in Reno. Then he'd use the shares as collateral for a loan. He could probably get 80 percent of their value, which would give him about three million dollars. The bank would hold the shares, but it wouldn't sell them — which was good, because they wouldn't show up on anyone's radar.

Sitting in the Admirals Club, nursing a tumbler of Johnny Walker Black as he waited for his flight to Vegas to be called. Wilson thought about all that he'd been through, including *the people* he'd been through. Bobojon and Hakim, Zero and Khalid, the kid at the diamond mine. *Life's a bitch*, he thought, *and then they bury you.*

243

20

LONDON MARCH 23, 2005

Ray Kovalenko sat in his office in the American embassy on Grosvenor Square in a state of rapt horror, reading and rereading the CAT scan report. He'd arranged to get the scan three days after learning that his best friend, Andy, whose birthday was only two days after Kovalenko's own, had been diagnosed with metastatic cancer. Liver, lungs, pancreas, colon. And Andy had felt fine! Jesus, your whole body could be going south and you wouldn't even know until it was too late.

Even as Kovalenko commiserated with Andy, he was looking up the number of his Harley Street internist. He insisted on a scan despite the doctor's opinion that a full body scan not only subjected the patient to unnecessary radiation, but often produced ambiguous results. False positives and the like, which could lead to unnecessary procedures.

Kovalenko's follow-up appointment with the internist was not for a few days, but a copy of the report had arrived from the imaging center in the morning mail. He took one look at it, felt the color drain from his face to his shoes, and got on his cell phone to Harley Street.

'I've got calcified granulomas in my lungs!'

'Not to worry — '

'Not to worry?! What about this nodularity on my liver! Is that supposed to be good?'

'Well,' the internist said, 'not 'good,' but — '

'And a lesion! I've got a lesion on my kidney!'

'Yes, well, it could be anything.'

'*Anything?!*'

'Or nothing. CAT scans are like that,' the internist told him. 'They show everything and, most often, it doesn't amount to much.'

Kovalenko's stomach tightened into a ball. And stayed that way.

All day.

★ ★ ★

The FBI's Legal Attaché program consists of fifty-three offices around the world, staffed by more than a hundred and fifty special agents, one of whom was Ray Kovalenko. Each Legat (or *Lee-gats*, as they were called) was part of the country team within the embassy.

Kovalenko's most important mission was to work with the CIA and British intel agencies to 'prevent, mitigate, and investigate terrorist attacks.'

The phone buzzed. And again. Reluctantly, Kovalenko put aside the CAT scan report (*mild atherosclerosis of the thoracic aorta!*) and picked up the telephone.

'Yes, Jean?' He'd asked her to hold his calls. 'I hope this is important.'

'It's Berlin. Mr. Spagnola. He said it was urgent.'

245

On top of his anxiety over the CAT scan, Kovalenko had a hangover, a nagging throb behind his eyes that the word 'urgent' seemed to propel into a new pain level. And it was just a couple of glasses of red wine! He cleared his throat, pushed the button on the phone, and forced his voice into friendly mode. 'Joey, heyyyy. What can I do you for?'

'Remember the guy the BfV took down?'

Kovalenko blinked. If he moved a certain way in his chair, he got a pain in his lower back. Probably the lesion.

Kovalenko remembered. Sighed. *Bobojon Simoni.* Who could have been a gold mine. And the Germans screwed it up. 'What about him?'

'Turns out, Simoni was like a switchboard for one of the al-Qaeda groups, posting ciphered messages on eBay,' Spagnola explained. 'One of their people needs a surveillance report on the White House? A wire transfer, or a recipe for ricin? All they had to do was check out the Korans from Akmed's Books.'

'You're kidding me.'

'No, I'm not. Anyway, I got half a dozen wire transfers in front of me. One of them's on your watch.'

Kovalenko picked up a pen, and began to make notes. 'Which one?'

'Looks like Mr. Simoni was feeding an account at the Cadogan Bank — '

'Cuh-dugg-in,' Kovalenko corrected.

'What?'

'It's the Cuh-*dugg*-in Bank, not the *Cad*-aggin Bank. Cadogan was — '

Spagnola cut him off. 'Whatever! It's a bank on St. Helier — and don't tell me it's 'Sont El-yeh,' 'cause I don't really give a shit! I got enough problems — I'm being sabotaged in my own house . . . by my own troops. Y'know what I mean?'

Kovalenko did not.

Spagnola took a deep breath. 'St. Helier,' he said. 'That's Jersey, right?'

'Right.'

'Okay, so . . . surprise, surprise! No name on the account,' Spagnola continued. 'All we got is a number. December 20 — twenty-five grand arrives. Via Bobojon Simoni, from an account associated with an off-shoot of al-Qaeda.'

'Which one?'

'They call themselves the Coalition of the Oppressed of the Earth.'

'Never heard of them,' Kovalenko said.

'Salafi jihadists,' Spagnola said. 'Same old shit. They want to go back to the seventh century.'

'They want to go back to the Stone Age, but they're using the Internet — eBay — to distribute money?' Kovalenko shouted. 'It's an outrage. Where's the ideological consistency?'

'Technically, it's the Agricultural Age.'

Kovalenko sighed. 'And what is this particular agent of the Great Satan supposed to do?'

'Well,' Spagnola said. 'I already told you the account is at the *Cuh-dugg-in* bank, St. Helier. Twenty-five K shows up on December 20. Numbered account.' Spagnola dictated the number. 'You need to find out who holds that

247

account. And where he is now. ASAP. Get back to me.'

Spagnola hung up.

Kovalenko sighed. *Jersey*. While not actually British (in fact, Jersey was closer to France than it was to England), the Channel Islands fell under Kovalenko's jurisdiction because they had a constitutional relationship with the U.K. Not unlike the relationship between the U.S. and Puerto Rico.

Banking was big business in the Channel Islands, but after 9/11, bank secrecy was not as impenetrable as it once was. He could at least hope for a bit of cooperation. Maybe he'd get lucky and they'd give up the name on the account.

Kovalenko thought about it and decided that he'd handle it in person. If he 'rang them up,' he had a feeling he'd be playing phone tag for days.

But how did you get to St. Helier? He buzzed Jean.

Ten minutes later, she called him back. 'About St. Helier, sir?'

He'd been trying to seduce Jean, but so far she'd been impervious to the old Kovalenkan charm. His invitations to 'have a drink' had so far been turned down. Probably a lesbian. And you had to be careful these days. No physical contact. A friendly hand on the arm and you were laying yourself open for a lawsuit. What a world.

'Yes, Jean.'

'How much of a hurry are we in?'

We? Wasn't *that* chummy. Maybe she wasn't a

dyke, after all. 'It's urgent.'

'Well, there's a flight from Gatwick. Orrrr
. . . we could have you there in about an hour by
helicopter.'

'Perfect. Let's do that, then.' One of the
bonuses of being in the antiterrorism business
these days was that no one had to stint. Five
years ago, a helicopter would have been out of
the question, but now, no one would blink an
eye. And that was good, because with the
chopper, he could be back in time for his Pilates
class. He'd only recently come to know how
important it was to maintain core strength. If
you let it go, sooner or later you'd face a whole
cascade of musculo-skeletal problems. Which he
did not need.

★ ★ ★

One thing he disliked about helicopters was the
noise. Buckled into his seat, it was like being
inside a vacuum cleaner. Terrible for your ears.
He made a mental note to buy some of those
earmuffs — the Princess Leia type that airport
workers wore. Guys who ran leafblowers,
construction workers, carpenters — they war-
ranted ear protection, but not the FBI's legal
attachés, who were on the front line of fighting
terrorism. He looked out the window. Above, a
leaden sky; below, the gray and choppy sea.

'Guernsey!' shouted the pilot, nodding toward
a landmass on the right.

Then he tilted his head to the left and
screamed 'Jersey!' Soon, they were yawing

249

toward the painted cross on the helipad and then they were down. Kovalenko ducked under the rotors and ran toward the black Mercedes that was there to meet him. (Jean was a marvel, lesbian or not.)

★ ★ ★

The banker, Jonathan Warren, was forty and handsome in that fragile British way. He wore a suit that was definitely 'bespoke.' Tasseled loafers. Manicured nails. 'Refreshment? A drink perhaps . . . '

'I'm all set,' Kovalenko said.

A faint whiff of citrusy aftershave wafted toward him as Kovalenko eased himself into a leather club chair. 'Is this an official inquiry?'

Kovalenko didn't reply. He simply reached into his breast pocket and removed the small leather portfolio that held his identification. He flipped it open with a flick of his wrist and slid it across the desk.

Warren studied the ID without touching it. Then he nodded his head slowly. 'I see . . . ' A frown creased his features. 'It's just that, well, you're an American.' Warren shifted uncomfortably in his chair. Another brilliant smile segued into pained speculation. 'If you don't mind . . . ' He picked up the telephone receiver.

'If you're reaching out to Five — ' Kovalenko began.

'Oh, I don't think we need to bother the spooks. I'll just call my director.'

Kovalenko leaned back in his chair. He

enjoyed exerting his power, enjoyed the unease he could inflict, especially on a huffy little prick like Warren. Just look at this room — all smoked glass and polished wood, elegant pen-and-ink sketches on the walls. An Aeron chair. The vast expanse of Warren's desk was occupied by a single blue iris in a slim, cutglass vase and an iMac. Kovalenko thought of his cluttered metal desk, his battered filing cabinets.

Across from him, the little prick was explaining the situation to someone with more authority. 'Yes, all right, I understand . . . ' He turned to Kovalenko. 'I'm happy to say we can accommodate you.' Bright little smile. 'Up to a point.'

'And what point would that be?'

'If I could see the account number?'

From his breast pocket, Kovalenko pulled out the plain white index card on which he'd printed the account number. He handed it to the banker.

The banker tapped a few keys on his computer keyboard, opened the drawer of his desk, extracted a gold pen, and scribbled on Kovalenko's index card, which he then handed back.

Kovalenko looked at it: *Thomas Aherne & Associates*.

'I'll need an address,' Kovalenko said.

'You understand: This isn't the account holder,' the banker said. 'That, I can't disclose. But Aherne and Associates are the registered agent. Which means they get all the mail, handle the inquiries. I'm sure they'll be happy to help you.'

251

'Of course they will,' Kovalenko told him, 'but I'm not asking them, I'm asking you.'

'I understand that, but . . . protocols aside, I don't actually have the information you're after.'

'You don't know who you're in business with?' Kovalenko asked.

Warren ignored the question. 'A number of our clients have arrangements like this one. Their affairs are handled by registered agents.' He tapped a few keys and a printer whirred into action.

Kovalenko looked at the paper handed to him.

THOMAS AHERNE & ASSOCIATES
210 COPE STREET
DUBLIN, REPUBLIC OF IRELAND

'Ireland,' Kovalenko muttered.

'Are you sure I can't get you something to drink?' Warren asked.

'No,' Kovalenko said. 'If you'll let me take a look at the account history — deposits, withdrawals — I'll be on my way.'

The banker shifted in his chair. Winced apologetically. 'No can do, I'm afraid.' Suddenly, he brightened. 'Unless, of course . . . you've letters rogatory?'

Kovalenko pursed his lips, and groaned inwardly. The FBI had no right to discovery in foreign countries, so the banker was correct in suggesting that letters rogatory would be necessary to compel the release of evidence. Which meant that it was almost impossible. Letters rogatory required fourteen steps, and each step required the attention of a lawyer or judge. *Letters rogatory.* The idea made Kovalenko woozy. It could take years. He sat up in his chair, and glared at the banker. 'This is an antiterrorism investigation.'

Warren blinked, but was otherwise unmoved by the information.

Kovalenko would appeal to MI-5 as soon as he got back to London. But he probably wouldn't get anywhere. Asking a Jersey bank for an account holder's name, Kovalenko realized, was like asking a priest for a transcript of someone's confession.

'I'm sorry,' Warren said, breaking eye contact. 'I'm afraid it's just not on. Our laws — '

'Your laws protect criminals and terrorists,' Kovalenko hissed. He could feel his face reddening, his blood pressure climbing. He tried to calm down, to 'center' himself, but it wasn't working. It occurred to him that this was just the kind of thing that triggered heart attacks.

★ ★ ★

The helicopter lifted off the pad, and swung away from the ground. Kovalenko watched the island dwindle beneath him. These offshore banks, he thought, are criminal enterprises. If he had his way, every corporation on earth, and especially the banks, would be 'transparent.' That would put a stop to a lot of crime, including terrorism. Just that one step. The only reason for bank secrecy was to wash money, hide money, or steal money. Put an end to funny money and

253

you'd go a long ways toward putting an end to funny business.

He forced himself to relax. Belly breathing, long on the exhale. At least he had the account number and, even more important, the name of the registered agent. That agent would have received any and all of the correspondence relating to the account, including transaction records. Either the agent forwarded the information to his client, or he held it for him.

Kovalenko hoped it was the latter. But whatever the agent had, Kovalenko would get. Because, in Ireland, they knew a thing or two about terrorism.

21

DUBLIN MARCH 31, 2005

It was all about which way you turned when you got on the plane. If you went left, you were on some kind of fast track, and if you went right, you were probably paying your own way.

Mike Burke had turned right, and now he was riding in steerage. Row 38, Seat A, ten rows up from the lavatories, but next to the window. Bound for Dublin.

He was returning from his sister Megan's wedding, which had taken place in a picture-postcard, country church in Nellysford, Virginia — Burke's hometown.

It was the first time he'd been back to the States since Kate died, and he'd done his best to be cheerful and agreeable. He'd assuaged the worries of his parents, and turned aside their questions. He was doing well, he was fine, the worst was over, it was behind him now . . .

Or so he said. In reality, he didn't fool anybody. To be around Megan and Nate, and give no hint of the way he felt, was . . . well, impossible. They were luminous with happiness, and he was . . . what? A walking reminder that 'things fall apart; the center cannot hold.'

Maybe it's time to move on, Burke thought. With the old man back on his feet, and business beginning to pick up, maybe it was time for Burke himself to get on with his life. If not right away, then soon.

After all the years he'd spent, going round and round like a ball bearing on a roulette wheel, he'd come to rest in Dublin with Kate. And it wasn't so long ago that he'd imagined spending the rest of his life there. But with Kate gone, Ireland no longer felt like home, much less like 'the future.'

Yet he was still in the same flat, *her* flat, with the eclectic furniture and the big sleigh bed they'd picked out together. Her clothes still hung in the closets. Her books stood in the bookcases. Her pots and pans dangled from a pegboard in the kitchen.

And then there was the old man, who never stopped talking about her.

It wasn't that Burke missed America, but somewhere in the back of his mind he'd begun to think of his trip to the States as a trial return. Maybe on his native soil, absent the daily reminders of Kate, he could imagine a fresh start.

But the experiment was over. He'd been in the States only a couple of hours when he realized there was nothing for him there. He was thirty years old, and he might as well have been the Flying Dutchman. The soft mountains of the Blue Ridge, black against the evening sky, meant nothing to him.

People kept telling him that it would get better, that his grief would ease. But that was just another way of saying that Kate herself would begin to disappear. They might be right, but it wasn't what he wanted, not at all. In some ways, his grief was all that was left of her.

Washington wasn't any better. He'd arranged to see a few of the people he knew but, once again, they hadn't known Kate. And so they seemed like strangers. For Burke, everything went through Kate, or it didn't go at all.

He couldn't get over thinking about the way they'd found each other. He'd actually fallen out of the sky — crashed and burned and damn near died, only to be delivered to her doorstep by a man who called himself Colonel Homicide. If that wasn't fate, what was it?

He shifted within the cramped architecture of his seat, his eyes on the video monitor overhead, displaying a cartoon Airbus inching its way across the Atlantic toward a map of Europe. He was exhausted by the efforts of the past few days, the strain of pretending he was fine.

Even so, he took some joy from Tommy's rebound. He'd had a part in that, a part in keeping the old man from dying of a broken heart. It was good to see him now, going out to the pub with his pals. They were busy again at the office, so much so that they'd hired a new secretary. These were boom times for Ireland, and now that Tommy was back, the firm would prosper once again.

Burke had kept the business afloat until the old man was on his feet again. But what really turned the corner for Tommy was a visit from Kate herself.

'She came to me,' he said, 'in the night. Stood

at the foot of my bed — Katie herself, mind you. 'Da,' she says to me, 'I canna stand the sadness! Do you understand me? Between you and Michael, I have no peace. You've got to stop.' And then she kissed me on the forehead and made me promise I'd be brave enough to get on with things. She promised that she would always be there, even if she was gone. Isn't that just like her?' Tommy asked. 'Still looking after us?'

Burke would have given anything for a glimpse of Kate. Even if it was an illusion, a hallucination or a dream, it would have sent a rainbow straight through his heart. After the vision, the old man looked so relieved, so suddenly at peace with himself and the world, that Burke felt a surge of envy. 'She hasn't come to me,' he said, as if Kate's ghost had betrayed him.

The old man gave him a warm smile, and touched his arm. 'Perhaps in time, Michael . . . '

★ ★ ★

As the aircraft began its descent, Burke awakened from his reverie to a sense of disappointment. It was one of those brilliant mornings that happen too rarely in Ireland, the bright green fields sweeping toward the Irish Sea, the sea alive with whitecaps under a Windex sky.

He would have preferred gloom. Darkness and rain. Instead, he found himself descending into a Hallmark card. As the plane banked into its final approach, he saw the flash of a dozen sails beneath the wing, and the long, furling wake of a fishing boat. It did not lift his spirits.

It was barely nine a.m. when he cleared Immigration, so he collected his car and headed for the M1 that would take him into the heart of the city. To his surprise, he caught himself smiling. There *was* something about Ireland. Maybe it was the scale of the place, the lilting voices in the terminal, the mischief in the brogue.

Without realizing it, he was beginning to feel at home in the maze of streets and parks that were Dublin. He'd missed the old man, and the routine of work, the rose-brick building on Cope Street and jogging along the quays beside the Liffey. It was, he grudgingly admitted, good to be back.

He parked in his spot at the rear of the building and took the steps to the second floor. It was barely ten in the morning when he arrived at the doors to Suite 210, only to find them locked — and a note.

It was thumbtacked directly to one of the wooden panels, which was a bit like nailing a Vermeer directly to the wall. The panels in the door were solid oak, and gleamed — the brass fittings were rubbed daily with a soft cloth. The old man would have a conniption.

Burke pried the thumbtack from the door, and read the note. It was an official notice, in Gaelic and English, dated the day after Burke had gone to the States for Megan's wedding.

**CLOSED BY ORDER OF AN GARDA SIOCHANA
(INTERNATIONAL COOPERATION UNIT)**

'Why didn't you call me?'

He'd gone directly to Dalkey, where he found the old man in the yard, pruning a rosebush. A tangle of thorny branches lay in a heap at his feet.

'Is it yourself, Michael?'

'It is.' A quick hug.

The old man shrugged. 'I knew you'd come back the second you heard — and would that be fair to your sister?'

Burke shrugged. His sister could take care of herself. 'What happened?'

'Well, I'll tell you what happened,' the old man repeated. 'This shower of cunts came stormin' in, like it was Ned Kelly they were after! Moira takes one look, goes into a swoon, if you can believe it, and this great eejit steps forward, flashin' one of them little wallets.'

Burke looked confused. 'What 'little wallets'?'

'Like you see on the box. With the badges inside. And it turns out, this one's not even Irish. He's one of your lot!'

'Who is?'

'The eejit I'm talkin' about. He's American! This shiny-faced palooka's come all the way from London — and the Garda, they're fallin' all over him, salutin' his every fart.'

'What did he want?' Burke asked.

'He's got a bug up his arse about some incorporation you did. I told him to feck off!'

Burke winced. 'What did he say?'

'Well, he didn't take that a'tall well. Touchy sort. Reminded me for the third time that he's

260

some bloody great FBI agent. Called himself a Lee-gut.'

'Gat.'

'Puh-*tay*-to, puh-*tah*-to . . . I told him I didn't care if he was Lord of the Rings. If he wants to look at one of our files, he'd better have his paperwork in order.'

'Well, yeah,' Burke said, 'but — which account was he after?'

The old man scowled. 'The Twentieth-Century Motor Company. Something like that.' He paused. 'Ring a bell?'

Burke shook his head. 'No.' He'd set up lots of companies at Thomas Aherne & Associates. Most of the time he didn't spend more than half an hour with a client.

'Manx registration?' the old man reminded him. 'Jersey bank?'

Burke made a gesture, as if to say, What else *is* there? Then he said, 'Hold Mail list?'

The old man nodded. 'What else would it be? Totally normal setup. But this Yank, he takes one look at the folder — '

'You *gave* him the file?' Burke asked.

'I "gave" it to the Garda.'

Burke was incredulous.

'It was a special unit,' Tommy explained. 'They had a court order.'

Burke's eyes rested on the harbor as he mulled over the old man's words. The confidentiality of the firm's files had always been absolute. For Tommy Aherne to give up a client was . . . unprecedented.

'Anyway,' the old man said, 'this Yank takes

261

one look at the client's name and, I swear to Jay-sus, he goes ballistic. Says we must have known it was bogus. That's the word he used. Bogus!'

'So what was the name?'

'A 'Mr. Francis D. Anconia.' Or something like that. I only saw the file for a second, and he was yankin' it out of my hands.'

The old man didn't have the name quite right. Burke remembered now. The client had asked him about his ear. Sounded American, but . . . 'Chilean passport?'

'The very one!'

Burke thought about it. Finally, he said, 'I still don't get it.'

'All I can tell you is, this Yank is steamed, he's squawkin' about money-laundering, terrorism — '

'Terrorism?'

'Swear to Christ, he's goin' from pink to purple, and back again. And just when I think he's going to keel over, he takes this Kerryman aside — thick as two planks, this one is — '

'Who?'

'The Kerryman! 'Inspector Doherty,' he's callin' himself — and the Leegut has a word with him, private like. Then this Doherty steps forward and announces that he's shuttin' us down, 'pending inquiries.' '

'What in-kwy-ries?' Burke asked. 'What's that supposed to mean?'

'Well, the short answer is *you*. This Kerryman says they're opening a money-laundering investigation, and they'd like to have a word with our Mr. Michael Burke, particularly since it's your

262

name that's on the file.'

Burke groaned. 'Then what?'

'Then? Well, then they threw me out of my office — my own office, if you can believe it, the one in which I've been diligently servicing a respectable clientele for — '

'What's the Legat's name?'

'Kovalenko.' The old man took off his gloves and laid his clippers down at the base of the rosebush. 'Come on, I've got their cards inside.'

There were three of them, resting on the marble top of a small table in the vestibule. The first card identified Sean Doherty as an inspector in the Garda's International Coordination Unit (ICU). The second card belonged to Ira Monaghan of the Garda's Financial Intelligence Unit (FIU).

The third card bore the FBI's logo, a gold-embossed American eagle, and the name Raymond Kovalenko. The card identified Kovalenko as a Legal Attaché and gave the address of the U.S. Embassy, Grosvenor Square, London.

'So what do we do?' Burke wondered.

'They expressed the hope that you'd get on the blower and arrange for a heart-to-heart.'

Burke didn't hesitate. He called Doherty's number, straightaway. The inspector put him on hold for what seemed like a very long time, and then, when he came back on the line, suggested that Burke should come down to his office the following afternoon.

'If it's all the same to you, I could come over right away,' Burke told him. The sooner he cleared things up, the sooner the firm would reopen — and the better it would be.

The receiver crackled with an emphatic *Tsk!* 'I'm afraid that won't work for us,' Doherty told him. 'Tomorrow afternoon would be the earliest. Would three o'clock be convenient? Pearse Street?'

'I was hoping — '

'Yes, well, I'm sure you were but, entirely on the q.t., of course, your man Kovalenko's awfully keen on this d'Anconia fellow. I've just this minute had a chat with him, while you were holding, and I can assure you he's determined to meet you in person. So that's something we can all look forward to!'

★   ★   ★

The next day, Burke went to the precinct house with his passport, which he'd been asked to bring. An identification tag was glued to his lapel, and he was escorted into Inspector Doherty's small and messy office.

Two men waited inside. The smaller of the two was a sandy-haired fellow with the frail physique of a heavy smoker. This was Inspector Doherty 'in the flesh' (or what there was of it). The second man was Ray Kovalenko. Six-two and solidly built, his even features were embedded in a pink complexion above a tiny, purselike mouth.

Kovalenko gestured to an empty chair, and everyone sat down. Burke assumed a helpful look, turning his face from one man to the other,

264

but neither of his interlocutors seemed in any hurry to begin.

The FBI agent removed a small plastic bottle of Purell from his pocket, and squirted a dab of the disinfectant into the palm of his hand. Then he rubbed his palms together, and studied his nails. Finally, he said, 'This client of yours — d'Anconia. What can you tell me about him?'

'Well,' Burke began, 'he had a Chilean passport — '

'We know that,' Kovalenko snapped.

His rudeness took Burke by surprise. For a moment, he didn't know what to say. So he began again. 'Well, anyway, as I said, he had a Chilean passport, but from his accent, I'd say he was from the States.'

'So you *knew* it was a bogus name.'

Burke shook his head. 'No.'

Kovalenko fixed him with a glare. 'You didn't think it was strange when a guy named 'Francisco d'Anconia' comes walking into your office, and wants to incorporate the Twentieth-Century Motor Company?'

'Well, the name was a little anachronistic,' Burke said, 'but — '

'Don't fuck with me,' Kovalenko warned.

Burke turned the palms of his hands toward the ceiling, and glanced at Doherty, hoping for an explanation. Doherty looked away.

Kovalenko's little mouth curled into a sneer. He leaned toward Burke. 'What about a Mr. Tim? Hypothetically, if a Mr. Tiny Tim came walking into your office — '

'Or Father Christmas,' Doherty suggested.

'Exactly! If Father Christmas came walking into your office, would you have a problem with that?' Kovalenko asked. 'Take your time,' he added, before Burke could reply. 'Because I really want to know.'

Burke looked from the FBI agent to the Garda, and back again. This isn't going well, he thought.

Kovalenko sighed. 'Let me ask you something,' he said. 'You a reader?'

Burke shrugged. 'Yeah. I read a little.'

The FBI agent looked pleased. 'How much do you know about Ayn Rand?'

The question took Burke by surprise. 'Wasn't she . . . she was some kinda *nut*, wasn't she?'

Kovalenko froze, as if he'd been smacked.

Uh-oh, Burke thought. *Wrong answer*. 'I mean, she was conservative,' he said. 'I seem to remember, she was pretty conservative.'

Kovalenko's jaws worked up and down, as if he was chewing on something. Spittle sparkled on his lips, but no words came. Finally, he leaned forward, eyes bright with venom. 'She was the most important writer of the twentieth century.'

'Really?!' Burke tried to sound interested and encouraging, but even to his own ears, the exclamation sounded skeptical and smart-ass.

'Yes, really! She wrote a little book called *Atlas Shrugged*,' Kovalenko snarled. 'Maybe you've heard of it.'

Burke said nothing.

'Francisco d'Anconia was the hero.' Kovalenko's brow creased in a frown, and he corrected

266

himself. 'One of the heroes. There were several.'

Burke tried to look fascinated. But Kovalenko wasn't buying it. 'Well, I guess I'll have to read it,' Burke said. He waited. A clock ticked on the wall behind him. From the street came the distant beep of a municipal truck, backing up. Burke cleared his throat. 'So, uhhh . . . how can I help?'

The FBI agent glanced at the Garda, his mouth open, jaws working silently. Finally, he said, 'Well, Mr. Burke, you can begin by telling me everything you know about your pal, d'Anconia.'

'Well, he's not a pal, actually. I mean, I saw only him for half an hour,' Burke said. 'Tops. You've seen the file. It's all there.'

'I want to hear it from you.'

With a shrug, Burke recited the details as he remembered them. 'The guy called. Came in. He didn't seem to know exactly what he wanted, but then, people *don't*.'

'They don't,' Kovalenko repeated.

'No. A lot of times, they don't. This guy wanted a corporation, a discreet bank account. I walked him through it.'

'*Discreet*,' Kovalenko sneered. 'That's one way to put it. The way I see it, you set up a shell corporation for this guy — who you *knew* was not Chilean . . . '

Burke interrupted. 'The passport looked genuine. The picture matched. And he looked kind of Hispanic.'

'And what made him come to Aherne and Associates?'

'He said he saw an ad,' Burke replied. 'The Aer Lingus magazine.'

'So. Not a planner. Kind of a last-minute decision.'

Burke made a gesture. *It happens.*

'And you never heard of the guy before?' Kovalenko said.

'No. I mean . . . I think he called from the airport.'

'We'll find out if there are any prior contacts. We're already looking into *you*, I can promise you that, Mr. Michael Anderson Burke.'

Burke shrugged. They knew his middle name. Wow.

Kovalenko sat back in his chair, and frowned, as if he'd been puzzled by a sudden thought. 'Why are you *here*?' he asked. Before Burke could answer, he clarified the question. 'I mean, what are you doing in *Ireland*?' The way he said it, the Emerald Isle could have been located in the Straits of Hormuz.

'My wife was Irish,' he explained.

Kovalenko's forehead descended into chevrons. '*Was*?'

Burke nodded. 'She died. About eight months ago.'

Kovalenko looked alarmed. 'Of what?'

Burke blinked in amazement. Finally, he said, 'Sepsis.'

Kovalenko drew in a sharp breath and let out a little *tsk* — though he didn't bother with any pro forma words of condolence. 'Eight months ago. And yet you're still *here*. For those of us with suspicious minds — and I'm paid for that

— it's just a little convenient, isn't it? You say d'Anconia had an American accent. Just like you. And here you both are, in Ireland. He just shows up out of the blue and you set up a phony corporation for him — '

'Look,' Burke said, trying not to lose patience. 'It wasn't a phony corporation. This is our business. We set up companies. It's what we *do*.'

'*Did!*'

Burke took a deep breath, but kept his temper in check. 'If laws are broken, if papers are not filed in a timely way, if there's a criminal enterprise or fraud, various authorities — *Irish* authorities — pursue those matters.' He turned toward Doherty. 'Tell me something. Why is the *FBI* hassling an Irish firm that's been in business for thirty years? What's going on?'

The Garda spoke up. 'International cooperation.'

'All we do at Aherne and Associates,' Burke said, 'is put together corporate entities and notify those connected to them about annual forms that have to be filed and fees that have to be paid.'

'That's *not* all you do,' Kovalenko insisted. 'You also set up bank accounts.'

'That's part of our service, yes.'

'Bank accounts in funny places. St. Helier. The Caymans — '

Burke shook his head. 'There's nothing 'funny' about St. Helier or the Caymans.'

Kovalenko made a gesture like an umpire, signaling *safe*. His eyebrows furled into a frown, and his face went from pink to red. He spoke in a muted snarl. 'I'll tell you what's funny. You know what's funny? Your tit's in a wringer — that's what's funny.'

Burke didn't know whether to laugh or cry. 'Excuse me?'

'This is a national security investigation,' the FBI man said, 'and your ass is dead center. What if I told you the bank account you set up received a wire transfer from an al-Qaeda operative? Hmm? Not a lot of money, at first, but . . . I'm guessing they were start-up funds. Because two months later, that same account has three-point-six mil moving through it. In and out, all in forty-eight hours.' He clapped his hands. 'Untraceable. Who has that money now? And what's he going to do with it?' He paused. 'Any ideas?'

Burke sat where he was. What was he supposed to say? 'Look, Mr. Kovalenko, we've given you everything we have. What more can we do? Try to understand that from our standpoint, this was a routine transaction. We probably do a dozen of these every month.'

Kovalenko drummed his fingers on the desk. 'There's nothing routine about terrorism,' he hissed. He paused to let this sink in, then sat back in his chair. 'Why don't we go through it again? You get a call from the airport . . . '

And so it went, for a second time and then a third. Doherty looked like he was dying for a smoke.

'Aren't you leaving something out?' Kovalenko asked.

Burke thought about it. 'I don't think so.'

The FBI agent slid a slip of paper across the desk.

It was a note from the file, written in Burke's own handwriting.

Esplanade
Belgrade

'Oh yeah,' Burke said, remembering. 'He was going to Belgrade for a couple of weeks. The Esplanade — that's a hotel. I sent the paperwork there.'

'It didn't seem odd that this was the only address Mr. d'Anconia provided?'

Burke shook his head. 'He said he'd be traveling. And he didn't want any other mail sent to him, just the banking papers. I put him on the Hold Mail list. A lot of our clients — '

'I'll bet!'

Burke was beginning to lose it. Turning in his seat, he asked Doherty, 'Tell me something: When did Ireland become the fifty-first state?'

The Kerryman chuckled. 'We've had our own troubles with terrorists, Mr. Burke. I'm sure you've read the papers. And after that unpleasantness of yours — I mean the World Trade Center, of course — cooperation seemed to be in order.'

Burke gritted his teeth.

Kovalenko snorted his contempt. 'There's only one reason to be on a Hold Mail list: to hide assets. Isn't that right?'

'No,' Burke told him, 'that isn't right. Different people have different reasons for

271

wanting to be anonymous.'

'Oh, I agree,' Kovalenko told him. 'Some of them are terrorists, some of them are drug dealers. Most of them probably just want to cheat on their taxes!'

Burke shook his head. 'There are lots of reasons to set up offshore, and there's nothing wrong with avoiding taxes. That's just common sense.'

'I'll tell you what's common sense,' Kovalenko promised. 'A little due diligence. You ever investigate a client?'

Burke shook his head.

'Not your business,' Kovalenko suggested.

'In fact, it's not.'

Kovalenko made a noise deep in his throat, and it occurred to Burke that the FBI agent was growling.

'You know,' Kovalenko told him, 'we had the chief of police in Belgrade visit the Esplanade.'

'Good,' Burke said. 'That's exactly what I would have done.'

'For your information, our Mr. d'Anconia stayed there for two weeks, and when he left . . . that's all she wrote. No one's seen him since.'

Burke had an idea. 'What about his passport? There's a photocopy in the file, I'm sure. Isn't there — '

'Some kind of emergency contact?'

Burke nodded.

'We thought of that,' Kovalenko assured him. 'The address in the passport turns out to be a restaurant in Santiago. El Pollo Loco. Which means . . . ' He turned to Doherty. 'Can you tell us what it means, Inspector?'

'Certainly,' the Kerryman said. 'It means the 'Crazy Chicken.' His emergency contact is the Crazy Chicken in Santiago, Chile.'

'I guess you didn't bother to check that,' Kovalenko added.

'No,' Burke said. 'I didn't check that.'

'He just walked in and out of your office — is that about it?'

'Something like that,' Burke replied.

'And that's everything you remember?'

'Let me think,' Burke said. But when he closed his eyes to concentrate, he was blind with fatigue. An enormous yawn convulsed him. He tried to stop it, but he couldn't. A tidal wave of jet lag rose inside him.

Kovalenko went over the edge. 'Let me see your passport!'

'What?'

'Your *passport.*'

Burke fumbled the passport out of his pocket and handed it over.

Kovalenko snapped open his attaché case. Removing an ink pad and a metal stamp, he rocked the stamp back and forth in the ink, then brought it down with a thump on the passport page with Burke's picture on it.

Burke gasped. 'What are you *doing*?'

'I'm endorsing your passport,' Kovalenko muttered, taking a pen from his pocket to sign and date the endorsement. Then he flipped the passport in Burke's direction, making sure it didn't quite reach him.

Burke retrieved the passport from the floor, and opened it. In burgundy letters, emblazoned across the page, were the words:

Valid only for travel to the United States

'Wait a second,' Burke sputtered. 'You can't do that!'

'I already did,' Kovalenko smirked.

'But . . . why?'

It was Doherty who answered. 'Because we'd like you to stick around for the trial. We'll need you to give testimony.'

'What trial?' Burke asked.

Kovalenko smiled. 'Republic of Ireland versus Aherne.'

Burke blinked. 'Aherne! Since when is Tommy on trial?'

'He got the papers about an hour ago,' Kovalenko announced.

'For what? What's the charge?'

It was Doherty's turn, and he seemed to be enjoying it. 'Money-laundering. One count.'

'What are you, out of your mind?! Tommy didn't have anything to do with it. *I* was the one who handled the paperwork. It's *my* name on the file. Tommy never even met the client!'

Kovalenko shrugged. 'Yeah, well, it's his name on the door.'

Burke came out of his seat like he was on springs, lunging at the FBI agent. Kovalenko shot backwards in his chair, its wheeled casters squealing across the floor. Doherty threw himself on Burke's back, locked him into a bear hug, and dragged him away.

Kovalenko sat in his chair with his back to the wall, breathing hard, rubbing at his arm. 'That's rich, you comin' after me.'

Burke looked him up and down. 'Yeah,' he said. 'Thinka that.'

22

DUBLIN APRIL 4, 2005

Burke couldn't believe it.

The company shut down, his passport void, the old man indicted . . . and all because this dick, Kovalenko, was an Ayn Rand nut with a hatred for offshore companies. The suggestion that he and Tommy were somehow in cahoots with d'Anconia, whoever d'Anconia was, was ludicrous. He could barely remember the guy. The real problem was that Kovalenko had taken an instant dislike to him. It was as simple as that.

And as complicated.

Burke had a way of rankling people in authority, people like Kovalenko who wore their self-importance like a badge of honor. There was something in Burke's stance, something in his attitude, or in his eyes, that just . . . *wound them up*. It would have been funny, it would have been a gift — but it tended not to end well.

Kovalenko was putting the screws to them because he *could*. The case would never come to court because, when you got right down to it, Burke had done everything by the book — no matter who the client was.

But in the meantime, Aherne & Associates was closed and the old man was in trouble.

Obviously, Kovalenko enjoying rattling people's cages — no matter who they were or what they'd done (or hadn't done). It was just an exercise in power. Like the business with Burke's passport. That was hardball. But it was hardball the way weenies played it.

★ ★ ★

Day after day, Burke did everything he could to persuade the Garda that it had made a mistake. He phoned, he wrote, he bombarded Doherty and Kovalenko with e-mails. He even showed up in person to plead Aherne & Associates' case. But none of it was of any use. He appealed to Inspector Doherty's sense of decency, but that only seemed to confuse him. So he tried a different tack: patriotism. Surely, *Irish* authorities could do something to protect *Irish* businesses. Surely, the Irish wouldn't let *a foreign power* push them around.

Doherty listened to it all, nodded throughout, and finally shrugged. 'It's outa my hands,' he said.

The thing was, the old man needed to work. After more than two weeks of idleness, he'd pruned all the roses, caught up on his correspondence, and played '108 holes of golf.' He was beginning to slip back into his old habits, getting bombed at the pub every night and talking, misty-eyed, about Kate.

In the States, the FBI was taking the time to contact Burke's friends, family, and former employers, to inquire about his political views,

277

acquaintances, and travels abroad. Burke learned of this when his father called to congratulate him on his application for a government job.

'What job?' Burke asked.

His father made a sound like a siren going off — a realization siren. 'Ohhhhhhh!' he exclaimed. And then, in a whisper: 'Cloak and dagger, huh?'

Since Ayn Rand and *Atlas Shrugged* loomed so large in Kovalenko's world, Burke checked it out online. Google gave him more than a million hits. The top-listed site was a web page supported by the Ayn Rand Society, which featured photos of the author, long excerpts from her works, accounts of her philosophy, links to Amazon, and more. In essence, Rand believed that self-interest was not only natural, but the secular equivalent of the state of grace.

It was kind of interesting — especially if you were out of a job and your passport had been revoked. Burke read biographical sketches of the author, including her sallies before the House Committee on Un-American Activities; reviews of her books; and explications of their plots. This was no ordinary author's website, but a mansion of chat rooms, with a library of blogs and long biographies of Rand's major characters. There was even an online dating service.

In 1957, eighteen years before Mike Burke was born, *Atlas Shrugged* topped the bestseller lists. A survey attributed to the Library of Congress and the Book of the Month Club deemed *Atlas Shrugged* as the 'second most influential book' for Americans — after the Bible.

At its heart, the book was the story of good and evil, capitalism and communism, light versus dark. Its plot was at once florid, complex, and more or less interminable. It involved an improbably named heroine — the lovely Dagny — and her efforts to rescue a railroad from unfair competition, shortages, and corrupt government manipulation. Meanwhile, Dagny searched for John Galt, the legendary inventor of a paradigm-shifting motor that was said to run on static electricity gathered from the atmosphere.

While Dagny struggled to keep the railroad going she noticed that many of the most talented CEOs of the time seemed to be leaving their jobs to 'spend more time with their families' (and possessions, Burke thought). Like the corporate Atlases they were, the best and the brightest were shrugging off the burdens society had placed upon them. In effect, the movers and shakers were on strike. They were sick of the government's interference, regulations, taxes, corruption, and incompetence.

Francisco d'Anconia was a robber baron on a secret picket line. A Chilean copper king, he decided to keep the metal in the ground rather than submit to regulations that squeezed his profits. His long-winded defense of this decision, 'Francisco's Money Speech,' was quoted in its entirety on various sites. The essence of the speech was simple: Money is the root of all good.'

And lots more, along the same line.

At the end of the book, Dagny crash-lands in a

wilderness canyon, a sort of Libertarian Shangri-la, where she comes upon the shrugging Atlases who have withdrawn from the world around them. Among them are Francisco d'Anconia and the mysterious John Galt, inventor of the world-transforming motor. Civilization founders in their absence.

It reminded Burke quite a bit of his father's blunt opinions about welfare, political correctness, and affirmative action. (No, no, and no.) In his dad's view, the government shouldn't be in the business of taking care of people. 'Folks are lazy,' he'd insist. 'They say there's no jobs — so how come all these immigrants are working *two* jobs, and looking for a third?'

But in reality, Larry Burke would have given you the shirt off his back. John Galt would have sold you sunblock.

It was two in the morning when Burke finished reading, and shut down his computer. He didn't get it. Whoever 'd'Anconia' really was, he had to be nuts. For whatever reason, he'd chosen to travel the world as a figment of someone else's imagination.

Obviously, he identified with Ayn Rand's hero. But why? And what did al-Qaeda have to do with it?

★   ★   ★

For nearly two days, Burke stayed in his room. He watched soccer matches, tennis games, the endless droning on the Beeb about Tony Blair's poll numbers. He ordered takeout from the

Italian place around the corner, and slept a lot, dozing in front of 'the box' (as the old man called it), only to wake up more tired than ever. He ignored the telephone when it rang, sinking deeper and deeper into his own lassitude. Occasionally, he wondered, *What now?* There was nowhere to go, and nothing for him to do. Or nothing he *could* do.

What roused him from this torpor was a visit from the old man. Together, they went to the Sun, where they sat at a dark and ancient table as far from the video poker machine as they could get and still be in the pub. Before long, each of them was deep into his third pint.

He felt like a bad influence, drinking with a man who was drinking too much. On the other hand, maybe it wasn't such a bad idea. A little convivial oblivion.

'I don't know what to do,' Burke remarked, not for the first time.

'Bastards,' the old man said. 'I don't know what to tell ya.' He took a long pull on his beer. 'I went to see Harrigan the other day.'

Burke sat up straight. Harrigan was the firm's soliciter. 'Oh?'

Tommy nodded. 'He says 'Hello.' '

'Did you happen to mention the business with Kovalenko and the Garda?'

'I did, indeed.'

'And what did he say?' Burke asked.

Tommy pursed his lips, then smacked them. 'He said . . . it's certain to cost a penny, but they don't have a case. Not a'tall. We'll win in the end.'

Burke nodded thoughtfully, and sipped his drink. 'Meanwhile . . . '

'We might have a bit of a rough patch . . . in the short term.'

Burke took a deep breath, and slammed his glass down on the table. 'You know what? I'm going to Belgrade!' He said it so loud, there was a dip in the room's noise level as people turned to look.

'And what do you want to go there for?'

'It's where d'Anconia went. I'll find the bastard and I'll bring him back.'

The old man's face screwed up into a caricature of skepticism. 'There's no point! That goony bird of your's . . . he already done that.'

'What goony bird? You mean, Kovalenko?'

'The very man! He's already checked it out. You'll just be wasting your time.'

Burke shrugged. 'Maybe not . . . ' After 9/11, Burke did not hold the FBI or the CIA in awe. As everyone knew by now, two of the hijackers had roomed with an FBI informant. Others had been trained in knife fighting by a retired Delta commando in Florida. The FBI had declined to examine one of the hijackers' computers, even after he'd been reported seeking to limit his flying lessons to steering jumbo jets in midflight (no takeoff or landing lessons required). Still other hijackers had been given visas to enter the United States even after the CIA had tracked them to a meeting in Kuala Lumpur, where plans had been discussed to put bombs aboard a dozen commercial airliners. This much Burke had read in the newspapers. Who knew what else was out there? 'I'm guessing they missed something,' he said.

The old man shrugged. Then had a second thought. 'And I suppose you'll be traveling on your driver's license, will ya?'

Burke shook his head, and finished his pint. Then he reached into the pocket of his battered waxed jacket, and produced an Irish passport. 'Dual citizen,' he said.

The old man cackled.

23

BELGRADE APRIL 11, 2005

Burke felt like a terrorist as he handed his virginal Irish passport to the man behind the glass. The Immigrations officer leafed through its pages with unconcealed boredom, then pushed it back without bothering to stamp it. With an airy gesture, he waved Burke on his way and nodded to the next person in line.

Burke felt the thrill that little boys feel when they've gotten away with something, especially when the getting away defeats the machinations of a martinet like Kovalenko. Through the wonders of dual citizenship, Burke was able to travel with impunity, a citizen of Ireland and the European Union.

Erin go bragh, he thought as he went outside to the taxi queue in front of the terminal. Soon, he was bouncing along in the back of a Zastava cab. The outskirts of the Serbian capital were like those of any other European city, an uneasy conglomeration of warehouses and farms, office buildings and apartment blocks. Heading downtown, Burke was impressed by an efflorescence of graffiti, the unfamiliar Cyrillic tags bristling with swastikas and crosshairs.

The city itself was a surprise. He wasn't sure what he expected to find — surly Serbs moving amid the ruins of NATO bombings, perhaps.

Instead, he found a graceful city at the juncture of two rivers, the Sava and the Danube. There was snow on the ground, but the fresh green of spring adorned the trees. The cabdriver apologized for the weather.

'Freak weather, this spring. Very cold. Now I am asking, where is global warming when you need it?'

The riverfront was lined with floating bars and restaurants, the populace seemed well dressed and prosperous, the streets were clean. The taxi chuffed past graceful and beautiful buildings from another era.

And then there was the Esplanade.

Boxy and utilitarian, the hotel was a concrete cube entirely devoid of architectural flourish or embellishment. As without, so within: Burke's room was a clean cell, redolent of some Serbian PineSol.

Why did d'Anconia decide to stay at this place? According to Kovalenko he had three or four million dollars coming in. You'd think he'd be ready to splurge.

Or maybe not. He hadn't seemed like someone who was used to having money. He dressed well, but the clothes looked new, and Burke got the impression that he was playing a role. He was definitely rough around the edges, staring at Burke's ruined ear and commenting on it. So maybe he was used to places like this.

* * *

The front desk was manned by Vuk Milic, a man of about Burke's own age. With his suit, tie, oiled hair, and earnest expression, Milic was someone Burke might have encountered at the desk of a Comfort Inn outside D.C. His English was good, if accented.

When he was talking about room rates and checkout times, Milic was fluent and almost chatty. When the conversation turned to one of the hotel's previous guests, a man named d'Anconia, Milic frowned. 'The particulars of guests cannot be discussed,' he said, tapping his fingers on the desk. 'This is not a possibility.'

Burke folded a twenty-euro note and slid it across the desk so that it came to rest in front of the desk clerk. Milic regarded the bill with a cold eye. 'You would like me to change this?'

Burke shook his head. 'No,' he said, 'I don't need any change.'

The bill vanished.

Milic began to type. After a moment, he flashed a smile, and said, 'Gaspodin d'Anconia has been here from twenty-four January to second February.'

' 'Gaspodin'?' Burke asked.

' 'Mister.' ' Milic returned his eyes to the monitor. 'He rents two films for TV: *La Genou de Claire*, and *Sorority Whores*.'

'Hunh . . . '

The desk clerk was unstoppable. 'Three times, he eats in restaurant, each time fish. Makes two telephone calls, long distance. One-two-three, five times he has drinks in bar. Always beer.'

Burke stared, dumbfounded. What if he'd

given the guy a hundred? Admittedly, none of the information was useful, but . . . 'Who'd he call?'

Milic peered closely at the monitor. After a moment, he scribbled some numbers onto a three-by-five card, and handed the card to Burke.

'That's it,' Milic said. 'There's nothing else.'

Burke believed him. He turned to go, then turned back again. 'You know why he was in Belgrade? I mean, was he on business or — '

'He is here for Tesla,' Milic told him.

Burke frowned. 'What's Tesla?' He seemed to recall, there was a rock band, but . . .

The desk clerk was looking almost hurt. 'Nikola Tesla,' he said. 'The inventor. He is Serb.'

Jackpot, Burke thought. 'So he was meeting this inventor?'

Milic snorted in derision, and shook his head. 'No, I don't think so. Tesla is dead, maybe fifty years.'

'Oh,' Burke said, the enthusiasm draining from his voice.

'Your friend — '

Burke started to correct him, but thought better of it.

' — he's here for meetings. I don't know the word in English. But many people come . . . '

'So, it's like a symposium,' Burke suggested.

The desk clerk shrugged. Then he cocked his head and peered at Burke. 'You don't know Tesla?'

Burke looked apologetic. 'I forgot,' he offered.

Milic couldn't believe it. 'But this is the most famous Serb of all time! He is more famous than — ' he looked up, as if searching the ceiling for the names of celebrated Serbs. Finally, he grinned. 'More famous than Vlade Divac!'

'Really!'

'Yes! Is true. He's inventing electricity!'

'I thought that was Edison,' Burke suggested.

The desk clerk scoffed. 'This is what you Americans say. But Tesla, he invents one kind of electricity, Edison invents the other, not-so-good kind. Then, Tesla is inventing many, many things. Twentieth century! This is his invention.'

Burke laughed.

The desk clerk scowled. 'Your friend, *he* knows about Tesla.'

'Does he?' Burke asked.

'Yes, he gives speech! At the symphony.'

Burke didn't know what he meant. Then he understood. 'Symposium.'

'Yes! First, he studies at the Institute — '

'What institute?'

'Am I talking to wall?' Milic demanded, as if Burke were a student with attention deficit disorder. 'Tesla Institute! After this, he goes to symphony, and gives speech!'

They were interrupted. First one guest, then another, came to request their keys. No card keys here. These were in the old European style, big keys attached to metal eggs so heavy that only the rare guest would be tempted to take his key along.

'So this symposium,' Burke asked. 'Where was it?'

But the spell was broken. Either the twenty euros had been used up, or Milic had decided that he'd said enough. He averted his eyes and began stacking some papers into a little pile. 'More, I don't know,' he said. 'Maybe in the cafe, someone knows.' He shrugged. 'Also there is the possibility of Ivo.'

'What's Ivo?'

'Doorman. He is back tomorrow.'

* * *

The bar was empty except for two women perched on stools at a tall table. A girl with spiky hair and bad skin stood behind the counter, rinsing glasses. She did not remember anyone named d'Anconia or, for that matter, an American by any other name. 'I'm here in the day,' she told Burke. 'Tooti, she's coming at seven. You could try her.'

Burke said he would, then asked if there was an Internet cafe in the neighborhood.

She lit a cigarette and gave him directions.

* * *

The Web was fantastic. He'd arrived at the Sava Cafe with nothing more than a name. And now, barely an hour later, he knew enough about Nikola Tesla — thanks to Google and the Wikipedia — to pass a third-grade Serbian science class.

A Serb born in Croatia, Tesla was a prodigious inventor, responsible (as the desk clerk had claimed) for alternating current, the Tesla coil, and scores of other devices. His patents numbered in the hundreds, and he was obviously something of a cult figure — and not just in Serbia. Tesla enthusiasts considered it a travesty that he had not been awarded the Nobel Prize, calling him 'the Leonardo of the twentieth century.'

After moving to the United States and working with Edison, Tesla became a rival to the American when he invented and championed alternating current, rather than the direct current that Edison favored. With the backing of the Westinghouse Corporation, Edison mounted a propaganda campaign to make alternating current appear dangerous. Dogs and cats, and even an elephant, were electrocuted onstage to make the point, while Edison asked men in the audience if they wanted their wives to risk their lives every time they plugged in the iron.

Edison's argument was false. Not only was Tesla's alternating current safer than Edison's direct current, it was more efficient and easier to deliver. Eventually, and with the backing of J. P. Morgan, the nineteenth century's quintessential robber baron, Tesla's technology won out.

It was the Serb who lit up the towns around Niagara Falls, and who won the contract to illuminate the 'White City' at the Chicago World's Fair.

In his heyday, Tesla lived in New York and was considered a trophy guest at the lavish gatherings of the gilded age. He partied with the Morgans, the Vanderbilts, and the Rockefellers, and hosted them and their guests in his Manhattan laboratory. A close friend of Mark Twain's, he astonished the writer and his friends with demonstrations worthy of Dr. Frankenstein. While Twain and other guests watched in amazement, Tesla would stand on an improvised platform, wreathed in lightning. He'd pace the lab with tubes of light that seemed to have no power source, while juggling balls of fire that left no marks on his clothes or skin. Where Edison was a chubby plodder, who wore his wife's smocks while he worked, Tesla was elegant and thin, a six-foot-six genius who performed his experiments in waistcoat and tails.

As quirky as he was brilliant, the inventor lived at the Waldorf-Astoria Hotel, where he dined alone each night in the Palm Room. There, he engaged in a ritual that involved a stack of linen napkins, with which he wiped clean every piece of cutlery, china, and glass on the table. That done, he could not eat until he'd calculated the cubic capacity of each vessel and, by extension, the volume of food before him.

It occurred to Burke that the Serb was a classic victim of obsessive-compulsive disorder.

And hypersensitive, as well. According to Tesla's biographers, the inventor had almost supernaturally acute hearing. He could hear a watch ticking several rooms away, and could sense a thunderstorm in another state. Acutely sensitive to pressure, he could not walk into a cave, through a tunnel, or under a bridge without suffering.

He was so plagued by the city's vibrations, by the passing of trucks and the rumble of trains, that the legs of his table in the Palm Room, like those in his laboratory, had to be sheathed in rubber. Sunlight pressed down upon him, and his vision was disturbed by flashes of light and auras that no one else saw. He counted every step he took, organizing the world around him in multiples of the number nine. He had a violent hatred of pearl earrings, and was horrified by the prospect of touching another person's hair. *But . . .*

It was Tesla, rather than Marconi, who first patented a method for wireless broadcasting, and it was Tesla who harnessed the power of Niagara Falls. He worked for years on ways of transmitting energy wirelessly across great distances, and claimed that he could capture electricity — free energy — from 'standing waves' at the earth's core.

He died in 1943, while the Second World War was at fever pitch in Europe. At the time, he was living in reduced circumstances at the New Yorker Hotel in Manhattan. According to reports, two FBI agents and a nurse were present at his death. When the inventor's relatives came to the hotel, they found that his safe had been drilled and his papers removed. Soon afterward, the Custodian of Alien

Property seized virtually all of Tesla's papers, though the Custodian's jurisdiction was questionable since Tesla had been an American citizen for decades. Those papers, which required a boxcar to transport, remained in limbo until the end of the war, when the American government uncovered Nazi documents in the course of an intelligence operation, code-named Paper-clip. The Nazi papers showed that German scientists and weapons designers had been developing new and frightening weapons based on Teslan principles and inventions. In 1945, Tesla's papers were officially classified Top Secret and taken to Los Alamos.

Eight years later, a nephew of Tesla's succeeded in gaining the release of some one hundred fifty thousand documents, and this trove became the founding archive of the Nikola Tesla Museum in Belgrade.

But the bulk of Tesla's papers (including most of the scientific notebooks, research papers, and experimental notes) remain classified to this day. Since Tesla was such a cult figure, many researchers had filed Freedom of Information Act requests for documents concerning the inventor and his work. All had been rebuffed. On one website, a scientist wrote that while working at Los Alamos, he was permitted to view diagrams and papers concerning the hydrogen bomb, *but not a page of Tesla's work.*

What could this scientist, who died more than sixty years ago, have to do with a bank account in the Channel Islands? For all Burke knew, Tesla was just a hobby, an interest of d'Anconia's that was relevant to nothing and to no one. D'Anconia might just as easily have been interested in orchids. Or UFOs. Or Civil War reenactments.

Only he wasn't. He was interested in Tesla.

Burke decided to take a break. Got to his feet and stretched. A girl with multiple piercings and blue streaks in her hair brought him a coffee that was strong and sweet. A pair of Israeli backpackers sat down at the terminal next to his.

Returning to his chair, he typed: 'Tesla Symposium Belgrade 2005.' Twenty-three hits, most of them in a language he didn't recognize. (Presumably Serbian.) But there were a couple in English.

The first was the home page for the Museum of Nikola Tesla, which contained a link to the symposium's site. He wrote down the museum's address, 51 Proleterskih brigada Street, then took the online tour, which guided him from room to room through the museum. Along with Tesla's ashes, personal effects, and correspondence, there were many photographs, original patents, and models of his inventions. The museum also housed the Tesla archives, which included the documents his nephew had obtained from the U.S. government.

He returned to the Google list and clicked on the site '2006 Tesla Symposium, Belgrade,' which included details of the program. He scanned through, looking for d'Anconia's name.

9:00–9:15:	I. Soloviev
	Smolensk Institute
	Patent #454622: A History
9:15–9:30:	D. DiPaolo
	University of Perugia
	Spark-Gap Oscillation: Implications for Wireless Communication
9:30–9:45:	S. Oeschle
	Gote University, Frankfurt am Main
	Geochronological Implications of Geomagnetic Decay
9:45–10:15:	J. Wilson
	Stanford University
	The Tunguska Incident: Calculating Vector Drag in Scalar Pair-Coupling
10:15–10:45:	James Re
	Diathermapeutics, Ltd., Bern, Switzlerland: The Debt of Ultrasound Therapies to Teslan Diathermic Technology
10:45–11:15:	S. A. Johnson
	Rensselaer Polytechnic Institute
	Scalar Electromagnetics in Weather Manipulation: The Woodpecker Signal and Global Warming
11:15–11:30:	E. Grobelaar
	King's College, London
	Tesla v. Marconi: A Short History
11:30–12:00:	A. Dobkin
	Massachusetts Institute of Technology
	Ball Lightning, Plasmoid Stability, and Nuclear Fusion: A Progress Report

And so on. Looking through the list, the vocabulary alone drove home just how far out of his depth Burke was. Nucleons, flux intensity,

Fourier frequencies, 'magnetostatic scalar potential.'

And no 'Francisco d'Anconia.'

He didn't get it. He could hear the desk clerk's voice, indignant that Burke had never heard of Tesla. But d'Anconia had. *'Your friend — he gives speech! At the symphony.'*

Then Burke had one of those realizations that begins with *duhhh*. He wasn't looking for 'd'Anconia.' He was looking for the man who had used that name as an alias, a joke, or an homage. If the guy he wanted to find had given a speech at the symposium, then he was one of the scientists listed in the program.

Burke sat back and sighed. *Geomagnetic decay? Scalar weapons?* This was not at all what he had in mind when he came to Belgrade, tracking 'Francisco d'Anconia.'

He printed a copy of the symposium's program, logged out, paid for the time he'd used, and began walking back to the Esplanade.

He was trying to get his head around it.

One point he had to give to Kovalenko: Some of Aherne's clients *were* a little dodgy. He was pretty sure one guy was running an online poker game. That was illegal in the States but not in Europe. He suspected that another client was bootlegging Microsoft DVDs. And there were dozens of customers engaged in 'creative' accounting where taxes were concerned.

D'Anconia didn't fit in with that crowd. In fact, Kovalenko had all but called him a terrorist.

But if d'Anconia was one of the scientists on

the list, well, it just didn't make sense to Burke. In his view, terrorists don't think about things like 'vector drag,' and they don't present papers at symposia.

They just *don't*.

24

It was dark and cold, and as Mike Burke walked back to the Esplanade, the snow was sifting down like flour out of the sky. The streetlights swarmed with snowflakes. Coming toward him, a woman in a long red coat walked with quick little steps, hunched against the cold.

The woman made him think of Kate and he found himself wishing that his wife was beside him. When the weather was like this, he'd put his arm around her, and pull her into the shelter of his shoulder. He could almost feel the warmth and weight of her. If she were here now, he would take her to one of the restaurants on the river, where they'd watch the light on the water, and drink red wine.

Snap out of it.

He turned the corner, and there was the Esplanade. He headed straight for the bar. Now that it was nighttime, half the little tables were occupied, with each one sporting a candle in a red glass. A brace of microphones on a tiny stage threatened live entertainment. He'd read in the guidebook that one of the musical specialties of Belgrade was a hybrid of techno and Serbian folk music called turbofolk.

The bar itself was more like a voodoo altar. A long blue mirror strung with Christmas lights looked down on dusty bottles of whiskey, gin, and vodka. Plastic cacti glowed green amid miniature Chinese lanterns, pink flamingos, paper angels, and bobbleheads of Marilyn, Jesus, and Elvis. A woman filled four mugs of beer, then turned to him with an inquiring look.

'I'm looking for Tooti,' Burke said, barely believing the words.

The woman behind the bar was forty, or maybe even fifty, with thinning hair and an unhealthy pallor. 'You found her.'

'There was an American who stayed at the Esplanade in January. The desk clerk thought you might have seen him. About my age.'

She arched a plucked eyebrow.

'He wore a hat,' Burke added. 'When I saw him, he was wearing a fedora, or whatever they're called.'

She smiled. 'He's gay, this guy?'

Burke shook his head. 'No. I mean, I don't know.'

Her lips came together in a pout. 'Then what do you care?'

He thought about lying, but the effort was almost too much. So what he said was: 'It's kind of complicated, but . . . my name's Burke. I've come a really long way. Y'know?'

She looked at him for a moment, and then she nodded, as if deciding something. When she smiled, Burke realized that she must have been a very pretty girl. 'His name was Frank.'

Burke lit up with surprise. 'You remember him!'

'We don't get so many Americans,' she explained. 'Mostly, they go to the Intercon.'

'You want a drink?' Burke asked. He put a

thousand-dinar note on the table. She poured herself a tumbler of Johnny Walker Black. Took a sip and frowned. 'You're not a cop?'

Burke shook his head.

'You don't look like a cop.'

'What's a cop look like?' he asked.

'Big muscles and little piggy eyes.' She leaned on the bar. 'Last week, two guys come from the RDB. They ask about this 'Frank' guy.'

'RDB?'

She rolled her eyes. 'State Security.'

'So what did they say?' Burke asked.

'Who cares? No one tells them anything.'

'Why not?'

'These same pricks are here two months ago. Arrest nice girls.' She paused. 'Okay,' she admitted, 'maybe they do prostitution. But no trouble, ever. Good tips, too.' She looked Burke in the eyes. 'You tip?'

Burke nodded. 'Oh, yeah. I'm always tipping.'

'Good! Because here, most people don't tip. I blame communism.'

Burke nodded in sympathy. Tossed another thousand dinars on the bar.

'Anyway,' Tooti said, 'nobody tells these cops nothing.'

'Y'know, your English is really good . . . '

'I'm in Chicago for twenty years. West side.'

'Really?! And then . . . what? You came back.'

'My mother was sick, so . . . ' She threw back her scotch, as if it were a shot of tequila.

'She get better?' Burke asked. 'I mean, is she all right?'

Tooti tilted her head and smiled, surprised

that he'd asked. 'Yeah,' she said. 'She's fine now. They cut it out.' She paused. 'Look, I don't mind telling you about this Frank of yours, but don't get excited. I don't know much.'

'You know his name. You call him Frank.'

She shook her head. 'He called *himself* Frank. He's coming in, has a couple of beers. He's not so friendly.'

'So what did you talk about?' Burke asked.

'I said, 'Hi. I'm Tooti.' And he said, 'Frank.' '

'That's *it*?'

Tooti nodded. The dinars vanished.

Burke felt as if he'd been had. 'He talk to anyone else?'

Tooti shook her head. 'No. And it's too bad. Good-looking boy like that. Some people flirt with him — girls, boys — he's not so interested.' She thought for a moment. 'Most of the time, he's writing.'

'Writing?'

'He has notebook,' she explained. 'Sometimes, he sits where you are, and I look. He's writing letters.' She frowned. 'But not Aunt Mary 'letters.' Letters and numbers.'

'You mean, like — '

'Algebra. I think maybe he's a student.' She tapped her glass with a finger and looked at Burke with an inquiring expression. He nodded and she poured herself another drink.

'He never talked about himself?'

She shook her head. 'One time, he danced.'

'Danced?' Burke asked.

Tooti nodded. 'This night, the band takes break. Not too much business. But Frank, he is getting loaded. So . . . he dances.'

'By himself?'

Tooti laughed. 'Yeah! And this dance, it's not the Twist, y'know? I mean, it's not like any dance you've ever seen! This guy Frank, he's kind of humming. Turning around. It's like he's floating. Very graceful, but . . . Anyway, he dances for a long time — five, ten minutes. After a while, the band stood there, watching him. Me, too.'

She looked at Burke. His expression told her that he didn't know what to make of the story. She shrugged. 'Anyway, when he stopped dancing, he gave me a big tip. Said he was going away.'

'Did he say where he was going?'

'No.' She tipped her glass back and downed the rest of her drink.

Burke turned to go.

'*Oh,*' she said. 'Wait. One more thing. He spoke Serb.'

'No shit . . . '

'The night he was drunk. His accent was terrible. I asked him if he was with NATO — sometimes, the soldiers pick it up. He just shook his head. So I thought, maybe he has relatives here. But no. He said he learned it from books.'

'In school?'

Tooti shook her head. 'No. He said he taught himself.'

Burke thanked her again and went up to his room, where he looked out the window at the snow. It was coming down harder now, turning headlights into opalescent beams as the cars crossed the city's bridges.

He lay in bed, watching the lights of cars slide up the wall and across the ceiling. It was all so weird. Nikola Tesla and Ayn Rand, talking Serb and crazy dancing.

With a sigh, he rolled over and closed his eyes. Beyond the window, a car was stuck in the snow, spinning its wheels. *Tell me about it*, he thought.

★   ★   ★

Seeing Burke in the lobby the next morning, the desk clerk nodded toward the doorman, a little guy in a magenta uniform with gold braid and epaulets.

Burke walked up to him. 'Ivo?'

The doorman turned, surprised that Burke knew his name. 'Yes?'

'Mr. Milic said I should talk to you.'

'Yes?'

Burke gave a little wave to the desk clerk, who returned the gesture with a smile. 'Yeah, he said you might be able to help me. I'm looking for a friend.' Burke handed him a folded ten-euro note. 'An American guy. Stayed here a while ago. About my age. Black hair.'

'This is Frank.' Ivo buried the ten euros in his pocket.

'Right! *Frank*. You know what happened to him? You know where he went?'

'Sure, he goes to airport. Bye bye.' Ivo held the door open for an elderly woman in a fur coat. Touched his hat, and smiled.

'Before that,' Burke said.

'You mean here? In Beograd?'

Burke nodded.

Ivo shrugged. 'Every morning, I find a cab for him. He goes same place.'

'Where's that?' Burke asked.

Ivo shivered. Then he stamped his feet in the cold, and looked away in the direction of the river.

Burke reached deeply into his pocket, and came up with a handful of dinars. 'It's all there is,' he said, and tucked the money into the door-man's coat.

'He goes to the Tesla Museum,' Ivo told him. 'More than this, I don't know.'

⋆ ⋆ ⋆

Burke paid the entrance fee to the pale man at the ticket desk, and grabbed one of the English-language brochures. He was about to tell the pale man that it wasn't really the collection he wanted to see, but then decided it might put him in a better light to take a turn around the place.

So he spent half an hour wandering around the museum, and the truth was, he could have spent hours. Knowing what he did about Tesla, the displays — working models, photographs, correspondence, patents and drawings, even the personal effects — were fascinating. The inventor really had been a genius. It was hard to believe his name wasn't a household word.

Eventually, Burke got back to the pale man at

the desk. 'Someone said there was a symposium here. A while ago.'

'Yes.'

'Is there anyone I could talk to about that?'

'Yes,' the pale man said in a whisper. After carefully moving the hands on a cardboard clock to indicate that he'd return in five minutes, he led Burke up the stairs and down a corridor to a small office.

'Here is Dragoslav Novakovic,' he announced, nodding to a man behind a desk. 'He is director.'

Novakovic looked up.

'This gentleman is interested in symposium,' the pale man said. With a courtly bow, he stepped back, turned on his heel, and withdrew.

Novakovic gestured to a wingback chair that had seen better days. He was a tall man with a carefully trimmed Vandyke beard, horn-rimmed spectacles, and graying sideburns. 'Please,' he said, exposing a gold-toothed grin. 'I am Drago.'

'Mike Burke.' They shook hands, and Burke sat down. Behind the desk, a computer clicked and whirred.

'I'm defragging the hard drive,' Novakovic told him, with a gesture toward the clicking CPU. 'This piece of shit — you'll forgive me — he's on his last leg.'

Burke smiled in a polite and understanding way, but the truth was he was nervous. He hadn't thought ahead about what he was going to say. And this was d'Anconia's turf. They spoke his language, and he spoke theirs. He'd even given a speech.

Novakovic saved him. 'So! you're interested in

the symposium . . . '

'Yeah, well . . . yeah!'

'We have abstracts, of course, but I'm afraid they're what you call 'sold out'! Even my copy, he is sold out. But no worries. We have more coming, two weeks' time.'

'Great.'

'I can send you a copy. But we have expenses.' He gave Burke a regretful smile. 'I think it's four hundred dinars — with postage — unless you wish express mailing. This is one hundred eighty dinars more.'

'By all means, send it express,' Burke said and, reaching into his pocket, removed a business card from his wallet. Pushing the card across the desk, he counted out the money and tried to think of a way to jumpstart the conversation.

Novakovic saved him again. 'So how did you learn about the maestro?'

Burke blinked. 'Well . . . ,' he said. And then it came to him in a rush of inspiration. 'I was flying to London, and I got to talking with the guy next to me — an American, like me. Turns out, he was on his way to Belgrade. Said he had to give a speech. I told him I was coming to Belgrade in a month or so, and he said, well, in that case, I should visit the Tesla Museum.' Burke laughed. 'I said, 'Who's Tesla?' And this guy, he couldn't believe it. 'The greatest inventor in history,' he said. 'That's what my speech is about — there's a symposium,' he said, 'and I'm speaking at it.' '

Novakovic nodded contentedly.

'Anyway,' Burke continued, 'this guy fills me in about Tesla and — '

'Now you're hooked!' Novakovic declared.

'Exactly! I am totally hooked.'

'And here you are!' Novakovic announced. 'That's wonderful!'

'The thing is,' Burke went on, 'I was hoping to get in touch with him again, but . . . I lost his card.'

Novakovic winced in sympathy, then brightened. 'But this is easy,' he said. 'We have only a few Americans giving speeches, so . . . ' He glanced at the monitor on his desk. 'If you don't mind — I think it's almost done. Then I get list of participants.'

'That would be great,' Burke replied.

Novakovic put his fingers together in a sort of steeple. 'So, what brings you here to Belgrade?'

'Oh,' Burke said. 'That!' He paused. 'I'm a photographer. I'm taking some pictures for *Travel and Leisure*.'

'Here? In Beograd?' Novakovic asked.

Burke nodded. 'They're calling it 'the New Prague.' '

Novakovic chuckled. 'Two years ago, Budapest was 'the new Prague.' Now, is our turn. Next year' — his hands flew into the air — 'Skopje! After that, who knows — Tbilisi!' The Serb giggled merrily.

'It's a beautiful city,' Burke said, running out of conversation.

'Yes, I think — ahhhhh! Now we cook with gasoline! I have liftoff.' The museum's director hunched over the keyboard to his computer, and began to type. 'I get participant list. We find your friend.' After a moment, he hit Return and the printer spewed out a list of speakers. Novakovic took a pen, and put a check beside half a dozen names. 'These are the Americans,' he said, and handed the list to Burke.

Johnson
Dobkin
Wilson
Para
Federman
Schrager

Burke studied the names for a moment, then laid the page on the desk. Shrugged.

'You don't recognize?' Novakovic asked.

'No,' he said. 'One or two of them sound familiar, but . . . this was a young guy.'

It was Novakovic's turn to shrug. 'Dobkin and Schrager, they're old men.' Suddenly, a thought occurred to him, and he wagged his forefinger back and forth. 'I don't give up!' He got to his feet, and crossed the room. Opening the door, he stuck his head into the hallway, and rattled off an order in a language Burke didn't understand. Then he came back to his desk, and sat down with a smile. 'This is what I am all about — to put together a Teslan from here and a Teslan from there. This is our mission — a part of our mission — at the International Tesla Society.' Once again, he folded his fingers into a steeple, and sat back in his chair.

A minute ticked by, and then there was a knock on the door. A young woman came in with a manila envelope. Handing the envelope to

Novakovic, she smiled at Burke and left the room.

The museum director reached into the envelope, and extracted a handful of black-and-white photographs. 'This is banquet, I don't know if your friend comes, but . . . ' He pushed the pictures across the desk.

Burke studied half a dozen pictures before he found what he was looking for: d'Anconia, standing with a drink in his hand, in earnest conversation with half a dozen others.

'There he is!' Burke said, pointing to the handsome face of the man who had stood in his office in Dublin.

Novakovic leaned over for a look. 'Which one? Him? But that's Jack! Jack Wilson!'

'Right!' Burke said. 'Jack Wilson.'

'I can tell you, it was *such* pleasure to meet him. We're in correspondence for *years*. And, finally, this year I meet. It's like seeing old friend.'

'That's great,' Burke told him, 'but . . . do you know how I can get in touch with him?'

'Of course!' the museum director told him. 'Everything is on computer.' He tapped a few keys, and scowled. 'Telephone number, I'm sorry, I don't have. But e-mail, yes! Address, yes!' He shook his head, chuckling. 'Jack Wilson!' The printer clacked and whirred and a moment later, Novakovic handed the printout to Burke.

Jack Wilson
P.O. Box 2000
White Deer, PA 17887
j–p482wl@midpa.net

'This is current?' Burke asked.

'Yes, of course! Is always same address. We are exchanging letters for years.'

'You think he's in Pennsylvania now?'

Novakovic shrugged. 'Yes, maybe. But from here, from Beograd, he goes to Lake Bled.'

'Is that around here?'

'No, no. It's in Slovenia. Bew-ti-ful place. Mountains, lake, the old hotels.' He bunched his fingers together and kissed them. 'Tito had villa there.'

'And you think maybe Wilson's still there?'

Novakovic made a face. 'No no no! He goes to see the notebooks. A few days, a week. Not months.'

'Notebooks?'

'Very special,' Novakovic said. 'All of Tesla's writings — the ones we know — we have them here. In museum. But not Top Secret writings. Your FBI takes these. Long time ago. Sends them on train to Los Alamos. Where they make bombs, you know? But Luka Ceplak, he has his *father's* notebooks. Every day, his father is writing. 'The maestro did this, the maestro did that' — for thirty years. I have seen them with my own eyes. And sometimes, Tesla himself makes notes on page. This is what Jack Wilson goes to see.'

Burke nodded, but he must have looked puzzled because Novakovic continued. 'Luka's father, Yuri Ceplak, was lab assistant who worked with Tesla in New York, then in Colorado Springs, and then again in New York. He writes hundreds of notebooks! And now they are

310

Luka's. But will he give them to us? No! He's stubborn old man. And lonely. Having note-books, people come to see him. Sometimes, they bring presents.'

'Like what?'

'Vodka.' Novakovic frowned. 'You know, your FBI, they lie about the maestro. They are saying he did not keep records, that he works in his head, that he makes no models, no step-by-step. So this is . . . ' he smiled, rolling his hand through the air, searching for the word. 'Bull-shit.'

Burke laughed. 'But this guy, Ceplak — '

'Yuri sees the war coming, and he comes home.'

'You're talking about the Second World War.'

'Yes, of course. *This* war. Yuri brings notebooks home. War ends. And we have cold war. Notebooks are going nowhere during cold war.'

'They just stayed with his son,' Burke said.

'No, Luka goes to Australia. Notebooks stay here. Luka's a physicist at university — in Perth, I think. He comes home only when his father dies. Sixty, sixty-five. Like that.'

'And after that?'

'He's teaching in Zagreb. But that was long time ago. I don't think he teaches now for ten years. So maybe we have different story.'

'What do you mean?' Burke asked.

'I'm hoping Luka will let us have the notebooks. I ask Jack Wilson to speak with him of this, but . . . I think Luka enjoys too much the visits he gets. People come to see notebooks, they

311

take him to lunch, they say, 'Luka this, Luka that . . . ' ' The curator made a what-can-you-do gesture with his hands.

When Burke asked, Novakovic looked up the particulars for Luka Ceplak, and wrote them on the same sheet of paper with Jack Wilson's address.

'This is so nice of you,' Burke said, as he got to his feet.

'No problem. You want me to send the abstract on Wilson's speech? You'll see, it's very very interesting.'

'*Is* it?'

'Yes, I think so,' Novakovic told him. 'But, I have to say, I don't approve. And I don't think the maestro would approve, either. Tesla, he was *heartsick* about Tunguska, so . . . all this talk about weapons? No. I don't think so.'

Burke frowned. *What's a 'Tunguska'?* he wondered. 'Is that what his speech was about?'

Novakovic nodded. 'Yes. He's talking about Tesla Cannon.' Seeing Burke's puzzlement, Novakovic smiled. 'Is particle-beam weapon. You know' — he made a gesture, his fists coming together and then exploding outward — '*Pffft* . . . gone!'

'Really?'

'Yes! Jack's paper corrects maestro's eigenvectors to get more accurate focus.'

Burke didn't know what the museum director was talking about. The whole thing got wilder and wilder. Tesla Cannons? Why not? Beam me up, Scotty. He thanked Novakovic for his help, and made his way downstairs and out to the

312

street. The main thing was, he had what he'd come for: d'Anconia's name and address. He'd give the information to Kovalenko, and that would be the end of it.

His elation faded at the Internet cafe around the corner from his hotel. An e-mail that he sent to Wilson, with 'Tesla' in the subject line, was bounced back almost as soon as he sent it. He checked the address that Novakovic had given him, but there was no mistake. And no Wilson.

Google wasn't a big help, either. The search engine generated twenty million hits for 'Jack Wilson,' which, Burke realized, was entirely predictable. Even so . . . He went through the first few tiers, and saw that most of the hits concerned a Pittsburgh Pirates shortstop, a fishing lure artisan in Montana, and some Indian who'd died in the thirties. He sighed.

He'd go through them all if he had to, but it didn't seem a promising path. He clicked on 'Advanced Search' and Googled 'Jack Wilson' and 'Nikola Tesla.' That took him to the page he'd already seen the day before, the list of presenters at the Tesla Symposium, 2005: 'J. Wilson/Stanford University/'The Tunguska Incident: Calculating Vector Drag in Scalar Pair-Coupling.' ' *Tunguska*.

Bingo!

Burke stared at the screen. *Stanford*.

If that was legit, knowing Wilson's alma mater should be useful. There had to be databases you could get to — or at least his sister could. (Meg was a genius at data mining.) Stanford alumni groups, enrollment and graduation records,

313

library cards — maybe even a published master's or doctoral thesis if Wilson had been a master's or doctoral candidate. And he must have been. Vector drag? Scalar pair-coupling? *I oughta get a Nobel just for typing them,* Burke thought.

His sister, Meg, worked for an environmental law group in Charlottesville, and she really knew her way around the Internet. Their dad, amazed by what his daughter could find out about something — or *someone* — joked that if Meg ever went over to the dark side, she'd make a great identity thief. *Cool,* she said. *I want to be Moby.*

But trying to find Jack Wilson via Stanford would take a while, even for Meg. Burke didn't know when, or even if, Wilson had actually gone there. Or if he'd graduated. Or what his degree was in — if he had one. Physics? Math? Engineering? Science fiction? Stanford was a big place. 'Wilson' was not 'Heimerdinger.'

He remembered the three-by-five card that the desk clerk had given him. Taking it from his pocket, he found two numbers. There was no reverse lookup on the Internet that gave you international numbers. But he Googled '386 country code' and saw that Wilson's first call had been to Slovenia. That was probably Luka Ceplak's number at Lake Bled. The second call had gone to the Ukraine.

His next stop was anywho.com. When the site came up, he put 'Jack Wilson' and 'White Deer' in the slots and . . . nothing. He tried 'John Wilson.' And again, nothing. The e-mail address

314

had been a phony, and the street address wasn't any better.

Burke was beginning to get a sinking feeling. Maybe 'Jack Wilson' was an alias, too. Maybe 'Jack Wilson' was a character in *The Fountainhead* — in which case, he could forget reopening Aherne & Associates. He tried again, using 'Wilson' by itself. Maybe the guy has parents there, he thought. Or a wife, or a cousin — This time, he got a hit. *Erica Wilson*. Must be a small town, he thought. Only one Wilson.

So he checked. And, in fact, White Deer had a population of 362. What were the odds that White Deer's only Wilsons, Jack and Erica, were related?

It cost a dollar a minute to make a telephone call from the Esplanade, so Burke bought a phone card at a kiosk near the river. He stood in a Plexiglas bubble that didn't do much to inhibit the cold wind, and tried to figure out how the hell you made an international call. The Cyrillic lettering was not a big help. It took him four tries to get the call through and by that time, his hands had turned to stone.

'Hel-looooo,' crooned the voice that answered. An old woman, Burke guessed, from the timbre of her voice.

'Hi!' Burke shouted. 'I'm trying to reach Jack!'

' 'Jack'? I think you have the wrong number!'

'Wait-wait-wait-wait-wait!' Burke pleaded. 'I'm in a phone booth in Belgrade.'

'Lucky you. I love Maine!'

Burke took a deep breath. 'Look,' he said, 'I'm trying to get in touch with a man named Jack

Wilson. I got your name off the Internet. You were the only 'Wilson' in White Deer, so . . . you know anyone named Jack Wilson?'

'There was a Hazel Wilson on Elm, but she's dead, four years. Maybe five.'

'I've got an address,' Burke told her.

'Well, that's the ticket!'

'Maybe not. It's just a post office box.'

'Oh.' There was something cautionary about the way she said it.

'Excuse me?' Burke said.

'Let me guess . . . is that Box two thousand?'

Burke fumbled open the sheet of paper that Novakovic had given him. 'As a matter of fact — '

'Well, that's your problem right there. If it's Box two thousand, that's the prison. All the inmates get their mail there.'

Burke didn't know what to say. 'It's a prison?'

'They call it a federal correctional institution. Most of us, though, we just call it Allenwood.'

25

ODESSA, UKRAINE APRIL 12, 2005

A plump woman stood behind the roping, wearing a pantsuit so closely fitted that she appeared to have been upholstered. She beamed a welcoming smile and held aloft a hand-lettered sign: ROMANTIC TOURISTS.

Jack Wilson joined the men around her, a collection of nervous males who joked too much and avoided eye contact. He'd tried to pick them out on the plane from New York, and he'd nailed all but one. As a group, they displayed the physical and social liabilities (bad skin, obesity, a piercing giggle, a stutter) that you might expect of men who'd surfed their way into the arms of Madame Puletskaya, their Internet matchmaker. Men who were shopping for a wife and willing to pay the freight.

Wilson was odd man out. For one thing, he was conspicuously good-looking. And while he hadn't been with a woman in years, there was a time, before his incarceration, when they had flocked to him. His easy athleticism and dark good looks made his youthful poverty ingratiating, his ratty cars adventurous, and his brilliance at math and science — which might have seemed nerdy — interesting. Thanks to Mandy, he had the cowboy manners of the Sundance Kid, all

Ma'am and Sir. He shook hands with a firm grip, looked folks in the eye, and never made excuses. Sharon, his Stanford girlfriend, had guided him through the mysteries of advanced cutlery, taught him the proper way to consume soup, conveyed a knowledge of wines and the ways of a valued houseguest. In her way, she'd polished him up like a piece of rough.

Wilson studied his traveling companions. They were really rather ordinary-looking. A cynic might suppose that they were there to get laid, but that wasn't it. Not really. There were easier and less expensive ways to do that. These men had flown halfway around the world, while submitting to the rigmarole of a staged courtship. Why? Wilson guessed that their resort to an Internet matchmaker was for much the same reason as his own. Like himself, they knew what they wanted, and whether from shyness or impatience, they were unwilling to look for a lover in the conventional ways. On the flight over, he'd met two of Madame Puletskaya's clients. The first was a fifty-four-year-old businessman who owned a lumberyard in Michigan, had never been married, and figured, 'It's now or never.' The second was younger and suffered from an illness he didn't identify, but which, he said, was certain to kill him. 'What I really want,' he said, 'is a kid. Someone to carry the name. So it isn't like I didn't leave nothin' or no one behind.'

Wilson faced the same dilemma as these other men. He didn't have the time or patience for seduction or courtship. Filling in the blanks for

Madame P. suited him just fine, a choreographed courtship that required no thinking, planning, or endeavor.

1. Flowers
2. Letters
3. Chocolates
4. Lingerie
5. Telephone calls
6. Visit
7. Marriage

He understood that the 'Ukraine Brides' would not be so readily available — would not have their photos on the Internet, would not be willing to leave home and family — if they were not desperate to escape a hopeless future. So it was that a beautiful and well-educated woman like Irina was, if not for sale, on offer. Not to anyone, of course. She had the power of rejection. But Wilson guessed that if push came to shove, she'd probably accept most of the Americans now standing in the lee of the formidable Madame Puletskaya.

As for Irina's appeal, well, she had it all. Even more to the point, once she was in Nevada, she'd be in a foreign country, thousands of miles from home. Which is another way of saying she'd be totally dependent on her husband, having no friends and nowhere to turn if and when the relationship went south.

She'd be his. Really his.

'Ah, Mr. *Wilson*,' Madame P. oozed now, grasping his arm. 'I recognize you *instantly*.'

319

Wilson glanced around at the others. 'Was it my name tag?' he deadpanned, gesturing to the red-rimmed HELLO badge stuck to his lapel.

Madame Puletskaya looked alarmed until she realized this was a joke. Then she broke into peals of girlish laughter.

'This one,' she said, giving him a poke in the arm, 'such a comic. He's looking even more handsome than his photograph. I promise!'

Wilson shook his head in a self-deprecating way. Madame P. counted heads, then efficiently swapped her welcome sign for a clipboard, extracting it from a huge, red tote bag. She checked off names in a methodical way, looking back and forth from the name tags to her clipboard.

'All here!' Madame P. enthused, herding them toward the airport exit. 'Now to van.' They walked out the automated front door, rolling their suitcases.

'We're like sheep,' one of them muttered.

'Baaaaa,' said Wilson.

A nervous eruption of laughter. As if this was one of the funniest things any one of them had ever heard.

A big man, wearing a FUBU T-shirt, tossed the suitcases into the van's rear compartment, then spoke into a cell phone. Madame P. tried to open the van's sliding door. Wilson stepped forward to help, earning another peal of delight from Herself. 'So strong, too,' she said.

Wilson rolled his eyes. 'Most of us are outstanding with minivans.' More laughter. *Christ*, Wilson thought, *it's like I'm Chris Rock.*

'Well, we're all here — so let's get going,' Madame P. said, suddenly in a hurry. She jammed her clipboard into her tote. Turning to the back of the van, she smiled. 'Surely, you must be tired and need to nap and freshen up before this afternoon's tea with the ladies. Two o'clock,' she said. Then she beamed a smile and wagged a finger. 'Don't be late.'

One of the oddities of the situation was that, in order to soften the commercial aspect of the arrangement, everything was done with a stultifying propriety. After months of obligatory letters, flowers, and chocolates, there would be a couple of hours of face-time — mediated by a chaperone. Then a 'touristic hour' the next day, and, after that, a dinner dance.

The 'romantic tourists' were booked into a second-class hotel on a noisy street just off the Vulitsa Deribasovskaya. Madame P. gave them three hours and insisted that they synchronize their watches. They might as well have been in summer camp.

★ ★ ★

The women were waiting at the appointed hour in the hotel's threadbare breakfast room, where an effigy of high tea was to be served. Irina blushed and smiled as Wilson took her hand and kissed it. Somewhere behind him, the man with the high-pitched giggle let out a whoop.

When the lukewarm tea and stale sandwiches had been consumed, Madame P. led the couples hand in hand on a stroll down a shady promenade along the Prymorsky bulvar. Irina seemed sweet and shy, although Wilson had no illusions about his ability to judge her correctly. He bought her an ice cream, he bought her a bottled water, he bought her a fake Gucci purse from a street vendor. She loved this, stroking it like a pet. Her English was not as good as he'd hoped — they'd spoken on the telephone very briefly — but it didn't matter. Her face was sweet with concentration as she labored to make small talk.

'I'm so happiness.'

'Happy.'

'Happy,' she repeated. 'Happy to make walk with you.'

'I think you're very brave,' he said. 'To leave your country, your family . . . ' Not that there was any mystery in it. Irina and the other women were willing to take a leap into the unknown because their prospects at home were so poor. Standards of living in the former Soviet Union were trending down for a lot of people, even as the economy grew and the 'oligarchs' prospered. Life expectancy was contracting, and so was the birthrate. Social services that were formerly taken for granted had all but disappeared. Irina and her family lived in a one-bedroom apartment — parents in one room with her younger brother, Irina and her sisters in the dining area.

'Some days, I am hope they come to visit,' she said. 'And I visit here, too, yes? This is possible?'

'Of course.'

Meanwhile, Madame P. and her staff were

busy making complex arrangements for the women to visit the States. Among other things, this entailed applications for K-1 visas — the so-called 'fiancée visas' required of people coming to America to be married.

In addition to the K-1 visas, the would-be brides would need an open-return ticket — and a traveling budget. Most of the men had taken advantage of Madame's boilerplate prenuptial agreement, but Wilson said that he wouldn't require one. This was taken as a gesture of love by Irina, but of course it was nothing of the sort. In the world to come — which Wilson was beginning to think of as *A.W.* (or After Wilson) — a prenup would be about as useful as an umbrella in a hurricane.

Sitting on a park bench under a beech tree, bright with spring leaves, Wilson described the ranch where they would live.

'It's paradise,' he told her. 'There's a stream where the deer come to drink, spectacular sunsets, the biggest sky you ever saw, hawks and fish, trees.'

'I am sure, very beautiful. Pictures you send, I put under my pillow. Such a big house. Is room for many children, I think.' She blushed.

Irina stroked the purse. 'Is dishwasher?'

Wilson nodded. 'Yes. And a big TV with a flat screen. Also . . . you'll like this: I bought you a car. A convertible.'

She squealed with delight, and then her face fell. 'But I am not knowing how to drive.'

'I'll teach you. It will be fun.'

'Is new car?' she asked.

He shook his head. 'No,' he told her. 'You don't want a new car. Computer goes on the fritz, and you're outta luck. Trust me.'

She frowned. 'Our home . . . in Nevada, yes?'

'Yes,'

'Is Las Vegas?'

He shrugged and smiled. 'We're out in the country, but . . . you'll fly into Vegas, and yeah, you'll get a chance to see it.'

She squirmed with embarrassment and then, at his prompting, confessed that she wanted to be married in the same 'chapel of love' in which Britney Spears had tied the knot. 'White Chapel. Is possible?'

He couldn't help but laugh. She was sitting there beside him, with her bright eyes and rosy cheeks, so eager, almost pleading. He couldn't help himself. He was charmed by her innocence, even if it wasn't that, even if it was just naïveté. Her infatuation with celebrity and stardom was as natural as it was predictable. Hollywood did that to people — even, it seemed, Ukrainian waitresses who'd never seen a copy of *People* or *Parade*. So why not indulge her? He'd been thinking of a simple ceremony, but . . . 'If that's what you want, why not?'

She smiled her demure dimpled smile, blushing with delight. 'Wait until I tell Tatiana.' She stroked the purse and turned her body toward him. Raising her chin, she kissed him on the lips. For the first time, he noticed her soft floral scent. Combined with the warmth of her breath and the look in her eyes, it excited him in a way that he hadn't been for years. Not since

324

they'd sent him to Supermax.

'I have something for you,' he said. 'Something to put in the purse.'

Her eyes widened. 'What?'

He handed her an airline ticket folder, which contained a first-class round-trip ticket from Odessa to Las Vegas, via Moscow and New York. He'd already spoken to Madame P. about the date and he'd been reassured that the K-1 visa would be ready in time. The paperwork was complete. All that was necessary was for Madame P. to submit evidence that Wilson had visited Irina in person. And this was as good as done. She'd taken his picture with Irina, and copied the visa stamp in his passport that very morning. Irina would fly into Vegas on June 16. This would give them time to marry, and still be at the ranch for the summer solstice.

The date was important. In a way, it was everything.

Irina gasped when she saw the ticket. 'First class!' she oohed, bringing him back to the moment. Then she saw the hundred-dollar bills that he'd put in the folder behind the ticket. 'Oh Jack!' she cried, surreptitiously counting the money. She kissed him again. Tears glittered in her eyes.

'You can buy a dress — or give it to your parents. An engagement gift. Like this.' He produced a ring from the pocket of his jacket, and slid it onto her finger.

Irina was dazzled. 'Oh, Jack. It's so beautiful.'

★ ★ ★

In the morning, Madame P. bundled them aboard a 'luxury coach,' which deposited them at the Nerubayske tunnels, home of the Museum of Partisan Glory. Madame P. doled out the tickets and issued a stern warning: 'Stay with tour. Do not be tempted to explore on your own. Each year, persons disappear into catacombs and never return.'

It reminded Wilson of his high school field trips. Indeed, the entire 'romantic tour' echoed those days, the awkward boys and giggling girls replaced by these self-conscious men and softly laughing women. Each couple was given a flashlight. Everyone held hands. Irina's hand was small and cool in his own.

Madame P. herself acted as the tour guide, explaining that the catacombs were created by mining for limestone — which had been used to build the city of Odessa. Over the years, the network of tunnels became a smugglers' maze.

Irina squeezed his hand.

'But here in Nerubayske,' Madame P. continued, 'lived small army of brave partisans during World War number two.' Various dioramas showed what life had been like underground for the fighters who lived in the tunnels in between attacks on the railroads and other efforts to thwart the Nazi advance.

At one turn, Wilson kissed Irina. She pressed her body into his. He turned off the flashlight. He was certain every other couple was engaged in a similar activity. He guessed that Madame P. had selected this excursion, rather than a visit to a well-lit museum, precisely to enable such moments. From the sounds of things, one couple off to the right was doing more than kissing.

Irina moaned and kissed him again. Her kiss was passionate if a little practiced — not that he had any illusions about virginity or a lack of sexual activity. The women had been tested for AIDS and for other STDs, and while a fertility test was not feasible, prospective grooms were reassured by medical exams and histories that showed no obvious impediments to motherhood.

Eventually they all followed Madame's waggling light to the exit. Irina blinked and rubbed her eyes as they emerged into the brightness of day. It reminded Wilson of stepping out of an afternoon movie. Matinee blindness.

'I am lucky one,' Irina said. 'Other men not so . . . ' She shook her head. And glowed.

★   ★   ★

Senior prom. That's what the dinner dance resembled, more than anything else — although there were only twelve couples in attendance. A small dance floor, tables for six with stingy bouquets, a flower-bedecked arch (for pictures). The men wore dark suits with carnations in the lapel; the women, fancy dresses. A three-piece band — the vocalist sporting a bright red mullet — cranked out an eclectic mix of music.

This might have been a faux prom, but Irina was real and palpable in his arms. 'You're a good dancer,' she told him, as he guided her around the little parquet dance floor. They had suffered through the chicken dinner, the cloying dessert, the clumsy toasts offered by Madame P. Now, the slow dances outnumbered the fast ones. The lights were dimmed. Madame P. and her diminutive husband had taken a turn on the floor, to a scattering of polite applause, and then retired to a corner.

Irina looked up at Wilson, a slight sheen of perspiration on her face. The guy with the mullet began to sing the Percy Sledge classic 'When a Man Loves a Woman.' Irina pressed herself into his arms. They did not so much dance, now, as sway together. 'I love this song,' she said, melting into him.

'Mmmmmm.' They swayed some more.

'I want to make love with you,' she whispered.

He pulled her closer, rocking from side to side. Slowly, his eyes began to close, then suddenly blinked open when he saw the herringbone mote glimmering in his peripheral vision, and realized that he would soon be blind. If only for a little while.

'Is good idea, yes?'

Wilson nodded distractedly.

'We make sure?'

'Yeah,' Wilson said. 'We should make sure.'

She sensed that something had changed, and worried that she had offended him. She drew back. 'What is wrong?'

'Nothing. I'm fine.'

She led him back to their table. Her dress was shredding into ribbons of color and he perceived her through a glaze of light — but he could still see the sweet little furrow in her brow.

'Is talking about love?' she asked. 'You don't like?'

He made a sound that tried to be a laugh but came out as something else. 'I get these headaches, sometimes — only they don't hurt. They just . . . make it hard for me to see. But it goes away,' he added, a little too hurriedly.

'This is vision migraine,' she announced, pronouncing the word 'meegraine.'

Wilson was astonished. 'That's right, but . . . how do you know that?'

'You forget, I'm in school of medicine before I must quit to work. I will see if Madame Puletskaya is permitting us to depart.'

Madame P. appeared, hovering above. To Wilson, she resembled the screaming figure in Edvard Munch's famous painting: a white face, surrounded by radiating auras of different colors. Next to her, Madame's husband was a sinister black figure, pulsating in the darkness. And then, it was almost as if he couldn't see at all.

Irina clutched Wilson's hand, speaking rapidly in Russian to their chaperone. Wilson couldn't understand a word, but the sense of the conversation was clear from Irina's tone, which segued from conviction to pleading, even as Madame's morphed from rejection to surrender.

Finally, Irina led him out the door. The cool night air felt like silk against his skin. She stroked his hair as they waited for the taxi. 'Is stress,' she said, in a low, firm voice. 'And sometimes, there is environmental factor.'

In the hotel, she demanded the key from the desk clerk. Once in the room, she did not turn on the lights, but sat with him on the bed. She removed his jacket and tie, took off his shoes, made him lie down. He heard her go into the bathroom. For a moment, he worried that she'd turn the light on, but she didn't. He heard the faucet run, and then she padded back to him across the floor.

'Is better, yes? The dark?'

'Yes.' He felt queasy, as he always did when one of the migraines came on, but Irina was a revelation — an angel of mercy, tender and caring.

She placed a damp washcloth over his eyes.

The room was stuffy, so she turned on the ceiling fan. But she didn't open the windows. How did she know that the noise from the street would bother him?

'It never lasts long,' he told her.

'Shhhhh.' She stroked his cheek with the backs of her fingers, the pressure so light, it might have been a breeze.

Every few minutes, she removed the washcloth. He could hear her turn on the tap, and wring out the fabric. Then she came back to his side and replaced the cloth, now cool, over his eyes.

It had been a long time since anyone had shown Wilson any kindness — in part, perhaps, because he hadn't allowed it. And no one had ever tended him during one of his migraines. He'd always hidden them, moving away from other people whenever they came on.

He congratulated himself on his intuition about Irina. She had heart. The other women might be mercenaries, even prostitutes, but Irina was the real thing.

The migraine was beginning to pass, though he was still a little dizzy, a little 'off.'

Her tenderness took on the aspect of a revelation. That he should find a woman as beautiful as this, and as gentle as this, augured well. And, in fact, everything was falling into place. With Hakim out of the picture, he had three times as much money as he thought he would — and no entanglements. The hard part, turning the hash into cash and getting out of Africa alive, was over. All that was left was the payoff.

He'd bought a ranch and started work on the apparatus. And it would soon be ready. The marriage 'transaction' that he'd entered into as a gesture to the future was looking more and more like a windfall, a blessing, a stroke of luck. Providence, or something like it, was smiling on him, readying the world for its cleansing and rebirth.

'It's almost gone.' He began to sit up.

'Shhhhh . . . ' With the tips of her fingers, she pushed him back down, and removed the washcloth. 'I'll be right back,' she said. 'Don't open your eyes.'

When she came back again, she stretched out alongside him, fitting herself to his body like spoons in a kitchen drawer. She leaned over him, stroked his cheek with the backs of her fingers, then kissed his neck.

'I remove my clothes,' she whispered. 'Is all right?'

'Perfect,' he said.

26

Mike Burke settled the telephone back into place. Wilson's address was a *prison*?

He jammed his hands into his pockets as he walked back to the Esplanade. The good news was that he had a name now, a real name — which was more than Kovalenko had. So he'd get points for that. He even had an address. Sort of.

But that was bad news, too. This particular address did not inspire confidence. On the contrary, it tended to reinforce Kovalenko's doubts that Burke had acted in good faith when forming a corporation for 'd'Anconia.'

On the other hand (there were a lot of 'on the other hands,' it seemed, as Burke tried to get Wilson into focus) his quarry was a Stanford man. So he couldn't be all bad, could he? Of course not.

The ridiculousness of this thought was not lost on Burke as he trudged through the cold-snap that was Belgrade. If Wilson graduated from Stanford, he'd undoubtedly done well on his SATs. But that didn't make him a saint. To go from the playing fields of Palo Alto to the Yard at White Deer suggested that our boy was either a very bad man, or a total fuckup.

Burke was hoping for Door #2.

At the hotel, it took Burke fifteen minutes to get through to London. When he did, Kovalenko wasn't there. His assistant, a Brit named Jean, offered to take a message. Burke said, 'Just tell him I can identify d'Anconia.'

'Who?'

He spelled it for her, and gave her his number at the Esplanade.

She repeated the details, then mouthed a little *tsk*. 'I must tell you,' she said, her voice clipped. 'Mr. Kovalenko is out of pocket at the moment. I'll do my best to get your message to him, but — '

'He's out of pocket?'

'Ye-esss.'

'Just how far out of pocket is he?' Burke asked.

She sucked a little air through her teeth in a display of regret. 'It could be several days.'

Burke groaned. 'This is kind of important,' he told her.

'I'm sure it is.'

' 'Urgent' is more like it.'

The secretary sighed. 'Maybe you should have a word with Agent Gomez. He's filling in.'

'By all means,' Burke told her. 'Put him on.'

There was a few seconds of silence, and then she came back on the line. 'I'm afraid he's away from his desk. Shall I have him call you?'

Do any of these people actually work? Burke wondered.

Replacing the handset in its cradle, Burke swung his legs over the side of the bed and sat up. As he did, he felt something crumpling in his pocket. It was the three-by-five card that the desk clerk had given him the day before. He sat for a moment wondering what to do. On the one hand, he was curious about who Wilson might have been calling in the Ukraine. But he was also smart enough to know that this was precisely the kind of thing that got cats killed. He should probably leave it to Kovalenko.

Right, he thought, and dialed the number. There were a couple of short rings, and then a recorded voice came on the line. To his surprise, it was a woman's voice, heavily accented and sexy:

You have reached Ukraine Brides. Please listen carefully to choose your correct prompt.

If you are interested to receive our brochure, please press 'one,' leave name and complete address.

If you are interested to speak to representative, please press 'two,' and leave telephone number to reach you.

Or . . . you may prefer to visit our complete website at ukrainebrides — all one word — dot org. Thank you.

Burke hung up. As he fell back on the bed, he thought: *He wants to get married?! Like this guy doesn't have enough problems?*

★ ★ ★

Gomez called the next afternoon. The first words out of his mouth were:

'You're in a lot of trouble, my friend.'

'What? Who is this?'

'Agent Gomez.' Suddenly, his voice changed. Became almost chipper. 'You mind if I tape this?'

Burke took a deep breath. 'What kind of trouble?'

A chuckle from Gomez. 'So the tape — it's okay, right?'

Burke gritted his teeth. 'Yeah,' he said. 'It's fine. What kind of trouble?'

Click. 'Well,' Gomez told him, 'I had a little chat this morning.' He paused for effect.

Burke waited. Finally, he said, 'Yeah — *and?*'

'I talked with Agent Kovalenko.'

'Great!' Burke declared.

'I gave him the message you left. Said you'd called from Belgrade. He was very curious as to how you managed to get around without your passport.'

Burke didn't know what to say. He started to mumble something about dual citizenship, then heard the weakness in his own voice and got angry — as much at himself as at Gomez. 'Y'know,' he said, 'I haven't done a fucking thing wrong.'

'Hey!'

'The only thing I've done is, I've been *helpful.*' He paused. 'So how come Kovalenko doesn't call me himself?'

A thousand miles away, Special Agent Eduardo Gomez stood beside the window in his office, looking through the blinds at the plane trees in Grosvenor Square. 'He's in the shop,' Gomez said.

'What?'

Gomez bit his lip. 'He's unavailable for a few days.'

In fact, and as Gomez well knew, Kovalenko was in the Mayo Clinic, having flown to the United States in a desperate bid to save himself — though from what was unclear. Kovalenko's own internist said he was fine, that the anomalies on his CAT scan were fairly typical, and nothing to worry about. But the Legat was not a man to take chances. Certainly, not with his own health. He wanted a second opinion — preferably from an American who had gone to Harvard. So he'd flown the coop — and the Atlantic.

The truth was: Ray Kovalenko was a hypochondriac. Everybody knew it. Nobody talked about it. In his absence, Gomez had taken the opportunity to avail himself of Kovalenko's office, where he'd checked out some of the websites the Legat had visited. And what he found was terrifying. Kovalenko surfed for diseases the way some guys surfed for porn.

The Centers for Disease Control, the World Organization for Animal Health, the User's Guide to Rare Diseases websites — each was just a click away at the top of the Legat's list of Favorites. The man needed help. But like a lot of people who need help, he did not want to hear about it. He was a medical paranoid who ran his life along need-to-know principles. And not just his private life. His professional life was equally opaque, perhaps because he understood that secrets were the hundred-dollar-bills of the Information Age.

So he didn't delegate well. Which meant that when Kovalenko was unavailable, certain cases did not move forward. And woe unto anyone foolish enough to step in where he wasn't wanted. In the end, Gomez thought, covering for Kovalenko was simple. You took messages and kept your head down. Anyone could do it.

Meanwhile, the guy on the other end of the line, the guy in Belgrade — Burke — was shouting: 'What does *that* mean? He's 'unavailable for a few days.' Do you even know what this is all about?' Burke asked.

'Of course,' Gomez lied.

A skeptical silence ensued. Finally, Burke asked, 'Did you tell him I can identify d'Anconia?'

'He knows that,' Gomez replied. 'His secretary gave him the message. That's why I'm calling.'

'But he couldn't call me himself?' Burke asked.

'If you'll just give me the information,' Gomez insisted, 'I'll pass it along.' He sounded almost bored.

Burke made a sound, somewhere between a gargle and a growl. If he told this guy that d'Anconia was an ex-con named Jack Wilson who'd done time in a federal prison called Allenwood, that would be the end of it. The FBI would get on with the case, and Burke would be left with nothing, twisting in the wind.

Maybe Kovalenko would do the right thing. Maybe he'd reinstate Burke's passport, and remove the sanctions against Aherne & Associates. Then again, maybe he wouldn't. When you came right down to it, the Legat did not seem like a stand-up guy.

'Y'know,' Burke said, 'I'm just gonna wait until I see him. It's kinda complicated, and . . . Tell Mr. Kovalenko I'll be in touch.' And with that, he hung up.

Falling back on the bed, he watched the lights fluttering across the ceiling. He thought about going back to Dublin. That would be the easiest thing. He could give the information to Doherty. But what was the point of that? This was Kovalenko's show.

And Kovalenko had left the house.

The best thing he could do, Burke decided, was find a way to improve his hand. Pick up as much as he could so that when it came time to sit down with Kovalenko, he'd have more to trade than a name.

He could fly back to Dublin that same night. But there was nothing for him to do there. If he returned to Ireland, he'd just sit around, missing Kate, and drinking with the old man.

But if he went to Lake Bled, he might actually learn something. D'Anconia — *Wilson* — was no doubt long gone. But this notebook guy, Ceplak, might know where he is. If Burke could find that out, Kovalenko would have to be more accommodating.

He reached for the three-by-five card that Milic had given him, and dialed the 386 country code for Slovenia. The phone rang and rang, and then a man's well-lubricated voice answered: '*Zdravo?*'

Uh-oh, Burke thought. And took a flyer. 'Mr. Ceplak?'

'*Jeste?*'

'I'm looking for Yuri Ceplak's son . . . ?'

'Yes! That's me!'

27

SLOVENIA APRIL 13, 2005

Lake Bled was only sixty miles or so from Ljubljana, but once Burke passed the city of Kranj, about halfway, sleet began to tick at the windshield of his rental car. Traffic slowed and the road grew slick as it twisted into the foothills of the mountains. Fog bleached and thickened the air. Two hours later, he skated into Bled, white-knuckled behind the taillights of a black Mercedes.

The setting was spectacular. A small town at the edge of an emerald-green lake, Bled rested in the shadow of an eleventh-century castle perched at the edge of a steep cliff. The Julian Alps loomed in the background.

The town was crowded with skiers so it was more than an hour before Burke found a room at the Grand Hotel Toplice, a faded white elephant that looked as if Agatha Christie had spent her summers there.

The room was more expensive than he would have liked, which reminded him that he was going to have to do something about money. He was running through his savings fast. Though he'd been the beneficiary of Kate's life insurance policy, he'd given it all to Doctors Without Borders.

In his room, he pulled aside the drapes that covered the French doors, and gazed through the falling snow at a gauzy sprawl of lights across the lake. He knew from an in-flight magazine that a seventeenth-century church was out there in the snow, standing on Slovenia's only island. In the campanile was a legendary bell. Ring it, and your wishes came true.

Burke took two miniature bottles of Dewar's from the minibar and emptied them into a tumbler. Going out to the balcony, he brushed the snow from a wicker chair, sat down and gazed across the lake.

Wishes were funny things, he thought, pulling his coat closer. To begin with, they were always in limited supply. No one ever had a thousand wishes. From the fairy tales that he'd read, you only got one — unless you were lucky, and then you got three. Either way, you didn't want to waste them. You didn't want to wish for something you could get on your own — like Lakers' tickets — or something you could *do* on your own.

Like bitch-slap Kovalenko.

Neither were wishes prayers. Prayers were for possibilities, however unlikely (Dear God, let her get well).

Wishes were for lost causes, or outright miracles.

He sipped the Dewar's and squinted into the wind, which was blowing toward him off the lake. In the distance, he could just make out the rough shape of the church, with its campanile. *Kate would have loved it here*, he thought. Then, looking toward the church, *Wish you were here.*

341

★ ★ ★

The morning was sky-blue, cold, and clear, sunlight knifing off the snow. To Burke's surprise, the road to Luka Ceplak's house was plowed, so it took only a few minutes to get there. Lugging two bottles of vodka in a Duty Free bag, he bounded up the neatly shoveled steps and rapped on the door. The air was fresh and redolent of woodsmoke. Beside the house, in an open-air shed, was a wall of wood so neatly stacked that it formed a flower at its center.

The man who answered the door looked like Geppetto. He was short, with a wiry physique and a pixie's face that went nova when he saw the Duty Free bag.

'Ahhhh,' he said. 'Mr. Burke? I see you come bearing gifts.' He rubbed his hands together. 'Always welcome. Please to come in.'

A woodfire crackled in a limestone fireplace as the old man removed the bottles from the bag. Discarding the tissue paper that enclosed them, he revealed, first, a blue bottle of Skyy ('Ahhhh'), and a bottle of Grey Goose, which he kissed. Grinning, he lifted one bottle, then the other, several times, as if doing biceps curls, then finally held the Grey Goose forward. 'Just a taste,' he said, 'to warm up our conversation — yes?'

Burke didn't drink in the morning. He was about to say no, when he thought better of it. 'Great.'

While Ceplak disappeared through a doorway, and puttered in the kitchen, Burke studied a

342

phalanx of framed photographs, sitting on top of the mantel. The pictures were black-and-white, and obviously quite old. In one of them, an elegant man in a three-piece suit stood in the foreground of what appeared to be a potato field. In the background was a structure that looked as if Eiffel had collaborated with Frankenstein to build a skyscraper. Rising above a low-slung brick building was a wooden tower that might have been about a hundred feet tall, capped by a gigantic metal hemisphere that would have gladdened the heart of Buck Rogers.

'So! Already, you've met the maestro,' Ceplak brayed as he reentered the room bearing the bottle of Grey Goose, two glasses, and a plate of crackers and cheese on a painted metal tray.

'The maestro?'

'Tesla! At the Wardenclyffe Tower, of course.' Ceplak handed him a glass, and raised his own. 'Na zdravje!'

'Cheers!'

The old man tossed back the vodka in a single gulp. Burke followed suit. Ceplak took a deep breath, sucking the fumes into his chest. 'Good, eh?'

Burke nodded. His throat was on fire.

'So!' Ceplak gestured to a Barcelona chair in front of the fireplace. 'Sit.'

It was a beautiful room, Burke thought, an eclectic mix of gleaming wooden antique and modern pieces. One entire wall was an expanse of glass with a view of the lake. Burke could see the island now, just off to the right. Tiny figures, blatant against the snow, moved between the shore and the island.

'Pilgrims,' Ceplak told him. 'Last year, in April, they row out. But this winter, I don't think it ever ends.' He gazed at the scene for a while longer, then turned back to Burke. 'And you! You're a pilgrim, too!'

Burke cocked his head. 'How's that?'

'You come to see the notebooks.'

'Actually . . . '

'My father, Yuri — maybe you know — for thirty years, he's Tesla's assistant. Is funny, this pair! The maestro, he's two meters — this is like basketball player! My father, he's like me: one point six meters! Practically a dwarf.'

Burke laughed, and loosened the collar of his shirt. The vodka within, and the fire without, were making him warm.

'You're probably wondering how they met, am I right?' Ceplak asked. 'Well, I'll tell you. My father comes to New York, it's 1885. He's fourteen years old, has maybe two dollars in his pocket. English, he has nothing. No words! Hello, good-bye, yes, no — this is tops! No friends, no relatives. But he knows about this famous Serb, right there in New York. So he goes to see him. Is Tesla, of course! And together, they're speaking Serb. For thirty years, my father's working for Tesla, they're speaking Serb.'

'Wow,' Burke said. 'Were you in New York then?'

Ceplak scoffed at the idea. 'No. I wasn't even born.' He paused, and posed, raising his chin in a noble profile. 'How old you think I am?'

Burke shrugged. 'Eighty?'

344

Ceplak's face fell. 'Yes, this is amazing guess! I am eighty.'

'So your father — '

'He stops working for Tesla in 1915. Bad time. No money. Tesla, by then he's moving from hotel to hotel. Always he's feeding pigeons in his room, always he's being thrown out. My father has job now at Con Edison, okay? And he gives Tesla little salary — just to live on.' He paused. 'Imagine, this great man! He invents everything — alternating current, radio, a hundred patents, plus! He's on cover of *Time* magazine — and he cannot pay hotel bill!' Ceplak shook his head and chuckled to himself. 'Ten years later, I am big surprise to my parents. We come back to Slovenia. End of story.' The old man topped off his vodka. 'Now,' he said, 'these notebooks — where do you want to begin?'

'Actually, I'm not here to see the notebooks,' Burke told him. 'I'm not a scientist. I probably wouldn't understand them.' He paused and corrected himself. 'I mean, I definitely wouldn't understand them.'

Ceplak rubbed his chin between his thumb and forefinger, peered narrowly at Burke. 'Youuuuu . . . are a journalist . . . or a writer. Perhaps, you are writing a book about the maestro, am I right?'

'No,' Burke said, his voice regretful. 'I came to ask you about someone else who was here, someone who *did* come to look at the notebooks. An American — maybe you remember him. A guy named Jack Wilson.'

A look crossed the old man's face, and Burke

tried to read it: distaste or apprehension. Maybe both. 'Yes, he's here,' Ceplak said. 'Long time. He sits where you're sitting. And he's reading. For days, he's reading reading reading. And he's making calculations.'

The old man got to his feet, and walked to the window. Lifting a pair of binoculars to his eyes, he gazed at the lake, and then began to chortle. 'Look at this!' he insisted, handing the binoculars to Burke. 'On the steps, up to the church. For newlyweds, if the husband carries the wife to the top, it's good luck for the marriage. But this poor fellow, he's smaller than me! Better *she* should carry *him*.'

Burke got the couple in view. The man was hunched over, dragging his bride up the steps in a sort of fireman's carry.

Ceplak refilled their glasses. 'Now that,' he said, 'is love!' He handed a glass to Burke, clinked it with his own, then downed his portion in a gulp.

Burke sipped his vodka as Ceplak went to the fire, and added a log. 'You know where Wilson went?' Burke asked.

Ceplak shrugged. 'He says he's going home. So, I guess he goes back to the States.'

'Any idea where?'

The old man shook his head. 'Tell me something,' he said. 'Why you are so interested in this man?'

Burke had a story ready — he'd thought it up on the plane. But he decided it would be simpler to tell the truth. 'We had a business arrangement. It didn't work out.'

346

The old man nodded, knowingly. 'He owes you money.'

Burke shook his head. 'No,' he said, 'it's worse than that. There's trouble with the police.'

'Police?' The old man's face creased with worry. 'He's criminal?'

Burke made a gesture. 'According to the FBI, he's a terrorist.'

Ceplak closed his eyes, put his head in his hand, and massaged his temples. 'You're sure?'

Burke reached for the vodka. 'I'm not sure of anything. All I know is, they shut down my business because of him.'

'And if you can't find him, what happens then?'

'I'll tell the FBI what I *did* find. Then it's up to them.'

Ceplak nodded thoughtfully. After a moment, he said, 'No good.'

Burke looked at him.

'Your FBI,' Ceplak muttered, 'they know Tesla. When he dies, they take his papers.'

'I know,' Burke said. 'I read about that.'

'They come here, it's not good,' Ceplak said.

Burke tried to reassure him. '*You* haven't done anything wrong.'

Ceplak looked worried. 'I think, these FBI, maybe they don't just read. Maybe they take the notebooks.' It could have been the light, but it seemed to Burke that the old man's eyes were wet with tears. 'Better they don't come here,' Ceplak announced. 'Better, *you* find him.'

Burke looked skeptical.

'Maybe I can help,' the old man said.

28

LAKE BLED, SLOVENIA APRIL 14, 2005

'How much do you know about Tesla?' Ceplak asked. They were sitting at the kitchen table, drinking coffee.

'The basic stuff,' Burke told him. 'Croatia, New York, Edison — '

'Yes, yes, of course! But what about his physics? You understand resonant frequencies? Scalar waves?'

Burke chuckled. 'No.'

'The Tunguska incident,' Ceplak said. 'You know what this is, right?'

The word was familiar, but . . . Burke shook his head.

Ceplak took a deep breath. 'Okay,' he said. '*Resonance*. You know word,' Ceplak insisted. 'It's an English word. Please, to tell me what it means.'

Burke thought about it. 'It has to do with sound. The way things vibrate.'

Ceplak squeezed his eyes shut and looked pained. 'This is true, but . . . not just sound. *Energy*.' Across the lake, the bell began to ring. Ceplak turned toward it. 'I guess he made it!' Then he turned back to Burke, and sighed. 'You didn't study physics?'

Burke shook his head. 'Science wasn't my thing.'

'But mathematics?'

Burke nodded. 'A little.'

'How little?'

'Math for Poets.'

Ceplak stared at him.

Burke looked sheepish. 'It was a class for kids who were not so good at math,' he explained.

Ceplak filled his cheeks with air, then released it in a rush. Leaning forward, he placed his elbows on the table and put the palms of his hands together, as if he were going to pray. 'To find Wilson, you need to understand Tesla, okay?'

Burke hoped not.

'Because Wilson, he's doing something with Tesla,' Ceplak said. 'I don't know what. But until you know what he's doing, you won't be able to find him. So, first I'm telling you Tesla is about resonance. This is key to all Tesla's work, okay?'

Burke looked uncertain.

'Don't worry!' Ceplak told him. 'I promise: Physics for Poets!'

'Okay.'

'So here we are: Tesla is manipulating electromagnetic energy — using *resonance*. Now, I ask again, what is this 'resonance'? You guessed it has to do with sound.' Ceplak sighed. 'And you're right, it does, but not only sound. Sound is what? A kind of 'wave.' Correct? Correct! But what is a 'wave'?'

Burke shook his head.

'Think of stone in pond,' Ceplak told him. 'Throw stone in pond, what happens? Waves move out in every direction. What *are* these waves?'

'I — '

'*Energy,*' Ceplak said. 'In the case of stone, impact creates kinetic energy, yes? And we can see this. Water was flat, stone hits, the energy radiates out from center, eventually dissipates on shore, yes?'

Burke nodded.

'Now I am telling you that electromagnetic spectrum — this is *all* waves. Twenty-four/seven, it's waves! X-rays, gamma rays, microwaves, radio waves, infrared waves, light waves — all forms of *energy.* Yes?'

Burke nodded.

'Now, pay attention, Mr. Math for Poets! Now I'm reminding you of quantum theory.'

Burke looked aghast.

'Don't worry,' Ceplak interjected. 'I give you one highlight. That's it. In quantum theory, *everything* is waves. *Energy?* Of course: is waves. But matter, too. Matter is waves.' He squeezed his face into a wince of a smile. 'Well, not 'waves,' exactly. Waves and particles — we might say 'wavicles.' '

Burke reached for the vodka.

Ceplak gave him an approving look. 'Alcohol can help. This table,' he continued, 'it looks solid.' He thumped his hands on the table, so hard that his coffee cup jumped. 'It *is* solid. But inside the molecules of the table, electrons are in motion — so we know table has resonant frequency.'

'Now you've lost me,' Burke declared.

Ceplak pressed his hands together. 'Just to listen, please. Will become clear.' He took a deep

350

breath. 'Every object has special 'resonant frequency.' Excite object, and object vibrates at that frequency.'

'Like a tuning fork,' Burke said. 'You hit it and — '

'Yes! This, exactly. Also a rock, a bridge, a glass, a wall. I don't care what! You give it the right push — maybe you hit it with a bat — it begins to vibrate. Put another way, we say it 'oscillates at its own frequency.' '

'Okay,' Burke told him. 'I get it.'

'Frequency in physics is number of waves per second, right?'

Burke nodded.

'Now 'resonant frequency.' ' Ceplak cleared his throat. 'For this, I give you classic example. Kid's swing. This is a *system* with single resonant frequency.'

Before Burke could say anything, Ceplak held up a hand. 'I explain! Swing is pendulum, yes?'

Burke nodded.

'Okay, suppose man gives swing big push. Swing goes up. Comes back. Goes up again — but not so high. Comes back — but not so far. Goes up . . . You see what's happening. Swing oscillates slower and slower as energy from push dissipates. Okay?'

Burke nodded.

'Now! Suppose man leaves, and swing is pushed by kid's sister. This sister, she's not so strong, she can't push swing so hard. Little person, okay? But even so, if she push swing at right time, swing goes higher and higher. Higher than man with big push, even. Because each little

351

push adds to energy already in system. We say, it 'adds amplitude.' In theory, swing could reach escape velocity, and bye-bye kid.'

' 'In theory,' ' Burke said, getting into the spirit of things. (The vodka was actually quite good.)

'You understand? Little girl can push swing higher and higher, but only if she has perfect timing. She has to be in step with swing's natural frequency. If she pushes when swing is only halfway back, she acts like brake, takes energy out of system, instead of adding to it.' Ceplak paused, and pursed his lips. 'She push too soon, she push off-center, she disrupts swing's natural frequency — and swing cannot oscillate smoothly. This is why we say swing is having only one resonant frequency.'

'Got it.'

'So! Each time, girl is adding a little bit of energy at just the right moment and in just the right spot. Okay?'

Burke nodded.

'Well, Tesla, too! He's doing same thing — amplifying resonant frequency of oscillating system. Just like little girl with swing, he makes precise inputs of energy to system in oscillation. In his case, electromagnetic system, which after these inputs is much more powerful. More energy, yes?' Ceplak smiled. 'Almost all maestro's key inventions based on this.'

Ceplak poured another vodka, and downed it. 'Last half of Tesla's life, he's working on the wireless transmission of electricity. He thinks he finds way to get free energy, using resonant frequency of earth.'

'The *earth* has a resonant frequency?'

Ceplak nodded. 'Think about it. Earth is a bundle of different energies.' He ticked them off on his fingers. 'Thermal energy from core. Gravitation. Plus gravitational pull of moon. Geomagnetic forces. Solar energy from sun. Gamma rays from outer space. Kinetic energy — earth rotating around sun, rotating also on axis.'

Burke nodded.

'Point is, Mother Earth, she's a ball of energy, yes? Tesla believed, and maybe proved, that earth has natural resonant frequency. That earth is producing 'standing waves,' waves that do not progress through space. Like all waves — these are form of energy, yes? And maestro believes that if you are driving blade of conductive metal down into earth, you can tap into that energy.'

'Okay.'

'Maestro thinks he can attract this energy and magnify or amplify it, then send it around globe to peoples everywhere, without power lines.'

'And how was he going to do *that*?' Burke asked.

Ceplak grinned like the Cheshire Cat. He gestured at the photograph of the strange tower. 'The magnifying transmitter! He starts with the standing waves from the earth — and amplifies that energy by adding small bursts of energy at precise right time.'

'But where are the 'small bursts of energy' coming from?'

Ceplak shrugged. 'Ordinary sources — generator using coal or hydropower. The point is,

353

maestro knows how to tap into energy from earth and amplify it — exact same way as girl pushing swing!'

Burke thought about this for a moment, then turned, and nodded toward the mantelpiece. 'The Wardenclyffe Tower — that was to hold this transmitter?'

'Exactly!' Ceplak beamed. 'He builds tower after years of experimenting in Colorado, where he has much smaller, simpler tower. In Colorado Springs, he's creating massive lightning bolts, he's giving electric charge to area for miles around his tower. Lightbulbs glowing even when their switches are off! Sparks coming off metal shoes of horses! Butterflies going around in halos of St. Elmo's fire!'

'Jesus!' Burke exclaimed.

'No! Tesla!' The old man was grinning from ear to ear as he contemplated this back-to-the-future scene in old Colorado. Then he cleared his throat and stretched. 'You hungry? Maybe you'd like something to eat? I'm thinking: Grand Hotel Toplice. Your treat.'

29

At Ceplak's suggestion, they walked. 'It's only three kilometers, we'll earn our lunch!'

Burke nodded, his mind elsewhere. He was thinking that the restaurant would be expensive, that he needed to change his airline reservations, that the trip to Lake Bled was probably a waste of time and money. How could Ceplak's physics and history lessons help him find Jack Wilson?

He followed the old man along a steep path that cut back and forth on the side of a forested hill, his loafers skidding on the packed snow. Ceplak was as nimble and sure-footed as a goat, decked out in hiking boots and armed with a walking stick. The pines around them were flocked with snow, their spiky branches rustling in the wind. Overhead, a cloudless blue vault, the air cold and clean. Burke took it all in with a photographer's eye.

Ceplak paused, and turned. 'I come back to Wardenclyffe,' he said, 'but first, *resonance* or to use another word, *vibration*. This can be destructive, no?'

'Well,' Burke said, 'if there's an earthquake — '

'Yes. Big release of energy, just like rock in pond, seismic waves radiate from epicenter. You feel earthquake sometime?'

'In California.'

'Then you know — you *feel* the oscillation of

the earth beneath you. The earth shudders, yes?'

Burke nodded.

'If shudder too strong, if oscillation too great, structures cannot tolerate. Buildings fall down. Rocks crack and crumble.' Ceplak stopped to toss aside a dead limb that lay in their way across the path. 'The lesson is: Resonance can be destructive. Another example is opera singer with crystal glass. Everybody is knowing this one. Singer with big voice hits note, holds note — glass shatters. Why?'

'Never understood it,' Burke said, hurrying to keep up with the geezer.

'I'm telling you before, sound is *wave*, sound is *energy*. Maybe, sitting drunk sometime, you run wet finger around top of glass. And it sings to you — like Buddhist monk! Ommmmmmm.' Ceplak cackled. 'Let's say tone of glass, its natural resonant frequency is 'F.' Fat lady sings same note — and voice is big enough — glass begin to vibrate. If sound is loud enough, if excitation strong enough — *pow!* Glass breaks.' Ceplak held up a finger. 'Caruso does this many times. Also Birgit Nielsen — soprano. Recording studio, they're telling her *please* to step back from microphone. Why? She's breaking *panes* of glass. Even she shatters gemstone one time! Think emerald. So, why is glass breaking?'

'Vibration,' Burke said.

'Yes. When sound waves from voice create vibration that matches natural resonant frequency of glass, oscillation is *amplified* — yes? Already glass *wants* to vibrate at this frequency, it begins to vibrate, you give it push with more sound wave' — he clapped his hands together — 'structure begins to come apart. It seem crazy that sound is breaking something as solid as glass, but always to remember, 'solid' is illusion. Glass is particles and waves like everything else. Move those waves too fast, excite too much, and glass shatters. Structure fails.'

Burke nodded as Ceplak pushed aside some branches, giving them access to a narrow road. They were still a hundred feet above the lake. Burke could see a plume of smoke rising from the Grand Hotel Toplice.

'Second example of destructive nature of resonance,' Ceplak said. 'Soldiers don't march on bridge. Why? If they march in time, bridge can collapse.'

'I've heard that.'

'Manchester, England, 1831,' Ceplak said. 'Suspension bridge. Soldiers marching in step. Bridge starts to shake. Soldiers don't take physics, they keep marching. Next thing' — his hands dropped in a gesture of collapse — 'all fall down. After Manchester, knowledge comes into military textbooks, into general knowledge.' He tapped a finger to his head. 'Destructive power of resonance. Since Manchester, military types know to teach: Soldiers must break step when they cross bridge. If not, they maybe not getting to other side.'

'Hunh.'

'You know the legend of Jericho?' Ceplak asked.

'The walls came tumbling down.'

'But why?'

'Joshua — ,' Burke began.

' — blows *trumpet!*' Ceplak said with an air of triumph. 'Blows *horn*. Walls of Jericho crashing down because of *sound*. Destructive power of resonance!'

'Right.'

'Okay, so back to Wardenclyffe. Early 1900s. Tesla makes partnership with J. P. Morgan — maybe richest man in world at time. Morgan thinks Wardenclyffe is radio tower, that this is what Tesla is building. Because Tesla, he's inventing radio, too.'

Burke laughed. 'I thought Marconi invented the radio.'

Ceplak wagged his head. 'Marconi gets Nobel Prize, but patents are Tesla's. Supreme Court decision in Tesla's favor.'

'Really?'

'Is true. Look it up! Anyway, Morgan gives Tesla money to build tower on Long Island.'

'And what does Morgan get?' Burke asked.

'Big share in Tesla's wireless patents. For Tesla, he hates to do this, but what choice? Maestro is needing money to build tower. Is big project. One hundred eighty feet tall, big metal bolt one hundred twenty feet into ground. But three years later, Morgan pulls plug because he is finding out this tower it's not for radio waves. Tesla plans to transmit power that he gets from earth. And he want to send it everywhere without wires.'

'But that would be great.'

'For mankind, yes. For Morgan, no. Morgan has big investments in Westinghouse and General Electric. He spends fortune building electric grid

358

— wires, meters, poles. Tesla is telling him we don't need any of this. We get power directly from earth, amplify it, and beam it everywhere. Peoples just need a cheap receiver to . . . *download* the energy.'

'Like radio antennas.'

'Exactly! But for Morgan' — Ceplak tapped his head — 'this new wireless energy is competition to existing business. And he's got big money still to pay off on infrastructure he's built, money that will come from electric bills.' Ceplak inclined his head. 'Business decision. Morgan cuts off further money to maestro.'

'What happened then?' Burke asked.

'Tesla has bright idea. If he can interest new investors, he doesn't need Morgan. So . . . he makes publicity stunt.'

'What kind of stunt?'

'First I'm remembering you that, at turn of century, world is crazy about Arctic exploration,' Ceplak said. 'You can't imagine! These explorers, they are like rock-and-roll astronauts. Famous, glamorous, always in big danger, exciting. They're big celebrities. And when they come back — *if* they come back — books, lectures, interviews. So anyway, Tesla has idea, goes to see his friend Admiral Peary.'

'The explorer?'

'Tesla knew everyone! Edison, Morgan, Peary, Twain. So, it's 1908. Already Peary has tried for the pole twice. He's getting ready for a third attempt, but Tesla can't wait. Maestro needs someone in the Arctic *now*, to witness publicity stunt. So Peary puts Tesla in touch with another explorer, Windjammer Steffannson.'

'Never heard of him.'

'Very, very famous at time. Exclusive deal with *New York Tribune* to follow his travels. Colorful character! He lives four and a half years as an Eskimo! Amazing story. And for maestro, happy coincidence! Windjammer leaving New York soon to start his adventure. So Peary introduces Tesla to Windjammer. And Windjammer agrees — he will be witness to maestro's publicity stunt. On June 30, Windjammer will visit Peary's old camp on Ellesmere Island. And he will watch sky for fantastic demonstration of Tesla's new invention.'

'And what's that?'

Ceplak leaned toward him. '*Fireworks*.'

'What do you mean?'

Before Ceplak could answer, they arrived at the steps to the hotel's terrace. Standing at the top, the maître d' greeted them as if they were prodigal kin, then guided them to a table overlooking the lake.

★ ★ ★

Leather-bound menus were brought, along with a silver bucket of shaved ice from which a bottle of Moët et Chandon leaned at an angle. A red-jacketed waiter filled two crystal flutes, then backed away. Ceplak raised his glass. 'To maestro!' They clinked.

Burke did his best not to look horrified, realizing the obvious: Lunch was going to be very expensive.

For a small and elderly man, Ceplak had a surprisingly large appetite. Burke ordered lake-fish and a salad, but the octogenarian required four courses, not counting a pink sorbet and an *amuse-bouche.*

Ceplak wet the tip of his finger with champagne, then trailed it around the rim of his glass. The glass began to sing. 'E,' Ceplak said with a chuckle.

'What was Tesla going to do with this Windjammer guy?'

'Maestro plans to make most spectacular display of northern lights ever seen. You ever seeing aurora?'

'No.'

'One time only I see,' Ceplak said. 'Is so beautiful.' He touched his chest. 'Makes you believe in God — even though we know the cause.'

'Which is what?'

'Solar wind. When it penetrates magneto-sphere, charged particles collide with particles in atmosphere.' He clapped his hands together. 'Negative particle meets positive particle. Dis-charge of energy! Light!' He sipped his champagne. 'Multiply by billions? This is northern lights.'

'But this Arctic stunt . . . what was Tesla going to do?'

'He was going to bombard ionosphere with charged particles. Billions and billions of them. Make fantastic display — like a god.'

'And he knew how to do this?' Burke asked.

'Of course. What is Tesla working on at this

time? *Wireless transmission of energy.*'

'Yeah. So . . . '

'So he's finding way to transmit energy without conductive wire. How does he do this?' Ceplak raised his eyebrows. 'Beam. Maestro creates beam of energy, beam of photons. From Wardenclyffe, Tesla targets beam for massive release of energy above Ellesmere. Particles hit particles — boom boom boom. *Big* light show for Windjammer, who will say Wow! Amazing! Windjammer will tell *New York Tribune* and investors will come running to maestro's door . . . '

'And it worked?'

Ceplak bobbed his head and shoulders, left to right, as if to say, *Yes and no*. Sipped his champagne. Then wagged a finger. 'First you must see that to create such beam is big accomplishment. Think of flashlight, searchlight, headlight. I'm reminding you that all light is same — stream of photons traveling at speed of light. But shine flashlight through dark and it's going only so far and then beam falls apart. We say 'beam loses coherence.' It loses energy to friction. For beam to reach distant point and retain coherence is almost impossible.'

'But Tesla did it.'

'He finds way to send beam of energy as paired waves in plasmoid sheath. Maestro eliminate friction. This allow beam to reach target with all energy intact.' Ceplak chuckled. 'If I can tell you how he does this, I'm winning Nobel Prize in physics.'

'Really?'

362

'Oh yes. Early days, in New York lab, maestro makes ball lightning many many times. Plenty of peoples witness. Maestro creates to amaze Mark Twain and others — like parlor trick.' Ceplak shook his head ruefully. 'They should have been more amazed.'

'What do you mean?'

Ceplak was effervescent with excitement. '*Because*: This is Holy Grail in plasma physics! To contain energy within stable form! Like ball lightning! Like sheathed beam from Wardenclyffe! This is key to fusion energy — because why?'

Burke shook his head.

'Think, Mr. Math for Poets! Energy escape, you cannot have fusion. Find way to keeping energy in . . . ?' Ceplak smiled. 'Nobel Prize. Hundred percent.'

'So Tesla didn't leave notes about this?'

Ceplak shrugged. 'FBI confiscates most of maestro's papers and put where? *Los Alamos!* I am sure scientists study maestro's notes. But no one figuring out how to do what he did with ball lightning or energy beam. Not yet.'

'I still don't understand the publicity stunt,' Burke confessed. 'Why would setting off a big display of northern lights in the Arctic interest anyone? What would it mean?'

Ceplak tapped his fingers on the table. 'Would mean that maestro could send and release a huge burst of energy — *without wire*. Peoples would understand that fireworks in sky were big discharge of power. If that power can be *downloaded* . . . ' The old man's hands opened wide, like a magician presenting an amazing trick.

Burke nodded. 'So this publicity stunt — it must have been huge . . . '

Ceplak shook his head. He looked somber. 'No! Stunt does not work. Is disaster.'

Burke blinked. *After all that . . . ?* 'It failed?'

'Not just *fail.*' A sigh. 'Please to listen, yes? I tell you what happened when maestro fires his beam. This is what your friend is interested in.'

'My 'friend' . . . '

'Yes. Wilson. He's interested in Tunguska.'

There it was again.

'This is what Jack Wilson studies,' Ceplak said. 'Tunguska, the beam, the publicity stunt.' Ceplak patted his lips with his napkin and leaned toward Burke. 'It's June 30, 1908. Nine thirty p.m., Eastern Standard Time. Tesla is at Wardenclyffe with my father. By now, maestro is broke. Money from Morgan all gone. Maestro having to borrow coal to start generator — this is how bad things are. The two of them climb tower. Maestro activates transmitter, aims beam at upper atmosphere, for release point west of Ellesmere Island. Same time, Windjammer is outside his igloo, looking at sky, waiting and watching.'

Ceplak took a long sip of water, and continued: 'My father's notebooks say at first they are not even sure beam is working. He and maestro, all they see is dim light. Then, there is owl flying into path of beam and . . . *pooof* . . . owl is gone. According to my father's notes, bird *vanishes.* After that, they switch beam

364

off. So, this is big disappointment. They see nothing. They hear nothing. Just . . . they are missing one owl.'

'And that's it?'

'At first. Tesla watches newspapers, because this light show should be big phenomenon in Europe. Windjammer is just *special* witness, yes? Windjammer has best view, and he knows in advance — so he can attest that this is caused by Tesla, that at nine thirty p.m., Eastern Standard Time, *exactly* comes promised show in sky.' He shook his head. 'But . . . nothing in papers. Then coming word from Windjammer — this takes few days — also sees nothing.'

'Nothing. So it — '

With a stern expression, Ceplak held up his hand like a traffic cop's. 'Couple days later, maestro happen to read about Tunguska.' The old man shook his head, knowingly.

'Which is what?' Burke asked.

Ceplak frowned. 'Tunguska is place in Siberia!' A little mirthless laugh. '*Was* a place. June 30, 1908, nine thirty p.m., Eastern Standard Time, explosion in Tunguska destroy half a million acres of pine forest. Everything leveled! Power of event is equal to fifteen megatons of TNT!' Ceplak peered at Burke, waiting for a reaction.

Finally, Burke said, 'Which is a lot. Especially back then.'

'Back then?!' the little man roared. 'A lot? This is stronger than Hiroshima! This is strongest explosion in history — *to this day*.'

'You're telling me this actually happened?'

Ceplak smiled. 'Google it.'

Ceplak delicately removed bones from his fish, forking morsels into his mouth. He patted his lips. 'So, maestro intends to create spectacular display of northern lights. Instead, he blows up big patch of Siberia. Reindeer, voles, birds, so on, trees — and also some people, nomadic herders living there.' He shook his head. 'Gone from face of earth.'

Burke said nothing.

Across from him, the old man sighed. 'So we are talking about big problems. One, power of beam in excess of maestro's prediction. Plus *two*, targeting.' He wagged his head. 'Targeting needs major work. Maestro is off by two thousand miles.'

'I can't believe I've never heard of this,' Burke said.

Ceplak shook his head. 'Is hundred years ago! Middle of nowhere! Much, *much* speculation about event at time. What *was* it? People hear explosion hundreds — maybe even *thousand* — miles away. Reporters from Tomsk go to see what happened. Is complete destruction! No one ever seeing anything like this. Is huge area. Trees, grass, animals — all gone. *Evaporated.*'

'And did people connect it to Tesla?' Burke asked.

'No,' Ceplak replied. 'He is by then marginal figure, eccentric, maybe a little crazy. And he does not step forward to take credit. He is horrified.'

'So how did they explain it?' Burke asked. 'The reporters.'

366

Ceplak shrugged. 'Scientists say maybe meteorite is hitting earth.'

'That's what I'd say.'

'Yes, except no impact crater. And core samples down to forty meters show zero nickel, iron, stone. These are components of all meteorites, so . . . theory number one goes out window and we get new one.'

'Which is what?'

'Since it can't be meteorite, scientists decide it must be part of comet.'

Burke nodded.

Ceplak shook his head. 'Can't be comet.'

'Why not?'

'Because astronomers don't *have* comet in vicinity. Plus, no one seeing it. No fiery mass falling from sky. Many many many . . . *hundreds* of witnesses report hearing explosion — but no one sees fireball? This is . . . not reasonable.' Ceplak shook his head and smiled. 'So! When all reasonable explanations fail, we are left with Tesla! June 30, 1908, nine thirty p.m., Eastern Standard Time, he launches his beam and at this exact time — because beam is traveling at speed of light, yes? At this exact time, on other side of the world, destruction of Tunguska.'

'Like the owl.'

'Yes. I am sure, my father was sure, Tesla was sure! He was responsible for Tunguska. Destructive power of resonance! And maestro is obsessed with this for rest of life.'

'Amazing.'

'Amazing that he does not try to exploit it. You can imagine the military interest.'

Burke nodded, but Ceplak knew that he didn't really get it because the old man leaned forward and spoke in a voice full of intensity. 'Not just destructive potential as weapon. Think, Mr. Math for Poets! Beam travels at speed of light, yes?'

Burke nodded.

'Powerful beam arrive to target at same time sent!' Ceplak said. 'How do you stop? How do you intercept? You understand there is no defense against this.' The old man folded his hands together.

'They would have thrown a fortune at him,' Burke said.

Ceplak held up his finger. 'Of course, Tesla is pacifist.'

By now, Ceplak was devouring a crème brûlée. Burke stared out at the lake, distracted. A wind stirred the new-fallen snow into white dervishes. Burke was thinking that, as interesting as all this was, an explosion in the wilderness nearly a hundred years ago, some marginal notations in some dusty notebooks held hostage by a lonely old man . . . How was any of this going to help Tommy Aherne — *his* lonely old man?

Across the lake, the wishing bell began to toll.

'Anyway,' Ceplak said, 'Tesla returned to this work for years, trying to find out where he goes wrong. He thinks he makes error in calculations of electrogravitational field. Many notations in my father's notebooks.'

'Did he ever test it again?'

Ceplak shrugged. 'I think he never has chance. After Tunguska, he dismantles transmitter. Works on equations, works on focusing mechanism in lab — but no money to rebuild. No money for anything. In 1917, tower at Wardenclyffe torn down for salvage.'

Burke nodded distractedly. *No more money for anything.* He was thinking about the bill for lunch.

'But your friend,' Ceplak said, his voice sharp and loud. 'I think, maybe Jack Wilson figures it out.'

'Figures what out?'

Ceplak didn't answer. 'He's here with me for twelve days. He studies notebooks in chronological order, starting in 1902. So he follows maestro's thinking. But, mostly he's looking at 1907, 1908, 1909, 1910. He reads other notebooks, yes, but these four are always in front of him on table. These four concern transmitter and corrections for targeting of beam.'

'Okay.'

Ceplak put down his spoon. 'I think Jack Wilson wants to build transmitter. Not to give free power to peoples, no. To build as *weapon*. He looks through notebooks for some little piece of data he's missing.'

'You think he found what he was looking for?

'Yes. On last day, he is so happy. He hug me, for real — not his way at all. And he's saying . . . ''it's time to dance.'' Ceplak raised his eyebrows. 'I ask what this means, but he doesn't explain.'

They were quiet for a moment.

'You think he's capable of building this thing?'

Ceplak expelled a soft puff of air, then met

Burke's eyes. 'I'm teacher, okay? My gifts? . . . they are limited. I can't judge who is capable of doing what in physics. Wilson is smart? Yes. Hard worker? Yes. Spent *lot* of time on beam equations? Yes. Could Jack Wilson build?' A pause. '*Maybe*. But I tell myself — *pffft* — not to worry.'

'Why?'

'I don't think he has resources to do something! He . . . ' Ceplak frowned, shrugged. 'He brings me cheap bottle of wine! He's not staying at Toplice. He stays at *cheap* hotel. He eats pizza pizza pizza. He's not having funds, this is clear. So, I take him for just another Tesla junkie with big ideas. He will write article on Internet about Tesla beam weapon and that is it. But then you come, you tell me — Wilson, suddenly he's rich person. And terrorist!'

Burke shrugged. 'That's what the FBI said, but you have to wonder. It's not like they really *pursued* this. I mean, Jesus, they didn't even find *you*.'

Ceplak leaned forward. 'Yes, but . . . maybe you're right. Maybe this is big exaggeration of your security services. Maybe they are playing game we don't know, but . . . I think you better find him.'

'Yeah, well, I'm doing my best,' Burke said, thinking *This is insane*.

Once he told Kovalenko what he'd learned, that a crazy ex-con from Stanford was planning to do God knows what with a 100-year-old 'invention' that never worked in the first place — or never worked properly — it was all over.

However you looked at it, Thomas Aherne & Associates would not be reopening anytime soon.

'Best is not good enough,' Ceplak said. The expression in the old man's eyes was grave. 'Tunguska was half million acres in Siberia. Pine trees, reindeer, a few nomads. But . . . ' His voice trailed away.

'But what?' Burke asked.

'I'm asking you: How big is Manhattan?'

30

JUNIPER, NEVADA APRIL 29, 2005

Wilson found it on the Internet, two weeks after he arrived in the States from Liechtenstein.

'A little piece of Paradise,' the B-Lazy-B was embedded in the Humboldt-Toiyabe National Forest, a discontinuous conglomerate of California and Nevada lands, comprising a vast wilderness of mountains and deserts, forests and meadows.

The ranch — its emblem consisting of one 'B' standing at attention, and the second 'B' snoozing on its back — had been created as a religious retreat in 1921. A back-to-nature movement had captured the imagination of Americans, who were beginning to question the direction in which industrialization was leading them. The wilderness was suddenly seen as a place where spiritual and physical renewal might be found.

With its big main house and a dozen spartan cabins, it had housed generations of Baptists on retreat. All was well until the 1940s, when the sect's accounts were looted by an evangelist with a green eyeshade, who then disappeared in the direction of Brazil. The bank foreclosed, and the retreat was sold to a Russian émigré, who'd always dreamed of owning a dude ranch.

With the dudes came electricity, and against all odds, both the ranch and the émigré prospered for years. A fifteen-hundred-watt diesel generator was brought in to eliminate the inconvenience of frequent power outages. To accommodate the generator and provide for the ranch's use in winter, underground storage tanks were installed to hold fuel and propane.

Eventually, the émigré suffered a midlife crisis, and decamped for Key West.

Soon afterward, the B-Lazy-B was sold to a dotcom mogul, who spent a small fortune refitting the rustic main house with Arts & Craft fixtures, Sub-Zero appliances, and a Viking stove. A tennis court was put in next to the bunkhouse, which now sported Poggenpohl cabinets and a glass-and-marble shower. Even the hot springs were gussied up, transformed from a single bubbling pool to a stone-lined spa, consisting of three smaller pools whose temperatures ranged from cool to very hot.

Once again, all was well until the NASDAQ crashed in 2001. Suddenly incompatible, the mogul and his much younger wife parted ways, and the ranch went up for sale. Unhappily for the mogul, it did not prove to be an easy sell. The dudes and the Baptists were long gone, as were a lot of millionaires who might have been interested in the ranch as a 'collectible.'

In their absence, the B-Lazy-B came to be seen for what it was — which was 'almost impossible to get to.' Though it had a helipad, it did not have a runway. To reach it, one needed a helicopter, a horse, or an off-road pickup truck with two spare tires and a winch. Even then, you really had to want to get there. From the nearest town, the B-Lazy-B was a bone-rattling forty-five-mile journey over dirt roads that twisted through the middle of nowhere to the far edge of that same place.

The ranch remained on the block for nearly two years, its asking price dwindling from four to three to two million dollars. Eventually, Wilson bought it for a million-six, putting ten percent down and arranging a mortgage with the same bank that held his shares of Roche.

No sooner was the ink dry on the contract than he began to lay in supplies, including enough propane to keep him warm for years, and enough diesel to run the generators — a collection of models, all built before 1975 — nonstop until the Rapture. An air cargo company, based in Sparks, delivered most of what he needed, including massive spools of electrical cable and bundles of iron rebar.

Not surprisingly, people began to talk. Specifically, they began to talk in the Bucket of Blood Saloon 'in nearby Juniper,' some sixty-three miles away. Seated around a card table playing Hold 'Em, a posse of locals chased shots of whiskey with glasses of beer. An aging hippie prospector, who called himself 'the Bat,' was the first to raise the issue: 'Whut the fuck's he doin' up there?'

The cowboy in the next chair, who happened to be a fan of singer Tom Waits, grinned. 'Yeah, what's he *building* up there?' The allusion went unnoticed.

Standing at the bar, a Ufologist named Vaughn Stein, who'd driven down from Provo looking for what he called 'Area 52,' chuckled knowingly. 'I heard he's one of them dudes that stares at goats.'

The Bat frowned. 'Say whut?'

'At Fort Bragg?' the Ufologist said. 'They kill goats, just by starin' at 'em.'

Groans of skepticism rose up.

In a corner of the saloon, a fertilizer salesman called 'Pilgrim' was feeding quarters into a slot, and pulling away at the arm. 'Bullshit!' he cried, without turning his head or breaking his rhythm. 'If that guy's doing anything, he's mining. Probably found himself a lode of silver — '

'Or uranium,' the Bat suggested. 'What I hear — '

'You don't hear shit,' said the bartender, pouring himself a shot of Drambuie. 'His name's Wilson, and he isn't doing any mining.'

The card players turned. When the bartender talked, they listened. He was a sensitive man who sometimes closed early if he sensed that people were ignoring him.

'Well, if he's not mining, what's he up to?' the Bat demanded.

The bartender smacked his lips. 'Well,' he said, 'he's like, an eccentric.'

The Bat gave him a raspberry, as if to say, *Tell us something we don't know.*

'Got himself some vintage motorcycles,' the bartender went on. 'Couple of Indians . . . one of them Norton Shadows.'

'That's a *hobby*,' the Ufologist declared. 'That doesn't tell us what he's *doing*!'

The bartender looked at him. 'Ain't no secret,' he announced. 'He's stargazing.'

Pilgrim froze. With an exaggerated look of incomprehension, he turned from the one-armed bandit and said, 'He's what?'

The bartender rubbed the bar in front of him with a dirty cloth. After a moment, he looked up. 'I was talkin' to Chopper Charley? Down in Sparks?'

'The helicopter guy,' said the Bat.

'Right,' said the bartender.

'He's crazy as shit,' von Stein laughed.

'Be that as it may,' the bartender told them, '*he* tells *me* he's flyin' in all *kinds* of crap to that ranch.'

'Like what?' the Ufologist asked, his voice thick with suspicion.

'Rebar, springs — '

'*Springs?*' Pilgrim asked. 'You mean like . . . spring springs?'

The bartender nodded. 'Big ones. Industrial ones, size of fifty-five-gallon cans.'

'What the fuck's he gonna do with that?' the Bat demanded.

'I already told you,' the bartender replied. 'It's for stargazin'.' By now, his customers were staring at him. None of them knew what he was talking about, which was just the way he liked it. Finally, the bartender heaved a sigh, and explained: 'That's why he's out here.' With a nod toward the ceiling, which was yellow with the accreted smoke of a million cigarettes, he said, 'No light pollution. On account of we're so remote.'

'But — '

'He's gettin' a telescope. Told Charley all about it. Not some rinkydink job, like you'd use for peepin'. This thing's some kinda Wernher Von Braun model. Got a forty-inch mirror, or somethin'.'

'What are you talking about?' the Ufologist complained.

'I'm just telling you what Charley told me.'

'And what's any of that got to do with *springs*?' the Bat asked.

The bartender sighed for a second time, letting them know that their obtuseness was trying his genius — and his patience. 'If you're lookin' at stars and galaxies and shit, you gotta have a stable foundation, or you ain't gonna see fuck-all. Any kinda disturbance — I don't care if a truck goes by or a mouse farts — that's it! Whatever you were lookin' at, you lost it! One second you're starin' at the Big Dipper, then the mouse cuts loose and you're lost in space, my friend. Lost. In. Space! Scope's shaking all over the place.'

'I still don't know what the springs are for,' the Bat said, sounding exasperated.

The bartender shook his head. His customers were the cross he bore. 'Let me spell it out for you,' he told them. 'He's jackin' up the lookout tower, and puttin' it on springs. So there's no vibration. It's like a private observatory.'

The Ufologist's eyes dilated with excitement. 'I knew it! It's like the embassy in Moscow! The spooks got a special room there. Put it on springs? That way, no one can eavesdrop on them.' He paused. 'Well, they *can*,' he said, 'but they can't hear anything. On account of there's no vibration. This guy, Wilson, he's probably some kind of spook himself.'

The poker players looked at one other, eyebrows raised.

The bartender lifted his glass. '*Klaatu verada nikto*, my man.'

★　★　★

It was a busy time for Wilson.

On a weekend trip into Reno, he put together a work crew of Mexican migrants, day laborers who waited with others each morning in the parking lot outside a 7-Eleven, making themselves available for work. There were four of them, and they didn't mind living in the wilderness for a few weeks, if the pay was right. And it was.

Meanwhile, he bought short-term supplies for himself, and a lot of things for the future: tires and seeds and freeze-dried foods. Tools and deep-cycle batteries, clothing, books, and staples. Flour, rice, and redundant systems for purifying water.

Outside the Busted Flush Casino, he found a whore pacing back and forth on the street corner. She was asking fifty bucks for a trick, but he gave her a hundred to introduce him to 'a writing doctor.' Two hours later, he had prescriptions for Percocet and Cipro, Valium, and half a dozen other drugs. Anything else he needed, he could buy over-the-counter.

378

What he couldn't bring in by truck was delivered by helicopter. Beside the cable, rebar, and storage tanks, he flew in a truckload of lumber, along with a pile of solar panels that might come in handy someday.

Guns were a bigger challenge. Because of his felony conviction, the Guns 'R' Us store in Reno was out. But this was more of an inconvenience than a deal breaker. He found an over-and-under shotgun, a Glock, and a Beretta at a Sunday-morning gun show in the Yerington High School gym. Even better, a classified ad in the Pahrump Valley *Times* offered an Ingram submachine gun ('barely used'). He didn't hesitate. These few weapons should be enough, he thought, to keep intruders at bay in the early days. After that, it wouldn't matter.

As for the house, he had a check-off list. Before *the* day he had to cut it off from the grid and make certain that his collection of generators were not even close to anything that might carry a charge.

The most important aspect of the B-Lazy-B, aside from its remoteness, was its proximity to a fire-lookout tower built by the Civilian Conservation Corps in the 1930s. Nine out of ten such towers had been torn down over the years, but in the late 1990s, preservationists acted to save the ones still standing. A lot of them had been restored and were actually available for rent — although only the adventurous were likely to be interested. Most lacked plumbing and running water, and staying in one was like staying in a lighthouse. You had to enjoy stairs.

Half a mile from the ranch house, Little Mount Baker Outlook was one of the last towers on the restoration list. Unlike some of the other towers, the cab atop Little Mount Baker had no amenities. Those who'd manned it had stayed in a wooden cabin (now tumbled down), a hundred yards away.

It was a world apart from the structure that Tesla had built at Wardenclyffe with J. P. Morgan's money. But at an elevation of seventy-two hundred feet, it had clear sightlines in every direction, and was almost perfectly suited to Wilson's purposes.

The weapon, as Wilson thought of it, wasn't a problem in and of itself. Tesla had built something very much like it more than a hundred years ago, and *he* hadn't had the Internet to help him. In effect, the Serb had had to invent or build from scratch what Wilson could buy with the click of a mouse from an electronics warehouse in Canada.

The problem was the lookout tower.

For the tower to serve its purpose, three things were necessary. At Wardenclyffe, Tesla had sunk a blade of metal 128 feet into the earth to capture the 'standing waves' of electricity that he needed for the magnifying transmitter. Wilson accomplished the same end with the help of a one-man show known as the Black Mountain Drilling Company.

Against the advice of its proprietor, Wilson suggested that he drill for water at a site directly beside the tower. The well man objected. 'There ain't no water there,' he said, 'or if there is, it's deep. And it's under a whole lot of ledge. Why don't we just — '

Wilson insisted. It was *his* money.

The well man complied. Over the course of a week, he broke five bits, cursing explosively each time. Wilson was terrified that he was about to strike water, and let him go as soon as he reached 130 feet. 'I gotta rethink this,' Wilson explained, paying him generously for his time and effort and all the broken bits.

With the shaft bored, Wilson arranged delivery of a truckload of custom-forged iron rods, each five feet long and four inches thick. One by one, he and the work crew lowered the rods into the recently bored hole, using gravity to create the conductive metal shaft that he required.

This done, Wilson supervised the Mexicans in spooling the cable from the generator to the base of the tower, half a mile away.

The third task was hardest of all. The tower — and, in particular, the cab at the top — had to be stabilized. This is where Tesla had an advantage. Stanford White was one of the great architects of his time. Taking Tesla at his word when the inventor insisted that the structure must be steady as a rock, White designed the Wardenclyffe tower in such a way as to make it as stable as an observatory.

Like Philippe Petit, the French aerialist who walked a wire between the World Trade Centers in 1974, White understood the problems of torsion and sway. As did Wilson. Any motion at all would derange the beam.

Like the dome on the Wardenclyffe tower, the

cabin atop Wilson's lookout rested on an open framework. With the Mexicans doing the heavy lifting, Wilson reinforced the framework with I-beams made of steel, and installed pressure transducers. Hooked up to a computer, the transducers tracked changes in pressure in the tower's framework. This allowed Wilson to pinpoint the places for damping mechanisms. Tuned to the resonant frequency of the tower, the dampers went a long way toward stabilizing the structure under the cabin.

To render the cabin itself motionless, Wilson rebuilt it as a 'floating room,' reseating the structure on an array of helically shaped compression springs weighing ninety pounds each. Like the iron rods, the springs were custom-made. With the dampers in place, the cabin was, for all intents and purposes, independently suspended within the framework of the tower.

The Mexicans had no idea what he was up to, nor did they care. They thought he was loco, and that was fine with Wilson. When the work was done, he paid them off in cash, and bought them tickets to L.A. The farther they were from the ranch, the better he liked it.

The one person who worried him was the helicopter pilot. A ponytailed Vietnam veteran with the gray teeth of a meth addict, Chopper Charley was as necessary as his curiosity was worrisome. 'Whatcha gonna do with *that*?' 'Damn! that's a lot of cable.' 'Lookit them springs! Why do you need . . . ?'

Wilson thought about arranging an accident.

382

It wouldn't be hard, but he hesitated to do it. Even the most transparent 'accident' would attract attention. The police would come to the ranch, asking questions, and almost anything could happen after that.

The solution came to Wilson one night when he was sitting on the porch of the main house, looking up at the stars, and thinking about Irina. The next day, he ordered a twelve-inch refractor telescope from a company in Texas, and arranged for Chopper Charley to deliver it. They unpacked the scope together, and the pilot was suitably impressed by Wilson's eccentric intent. And he was delighted when Wilson promised to invite him to 'a star-party, just as soon as I get the tower stabilized.'

Meanwhile, he set about building the weapons. The big one had been trucked in pieces to the lookout tower and hoisted up to the platform before he could even begin to assemble it. It was coming along, and its smaller mobile counterpart was actually ready.

The portable weapon was needed for tests, to ensure that he'd solved Tesla's focusing problems. Just like the large one, the weapon itself had posed no challenges. Again, the issue was vibration and stability, providing it with a suitable base.

Toward this end, he bought a Cadillac Escalade (the pickup version, with the shortbed) and installed an array of special shock absorbers and damping mechanisms. The changes made the truck even heavier, so that it handled like a pig. But it worked well enough for his purposes.

Although the online topo maps were helpful, target selection was a problem that couldn't really be solved until he went to the sites with a GPS. He'd purchased a Garmin watch for just that purpose. It had a built-in GPS system, so he could take readings unobtrusively.

He had a hierarchy of 'small targets,' headed by Joe Sozio, the U.S. attorney for the Northern District of California. But he didn't want to start with them. That would be like eating dessert before the main course.

The Patent Office was an obvious candidate for his tests, but the impact of the exercise might not be widely reported. The Patent Office was a bit like a tree falling in the forest. If nobody saw it fall and nobody heard it, what was the point? The New York Stock Exchange was a better choice in terms of impact, but its location was problematical. The sightlines would be terrible. Ditto the chances of getting away in the traffic.

He considered knocking out a satellite, but rejected the idea. For one thing, he wasn't sure he could do it. For another, the incident might not be publicly reported. Then, too, he didn't want to interfere with airline traffic before Irina arrived.

Yet another target, and a tempting one, was the Church of Latter-Day Saints — the Mormon Temple. For one thing, it was close, a straight shot, maybe four hundred miles east on the loneliest road in the world. More to the point, he had a grudge with the Mormons: They'd all but run the Paiutes off their traditional lands. It would be wonderful and fitting to trash the genealogical archives that were the Church's bedrock. But it wouldn't have much of an impact. Mormon researchers would be inconvenienced, and forced to work with paper until the records were restored. That would lead to fewer baptisms in the short run, but if you weren't a Mormon, why would you care? Wilson didn't.

That left SWIFT.

This was the acronym by which the Society for Worldwide Interbank Financial Telecommunication was known. A nearly invisible enterprise of massive import, SWIFT linked about 8,000 financial institutions in 194 countries, processing messages among them involving transactions adding up to more than six trillion dollars per day. And it wasn't in New York.

It was in Culpeper, Virginia, a sleepy town in the shadow of the Blue Ridge Mountains. Even better, Culpeper would be a twofer, because another important financial institution was located there — the so-called Culpeper Switch, the central node in the U.S. Federal Reserve banking system. Why these two important institutions had chosen such an obscure place to call home was a mystery. But it was a bonus for him. More buck for the bang, you might say.

He was guessing that in Culpeper, sightlines would prove no problem, and what's more, he'd be using the weapon in the same way he intended to use it on June 22.

It was fun to think about where to strike. The beam was flexible, and he hadn't decided exactly what degree of damage to inflict. Certainly, he didn't want to create a new Tunguska — not

385

with these targets. That would draw too much attention, too soon. Ideally, the tests should be less than catastrophic, a little ambiguous, even a bit subtle. Let people wonder: Was this an accident? Some kind of natural occurrence — or what? How had it happened? Once he deployed the weapon in the tower, everything would come apart at the seams — and America would know that it was under attack. Or had been. Because, by then, the war would be over. And there would be nothing subtle about it. (Nor would there be anything subtle about what was going to happen to Robbie Maddox. But that was different. That was personal.)

All of the hard physical work had transformed Wilson's body. After two months at the B-Lazy-B, he was ripped. A healthy diet, along with the lifting and climbing and hauling, had turned his body hard. He'd never been this fit, not when he was running track and playing ball — not even when he was lifting weights in Allenwood.

It was a good time. Moving from one thermal pool to another at the end of the day, it occurred to Wilson that in many ways he'd never been happier. Lying back in the water, he luxuriated in its heat, the air on his face crisp and cold, redolent of pine and sulfur. Looking up through a canopy of trees, he saw a jet sliding silently across the sky, heading west — and the future flashed before his eyes, like so much spatter. Because, of course, it was going to be an abattoir. There was no way around it. He was an instrument of the past. Nothing more, and nothing less — the fulfillment of a prophecy.

He had been named for the man who created the Ghost Dance. At least, that's what he'd been told. He'd never lived on a reservation himself, though Mandy had taken him to a few, insisting that he should be proud of his heritage — but that was wishful thinking. Until he'd gone to prison, he'd more or less seen his Indian identity as something to overcome, a stigma.

Mandy had to drag him to the one ritual that truly made an impression on him — the reenactment of the Sun Dance. At the time he'd complained about it. Getting up at dawn? Watching a bunch of old men sing and dance? But to his surprise, something about waiting in the cold and dark, something about the solemn anticipation in the midst of so many others who looked like him, had been a powerful and exhilarating experience.

It seemed as if he'd been almost ready to claim his cultural inheritance — but a few weeks afterward his life came apart and the opportunity was lost. The State took him away from Mandy, and he got caught up in trying to survive at his new foster home, with its God-squad parents and seven foster siblings. The closest he got to the Sun Dance again was to write a paper about it.

Until he'd gone to prison, 'Jack Wilson' was just a name, a nod to history — like George Washington or Martin Luther King.

This changed once he found himself behind bars, stripped of his invention and his future. Then he realized there was a reason for the name: He was the reincarnation of Jack Wilson. He was the Ghost Dancer.

Suddenly, he understood that what happened to him wasn't an aberration. It was a logical extension of the earlier genocide of Native Americans. Wilson's imprisonment was inevitable. If anything, he thought, he was doubly doomed — once for his heritage, and again for his genius. Because, of course, the invasion had long since turned in upon itself, so that the whites were now devouring their best and brightest. Ayn Rand had taught him that.

Lying in the water with his eyes closed, wearing only the ghost shirt that was his skin, it occurred to Wilson that if revenge is a dish that's best served cold, after ten years — *a hundred years! two hundred years!* — the temperature should be about perfect.

31

LONDON MAY 15, 2005

Mike Burke stood by himself in a rainy breeze on the corner of South Audley Street and Grosvenor Square, watching a door at the side of the U.S. embassy. The day before, he'd seen a flood of workers pour out that door at the end of the day, avoiding the public entrance at the front. So he guessed this was the exit that Kovalenko would use.

It was almost five o'clock, and Burke had already been there for more than an hour. It would have been easier, of course, to wait outside the FBI agent's apartment. It was probably somewhere around here, or over in Knightsbridge. But Kovalenko wasn't listed in the telephone book or in any of the online directories Burke tried. To get an address, Burke would have to hire an investigator or sweet-talk someone who had access to the embassy's internal directories. That would take a while, and he didn't have the time.

So here he was, getting wet.

The line in front of the embassy snaked halfway around the block, organized by an airport-style rope-and-pole system. The queue was remarkably patient, almost docile, under a conga line of umbrellas. It was like a temporary village, linked to the outside world via dozens of cell phones. People were eating and playing cards, talking, reading, and changing diapers. Every so often, someone would dart around the block to use the facilities, then jog back to thank whoever it was that saved his place in line.

The day before, Burke had waited three hours to see Kovalenko, only to learn that the Legat was unable to 'fit him in.' The soonest an appointment could be arranged, he was told, was in three weeks.

Three weeks! Meanwhile, Aherne & Associates would remain shuttered, the information about Wilson would go nowhere, and the old man would probably finish the job of drinking himself to death.

Burke had returned from his travels to Belgrade and Ljubljana to find Kate's father wallowing in self-pity. 'I'm like a clock that you wind with a spring,' he said with a chuckle, 'and I can feel myself winding down . . . ' Lest Burke didn't get the point, he repeated the phrase with a raised eyebrow: '*Winding down*.' Burke hadn't been gone for more than a week, but in that week Tommy had reached a point where sobriety was a foreign state. He'd taken to having an eye-opener with his morning coffee, which was a bit like kick-starting a Harley. Most afternoons, he had to be escorted home by one of his friends.

The way Burke saw it, a meeting with Kovalenko was urgent, regardless of any threat Wilson might pose.

From where he stood, Burke made repeated

calls from his cell phone to the embassy, asking to speak with the Legat. Each time, he was told that Mr. Kovalenko was in conference, or 'away from his desk,' or simply not taking calls. Each time, Burke left a message, assuring the assistant that his business was urgent.

But nothing happened.

If it had been up to Tommy, that would have been the end of it. The old man was of the firm opinion that they should leave the matter to the Irish courts. Their solicitor was confident that Aherne & Associates would prevail, since they'd done nothing wrong. But it might take a while for the case to be heard.

'How long?' Burke had asked.

'With luck,' the solicitor replied, 'we should be on the docket by the end of June.'

'*June!*' Burke and Tommy shouted in unison.

The solicitor had winced. 'Or July.'

Which was why Burke was standing in a flying drizzle outside the embassy. He'd waited and waited, and called and called. Now, he was stalking the sonofabitch.

He'd met Kovalenko only once — at the 'interview' in the Garda's office. But he'd recognize him in an instant. The doughy face, the purselike mouth, the piggy little eyes . . . Time after time, he thought he saw the G-man coming out. But it was always someone else.

Surveillance was an odd business. It was deeply boring, except when it wasn't, and then it was pure adrenaline. It required the same kind of unfocused attention that long drives demanded.

You had to be there and not be there at the same time. Like Schrodinger's cat.

Burke was beginning to feel conspicuous. It was only a matter of time before a marine guard or a bobby would ask him what he was doing there.

To this worry was added the fear that he might have missed his quarry, that Kovalenko had exited through another door. There must be a parking lot somewhere, behind the building or underground. Maybe Kovalenko had a car, in which case Burke might never see him. He'd almost talked himself into giving up, when Kovalenko came around the corner.

Burke was pretty good at spotting cops. There was something about the way they held themselves, the way they walked. And Kovalenko might as well have been wearing a uniform. In a sense, he *was* wearing a uniform. His hair was actually *combed*, and combed in a way that the comb's teethmarks were embalmed in gel. He wore the regulation Dick Tracy suit, blue shirt, and striped tie. In his right hand, just below the requisite Rolex, was a shining black attaché case. His stride was that of a man who was privileged to carry a gun in a country that despised them.

Burke followed him around the corner and into the Nightingale Arms, a small pub that was all mahogany and cut glass. The place was crowded and smoky, with a mix of young men talking equities and Bond Street shop girls being beautiful.

People were two deep at the bar, where Kovalenko stood. Burke watched him catch the bartender's eye. Money changed hands and, a moment later, the Legat held a glass of red wine. It was obvious from the interchange that Kovalenko was a regular. He probably came here every night after work.

The FBI agent sat down on a banquette at a small table in the corner, next to a young couple staring into each other's eyes over pints of lager. Burke touched a chair no one was using.

'Okay if I sit here?'

Kovalenko made a magnanimous gesture: *Be my guest.*

It annoyed Burke that the G-man did not recognize him, but sat where he was, studying his nails. Which, Burke saw, were neatly manicured.

The crowd was a roar around them, the noise rising and falling like a chorus of cicadas in late summer. Inexplicable crescendoes and fades.

Burke leaned forward. 'I followed you here,' he said.

Kovalenko's eyebrows knitted together. He must have misunderstood. Leaning toward Burke, he cocked his head to the side, the better to hear. 'Sorry?'

Burke got up from his seat, and squeezed onto the banquette next to Kovalenko, who suddenly found himself boxed in. 'I followed you here,' Burke repeated.

Kovalenko blinked. Frowned. His eyes jumped left and right, then came to rest on Burke's hands. Seeing them on the table, the Legat seemed relieved. 'Why did you do that?'

Burke shook his head, and chuckled bitterly. 'You don't even remember who I am, do you?'

Kovalenko lifted his glass. Took a sip. Set it back down. He looked Burke up and down. Then he chuckled. 'Dublin,' he said.

'Right.'

'You're the Ayn Rand guy. It's Burke, right?'

'Right.'

Kovalenko gave Burke an appraising look. 'Okay, so . . . what can I do you for, Mr. Burke?'

'Well, I was hoping . . . maybe you'll recall. You shut us down. My father-in-law's company. I was hoping we could fix that.'

Kovalenko relaxed. He leaned back against the wall, and all the tension went out of his body. He looked at Burke as if Burke were a pane of glass, and sighed.

Which made Burke even angrier. But he kept it in. Reaching into his pocket, Burke pulled out a three-by-five card on which he'd carefully printed the following information:

Jack Wilson
P.O. Box 2000
White Deer, PA 17887
(Allenwood Prison)
Stanford University
'Calculating Vector Drag in Scalar Pair-Coupling'

'You were right about the guy you're looking for,' Burke told him, handing the card to Kovalenko. 'He's dangerous.'

Kovalenko glanced at the card. 'This is Mr. d'Anconia?'

Burke nodded.

'But I'm guessing this isn't his current address,' Kovalenko said. 'If it was, he wouldn't be a problem.'

'No, he got out — '

'What's this?' the Legat asked, holding the card up for Burke to see, snapping it with his finger. 'Vector drag — what's a vector drag?'

'That's the reason Wilson went to Belgrade,' Burke told him. 'He was researching a man named Tesla.'

'The inventor?'

'Right.' Burke was surprised the FBI agent had heard of him.

'So what does Mr. Wilson want with a dead inventor?' the Legat demanded. 'Some kind of science project?'

Burke ignored the sarcasm. 'I think he's trying to build a weapon.'

Kovalenko chuckled. 'A weapon! Well, that's just great. Maybe he'll invent the catapult.'

Burke acknowledged the joke with a smile, and a nod. He wanted to tell the man in front of him why Wilson should be taken seriously, but when Burke began to explain, the Legat cut him off, holding his hand up like a traffic cop.

'So, if I wanted to talk to Mr. Wilson, where would I find him?'

Burke shook his head. 'I don't know.'

'You don't know.'

'Not exactly.'

'Well, how close can you get?' Kovalenko asked. 'Is he in China? Brazil?'

'I don't know where he is. What I gave you — his name — Allenwood — Stanford — that's

395

it. And it wasn't easy to get.' He paused. 'Look,' he said, 'I think you should take this guy seriously. He's — '

'Let me tell you something,' Kovalenko said in a bored voice. 'I've got a lot on my plate. I got terrorist cells — real guys with bombs — up north. I've got problems with container ships and dirty bombs, snake-heads and Chechens. Not to mention the Nigerians, who are into everything. And guess what? I'm facing surgery. On my gallbladder! You realize how serious that is?'

Burke wanted to kill him. 'How serious what is?' Burke asked. 'The bombs or your gallbladder?'

Kovalenko smiled, as if Burke had just given him permission for something. 'Let me explain it to you,' he said. 'What this is all about — you and me, sitting here together, having a chat like we are — is cooperation. You want your business open? You want the indictment dropped? Help me find the guy.'

'I *have*,' Burke told him.

Kovalenko shook his head, and sighed, feigning infinite patience. 'Not really.' He took another sip of wine. 'Truth is, yes! I'd love to have a chat with Mr.' — he glanced at the card — '*Wilson*. But I got to be frank with you. He's nowhere near the top of my To Do list. And anyway,' he said, waving the card as if to dry it, 'what good does *this* do me? It's yesterday's news.'

'It's his *name*. The prison must have records. Stanford . . . You could *find* him.'

Kovalenko shrugged. 'Maybe. But how does that help *you*? If *I* find him?'

Burke couldn't believe it.

Kovalenko laughed. 'You want to reopen, right?'

Burke nodded.

'Okay,' Kovalenko said, 'what's it called?' He frowned, pretending to think hard. 'Asshole Associates, right? Something like that. You want to reopen Asshole Associates. No problem. Here's what you do: You find your client! But find him before I do. Because if I find him first, it doesn't do fuck-all for you. You understand what I'm saying? Don't tell me where he was a couple of months ago. Because that doesn't help me.'

Burke took a deep breath, and counted to five. 'Let's say I do find him — '

'Then we'll have a deal,' Kovalenko told him, suddenly magnanimous. 'I'll tell the Garda to back off, and you can go back to doing what you do best: setting up fronts for people who cheat on their taxes.'

Burke took an even deeper breath. He wanted to hit the guy. Instead, he said, 'How do I know you'll do what you say?'

Kovalenko shrugged. 'Because I *always* do what I say. Meantime, don't call me. Don't harass my assistant. She's busy, and, as incredible as it may seem, I've got other priorities.'

Other priorities. It was all Burke could take. He sat where he was, watching the red mist descend in front of his eyes, trying to decide

397

whether to bitch-slap the guy or head-butt him. It wouldn't help things, he realized that, but it would give him a feeling of great satisfaction — if only for a little while.

Kovalenko had no way of knowing, but Burke had a temper. The kind that was hard to control. His parents had worked hard to exorcise it, taking him all the way into Charlottesville for karate lessons, where the civilizing effect of bowing to one's opponent soothed his mother.

If I smack this guy in the face, Burke thought, *there won't be any real damage, not really. Unless he pulls a gun, and blows my head off. So maybe I should just put him out: grab him by his fucking tie, give it a jerk, and head-butt him.* For a moment, this seemed like a plan. But only for a moment. Assaulting an FBI agent could only end with Burke behind bars and the old man totally banjaxed. Even so . . .

He was still thinking about it when he saw the young girl next to him, cringing toward her boyfriend, practically crawling into his lap. She looked terrified. And so, Burke saw, did Kovalenko, though he was better at hiding it.

He got to his feet. The adrenaline fade left him jangled and disoriented. Turning, he pushed his way through the crowded pub, and out to the sidewalk. For a moment, he stood there with his eyes closed, face turned to the sky, feeling the drizzle.

★ ★ ★

A rough day on the Irish Sea. The ferry pitched and plunged in the rain, plowing through a sea of whitecaps. Burke stood by the rail on the deck, shivering in the spray from the bow. His eyes were on the water, but his mind was in London. It would have been grand to inflict a bit of bodily harm on Kovalenko — a mistake, yes, but a delicious one. Now, he'd probably never see him again.

The main cabin of the ferry was filled with uniformed schoolkids returning from a trip to the big city. They were filled with youthful energy, teasing and flirting, relentlessly mobile, whooping with laughter.

Not so, himself. He felt like a hermit crab, hunkered into his Burberry, dark thoughts behind his eyes.

32

DUBLIN JUNE 5, 2005

Back at home, Burke fell into a dark funk, one pointless day collapsing into the next. More than two weeks slid by as Burke did nothing but watch the tube and drink. Most nights, he slept in his clothes.

He felt trapped.

He was furious with Kovalenko, yes, but his anger extended to Jack Wilson, too. The moment Francisco d'Anconia walked into Aherne & Associates' offices, there was only one way things were ever going to work out, and that was with Mike Burke holding the bag.

But it wasn't just anger he felt. Beyond that, he was worried. All of a sudden, Kovalenko had more important priorities than Jack Wilson, not the least of which was his gallbladder. How long had *that* been going on? Burke wondered. Then he remembered the phone conversation he'd had with Kovalenko's subordinate, or whoever he was: *You're in a lot of trouble, my friend.* Were they all like that? Was it in the job description, that you had to be a dick? What was it he'd said about Kovalenko? *He's in the shop.*

It hadn't made sense, but now it did. Kovalenko was in the hospital, or at the doctor's, or something. And now he was having surgery.

Christ, Burke thought, *Kovalenko's not even paying attention.*

And if Kovalenko wasn't worried about Wilson, who would be? Burke might take the story elsewhere, but . . . where? He didn't have enough to persuade anyone who could do anything about it that Wilson was dangerous.

On a few occasions, when Burke had managed to tear himself away from the tube, he'd done a little research into particle beam or 'directed energy' weapons — enough to know that, even in the midst of the Iraq war, the Pentagon was pouring money into it. A firm in Virginia was developing something called StunStrike, a device that worked off a Tesla coil and delivered a small bolt of lightning to blind and stun combatants. Raytheon was doing its own work in the field, devising weapons that could knock out the electronics of things like Stinger missiles, land mines, drones, and even aircraft.

Another project, based on the same basic technology, involved a beam that could microwave a crowd — or the inhabitants of a building. Essentially, the beam heated the water in the human body to a point where victims felt as if they'd received an instant sunburn. It more or less stopped them in their tracks, and the beauty of it was that afterward, they were fine. So it had civilian applications. Crowd control. Preventing stampedes. And then, if the people in front of you *didn't* stop, you could ratchet up the setting until they felt like they were on fire. Jack it up a little more, and you'd boil them until their skin split.

401

Kovalenko might have known about these Pentagon efforts, but he wouldn't connect them to Tesla, whose heyday had been more than a hundred years ago. The truth was, Kovalenko didn't know enough to worry about Jack Wilson.

And . . . he wasn't interested in learning. To the FBI agent, Jack Wilson was about as worrisome as a Nigerian con game.

★ ★ ★

And then one morning, Burke got up early and in a fit of masochism took a cold shower. To his surprise, it made him feel better. Virtuous, even. Then he made a cup of coffee for himself, and carried it to his computer. Sitting down before the monitor, he told himself to *Get it together*.

He was tired of treading water while the world wound down around him. If he didn't do something soon, he'd drown. *So watcha gonna do, boy? Join the circus, learn the guitar? Look for a guru in old Siam?*

How about: *Find Wilson*.

Now that's an idea, he thought. *I could find Jack Wilson. But what would he do with him? He could FedEx the sonofabitch to Ray Kovalenko, and it wouldn't do any good. On the other hand, they deserved each other. They might even be good together. And then, at least, this would be over — and I could move on.*

So he typed a search string into the Google bar: '*jack wilson*' *stanford indicted*.

Somehow, Wilson had gone off the deep end,

402

matriculating from a dormitory at Stanford to a cell block in Allenwood. That was quite a transition — and maybe enough to have made the papers.

The cursor changed to an hourglass and, in an instant, the screen refreshed.

There were dozens of hits.

He clicked on the first one, which was dated November 22, 1995 — a news story from the *San Jose Mercury*.

STANFORD MAN GUILTY
By Judi Whitestone

San Francisco Bay Area inventor and Stanford graduate Jack Wilson was found guilty in federal court today of soliciting the murder of U.S. Attorney Joseph Sozio.

Sozio's office indicted Wilson last year for violation of the Invention Secrecy Act.

A summa cum laude graduate of Stanford's prestigious School of Engineering, Wilson listened impassively as the verdict was read.

The prosecution's case was based on surreptitious tape recordings made by Wilson's former cellmate, Robert Maddox, who also testified at the trial.

Sentencing is expected next week.

Jesus, Burke muttered. *And I thought I crashed and burned.*

He spent an hour trawling for details on the Net. And what he found was enough to make you weep: Horatio Alger hitches a ride with Icarus . . .

The story had been well covered in the Silicon Valley press, where Wilson came to be seen as a golden boy with feet of clay.

According to the papers, Golden Boy was an orphan. In 1969, he was found in a box outside the emergency room of the county hospital in Tonopah, Nevada. Attached to his blanket was a round sticker with a smiley face. Under the word, HI!, someone had printed the words I'M JACK WILSON.

Wilson's defense attorney played the orphan card and the Horatio Alger card as if they were a pair of aces. Brought up in a series of foster homes, young Jack Wilson was both prom king and valedictorian of his class at Churchill County High School in Fallon, Nevada. A national finalist in the Westinghouse science competition, he won a full ride to Stanford. Graduating at the top of his class, he was awarded the Ratner-Salzberg Prize (an inscribed pewter bowl and a check) and carried the Engineering School's banner at commencement.

Other awards followed as he went on to earn a doctorate in electrical engineering. In 1993, he formed Wovoka Enterprises, applied for his first patent, and began to approach venture capitalists.

Patent? What kind of patent? Burke wondered. He searched a dozen different ways, but there was nothing about it.

It was at this point that Wilson's seemingly unstoppable ascent to fame and fortune came to an end. In July of 1994, the Stanford man was indicted for violating the Invention Secrecy Act of 1951.

According to a trade publication called *Silicon ASAP*, Wilson's invention had been seized by the U.S. government through the process of eminent domain. That is to say, it had been taken in the same way that the government seizes real estate in order to build a highway or railroad. Washington declared Wilson's patent government property, remitted a check for what it considered appropriate compensation, and classified the invention 'Secret.'

Relying upon the U.S. attorney's complaint, *Silicon ASAP* reported that Wilson attempted an end run around the Invention Secrecy Act. Ignoring the seizure of his patent, Wilson attempted to raise mezzanine financing with a presentation at the offices of a venture capital firm in San Francisco's financial district. According to an executive who witnessed the presentation, Wilson intended to produce the invention at a manufacturing facility offshore. Anguilla was mentioned.

FBI agents arrested Wilson as he left the meeting. The next day, he was indicted for violating the Invention Secrecy Act.

Burke found out what that was through the Federation of American Scientists' website. The act was passed in 1951, and established protocols for the government's seizure of inventions deemed vital to national security. Within the Patent and Trademark Office, special examiners look over all patent applications to determine if there is a national interest. Qualifying applications are referred to boards in the affected precincts — most often, the Department of Defense and the Department of Energy. Their recommendations are usually final.

In most cases, the seizure of a patent is not a hardship for the inventor, because the patent was developed with government funding. But for some inventors it *is* a hardship. In 2003, for instance, nearly half of the one hundred fifty patent secrecy orders related to private, or so-called John Doe, inventions.

The inventors' appeals almost always failed, as did their complaints of insufficient compensation. How do you establish the commercial value of something that has never come to market — and never will? How do you make your case when you're forbidden by law from discussing the invention itself?

Burke rocked back in his chair. Now he understood Wilson's affection for *Atlas Shrugged* and Francisco d'Anconia. But what did Wilson invent? Given his interest in Tesla, and the government's assertion of eminent domain, it was probably a weapon.

Burke went back to the well.

Following his arrest, Wilson was transported to San Francisco County Jail #1, where he shared a cell and small talk with a motorcycle thug named Robbie Maddox. Before the despairing Wilson was able to arrange bail, Maddox met secretly with sheriff's deputies, insisting that his cellmate was planning to kill the U.S. attorney.

Two days later, Maddox initiated another

discussion with Wilson. This time he was wearing a wire.

At Wilson's trial on charges of solicitation of murder, the following exchange was played for the jury:

Sozio? Yeah, I would definitely . . . like to see that sonofabitch go down.

How much would that be worth to you?

You gotta be kidding!

No, really! How much?

Christ, I don't know . . . Why? . . . You know someone who could do it?

I could do it . . .

Get outta here . . .

. . . is that a deal?

. . . yeah, sure . . . deal.

Wilson's defense attorney, Jill Apple, agreed that her client was angry at the government for seizing his invention. And yes, he had undoubtedly vented that anger to Maddox. But, she argued, the government's assertion that Wilson's remarks constituted a threat, much less a contract, was ridiculous. If Wilson was conspiring to murder anyone, where was the overt act to further the conspiracy? It didn't exist. He didn't do anything. All her client had actually done, Apple insisted, was shoot off his mouth — because his world was crumbling around him. That was a mistake, she said, but it was not a felony.

She argued that her client was a victim of entrapment, and insisted that Wilson's remarks had been taken out of context. Apple called Maddox a 'provocateur,' and pointed out that

407

after Wilson was charged with solicitation of murder, the U.S. Attorney's Office moved to dismiss Maddox's indictment in a drug case.

The jury didn't buy it. Wilson was convicted. And because his target was the U.S. attorney, he was sentenced to 'the Alcatraz of the Rockies' in Florence, Colorado.

There he spent his first year locked down in a six-by-ten concrete cage, doing time beside the likes of the Unabomber, the Shoebomber, Terry Nichols, and Ramsay Yousef. Condemned by Amnesty International for violating the United Nations' minimal rules for prisoners, the Supermax prison in Florence was brightly lighted twenty-four hours a day. But not by the sun. The only daylight the prisoners could see was a segment of sky, high up on the wall. Like everything else, this was a security feature. In the absence of a landscape, escape became psychologically impossible. All that was left to the prisoners was a toilet, a sink, and a slab of concrete to sleep on. That, and a TV screen embedded in the wall, tuned to insipid programming.

Burke rocked back in his chair. *Supermax*, he thought. *Jesus!*

There were only two Supermax facilities in the federal system, he read, though six others were planned. Of the two, the one in Florence was newer. And therefore crueler. More state of the art. The inmates were effectively buried alive.

Burke had been brought up on movies of convicts pumping iron, playing football, or running on a guarded track. But there was none

408

of that for most of the prisoners in Florence. Their first year, and sometimes two, was spent in their cells with virtually no opportunity to exercise or interact with others, including the guards. If their behavior changed — if they embraced the hopelessness of their situation and surrendered to apathy — they might someday be released into the larger population of less dangerous inmates. Until then, they might just as well be frozen in amber.

It was all about isolation.

Guards slid the prisoners' meals into revolving 'food wickets,' so that the trays appeared in the cells with no apparent human intervention. Drains and drainpipes, which inmates used to communicate in other prisons, were damped. You could bang on the toilet all day long, and no one would hear you. Cells were soundproofed, and sealed off by two doors, one barred, the other solid.

Even as the inmates were denied a view of the surrounding landscape, visitors were equally clueless of the terrain. The only approach to the prison was through a long, winding tunnel. As with the meals in the cells, visitors arrived out of nowhere to find themselves in a hermetically sealed, antiseptic hell, surrounded by walls gleaming with razor wire, monitored by pressure pads, motion detectors, and dogs.

It was, Burke thought, a long way for Wilson to fall, and a hard place to land. He glanced at the notes he'd made, then worked the Internet to find telephone numbers for the U.S. Attorney's Office in San Francisco; Wilson's lawyer, Jill

Apple; and Robbie Maddox.

He gave up on Maddox right away. Anywho-
.com didn't have a listing for him in San
Francisco, which meant that he could be
anywhere. Sozio was easier to locate. He was a
judge now, working out of the same federal
building in San Francisco where he'd previously
worked as a U.S. attorney, but there were so
many layers of insulation between him and the
public that getting an interview would be
virtually impossible. That left Apple.

He found her number the old-fashioned way,
through information. Half an hour later, he was
lying to her. He told her he was a journalist who
wrote for *Harper's*, Counterpunch, and Salon.
He mentioned some of the stories he'd covered
(as a photographer), and said he was thinking of
doing a piece about the Invention Secrecy Act.
He was calling her because he'd become
interested in one of the cases she'd handled.

'Jack Wilson,' she guessed.

'Right!'

She was a friendly woman with a warm
southern voice. 'Are you in touch with Jack?' she
asked. And then, in a rush of realization: 'He
ought to be out by now!'

'Yes, he's been released but, no, I don't know
where he is,' Burke told her. 'I was hoping — '

'Well, I can't help there,' she said. 'We didn't
stay in touch.'

'No?'

'No. We appealed, but . . . I imagine he's a
different person, now.'

'Yeah, well, he would be.'

410

She sighed. 'It was heartbreaking, really.'

'How's that?' Burke asked.

'I don't know how much you know about Jack's life, but — he achieved so much, and then . . . it was just so sad. And unfair, too.'

'Unfair?'

'Bad luck.'

'How so?'

Apple sighed. 'About a month before Jack went to trial, some lunatic walked into a courtroom in San Jose, and just opened fire. Shot the judge, a bailiff, and a popular young attorney on the prosecution team. Then he turned the gun on himself.'

'How'd he get into court with a gun?'

'The papers said it was a Glock. Lots of plastic parts, though I guess it's mostly metal by weight. Anyway, you have to be trained to recognize it on a scanner if it's disassembled. I guess he put it together in the men's room. But the point is, if it wasn't for San Jose, I don't think Jack would have been prosecuted. They didn't have a case, but they really wanted to send a message.'

'I read what Wilson said on the tape,' Burke told her. 'It sounded like — '

' — bullshit. Which is what it was. He was angry. Who wouldn't be? But *murder*? No way. If you'd seen that sleazeball on the stand . . . what's-his-name? I've blocked it out.'

'Maddox?'

She made a disgusted sound. 'This is the man they're talking about when they talk about someone with 'a record as long as your arm.' So, of course, he was a professional snitch, and Jack,

411

well, Jack had never been inside a jail before. So he was easy pickin's.'

'Why was he in jail, anyway?' Burke asked. 'Couldn't he make bail?'

'He was arrested on the weekend, and I don't think they arraigned him until Monday afternoon. He had a public defender at that point, and I think he was trying to arrange a loan, using his condo as collateral. But it took a few days and . . . Maddox happened. It was bad luck. Like I said.'

'You also said he was easy pickings,' Burke reminded her.

'Right. Maddox set him up. I can imagine how it went down. If you listen to the tape, there's no context for anything. All of a sudden, Jack says, 'Sozio,' like it's a revelation. And the conversation isn't continuous. There are all these gaps. I had an expert witness examine the tape, and he suggested Maddox was manipulating the microphone. But we couldn't prove it. And in the end, the jury didn't buy it.'

'Did you call Wilson to the stand?'

She hesitated. 'I did, and it was a mistake. Jack was . . . he's very charismatic, one on one. Handsome as hell. But on the witness stand? I wanted a *victim* up there, but what I got instead was John Galt!'

'The Ayn Rand thing,' Burke said.

'You know about that!'

'Yeah.'

'Well, it wasn't helpful,' Apple told him.

'I'm surprised you let him talk about that — '

'I didn't! I cut him off as soon as he got

started. But the prosecutor picked up on it, and jump-started the whole thing all over again on cross. And he just hung himself. He actually told the jury that it didn't have a right to judge him because they weren't his peers.' She paused. 'This did not go over well.'

Burke laughed. 'Meanwhile — '

'Meanwhile, I'm trying to keep the jury focused on the throwaway Indian boy who was left on a doorstep in a cardboard box. You know, he didn't even know who he was named for until he was ten years old. I mean, he *looked* Indian, but he had no idea what tribe he was or anything like that. That's when he got a foster mother who finally did some mothering. She helped him find out who he was, and where he'd come from.'

'When you say he was named for someone,' Burke asked, 'who are we talking about? Who's 'Jack Wilson'?'

'The Paiute. You never heard of him? He was famous! Invented the Ghost Dance. You should put that in your story. He lived in Nevada way back when.'

' 'Jack Wilson' doesn't sound like an Indian name,' Burke said.

'That was his white name — the name of the family he grew up with. His native name was 'Wovoka.' '

'Like the company,' Burke said. 'Wilson's company.'

'That's right! I'd forgotten that.'

The connection had been there all along. Burke had seen it in a list of Google cites, but he hadn't paid attention. It seemed irrelevant. Jack

413

Wilson . . . the Ghost Dance . . . He thought it was a coincidence, if he thought about it at all. But there was that woman, the one in Belgrade — Tooti! She'd said something about Wilson dancing. And Ceplak, talking about Wilson's last day with him: *Time to dance.*

'Let me ask you a question,' Burke said.

Apple chuckled ruefully. 'I think we've probably talked enough. I've got a lot of work to do.'

'What was the invention? The invention that started it all?'

The lawyer laughed. 'Well, that's the sixty-four-thousand-dollar question, isn't it? Or does that date me?'

'It's pretty important for the story,' Burke told her. 'I mean, it's at the heart of everything.'

'I suppose it is,' she replied, 'but that's why they call it the Invention *Secrecy* Act.'

'I'm not trying to find out how it works, or anything. I'm just curious — the readers are going to be curious — about what it is.'

'Well . . . '

'I'm guessing it's some kind of weapon. I mean, for the government to seize it like that, it would have to be.'

The lawyer sighed. Finally, she said, 'Can we go off the record here?'

33

NEVADA JUNE 5, 2005

A road trip.

In a few weeks, such a thing would no longer be possible, so Wilson resolved to take his time as he drove east. He wanted to savor every last moment: the subtle changes in the land, the search for decent road food, even the chance to gripe about the weather and the price of fuel with waitresses and other strangers. It would have been fun to drive cross-country with Irina, he thought, show her the diverse beauty of the country, just meander west and take it all in.

Not possible, of course. After June 22, the pleasures of this kind of driving — of any kind of driving, really — would come to an end. The intricate web of highways and roads and streets that knitted the country together would, in an instant, be useless. Virtually every vehicle on the road would come to a stop. Their engines would sputter and die. And they would never start again.

Vintage cars and a few diesels, like the ones back at the B-Lazy-B would still be capable of travel, but their range would be limited by the dead cars littering the roads.

Even if the occasional old car could get around, most of the fuel would be trapped underground in tanks, inaccessible without the electricity needed to work the pumps.

Bicycles would become quite valuable.

★   ★   ★

Although he'd modified the suspension, and created a sort of gimballed cocoon for the weapon, he winced as the Escalade shuddered over the rough road from the ranch to Juniper. He felt better when he hit Route 225.

Now that the road was smoother, he tapped the dashboard controls to select the Russian language CD. When it came on, he spoke out loud at the prompts, mimicking the recorded voice.

Thank you: *Spashiba*

You're welcome: *Pajalsta*

Sorry: *Izvinche* (to strangers); *Izvinit* (to friends)

As well as making this effort to learn Irina's language, he'd purchased more than a hundred books in the Russian — everything from dictionaries to poetry to classics, contemporary fiction, and children's books. He'd bought an array of DVDs, as well, along with several icons, a samovar, and sets of matryoshka dolls for their children. He didn't want Irina to feel cut off from her culture.

After an hour or so, he switched off the language CD. Time for some music. He used to sing aloud in Florence all the time because music was one of the things he missed the most. It was amazing how many tunes he knew just as fragments. And locked up in solitary, that could drive you crazy if you let it, the way the rest of a tune stayed out of reach, closed off in some neuronal backwater. In the beginning, it maddened him that there was no way to fill in the blanks. It wasn't as if he could go online and download the song or go out and buy the CD to satisfy his curiosity.

So he went crazy buying CDs after he got back from Africa. He filled in *all* those blanks and more. The B-Lazy-B had a catalog of more than three thousand CDs — and a state-of-the-art sound system. It was an eclectic selection — he couldn't be sure how his tastes might change as time went on.

The Escalade had a pretty good sound system, too. By the time he reached the Utah border, he was rapping along with Eminem.

'*Oops, there goes gravity.*'

34

DUBLIN JUNE 5, 2005

'It wasn't a weapon, at all,' Jill Apple told Burke.
'It was a battery.'

Burke thought he'd misheard. 'Sorry . . . ?'

'He found a way to make a better battery. A
lightweight, long-lived *battery*.'

'You're kidding,' Burke said.

'I'm not. These things made the Energizer
Bunny look like a fruit fly.'

Burke laughed.

'You can imagine how excited Jack and his
partner were,' Jill said.

'What partner?' Burke asked.

'He had a partner. Eli something . . . *Salzberg!*
They went to grad school together. I think Eli
was getting an MBA. Very smooth. He was
putting together the venture-capital meetings,
when Jack got the letter.'

'From?'

'The patent office. DOD decided the application should be secret. So that was that. No
patent. They offered compensation — I think
they came up with $ 150,000.'

'And how much was it worth . . . actually?'

'Eli thought he could get twenty-five million
for a ten percent equity interest. That's what they
were asking.'

'Jesus! So what did they do?'

'They came to me,' Jill told him. 'And we took it to court,' Jill replied. 'But no one ever wins these kinds of appeals. The hearings are closed, and the government doesn't have to justify itself. They just say it's in the national interest and that's that.'

'No wonder he's pissed,' Burke said.

'It's eminent domain applied to intellectual property. If the government wants to put a highway through your living room, all it has to do is assert the public interest. And it's the same with patents. The Invention Secrecy Act (it's 35 U.S.C. 17, if you want to look it up) goes back to the cold war.'

'So how many patents have they seized?' Burke wondered.

'Something like ten thousand.'

Burke laughed in disbelief. 'It's like the X-Files!'

'Well, yeah, it is!' the lawyer replied. 'There are all kinds of rumors — indestructible tires, nonaddictive opiates . . . Jack's mistake was trying to make an end run around the Pentagon. That's what got him arrested.'

'And that's when he ran into Maddox.'

'Right.' There was a quavering noise on the line. 'Can you hang on?'

'Sure.'

She came right back. 'Listen, I'm supposed to be in court in ten minutes — '

'Oh, I'm sorry, I — '

'You know, you really ought to talk to Eli!'

'I'd love to. You got a number for him?'

419

'No, but he won't be hard to find. He was on Bloomberg the other day, talking about Argentina. He's got some big job with the World Bank. I think he's based in Washington.'

★　★　★

Taking his laptop into the kitchen, Burke set it on the table, and prepared dinner for himself. Uninterested in cooking, he'd taken to 'freebasing' ramen. This involved crushing the noodles in a baggie, and sprinkling them with the powder in the seasoning packet. The noodles would then be thoroughly shaken in the bag, after which they would be ready to eat. Uncooked, the ramen had the same texture as the crusher-run at the bottom of a bag of Cheetos.

Sitting down to his laptop, with the ramen to his left and a bottle of Jameson's to his right, Burke went online to see what he could learn about Wilson's namesake and his people.

The Indian messiah, Wovoka, arrived on the scene after more than fifty years of serial catastrophe and genocide. In 1830, the tribes of the east had been driven west by the Indian Removal Act. This forced migration, infamous as the Trail of Tears, confined the tribes to 'Indian Territory' in what is now a part of Oklahoma. As the frontier moved west, the tribes of the Plains and the Great Basin found themselves incarcerated in open-air prisons called reservations, where they survived in a fever dream of alcohol, desperation, and disease. Nomads who had once survived — and thrived — by hunting and foraging now found themselves on unfamiliar ground, with many of their customs and religious rites forbidden by law. The desperation that resulted was compounded by a succession of 'renegotiated' treaties that amounted to land grabs. Finally, the Indian tragedy verged on cataclysm when the government cut back on its deliveries of rice and wheat in the midst of a withering drought. Simply put, the Trail of Tears delivered the Indians to what they called the Starving Time.

Enter Wovoka.

It was said that he came from a family of shamans, and maybe he did. But what was certain was that he grew up on a Nevada ranch owned by a man named David Wilson, who called the boy 'Jack' and gave him his own last name. In about 1889, Wovoka began to speak of a vision he'd received.

I bring you word from your fathers, the ghosts, that they are now marching to join you, led by the Messiah who came once to live on earth with the white man, but was cast out and killed by them.

In Wovoka's vision, the white man would be driven from the Indians' lands. The earth would be restored to abundance and plenty, and the Indians' ancestors would return to live among them.

Wovoka preached that new land was being prepared. It would arrive from the west in the spring of 1891. The new land would cover the old land 'to the depth of five times the height of a man.' In the meantime, the tribes must live in

421

peace with themselves and the white man. Just before the new land arrived, the earth would tremble and shake, but the Indians should not be afraid. Death, disease, and the white man would vanish. *The new lands would be covered with sweet grass and running water and trees, and herds of buffalo and ponies will stray over it, that my red children may eat and drink, hunt and rejoice.*

But Wovoka's revelation wasn't only descriptive. It commanded the tribes to dance in a particular way at particular intervals. This would help to bring about the end, and the new beginning that would follow.

Almost every website used the same expression. The movement spread 'like wildfire.' It was an apt simile, Burke thought. Just as forest fires jumped from one stand of trees to the next, the ghost dance religion leaped from one tribe to another. Indian leaders (among them, the Sioux's Red Cloud and the Lakota's Kicking Bear) traveled enormous distances to visit Wovoka in western Nevada.

Even as the message spread, it changed (as 'messages' are wont to do). The new land would roll in just as Wovoka promised. But it would not just push the white man out. It would bury him.

As reports of their impending demise began to circulate, whites decided that a revolution was in the works. The 'ghost dance,' they told themselves, was actually a 'war dance.' The Indian vermin were planning to murder them all in their beds.

Then ... Wounded Knee. Winter of 1890.

Sitting Bull, an advocate of the Ghost Dance and the most renowned of all Sioux chieftains, had just been assassinated by government agents. Fearing an insurrection, the 7th Cavalry (General Custer's old regiment) was sent to arrest Indian 'agitators' in South Dakota. To escape arrest, a band of Lakota made their way by night through the Badlands. Their aim was to find shelter and protection on the Pine Ridge reservation.

The army tracked them, and forced the Lakota to the banks of Wounded Knee Creek. Surrounded and outnumbered, the Lakota displayed a white flag, signaling their surrender. While the Indian's leaders were being interrogated, the order was issued to confiscate the Indians' weapons. According to contemporary accounts, some of the Indians began singing Ghost Dance songs. A medicine man threw a handful of dirt in the air, which some of the soldiers (drunk) imagined to be a signal. A gun went off, and though the shot hit no one, the cavalry opened fire en masse. Four Hotchkiss cannons, positioned on a hill overlooking the encampment, each capable of firing fifty explosive rounds a minute, loosed a murderous barrage.

Hundreds of Lakota — men, women, and children were blown to pieces. Some came forward with their hands raised, only to be executed where they stood. Still others were hunted down in the woods, or froze to death escaping the soldiers.

In the end, the army lost twenty-nine of its

own men, almost all victims of 'friendly' cross fire. Congress doled out twenty Medals of Honor to soldiers who'd taken part in the massacre.

Burke drained his whiskey, poured another, and drank deep. He knew a little about Wounded Knee. Knew where it was, anyway. In 1973, a couple hundred Indian activists occupied the village to publicize a long list of grievances, including corruption on the reservation, racial discrimination, and the sale of Indian lands to developers.

The FBI and National Guard repeated the past by laying siege to the town, cutting off its electricity and water. Gun battles broke out and, for seventy-one days, a war raged, with the American Indian Movement and its followers massively outgunned. According to some reports, more than five million rounds were fired into the village. For their part, AIM fighters had two automatic weapons, which they used to great effect, running from one location to the next, firing short bursts that made it seem as if their numbers (and firepower) were much greater.

It was inevitable that they would lose the battle, and they did. But just as certainly, they won the war. The siege at Wounded Knee created a renaissance of interest in Native American traditions, while casting a cold light on the federal government's malignant neglect of the reservations and those who lived on them.

Incredibly, despite the millions of rounds that were fired, only two of the fighters at Wounded Knee were killed. One of them was a kid from

Nelson County, Virginia, where Burke himself had been raised. People used to talk about it when he was growing up. Frank Clearwater, they said. Died fighting.

Burke got to his feet, stiff from sitting in the same place for so long. He was thinking about the day Jack Wilson had knocked on his door in Dublin. They'd shaken hands, and Wilson had introduced himself as Francisco d'Anconia. Burke thought he was talking to a businessman, but now he saw how wrong he'd been. Jack Wilson wasn't a man at all. Not in his own eyes, anyway. He was a tidal wave of new land, looming toward his enemies.

35

'Salzberg.'

There was a TV in the background. Burke could hear it, the unmistakable white noise of Americans cheering.

'Yeah, hi, it's Mike Burke — I got your number from Jill Apple — you know, Jack Wilson's lawyer.' Burke affected the chipper voice of a journalist who (1) expected everyone to recognize his name, and (2) was 'just doing his job,' cold-calling someone he hoped would be a source. 'I'm doing a story on the Invention Secrecy Act — '

'For . . . ?'

'*Harper's*,' Burke replied, panicking for a moment because he always confused the magazine with the *Atlantic*, and didn't remember what he'd told Jill Apple.

'Okay, so how can I help you?'

Burke repeated the song and dance he'd given to Apple.

'So he's out,' Salzberg said.

'He is. And I'd really like to talk to him, but . . . no one seems to know where he is.'

'Well, I can tell you he has not called this old friend.' He paused. 'You talk to Mandy?'

'No,' Burke said. 'Who's Mandy?'

426

'His foster mother, Mandy Renfro. Although . . . Jeez, she might be dead by now.' A fatigued sigh.

'Do you know where she lives?'

'Fallon. Where Jack was from — in Nevada. But she was in her sixties, so . . . '

'I'll check it out,' Burke promised, 'but, look, Mr. Salzberg — '

'Call me Eli.'

'*Eli!* I know you can't tell me about the invention — '

'The hell I can't! I just can't tell you how to *make* it — not that I ever could.' He paused. 'You mind hanging on for a second? I'll be right back.' The noise from the television cut out, and for what seemed like a long while, nothing could be heard but the low hum of the transatlantic cable. Then, the rattle of ice in a glass. 'I'm back,' Eli announced.

'I hope I haven't ruined your game,' Burke told him.

He laughed. 'No,' Eli said. 'I've got TiVo.' Then his tone changed, and he was all business. 'So what do you want to know?'

'Well,' Burke said, 'I know what *Jack's* role was, but . . . '

'Me? I was the money guy,' Eli told him. 'Start-ups are expensive, especially manufacturing ones. My job was to find the venture capital, which, trust me, was not going to be hard, not with the product we had.'

'So what happened?'

'*Shit* happened! The government destroyed a brilliant guy. They made me testify against him.

427

Did you know that?' The economist's bitterness was almost palpable. 'I think Jack was probably my best friend. I still can't believe it.'

'What do you mean?'

'You'd think Jack had invented . . . I don't know, some kind of bomb or something. That's what you thought, right? That's what everyone thinks.'

'Apple said it was a battery.'

'Right! A *battery* — a battery that would last ten times longer than anything else out there. With pretty much the same components. You'd think they'd *want* that on the market. I mean, just from an environmental perspective, it would have been a huge plus for everyone. But no. The national interest is apparently better served by pollution.' The economist paused. 'Do I sound bitter?'

'A little,' Burke told him.

'Well, maybe that's because it cost me about a hundred million bucks! Not to mention the fact that we were going to change the world. At least, Jack was. He wanted to start a foundation. For indigenous peoples.'

'Native Americans.'

'Native everythings. They have the same problems in Brazil that we have here,' Eli insisted. 'Australia, Africa — it's the same story. You should make that a part of your article.'

'I will,' Burke promised. 'But I'm still trying to figure out why the government went after your invention.'

Eli snorted. 'I think they thought it would give them an advantage on the battlefield. But who

428

knows? This was going to be a very big product. It was going to make waves in the marketplace. I don't want to get into specifics, but it would have had a negative impact on certain manufacturers and mining interests. Some of those interests are big contributors to people's campaigns. So maybe that was a factor, but . . . who knows? They don't actually give you a reason. They just take what they want.'

'Apple said Jack made an 'end run' — '

'Around the government, yeah. He did. And got clobbered — they had to carry him off the field.'

'What happened?'

'Well, he filed for the patent. And here's what happens when you do that. You file your specification, say what your invention does, submit drawings, sometimes models, and you send it off. Then the patent examiner evaluates it. Is it original, or does it significantly improve the state of the art? Well, Jack's battery relied on certain insights . . . ' Eli paused. 'He always said he was standing on the shoulders of giants, and one giant in particular, a Serb — '

'Tesla.'

'Ri-igght! You *have* done your homework. Anyway, Jack's battery took advantage of some of the insights Tesla had, and relied on one of Tesla's lesser-known patents. So it wasn't original in the technical sense. But did it improve on the state of the art? Oh yes! It did. It really really did.'

'So what did you do?'

'What do you think? We formed a corporation.'

'And you were successful?' Burke asked.

'Yeah. Kleiner Perkins put up half a million in seed money when we didn't even have a business plan. Not a real plan, anyway. They just listened, looked at the prototype, and wrote a check.'

'Then what?'

'When we got a little further along, I set up a meeting with Morgan Stanley.'

'And what happened?'

'Well,' Eli replied, 'what *happened* was, we got a letter, a certified letter, from the commissioner of patents. I think it was three lines long. Basically, it said there was a national security interest in the application. As a consequence, they were impounding it under the terms of the Invention Secrecy Act. Enclosed, please find a check for a hundred fifty-two thousand dollars. That's what happened.'

'Christ,' Burke said. 'What did you do?'

'What did I *do*? I talked to a lawyer, and then I took her advice.'

'Which was . . . ?'

'Forget about it. I actually flew to Zihuatanejo, Mexico, and stayed plastered for a week.'

'And Wilson?'

'Jack . . . reacted differently. That meeting I told you about — the one with Morgan Stanley? He flew to Boston and gave the presentation, as if nothing had happened. The only thing he changed was the manufacturing venue. He was going to set up offshore.'

'And the government found out,' Burke said.

'One of the people at the Morgan Stanley presentation is a director of In-Q-Tel, so — '

'What's In-Q-Tel?'

'It's actually a CIA proprietary,' Eli told him. 'But it's not what you're thinking. It's not covert or anything. It's a straight-up venture-capital firm that happens to be owned by the CIA. They have headquarters in the Valley. A sign on the door. The whole nine yards. The idea is, they put up money for start-ups that deal with problems the Agency has an interest in. I don't know — a data-mining program for Arabic text, a new kind of body armor, whatever.'

'Or a battery,' Burke declared.

'Right.'

'So you think In-Q-Tel went to the feds — '

'No. I think In-Q-Tel learned about the presentation at Morgan Stanley from one of its directors and got excited. I think they realized this product had some serious applications. And I think they let their principals know that they wanted to participate in our little venture.'

'And then — '

'The shit hit the fan,' Eli said. 'The Pentagon got wind of it, and the next thing you know Jack is being charged by the U.S. attorney. I mean, he's arrested, *cuffed*. And he's facing two years and a two-hundred-thousand-dollar fine. Me? I'm mortgaging the condo to make the bail.'

'What about the check you got?'

'The hundred fifty-two grand? We didn't want to cash it. Because once you cash the check . . . '

'So that's when Jack met Maddox.'

'Right.'

Burke sighed. 'Did you ever see Jack — inside?'

'In *jail*, yes. In *prison*, no. The last time I saw him, they were leading him away. I tried to visit him in Colorado, but . . . he wouldn't see me.'

'You mentioned a foster mother . . . ,' Burke said.

'Mandy. She was living in a trailer in Fallon. But, like I said, she was pretty old . . . '

Burke was out of questions. 'Look,' he said, 'I want to thank you — '

But Eli didn't want to let it go. 'The thing is,' he said, 'Jack and I . . . we roomed together. And then, when he went away, it was like he was gone. I mean, totally gone. Long gone.'

'What do you mean?'

'He didn't answer my letters. He wouldn't talk on the phone. I went to Florence, thinking if I'm *there*, if I've driven hundreds of miles, he's *got* to see me. And let's face it, it's not like he had anything else to do. That place in Colorado — it's like a mausoleum. Except they feed you. The whole idea is to grind people down through isolation. And Jack was actually turning people away.' Eli paused, and laughed. It occurred to Burke that he might be a little drunk. 'I keep thinking back to the last time I saw him . . . '

'When was that?' Burke asked.

'In San Francisco, when they led him out of court. He was in shackles, y'know? Had his hands cuffed to his waist, his feet hobbled. I felt like crying. Because this guy was like . . . the Prince of Palo Alto! Or *coulda* been, or *shoulda*

432

been. And I kept thinking, 'It's like that song.' '

Burke didn't know what he meant. 'What song?'

'That *song!*' Eli insisted. 'The one about the music. You know — '*The Day the Music Died.*' '

36

JUNE 6, 2005

Yesterday: *Cheerah*
 Tomorrow: *Zaftra*
 I love you: *La ti tiya yi blue*.
 Wilson pulled off Route 29 and took the
country road that led into Culpeper.

The outskirts were the usual mélange of hair
salons, car washes, automobile showrooms, and
plant nurseries. The town's rural position was
emphasized by two large businesses selling
farming equipment — vast lots of tractors and
mowers and balers. He passed a bunch of
franchises: Wal-Mart, Lowe's, Ruby Tuesday,
Dairy Queen. Then he arrived at the heart of this
sprawl, Historic Culpeper — a few leafy blocks
of brick buildings with informational plaques.

Wilson surveyed the array of motels available,
choosing the Comfort Inn for its elevation and
location — half a mile outside his target area. He
opted for a suite. Ever since Florence, space had
become important to him, a luxury he could
now afford.

SWIFT was just across Route 29. He'd
obtained the location online from the town's tax
records.

Set between farms with red barns, the banking
epicenter kept a low profile. There were no signs

434

identifying it, just placards that read NO TRESPASSING and PRIVATE PROPERTY. Still, there was no mistaking the place. The grounds were double-fenced, the fences topped with razor wire. There were security cameras between the fences and a guardhouse with a motorized gate.

Wilson pulled up to the guardhouse and asked for directions to Wal-Mart. A parking lot was visible, but behind the double fence, a large earthen berm obscured the view of whatever structure was back there. While the guard gave him directions, Wilson took a GPS reading on his watch.

The Culpeper Switch was less than a mile away. Formerly housed in a bunker called Mount Pony, it resembled the campus of a small school. Once again, security was blatant. He stopped for a moment on the road that ran along the perimeter of the facility, adjusted his seat belt, and took a second GPS reading.

That evening, he ate dinner at Ruby Tuesday's. When he got back to the motel, he sat at the dinette table in the little suite's kitchen and plugged in his laptop. He fed in the GPS coordinates of the Escalade's parking place, along with the coordinates of SWIFT and the Culpeper Switch. The software program interfaced with a topographic map of Culpeper and environs. In four minutes, he had the focusing parameters.

★　★　★

435

Part of the fun was that Wilson wasn't entirely sure what would happen. That is to say, he couldn't be sure of *everything* that would happen. There would be a cascade of consequences whose end might be observed — but not predicted.

Culpeper itself would be paralyzed, yes. Its cars and tractors would be inoperable, its microwaves and television sets dead. There would be no light, no water, no working sewage system. ATMs, gas stations, bank vaults, security alarms — these would all go down. And they would not come back up.

He wondered how long it would take before anyone would realize the extent of the damage. People were used to power outages and computer crashes. But this would be different, the damage structural, pervasive, and permanent.

It occurred to him that the effect of the pulse would be the opposite of a neutron bomb. A neutron bomb would kill the living things and leave the infrastructure viable. His pulse would destroy the infrastructure without directly impacting anything that lived and breathed.

The local impact would be ironic in at least one way: A small town that just happened to process more than two trillion dollars in transactions per day, would be without access to any cash.

Not that there would be any way to spend it. Cash registers, credit card machines — none of these would work.

Doors would not open, except by hand and

key. Those controlled by chips would have to be taken off their hinges. He wondered about the county jail. If the cell doors were locked by computer, would they stay locked when the systems crashed? Or would the inmates simply be able to stroll out.

Gasoline pumps would not work either, although, for a while at least, there would be little need for gasoline. Vehicles would simply come to a stop as their computer-driven systems stopped firing the fuel injectors. Power brakes and steering would shut down, much as if the drivers had turned off their ignitions. Strong drivers with good reactions ought to be able to bring their vehicles safely to a stop, but it was inevitable that many would lose control.

Trucks? He didn't think they'd fare so well, despite the skill of their drivers and their hydraulic braking systems. Trucks would be in the grip of Newtonian forces aligned against them. The greater mass of the vehicles — and hence their velocity — coupled with the failure of the steering and braking systems, would probably send them out of control.

They'd become unguided missiles.

There would be fires from the exploding fuel tanks and possible HazMat spills. It all depended on which trucks, hauling which loads, were *where* when the EMP — the electromagnetic pulse — hit.

There would be a number of immediate fatalities — and not just from car crashes. Aircraft unlucky enough to be traversing the affected area would drop from the sky.

Pacemakers would go down. Hospitals would become . . . inhospitable. Their generators — backups that automatically cut in during power failures — were hooked up to the building's electrical system, so they would be destroyed by the pulse. Intubated patients in the midst of surgery would die. Monitors and electronically controlled breathing apparatus and drug delivery systems would fail. Locked pharmacies would not open to electronic codes. Elevators would stall between floors.

The most prolonged effect would be caused by damage to the basic infrastructure, especially the roads. Before anyone could address the replacement of the power grid or the restoration of water and sewer, Culpeper's streets would have to be cleared. And they would be choked with inoperable cars. Cars that would never work again.

As for the banking facilities themselves, Wilson was less sure of what would happen. Of course, they would be hardened against EMP. But they would not be able to withstand the pulse he'd be unleashing — a scalar pulse far more potent than the EMP from a nuclear detonation at high altitude. The only defense would be a Tesla shield — and no one had that.

And how would the world financial community react to an attack of this sort? He didn't know. The big systems — Fedwire and CHIPS and SWIFT — were undoubtedly fail-safe. They had to be. The trillions of gigabytes flowing between banks represented real money, with electronic tracking the only records of the transactions.

But Culpeper was a big cog. Even if it was only down for a minute, it would rattle the world's financial markets. Because, of course, if Culpeper could be hit, so could the backups.

Wilson would bet that the stock exchanges and central banks would have to close. Would people panic? He didn't know. He'd be listening to the radio as he drove west.

* * *

Study of the effects of EMP dated back to the days of nuclear tests in the atmosphere. When the Los Alamos boys began to get too much flack for detonating devices close to the ground in Nevada, the tests were moved to isolated islands in the Pacific.

People still squawked. The thermal and blast damage might not be important in these out-of-the-way locales, but the radiation, and its persistence in the soil, was still a problem. The areas would be closed to humanity for decades. Maybe forever.

And there was another problem: Fishermen or nomads had a way of stumbling into harm's way, then to become public relations nightmares, living (or dying) examples of the effects of radiation on the human body.

So the scientists took to the skies.

The way they figured it, tests at high altitude would inflict little blast or thermal damage, and the radioactive fallout would be dispersed over a large area. In this diluted state, the radiation would cause relatively little harm. What they hadn't counted on was a side effect of high-altitude detonation: the electromagnetic pulse.

What happens during a nuclear detonation at altitude is that gamma rays released by the explosion crash into molecules in the atmosphere — oxygen and nitrogen — causing a discharge of high-energy electromagnetic radiation.

When such a pulse hits any conductive material — wires, power lines, antennas, cables, radio towers, railroad tracks, pipes, metal fencing — it is carried along. If the EMP hits an antenna leading to a radio, the radio is fried by the ensuing surge. If the antenna leads to the interior of a reconnaissance airplane, the EMP will destroy the aircraft's instruments. If the railroad track leads to a switching mechanism — or a train — it will burn out the controls. If the pulse hits a building, all its electrical circuits will melt.

Los Alamos physicists found out about EMP's destructive potential in 1962 when they detonated a 1.4 megaton device called Starfish Prime over Johnston Island in the Pacific. On Hawaii, more than seven hundred fifty miles away, electronic systems collapsed. Streetlights flickered out in Oahu, telephones went down in Kauai. Airplanes in the vicinity lost instrumentation. Radio communications were disrupted more than eighteen hundred miles from the blast.

The Russians had similar experiences: power

440

lines blown out of commission, communications systems destroyed, villages darkened.

There were fears that a single high-altitude blast detonated over Kansas would generate an EMP that would destroy all electronics in the lower forty-eight.

Scientists were already so worried about EMP damage in the sixties — when computers were few and digital technology was in its infancy — that nuclear testing went underground after the Johnston Island blast.

Now, computers were ubiquitous and digital technology was behind everything from missile guidance systems to espresso machines.

As a result, the effects of a high-altitude Electromagnetic Pulse would be so profound as to be irreversible. Wilson believed that the pulse he intended to launch from the Nevada fire lookout tower would destroy the entire infrastructure of the continental United States. In one second, the world's only remaining superpower would be a third-world country on par with . . . Angola.

But first, the test. First, Culpeper.

37

DUBLIN JUNE 6, 2005

Burke retrieved Miranda Renfro's address from the town of Fallon's website, which listed the property owners and the amounts of their assessments.

Miranda Renfro owned lot 7B, Echo Village, 3 Fred Brigham Road. With data from the same site, he tried calling her immediate neighbors to see if he could persuade one of them to bring her to the phone.

But no. Two of them thought he was a scam artist, the third didn't speak English.

That night, he drank beer and sat in front of the box. He watched Man United play to a draw at Man City. Then the news, then a program about the Crusades.

He was still drinking too much and it worried him. But it didn't stop him from grabbing another beer. He paced around the room, thinking about it, and finally, he made a decision. If the mountain wouldn't come to Muhammad, Muhammad would go to it. He sat down in front of the computer, and turned it back on. He typed 'Travelocity' into the search bar.

★ ★ ★

As it turned out, making travel arrangements was easy. Explaining to Tommy wasn't.

Burke was telling him about the trip when he realized how obsessive his quest for Wilson must seem. Belgrade was one thing, a little side trip to Slovenia, okay, maybe, but following a slender lead thousands of miles to *Nevada?* This was going too far — geographically, and in every other way.

He could read this in Tommy's eyes, both skeptical and worried. 'What you think you're going t'find there?'

'Jack Wilson, if I'm lucky.'

'Nooooo,' Tommy said. 'You don't believe that, do you?'

'Maybe this Mandy woman will tell me where I can find him. And I can tell Kovalenko.'

'You think so, lad? If someone like you comes here looking, I'm going to tell them — oh, yeh, Michael's over in Dublin, let me gi' you his address?'

'Well — '

'And if you do find him, what you gonna do, hey? 'Jack Wilson, come wi' me to the FBI?' 'The old man frowned. 'And you think he'll toddle along? This man is a *criminal.* No, it's madness, Michael. If you're doing this for the business, forget it. We wait, we take our chances wi' the courts, I canna have you racing around the *globe.*'

Burke said he'd think about it. And he did. In fact, he slept on it.

And in the morning, he took a cab to the airport.

38

It occurred to Wilson that if he waited until night, he could see the town wink out. Which would be interesting, but he wanted to strike during banking hours.

He drank his coffee and packed up. Had some Cheerios and a banana for breakfast. Checked out. Looked at his watch. Nine thirty.

Might as well go.

He started the Escalade and flicked the switch to engage the step-up module (a glorified Tesla coil) with the vehicle's V-8 engine. This comprised the weapon's power source.

He left the car running, and stepped outside. The Escalade's short bed had a rigid cover. This he removed, and set down next to the truck. He dismantled the gimbal rig and moved aside the pieces of the foam cocoon, then connected his laptop to the device. The software that controlled the weapon elevated the barrel and then the focusing program kicked in, swiveling it into position. It was almost noiseless: a faint whir.

If anyone had asked, he would have told them that the weapon was a surveying device. But he was parked near the lot's perimeter and there was no one in sight.

He touched the tattoo on his chest for luck,

then flipped the toggle switch that fired the weapon. He could not detect the beam at all. He heard nothing and, like Tesla and Ceplak before him, he wondered if it had worked.

But unlike Tesla, Wilson did not have to wait weeks for news reports from Siberia. Even as he watched the barrel retract and fold in upon itself, a 727 heading for Dulles slid by directly overhead in complete silence.

Its momentum and glide had taken it beyond the target area. The engines were dead and it was already losing altitude. He wondered how far it would glide. He wondered if he'd hear the impact and explosion.

The plane represented another part of the Culpeper experiment. As the agent of death for innocent people, what would he feel? Would he be repulsed?

The plane yawed to the right.

He hadn't been entirely sure about planes. In trim, with the ailerons and landing gear tucked in, they could glide for quite some distance. And some had backup hydraulic systems that might allow a very good pilot to bring a plane down safely.

But not this aircraft. It was entering a dive. Without the thrust of the engines, it was basically a flying rock.

Wilson lost sight of it for a moment. Then he heard a concussive thump, and black smoke billowed on the horizon.

He felt a strange mix of remorse and elation. He'd been on a lot of planes, and knew what really bad turbulence could do to people. He could imagine the terror of the crew in the cockpit and the passengers' panic. It was probably a bit like Wounded Knee, with death in your face and nowhere to run.

In any case, Wilson thought, it was all in a good cause — and besides, it was fate.

Theirs and his.

★   ★   ★

The random nature of the destruction intrigued Wilson and he would have liked to stay in Culpeper to witness the cascade of events firsthand. But no.

The Comfort Inn was beyond the impact area and he'd been careful to map out an exit route, because it wouldn't take long for the gridlock to ripple outwards. He didn't want to get caught up in that. And besides, he had other business to attend to. He could listen to the news while he drove.

There was a bad moment when he turned the Escalade's key and nothing happened. A rush of sensation in his chest. Maybe his own car hadn't been out of the target area! Had he miscalculated?

But no, his watch was still working. So he tried the key again. This time the engine started with a roar.

★   ★   ★

As he approached an intersection almost thirty miles from the motel, he saw that the traffic

446

signals weren't working. Cars edged through, one at a time.

He wasn't surprised. An EMP hitting Culpeper was certain to cause peripheral damage. He'd had no idea how extensive the damage to the power grid would prove to be, but he knew it could be considerable. The excess voltage from the pulse would fly along the conductive electrical lines, burning out everything for some distance. And as far as the grid was concerned, despite the big outage of 2003, little had been done to improve its stability.

And the truth was that electrical substations were not created equal. If the Culpeper substation was a node that carried a heavy voltage load, its failure would propagate for hundreds of miles. Those outages would be short-lived. The utilities would have things up again in a day or two.

But not in Culpeper. Culpeper was dark. Culpeper was fucked.

He listened to the radio.

The first reports were about events that took place *outside* Culpeper: the plane crash, the spectacular traffic jams. That made sense, of course, because there was nothing coming out of Culpeper itself. Getting TV trucks and communications gear into the little town would be impossible until the traffic jam could be untangled and tow trucks could begin to pick away at the permanently stalled cars.

By the time he reached Pennsylvania, he knew that the banking facilities in Culpeper had not proved capable of withstanding the pulse. The

447

financial markets had closed early — due, it was said, to 'technical problems.' Breathless reporters speculated about 'computer viruses and Trojan horses,' while a White House spokesman dismissed as 'conspiracy theorists' those who suggested that the plane crash was somehow related to the problems Wall Street was experiencing. 'The next thing you know,' he said, 'they'll be dragging in the traffic jams we're seeing outside the Beltway.'

No one said anything about Culpeper. Culpeper wasn't a story yet.

'But this wasn't just any hacker or virus,' one reporter insisted. 'This was financial terrorism.'

Banks in time zones to the west closed early.

International correspondents from Asia to Europe reported that trading had ceased on their exchanges.

The Fed chairman came on the air to announce that there was a 'glitch' in the system. He reassured the public that computerized banking networks were built with safeguards and 'redundant systems,' and that things would soon be up and running again.

And what about the plane? Had it been attacked? Or was the crash just a coincidence?

The vice president urged calm from an undisclosed location.

It was almost dinnertime, and Wilson was nearing Pittsburgh when the first news emerged from Culpeper itself.

Hysterical residents sketched a picture of a town littered with dead vehicles, where nothing electrical or electronic worked.

Those who'd made their way out of Culpeper brought the scene alive. Fires were blazing out of control, most of them ignited by truck or car crashes. Fire trucks and ambulances found it impossible to get to the scene.

Wilson hadn't even considered fire, but of course he should have. The great quake that struck San Francisco in 1906 had done some damage, yes, but it was fire that wrecked the city.

It was shortly after Wilson crossed the border into Ohio that a voice first mentioned the possibility of an 'electromagnetic pulse.' On an NPR talk show, a roundtable of experts batted the subject around. One panelist, a retired nuclear physicist, did his best to explain the phenomenon. But when he started talking about 'Compton recoil electrons,' the host interrupted him.

'But what would cause it? That's the concern.'

'Well, it's very strange that the effect is so localized,' the expert said drily. 'I can't begin to explain that. But generally we see an EMP as the side effect of a thermonuclear detonation.'

Panicked callers swamped the switchboard. The expert backpedaled. Yes, it could have been something else: a solar flare, perhaps, or some kind of 'anomalous lightning storm.'

Within minutes radio stations were airing reassurances by government officials: No radiation had been detected in or around Culpeper.

Media helicopters surveyed the afflicted town, providing updates about the fires and traffic jams and immobilized vehicles. Medevac helicopters swept in and out of the town's airspace, ferrying

449

patients from the regional hospital to facilities in Washington.

Eventually, a handful of Culpeper residents found their way to the airwaves. And that's when some of the wilder reports began to circulate. The sun had blinked out — just for a moment — and then the cars died.

Wilson was near the Indiana border when he first heard that a swarm of black helicopters had been seen just before the pulse hit. Another resident mentioned the sighting of a chupacabra. A third reported seeing 'a saucer-shaped vehicle in Rick Marohn's cornfield.'

On the outskirts of South Bend, he stopped for a six-pack and a Subway sandwich, then took a room at a Ramada. By then, it was all Culpeper, all the time.

39

ATLANTIC CROSSING JUNE 8, 2005

Cruising along at thirty thousand feet, Burke had to agree with Tommy. It was a fool's errand, no doubt about it. He was headed for a trailer park in Nevada to look up a woman who was very unlikely to help him.

Still, above the clouds and power lines, it felt *right*. It was the next logical step, and he had to take it. He looked out the window, into the plain blue sky. He wouldn't admit it to Tommy, because he knew it sounded crazy, but it seemed to him that his search for Jack Wilson was being driven by forces outside himself. That he and Jack Wilson were fated to come together, like blips on a radar screen. What would happen when they met, he didn't know. He couldn't worry about that yet.

What he *did* worry about was getting through Immigration.

The rules for dual citizens holding U.S. passports were clear: You must travel on your U.S. passport when entering or leaving the United States. He thought about taking a chance and using his Irish passport, but Kovalenko had probably put him on some kind of lookout list. Using his Irish papers would be breaking the law

451

— and if they caught him, they might not let him in.

Or worse.

When it was his turn to step over the yellow line, the Latina at his entry station took one look at the VALID ONLY FOR TRAVEL TO THE UNITED STATES stamp, and immediately picked up the telephone. She seemed nervous, punching numbers into her computer. She slid his passport through a scanner, and then gave him a worried look. 'We have to wait for my supervisor.'

A big man in uniform came over to consult. There was a certain amount of keyboarding and then the big man shrugged.

'He doesn't need a passport to travel *inside* the country. Stamp it,' he said, and the Latina did. To Burke he said: 'You can't leave the country on that passport. You do understand that?'

He did.

★ ★ ★

During the plane's long taxi toward the arrival gate, the captain had aired a vague announcement about 'delays.' Aer Lingus personnel would be standing by to advise. Burke hadn't really paid attention. Once he'd cleared Immigration and Customs, he had to get to a different terminal and catch a flight to Reno on America West.

But it was evident inside the terminal that something had happened. The place was thronged. There were crowds around the few TV monitors. People were talking, and even without listening to what they were saying, he could sense the excitement and alarm in their voices, the whine of anxiety.

'I think it's terrorists,' pronounced a man in blue jeans and a Nuggets T-shirt.

'They're saying it's one of them solar flares,' his wife insisted.

Those who had been in the air when it happened, like Burke himself, had to play catch-up. All flights were grounded. Bunchy lines of impatient travelers waited to harry airline agents, seeking vouchers and information.

Mostly there *was* no information. Everyone watched the news, glued to small screens featuring wall-to-wall coverage of a complex nightmare that had already been condensed into a single word: Culpeper.

It took Burke a few minutes to grasp the parameters of the story and when he did, he realized what had happened — and who, and what, was behind it.

He made his way to Terminal 7 and found a little square of territory on the floor. He sat on his suitcase and waited, his eyes on a television monitor.

Helicopter footage showed the hundreds of stranded cars, some of them charred wrecks, and then a montage of burning buildings. The chopper flew low enough so that Burke could see people standing in the street, waving at the camera. Abruptly, the coverage shifted to the site of the airplane crash. Huge pieces of wreckage

453

were being moved by machines. A different reporter interviewed family who'd been waiting for the plane at Dulles. The crawl at the bottom of the screen said that eighty-seven passengers and eight crew members were presumed dead. In Culpeper again, a handheld camera showed shaky footage of men with crowbars trying to pry open an elevator. Inside a hospital corridor, a weary doctor spoke, while the crawl noted that fourteen persons had died, four in mid-surgery and the remainder when life-sustaining equipment failed.

★ ★ ★

At three a.m. — late morning in Slovenia — Burke called Luka Ceplak.

'Michael!' Ceplak roared. 'I *missss* you. How are you?' A heavy sigh. 'I know why you call,' he said, his voice somber now.

'You do?'

'Culpeper, yes? You want to know is our boy?'

'I wondered . . . '

'Is him. These facility — aircraft, too! — *protected* against ordinary EMP. But not scalar EMP. You can't stop it.'

'But I thought if Wilson used the weapon it would be . . . Tunguska.'

'It's different way. You think this town is back in business soon? No no. *Years.*'

'So he struck out at the banks. You think that's it?'

'No,' Ceplak said. 'I think, now he knows it works, he will go again. Bigger.'

454

40

KUALA LUMPUR JUNE 9, 2005

Andrea Cabot worked her way through her morning yoga routine. Her instructor discouraged listening to the news, and in fact recommended 'soothing music,' but Cabot was too busy not to multitask. CNN was on in the background.

She had to agree that the broadcast was not conducive to concentration. It was hyperactive, scattershot coverage of the Culpeper incident: the plane, the inoperable cars, the power outage, the 'down' banking centers, the fires.

As Cabot executed the transition between Downward Dog and the Baby pose, the breathless reporter gave way to the first in a parade of experts.

'Remember that old movie? *The Day the Earth Stood Still*? A man arrives from outer space, and as a display of power, he causes every motor and engine in the world to stop for half an hour. That's what happened to Culpeper. The world just . . . *stopped*.'

Andrea Cabot tuned out. She already knew more about Culpeper than she wanted to, thanks to an avalanche of flash cables that started to arrive within minutes of the event and had not yet diminished. She knew more than the expert or the reporter or the crazed eyewitnesses or the spokespersons for NOAA, FBI, and FEMA.

She knew that Culpeper had been deliberately attacked, that the array of disasters was not the result of a 'solar storm' or 'geomagnetic anomaly' or 'coronal mass ejection.'

It was the result of an electromagnetic pulse of precise dimension and unusual power, probably from an E-bomb, but an E-bomb of 'an unprecedented level of sophistication and precision.' What really stunned the analysts were two facts. The first was the power of the pulse. The banking facilities in Culpeper had been hardened against conventional EMPs, as was true of most sensitive facilities. *This* EMP had overwhelmed state-of-the-art shielding. The second thing the analysts couldn't get past was the 'surgical' nature of the attack. That *was* alarming. That meant the attack involved technology that the Pentagon itself did not possess.

In some ways, though, the assessment had set her mind at ease. It meant that Culpeper had nothing to do with her — and a good thing, too, because she already had a lot on her plate.

She came out of Baby and lifted into Cobra.

Two weeks ago, she'd picked up chatter about an upcoming chain of attacks against 'Western' hotels in Bangkok and Kuala Lumpur. Something spectacular and coordinated in the Qaeda style.

But the boys over here would not be employing anything like the Culpeper device — whatever it was. They'd attack with fertilizer bombs. Or with improvised explosive rigs strapped to the chests of young men with Down's syndrome.

Which was another way of saying that Culpeper was somebody else's problem.

41

Wilson took a long shower, shaved carefully, then dressed with the care that people reserved for important occasions. It was part of the process of readying himself, a way to bring focus and gravity to what he was about to do.

His clothes were an exercise in misdirection: a cheap pair of athletic shoes and a dark blue jumpsuit with an oval patch containing the name 'Jim.' He had a clipboard as well, and a plastic pocket protector with a couple of ballpoint pens. The K-Bar knife from the army-navy store fit comfortably into the large pocket of his jumpsuit. Unlike the rest of his outfit, the knife had nothing to do with misdirection.

He smiled at the workman in the mirror.

Then he put on his watch — not the Garmin, but the watch they'd returned to him the day he'd left Allenwood. It had been taken from him in San Francisco nearly a decade earlier. The feds had put it in a box, and the box had followed him on his long journey through the prison system.

And while he was doing his time, and the watch was running down in the company of his 'personal effects,' what had Robbie Maddox — the sleazeball who'd set him up — been

458

doing? While Wilson had nothing to look at but a slice of sky, where had Maddox been and what had he seen? How many meals had he eaten with friends, while Wilson had his food shoved at him through a *wicket* in his cell door? How many women had Maddox known while Wilson sat by himself, talking to the wall? How much music had Maddox listened to while Wilson tried, and failed, to shut his ears to the constant slam of sliding cell-block doors and the incessant patter and shouts and cries of men without hope?

These were rhetorical questions with a single answer, and Wilson knew what it was. Most of the time, Robbie had been in the joint himself. Two years here and there, a year somewhere else. It was all in the report he'd commissioned from a P.I. named Charley Fremaux, in Chicago.

It took Fremaux less than a week to find the snitch. He was living in Waverly, Nebraska, a suburb of Lincoln, where he had been for more than a year. Injured in a car crash that the police thought was part of an insurance scam gone bad, Maddox had moved in with his older sister, Lynn, a librarian who lived alone. Long since recovered from his injuries, Maddox continued to enjoy his sister's room and board.

Wilson studied himself in the mirror. He knew that what he was about to do was self-indulgent. It wasn't part of his larger plan. If anything, it put the plan at risk.

But Robbie Maddox had buried him alive. He'd lied and cheated, bartering Wilson's life for a few weeks on the outside. There was no way for Maddox to repay the time he'd stolen.

Wilson worked to quiet his mind. He held the image of a leaf in his mind's eye: a green leaf, caught in a spider's thread, the leaf spinning and fluttering in the invisible wind.

And then he headed for the door. For Robbie Maddox, time had run out.

★　★　★

Broad daylight. Not just any daylight, but *broad* daylight, the kind of daylight in which banks get robbed and people get gunned down.

The phrase interested Wilson. Included in the account of a crime, it always carried a note of outrage. It suggested a state of illumination so thoroughly bright and all-encompassing that wrongdoing should be inconceivable. A light that cast no shadows and left no place to hide. Any crime committed under its auspices was all the more horrific.

At one o'clock in the afternoon, Wilson stopped at a pay phone outside a convenience store to call the library where Maddox's sister worked. He asked to speak with her, and when she came on the line, he hung up.

At one fifteen, he parked the Ford Escort he'd rented around the corner from the little rancher at the address Fremaux had given him. Clipboard in hand, he walked to the front door. A motorcycle sat in the driveway, which suggested to Wilson that he was in the right place at the right time.

He knocked.

When the door swung open, Maddox had

about half a second to get away. But it took him a full second to recognize the man in front of him. By then, it was too late. Wilson threw an overhand right that shattered the bones around Maddox's left eye, and sent him reeling into the living room. Wilson followed him into the house as Maddox, stooped in pain, screamed, 'What the fuck?!'

There was a poker standing beside the fireplace with some other tools, and without thinking, Wilson grabbed it. Maddox staggered backwards in a panic, stumbling against a coffee table, hands in front of his face.

'Hey — ' he said.

Wilson drove the poker into the side of Maddox's knee, dropping him to the ground with a scream that kept on giving. He looked around. The door was still open, but it didn't matter. This wasn't going to take long. He slammed the poker into Maddox's shoulder. Then the other shoulder. And again.

Tossing the poker aside, he got down on his haunches beside the man who'd set him up. 'Jesus, Robbie, it's been a long time! How you been?'

'Ohhh, man . . . ' Maddox's voice was a low quaver, a mixture of terror, pain, and recognition. His speech came breathlessly, in gasps. 'I didn't *know*! I mean, what I was doing, I — I'm sorry, man! I'm really — '

Wilson reached into his jumpsuit, withdrew the K-bar knife.

Maddox saw it, and sunk deeper into the shag rug. 'Please . . . '

461

Wilson buried the knife to its hilt in Maddox's chest, then pulled it out and made sure of things. Grabbing him by the ponytail, he jerked the snitch's head to the side, and back, and slashed his throat.

Then he got to his feet, surprised to find himself out of breath, watching the dark blood pool around his shoes. As he started to leave, a thought occurred to him, and he turned back. *I really ought to take his scalp,* Wilson thought. *It would be, like, an homage.* He considered the idea for a long ten seconds, standing in the doorway with the knife, dripping in his hand.

But in the end, he decided against it. He wasn't a savage, after all, and besides — where would he put it?

42

KUALA LUMPUR JUNE 10, 2005

After a long, long day, Andrea Cabot was drifting in a pleasant half sleep that promised to deepen into the real thing when something began to nag at her. She shifted position and tugged at one of her pillows. She'd already pulled two all-nighters this week, and she was dead tired. She longed to be unconscious.

And so she drifted down, a delicious, lolling descent into a real *slumber* . . . when a bolt of realization jerked her upright.

It's a test! Culpeper was a test!

The phrase swam up from her memory. She'd been with 2-TIC at the time and she'd been looking at surveillance footage with a Brit from MI-6 and that chubby guy from the Bureau — what was his name?

Kovalenko.

The three of them watched it over and over: the man with the hat and the sling, the man who'd left a pair of suitcases packed with newspapers near the British Airways counter and then departed. Which had caused the evacuation of the terminal.

It's a test, Kovalenko said, after they'd screened the footage for about the tenth time. And he was right. Andrea knew he was right.

463

The Brit didn't get it. If you want to blow up the airport, why not just do it? he'd asked. *Why practice?*

But the Brit had been missing the point. The test was not to see if the man in the sling could get the suitcases into a dangerous position. The test was to see if the man would do it. The *man* was being tested, not the plan.

Woven through this recollection was everything she knew about Culpeper — what she'd seen on CNN and what she knew from the cables and gossip. Culpeper was a black hole. But why Culpeper? Why *just* Culpeper?

Everyone thought it was because of the banking nexus there, that it had been a strike at the financial heart of the west. But Cabot didn't buy that. The presence of SWIFT and the Federal Reserve installation may have played a part in target selection, but she thought the attack was confined to Culpeper because it was a test.

But a test of what?

This was where the third, truly alarming, train of thought came in. This one involved Hakim Mussawi, lying on the table, coming off the Anectine paralysis. She'd check the transcripts, but she didn't think she was mistaken in her recollection.

'There's an American!' he'd gasped, spitting out the words as if they could save his life. 'He's *building a machine.*'

What kind of machine? she'd wanted to know. Thinking, of course, a bomb.

But no. Mussawi said that the American was

464

building a machine that was going to stop the world.

Or not exactly that. It was going to *stop the motor of the world.*

It was this phrase, gasped out in extremis, that now caused the hair on the back of her neck to stand up.

What had the expert on CNN said that morning? He'd been talking about an old movie, but what he'd said was: 'For Culpeper, the world has stopped.'

Andrea squeezed her eyes shut. There was something else: that fuckup in Berlin, the Bobojon Simoni mess. The follow-up intel from that fit into this somehow. She threw on her clothes. Was she crazy? Did this shit actually *fit?*

Though she almost never drove herself, she was in no mood to wait for her driver. Getting the BMW from the garage, she launched the car into the chaos of KL's streets, where even at two a.m., there was a surprising amount of traffic. Despite the hurry she was in, she took the time to make sure she wasn't being followed. Keeping her eyes on the rearview mirror, she made a series of left turns, effectively turning in a circle over the course of a dozen blocks, then reversed her course with a U-turn in the middle of a crowded intersection.

She ought to call Berlin, she told herself. Pete Spagnola was the guy. She'd pick his brain, try to nail it down: What was it about the Simoni incident that set off the alarm in the back of her head?

Then there was Mussawi. He was being held

465

on an aircraft carrier in the Sea of Japan. She was going to need another session with him. She'd need to chopper in.

And last but not least, Ray Kovalenko. That thing with the suitcases. There was no reason to think that the man in the sling had even been a U.S. national, let alone the 'American' Mussawi was screaming about. But the surveillance footage from Dulles nagged at her and it wouldn't hurt to touch base with Ray.

★   ★   ★

Cabot glanced up at the array of clocks — nine p.m. in Berlin. Unless there was something special happening, Pete wouldn't be there. She called the switchboard. They could give her Pete's home number.

But, no. He'd been 'rotated' back to Langley. 'His duties are being handled by Ms. Logan. Shall I connect you . . . ?'

'Madison Logan.'

'You're working late,' Andrea said.

'No, *you're* working late,' said the preppy voice at the other end, displaying an impressive understanding of Cabot's whereabouts.

'Yes, well, a thought woke me up and I wanted to talk to Pete. About Simoni? I'm assuming you — '

'I'm well briefed on that,' Logan reassured her. 'How can I help?'

'Those steg files on Simoni's computer. I'm talking about the bank accounts that received Qaeda money? I can't quite remember, but

466

didn't one of them walk back to a U.S. national?'

'Well, that's the thinking, although I'm not sure there's actual proof. It was an account at the Cadogan Bank on St. Helier. Is this important?'

Cabot ignored the question. 'Who handled the investigation of the account?'

'It was the FBI Legat in London,' Logan said. 'Kovalenko.'

'Ray!' Cabot said.

'You seem surprised.'

'No, no,' Cabot reassured her. 'Just a small world.'

★   ★   ★

As Kovalenko listened to Andrea Cabot, his stomach churned. And the longer he listened, the worse he felt.

She was giving him intel from a rendition, the interrogation of some raghead. And what she was saying made his heart stagger in his chest.

' . . . 'stop the motor of the world,' ' she said. 'That's what he said: 'there's an American who wants to stop the motor of the world.' Now I'm thinking — that sounds like an EMP. That sounds like Culpeper.'

'Andrea,' he gasped.

'Wait wait wait,' she said. 'Let me just get through this before it all just . . . disassembles in my mind. Now the guy we picked up in KL — he's the one who gave up the Qaeda operative in Berlin — the one who got shot.'

'Bobojon Simoni.'

467

'Right. And Simoni's computer was the source of a list of bank accounts.'

Kovalenko's heart was sinking. Not just sinking, *hurting*, a burrowing pain in his chest. This is the way it could happen: heart attack.

'And you got sent out to check on one of those accounts, am I right, Ray? Cadogan Bank, St. Helier?'

'Andrea,' he said. His voice had barely enough velocity to make it out of his mouth.

But the bitch kept talking.

'Didn't you find out that account belonged to an American? An *American*, Ray . . . you see where this is going? An American who got money from Qaeda, who wanted to build an engine that would stop the world. Well, I think he's made a start. So we have to talk to that American. *Right away.* Who is he, Ray? Where is he? Whatever you've got — gimme, gimme, gimme.'

Kovalenko's mind was whirling. *Stop the motor of the world*. Straight out of *Atlas Shrugged*. 'Francisco d'Anconia,' who once had an account in St. Helier, was the guy who did Culpeper — he had no fucking doubt.

And now his mind presented him with a scene in the Nightingale Arms where the man from the firm in Dublin was trying to give him the data he'd collected on d'Anconia. Biographical details. D'Anconia's *real* name. What was his name? Bork? Burke. That was it — *Mike Burke*. He'd actually *written it out* for Kovalenko. On an index card. All he wanted was to have the restrictions lifted on his father-in-law's firm.

And what did he, Ray Kovalenko, do with this gift of information? He'd glanced at the card, yes, but what did he *do* with it? *He didn't remember.*

The information had seemed unimportant. He'd intended to send it to Washington, but . . . he hadn't done that. The truth was, he didn't remember doing *anything* with the card.

It must be in the office, he told himself. *Or* — what had he been wearing? Maybe it was in some pocket. The truth was he had no idea where it was. It was possible — *no, he wouldn't do that, would he?* — that he'd thrown the card away.

At the Nightingale, Kovalenko remembered telling Burke that the information on the card wasn't worth much. He remembered making Burke so mad, the fuck looked like he was going to head-butt him.

And now, unless Kovalenko could find that card, he was going to have to go crawling back to Mike Burke. *Begging* him.

'Ray?' Andrea said.

'I don't have it. But I'll get it.'

'What do you mean?'

'I'll get back to you.'

He heard her shriek as he was putting the phone down: '*Ray!*'

43

JOHN F. KENNEDY AIRPORT
JUNE 12, 2005

By the time flight restrictions were lifted, fourteen hours after Burke's arrival at JFK, the terminal was a wreck. People were surprisingly patient and cheerful, but there was no water or food and the restrooms were alarming. It was six more hours before Burke got a seat on a flight to Reno. By then he was willing to go anywhere within a thousand miles of his destination, but since this flexibility was shared by virtually everyone in the terminal, it did no good.

Once in Reno, though, he rented a car, intending to drive to Fallon. But when he started nodding out behind the wheel, he pulled into a Travelodge outside of Sparks, and collapsed into bed.

The next day, it took him two hours to get to Fallon, a time he spent rehearsing his spiel for Mandy Renfro. He was a reporter, writing a piece for *Harper's* . . . .Somehow it didn't sound particularly convincing. But it was the best he could do, really, so he drove on, relying on the Mapquest directions to get him there.

The trailer and its setting were tidy and neat, surrounded by a low white picket fence. He stood on the doorstep, holding the wilted bouquet he'd bought that morning at a convenience store, and rapped on the door. It was opened by a very old woman in jeans and a gingham shirt. Her eyes were a startling pale blue.

'Help you?' she asked, but his reply was drowned out as a pair of navy jets roared overhead. He'd read in the guidebook that Fallon was the location of the Top Gun pilot training program.

Mandy Renfro smiled and held up a finger. 'You get used to it,' she shouted. Once the noise died down, she asked, 'Now, how can I help you?'

Burke told her that he was writing a story for *Harper's* about the Invention Secrecy Act.

'I see,' she said, and frowned at the flowers. 'Those poor things need help.' She gave him an assessing look. 'You might as well come in. *You* look thirsty, too.'

She invited him to sit in the tiny living room. At one end of the room was a shrine to Jack: a shelf of trophies, a couple of photos, some certificates, and a Stanford pennant.

Mandy put the flowers in water, and came out after a few minutes with two tall glasses of iced tea. Only when she had stirred in the sugar with a long-handled spoon, and put their glasses on the coffee table, did she herself sit down.

Every minute or so, a jet put their conversation on hold.

'So who did you say you're doing the story for?'

'*Harper's*,' Burke replied.

471

Mandy Renfro gazed at him with her bright blue eyes. 'Young man,' she said, 'I don't b'lieve you're telling me the truth.'

'Well — '

'It doesn't matter,' she said, 'I can't help you with Jack anyway. I know he's out of prison because I make it my business to keep up with him.' She glanced down at her hands. 'But he does not make it his business to keep up with me.'

'So the last time you saw him was in the courtroom?'

'That's right.'

'Like everybody else.'

She took a dainty sip. 'You look awful tired. Why don't you tell me why you're really here? What's your interest in Jack?'

Burke was tired of lying. He told her the outlines of the story, but left out the part about Culpeper. 'I think he's building a weapon,' Burke told her. 'A powerful one.'

She closed her eyes and shook her head. 'Lotta anger in that boy, and why not? After all those years in that terrible place.'

Burke nodded.

'There's two ways animals get when they been hurt bad — and Jack's been hurt bad, you know. Some critters will curl up and pretend to be dead and just kind of keep a low profile and ride it out. The others? You hurt them and they want to hurt you back. They attack. Or they wait, and *then* they attack. Even dogs been known to hold grudges. Coyotes, too.' She took a sip of tea.

'You think Jack is going to retaliate.'

'Jack was done wrong. So, yes — I worry about what he might do, smart as he is, strong-willed as he is.'

'I worry, too.'

'What will you do if you find him?'

'I'm not sure,' Burke said. And it was true; he really didn't know. 'You think he'll come here?'

'This little trailer was his special spot, but if he isn't here by now, he's not coming.' A sigh. She stirred her tea. 'You've heard about it, I'm sure, that he was found in a box at the door to the hospital, with his name on one of those stickers.'

Burke nodded.

'That put Jack to feeling bad about himself — he was abandoned, no two ways about it. But I explained that sometimes a child is left like that to protect it from harm. And I told him it was a beginning in life that he shared with some mighty powerful figures. Moses for one, drifting in his little basket. And Sargon — he was the king of Mesopotamia — also found in a basket. I told Jack his start in life was right out of legend.'

Burke nodded.

Mandy had a little smile on her face. 'You're thinking how's a lady lives in a trailer know about ancient Mesopotamia. Before I met Alan, my husband, I had two years at Boise State. And I'm a great reader. I gave that to Jack.

'Anyway, Jack came here when he was ten and we never did find out about his parents. One white, one Indian — that was clear from looking at him. He was a half-blood. Half Paiute, you might guess, because Paiutes are mostly what you have in Nevada. And then there was the name — that pretty much sealed it. Anyway, Alan and I — Jack, too, when he was older — we looked and looked to try to discover who his parents might be, all the local history in the papers and so on. Anybody pregnant, any young woman who disappeared.'

'But you never found out.'

'Nossir. Somebody with some schooling, you might think — else they never would have heard of the first Jack Wilson. And that was interesting, too, that his mama, or maybe his daddy, chose to honor an ancestor, but chose the white name instead of the native one.'

'Wovoka.'

She looked up, her eyes sharp. 'So you have done some lookin' around.'

He nodded.

'Whoever Jack's parents might have been, it was a dandy genetic combination. Jack was just *beautiful*. Oh lord, with his shock of hair and big dimples and those frying-pan eyes — folks just couldn't take their eyes off that boy. And smart? Just as bright as a penny.'

'I've heard that.'

'You have no idea. When he came to me as a foster child, he was still a boy, really — small for his age. He'd already been through half a dozen foster homes. Nothing against the system, they *try*, they really do, but they've got some crazy rules and they've got some foster parents prob'ly shouldn't be parents at all. Some of these people take children in as a moneymaking proposition.'

'Really?'

'Oh lord, yes. They'll have eight, ten kids

— and that's a lot, isn't it? Especially when these are kids with issues.' She sighed and sipped her tea. 'Jack got slapped around by one foster mother's boyfriend, and then he was in a couple of these warehouse-type deals. When he came to me and Alan, he was . . . *guarded*. It took a while to win his trust. But then . . . ' She shut her eyes and Burke saw tears glitter in the corners. 'We really *did* become a family.'

'How long was he with you?'

'Until he was sixteen. Six years. Alan and I . . . we helped him look into his heritage and made sure he knew about Paiute history. I took him to Pyramid Lake and introduced him to the people there. Would you like to see a picture?'

'Sure.' Burke followed her into a tiny room.

'This was Jack's room,' she told him. 'And that's Jack with Peter Whitecloud.' She pointed to a framed photograph of a twelve-year-old boy smiling beside an older man in blue jeans and a sweater. 'Peter was head of the tribal council then. A real V.I.P.'

'Is he still around?' Burke asked.

'No,' Mandy said. 'He passed a few years ago.'

There was a posterboard next to the bed, and Burke went over to it. 'What's this?' he asked.

'Oh, that — that was a ninth-grade project Jack did. He got an A plus!'

Under the heading *200 Years of Losing Ground* was a series of beautifully drawn maps of the continental United States. Burke looked closer and saw that color-coded areas represented the lands of various tribes. There were six maps in all, starting in 1775 and ending in 1975.

475

Sidebars in small boxes noted the enactment of laws and treaties affecting the Indians, mostly for the worst. The maps dramatized the rapid diminution of land belonging to Native Americans.

In the last map, there were only a few specks of color east of the Mississippi. In the West, the biggest chunks of Indian land were in the Dakotas and in the Four Corners region. Even in Oklahoma, the whole of which had been declared 'Indian Territory' in 1835, reservation land was now but a tiny fraction of the state.

'They're *still* suffering,' Mandy said. 'Folks think the casinos have changed it all, but the truth is, Native Americans are *still* the least healthy, least wealthy, and least educated of all the peoples in the United States.' She sighed, and led him back to the living room. 'I don't mean to rattle on,' she said.

'What happened when Jack was sixteen?' Burke asked. 'Where did he go?'

The old woman squeezed her eyes shut. 'My husband got liver cancer. They can't really do a damn thing for it — except, maybe, a transplant. Alan was on the list, but . . . we ran out of time.' She sighed. 'Anyway, when Alan was diagnosed, I didn't let on about it. I should have, I know, but I was afraid they'd take Jack away.'

'You mean Child Services? Why would they do that?'

'Because we were old — or not 'old,' but old to be Jack's foster parents. I was fifty-five and Alan was sixty when he came to us. It was just pure old-fashioned luck that we got him. They had to place him, we were willin', and at the time, they had nobody else. But when they found out that Alan was sick and that I was spending a lot of time taking care of him, that was that.' A quick intake of breath.

'I'm sorry.'

She dabbed at her eyes with her knuckles. 'He didn't want to go. We were all the family he had, plus he knew I couldn't take care of Alan by myself. Without Jack's help, Alan would have to go to a hospice. And that's what he did.' A sigh. 'I had to be real firm with Jack. I knew he'd try to run away and come back, but I made him promise not to. I told him that it would be the death of me if he spoiled his chances. Even back then, he wanted to go to Stanford, and I knew he had a real shot at it. But not if he got into trouble. And 'running away,' they treat that like it's a felony, you know?'

Burke nodded.

'Jack got to a place in town that wasn't too bad — lots of kids and they made him pray all the time. But Jack was old enough by then to look after himself. And he got to stay at the high school, which was great. He went with me to visit Alan most weekends, and I met him at the library a bunch of times. We did his college applications there.'

'But they didn't let him come back after your husband died?'

She shook her head. 'I was too old to look after him — that's what they said.'

'But he got into Stanford.'

'I was so proud! Bright as he was, it was still a

miracle. And then to do so well. And that invention! He was *so* excited! It would have been a tremendous boon. He was going to buy me a house, which I didn't need. But he would have *loved* to do that. It would have made him feel . . . I don't know. Real good about himself.' She sighed and her shoulders slumped. Suddenly, she looked very tired. 'I still can't believe what happened,' she said. Her eyes teared up, but she didn't cry. 'Now, maybe he was mad — he certainly had the right to be mad — but he never would have hurt anybody. Not my Jack.'

'Not then, but . . . what about now?'

She shook her head. 'I don't know.'

Burke leaned toward her. 'What worries me is . . . I think he might be involved with this Culpeper thing. And that Culpeper might not be the end of it.'

'Oh my God — ' Her hand flew up to her mouth. 'I'm sorry. I just don't know a thing that could help you.' Her damp eyes shone like crushed jewels. 'I don't know him anymore. I only know the person he used to be. Even in court, even by then, he was different. You could see it. Eyes closed down, hard as a stone.' She shook her head. 'He's been out for months now, and he hasn't called.'

'But if he does . . . '

She pursed her lips, and nodded. 'If he does, I'll call you.' She offered a square of paper from a basket. It was the reverse side of a page from a one-a-day calendar of flower photos. He gave her his number in Dublin, and told her he'd check his messages each day.

478

He was saying good-bye, on his way out the door, when her voice stopped him. 'You know . . . ' she said.

When he turned, she was looking at the calendar page.

'I don't see how this can help,' she told him, 'but if Jack . . . *does* something . . . I can guess the date.'

'When? How?'

'June twenty-two. It's an important date for a lot of Native Americans. Because it's the solstice.' She pressed her lips together. 'You say 'sundance' now and everybody thinks of Robert Redford. But the Sun Dance was the biggest ceremony of the year for many tribes. The government outlawed it way back when — and I know Jack wrote a paper about it in high school. He said it was like outlawing Christmas.'

'Why was it outlawed?' Burke asked.

She shrugged. 'Because it was bloody — for *some* of the tribes, at least. White people were repulsed by it.'

'What did they do?'

'It was different from tribe to tribe, but it always involved a lodge pole, like a May Pole, but bigger, standing in the ground. The Plains tribes would attach a buffalo skull to the pole, and stuff it with offerings of grass. Other tribes tied a buffalo penis to the pole. But the idea was the same: The land should be fertile, and the people, too. There was always a lot of drumming and dancing and singing, and, well, this is the part that got so many whites upset. Some of the men would be tethered to the pole by straps attached to hooks in their chests or backs.'

'Jesus,' Burke exclaimed.

'Well, you can imagine,' Mandy said. 'They'd fast and suffer for days, dancing in a circle around the pole, pulling against their own flesh, hallucinating and having visions. The way Jack explained it in his paper, it was a symbolic death, part of the great cycle. When they finally broke free from the pole, it was like . . . a resurrection.' She frowned. 'Anyway, Jack's essay won a prize and all. I'm thinking that if he was going to make a gesture, that's when he'd do it.'

Burke frowned. Today was June 13.

Mandy saw the look on his face, and guessed what he was thinking. 'I know,' she said, 'it's not even ten days.'

44

The city at night. It took your breath away.

Wilson drank it all in as he headed into town. The hills tumbling down to the water. The contours of land, made visible by the city's lights, ending at the harbor's inky edge. It was gorgeous, and it just got better the closer you came. A galaxy of skyscrapers glittered against a backdrop of stars, the Golden Gate ablaze with the lights of cars.

The natural setting was spectacular, but it was technology that made the city beautiful at night. Wilson smiled at the irony. The glittering world in front of him was a direct descendant of the first illuminated metropolis: the White City of the Chicago World's Fair, which Tesla's inventions had helped to light.

Ironically, Wilson thought, it was Tesla's technology, improved upon by himself and manifest in the transmitter atop the lookout tower in Nevada, that would put out the lights forever. America was about to return to more natural, diurnal rhythms.

How long, he wondered, until the cars disintegrated? Decades, he guessed, even in the Bay Area's moist air. Some of the metal might be scavenged. The rest would oxidate. But the

481

plastic? The rubber? It would be there for centuries, an eyesore and a reminder, except in the country's more fecund climates, where it would disappear in the midst of encroaching forests.

And the bridges? The bridges would remain until an earthquake pulled them down.

Driving into the city, he felt the lure of it: the normal life. He and Irina could be happy here. He could sell the ranch and buy a house. Get a job, or start a business. Felon or not, a good engineer was a rare commodity. He could introduce Irina to the silver-dollar pancakes at Sears, and watch her dimpled smile as she enjoyed the role reversal of being waited on. They could go to Chinatown and Golden Gate Park. Their kids would play t-ball and soccer. He'd buy her a minivan, and head north along the coast to the Russian River, where people from her part of the world settled a century ago, trapping and fishing.

Right, Wilson thought. We'll do that. And then we'll hold hands and sing 'We Are the World.'

He pulled up in front of the Nikko, and let the valet park the Escalade. The transmitter he'd used in Culpeper was locked down under the bed's cover. Then he checked in, went to his room, and cleaned up.

He grabbed a bottle of water from the minibar, dropped into a comfortable chair, and removed the tiny photograph of Irina from his wallet. He looked at it for a long time. There was something almost inscrutable about her expression, a mixture of sadness and hope . . . and something else. He couldn't quite figure it out, but that was okay, too. She'd be flying into Vegas in a few days, and after that, he'd have a lifetime to learn her secrets.

★ ★ ★

It was raining the next morning. Brake lights bled onto the slick black pavement. The Escalade's wheels hissed as it rolled along a network of one-way streets, arriving, just a few minutes later, at the courthouse.

The building didn't open until nine, but he wanted to get to it early, so he could scope out the parking. He needed exact GPS coordinates for both the spot where he'd be parked and the courtroom he was targeting. Culpeper had been a more amorphous target, and therefore comparatively easy.

The awkward part was the need to expose and elevate the weapon. It didn't look like much, it didn't even look like a weapon, but it looked strange — there was no question about that. And while he needed clean sight lines, he also needed to park in a spot where no one was likely to notice the truck for the few minutes it would take to do what he had to do.

In the end, any number of places might have been suitable, but the decision as to which was best was a no-brainer. He smiled as he pressed the button and retrieved the ticket for the Turk Street garage. It was so early that only the first two levels were occupied — with a sprinkling of cars on the third. After that, nothing.

Wilson drove straight to the roof. Rain pounded the windshield as he emerged into the open air. It was clear at a glance that at eight a.m. on a weekday, level five was likely to be empty.

After checking the locations of surveillance cameras, he backed into slot 952.

Standing at the truck's rear, Wilson looked out directly at the courthouse. The CCTV cameras would be able to see the bed of the truck, this was true, but one camera's visual field would be partially impeded by a post and the other would be somewhat obscured by the truck's cab.

He considered it. He could spray-paint the lenses. Or he could go with the probabilities. There were four cameras on each level. That made twenty cameras in all. There was probably a bank of monitors somewhere on-site. But most of the time, absent a disturbance, no one would be looking at the feed from the surveillance cameras. The footage was primarily for later use, if there was a theft or some other crime.

What were the odds, Wilson wondered, that a security guard would be paying attention to the camera covering slot 952 during the five minutes Wilson needed to deploy the weapon? And what, in any case, would the guard see? Surveying equipment, or something like it, in the back of a Cadillac Escalade.

He took the elevator to street level and crossed to the Philip Burton Federal Courthouse. It was a huge structure. He'd read that there were eighty assistant U.S. attorneys, six federal magistrates, and thirteen district judges walking its halls. Fed Central, in other words.

One of the district judges was former U.S. Attorney Joe Sozio, who had brought the solicitation of murder charge against Wilson. Sozio had been appointed to the bench by President George W. Bush in 2003. He was currently presiding over a case in Courtroom 3.

Wilson signed in, and showed his ID. He placed his jacket and hat on the conveyor belt, and put his wristwatch and change in a plastic bin. The guard waved him through.

The case in Courtroom 3 seemed to involve a Central American gang. Wilson scanned the crowd. The benches closest to the defense side of the courtroom were packed with Salvadorans. At least, he thought they were Salvadorans. Their skin was darker than Wilson's own, and they had the distinctive features of the region. Wilson noticed that the older observers — parents, aunts, and uncles, he supposed — were modestly but respectably dressed, while the younger males wore the big shirts and droopy pants of gangbangers.

Like Wilson, they were Indians or, what was more likely, mestizos — a mixture of Indian and European blood.

'All rise.'

Wilson got to his feet with the others while the bailiff called the court to order. He took a GPS reading from his wristwatch, and noted it on a pad. It was nine thirty-two.

Wearing his robes, Judge Sozio entered the room with the air of a celebrity, striding to the thronelike chair on which he sat in judgment on

485

mere mortals. He was the patriarch, and it was only when he had taken his seat that the rest of them were allowed to do the same.

Wilson watched him with a cold eye. His hair had thinned and gone to gray, and his chin was beginning to sag. But, otherwise, he looked much the same. His light brown eyes still had the predatory gaze of a raptor. For a moment, they flicked Wilson's way, and Wilson felt his heart do a little dance in his chest. But there was no gleam of recognition in Sozio's eyes.

One of the Salvadoran kids was sworn in. 'I do,' he said in a high-pitched whispery voice, following the bailiff's bored recitation.

The prosecutor, a Latina in a pale blue suit, got to her feet at Sozio's prompt and swerved toward the kid like a cruising shark.

Wilson didn't want to call attention to himself. He waited until the court went into recess, and returned to his hotel.

There, he typed the GPS coordinates that he'd taken into his ThinkPad. Then he set about logging in the equations that defined the beam.

This was one of the amazing things about the weapon, something Wilson had learned from a marginal note of Tesla's. The beam was versatile, capable of emitting paired waves from any part of the electromagnetic spectrum. In one manifestation, it caused total destruction of the target mass — Tunguska, in other words. But with a relatively simple focal adjustment, he could unleash an electromagnetic pulse like the one over Culpeper.

For Sozio, however, Wilson had something else

in mind. With a tweak, he could irradiate the courthouse with energy from a different part of the spectrum, one that had much longer wavelengths and lower frequencies than gamma rays. Microwaves, in other words.

He was a kid when microwave ovens first became popular. People hadn't understood how they worked. Not that they understood them now, but at least they knew enough not to put poodles in them to dry after a shampoo. Most people also realized that positioning was critical in a microwaved environment. For even cooking, you had to rotate the dish, or place it on a revolving turntable. Volume was important, too. The more you had in the oven, the longer it would take to cook. And metal was out: Even little kids knew that it would blacken, pop, and burn if you microwaved it.

Like poodles, people are mostly water. Put water in a microwave, and it will boil.

Or at least some of it will. Because of the building's structural complexity and the nature of microwaves, the damage to people in the courthouse would not be uniform. Some would get a sunburn, probably a bad one. But others would be hit harder. They'd see their skin split open like the casing of a steamed hot dog. It would be terrible. And it would be even more dramatic in Courtroom 3, where everyone, but most especially his Honor, Judge Sozio, would explode like so many balloons.

★　★　★

He got up early the next morning and exercised for an hour in the Nikko's gym. After he showered, he put on the hotel robe. Out of habit, he picked up the sewing kit and dropped it into his suitcase. In the old days, he used to save that sort of thing for Mandy. Her eyes had been starting to go and she loved the little plastic containers: the prethreaded needles lined up in an array of colors.

Mandy. She had been the hardest one to turn his back on, harder than Sharon, even. A couple of times he'd been tempted to drive out to the trailer and see her. He could imagine her, sitting outside in the white Adirondack chair he'd given her on her birthday. Iced tea perched on the armrest. A book in hand.

Forget it, he told himself, and called down to the front desk for his car. Then dressed and packed his bag, left a tip for the maid and headed out.

It was one of those quintessential California days, sparkling and clear, the air rinsed clean by yesterday's rain. He drove to the garage on Turk Street and made his way to the roof.

His was the only vehicle there. He backed into the chosen slot and with the engine running, unsnapped the cover, pulled aside the Styrofoam that held the weapon in place, and attached it to the laptop. Then he waited for the barrel to telescope into position. When the green diode began to blink at its base, he took a deep breath, and flipped the toggle switch.

That was that.

Thirty seconds later, he toggled the switch a

second time. The light blinked off, and the barrel telescoped into itself. He reset the Styrofoam blocks, buttoned the cover over the Escalade's little bed, and got back in the truck. Then he wound his way down to the ground floor of the garage, forcing himself to drive slowly so his tires wouldn't squeal on the floor.

This was the one drawback to parking on the roof. It took a while to get down and, when he did, he was hyperventilating. There were two cars in front of him, waiting to pay, and they took their time about it. When he finally pulled out of the garage into the street, people were staggering out of the federal building in droves, hysterical and screaming. Some fell to the ground and rolled. Others stutter-stepped, first one way, then the other.

Their flight was pointless and reflexive, like insects sprayed with poison. There was no escaping what had happened to their bodies, but escape they must, so flee they did. It was useless, of course. And these were the survivors! (At least, for now.) The scene *inside* the courthouse would be unimaginable.

Wilson turned toward the corner, only to find himself at a red light. He was desperate to get away. In a minute or so, the area would be in gridlock as emergency vehicles rushed to the scene and passersby panicked at what they were seeing. Wilson watched in horror as a sightless woman with suppurating skin ran blindly into the Escalade, then reeled away in the other direction, her mouth open in a silent scream.

His own vision was beginning to fray at the

edges. It was just a flicker at the side of his eye, but he knew where it was going. The pattern was intricate and beautiful, scalloped and iridescent. In a couple of minutes, he'd be half-blind.

He heard sirens now, wailing in and out of harmony with the quavering cries of those who'd fled the courthouse. Already, traffic was grinding to a standstill as people got out to help, slowed to gawk, or succumbed to fender benders. On impulse, Wilson, turned the Escalade into the entrance to an underground parking lot that served the Civic Center.

Grabbing a ticket, he spiraled down to the third floor, pulled into a space, and sat, waiting for his sight to come back. It didn't seem like a good idea to sit in the truck so close to the scene. Even in the garage, under tons of concrete, he could hear the sirens, a layered wailing effect that sounded like women ululating.

He stayed in the Escalade for what seemed like a long time, although he couldn't be sure of the duration. Neither his watch nor the digital numbers on the dashboard were legible to him. A waterfall of light danced in front of him.

Taking out his wallet, he fumbled for the picture of Irina that he carried. Holding it in the palm of his hand, he tried to focus on it.

At first, he couldn't be sure if he was looking at the picture, or at its back. But then, her face began to appear, almost like a simulacrum. Finally, it snapped into focus. The almond-shaped eyes, her bright smile.

When he looked at his watch, he almost laughed. He'd been disabled for less than ten minutes. Even so, he'd hoped to be on his way to the airport by now, the idea being to abandon the Escalade in a satellite lot and rent something else for the drive to Vegas.

That was out of the question now. Traffic would be frozen for hours around the court-house and Civic Center. The best thing to do, he decided, was to leave the Escalade right where it was. Walk to the BART station, and get to the airport that way.

On foot, there was nothing to incriminate him. His laptop looked ordinary enough, and his suit-case could stay where it was, locked in the truck.

Plan B, then, Wilson thought, and walked quickly to the elevator.

Once outside, he kept going, head down, walking quickly. It was hell on a beautiful day. At the BART station, a red-haired woman was bab-bling about 'a freak fire at the courthouse — they say a boiler blew, and lots of people were burned.'

A black man in a Zegna suit and Hermès tie nodded knowingly: 'Superheated air.'

At the airport, people were clustered around television monitors, shaking their heads incredu-lously. On-screen, a platinum blonde reporter stood in front of the Civic Center, commenting on the scene in a smaller screen that showed people in spacesuits, or what looked like space suits, toddling in and out of the courthouse. The reporter was doing her best to keep her composure, but she was breathless and obviously rattled by what she'd seen. 'No one — I can't find *anyone* — with any idea about who, or what, is responsible for this.'

45

Still weary with jet lag, Burke decided to spend the night in Fallon. He took a room at the Holiday Inn Express and ate dinner at a Mexican joint called La Cocina. Returning to the motel, he went to bed at ten, thinking he had traveled thousands of miles to see Mandy Renfro. For nothing.

He didn't have a clue as to what he was going to do in the morning. Go to the casino. Put whatever he had in his wallet on red, and watch the ball go around and around. Or maybe he'd just play blackjack until the world came to an end. That would be a plan.

As it turned out, he slept nearly twelve hours, waking up a little before ten. When he stumbled downstairs to see if he could still catch the free continental breakfast, he knew right away that there had been another event. Despite the lateness of the hour, a dozen people were still in the breakfast room, clustered around a television.

On the screen, figures in HazMat suits were carrying stretchers to a fleet of ambulances standing haphazardly at the curb, while police kept a crowd at bay in front of what looked like a government building. Paramedics were treating people on the sidewalk.

'Where *is* that?' Burke asked. Never taking his eyes from the screen, the man next to him replied, 'Frisco.'

'What happened?'

The man just shook his head. 'A lot of people are dead.'

The screen shot changed to a press conference, where the city's mayor, standing next to the chief of police, was insisting earnestly that there was 'no evidence of biological agents.'

A reporter asked: 'Was this a terrorist attack?'

The chief of police rambled through a series of evasions.

An elderly woman close to the TV spoke up. 'Someone said the temperature went through the roof. They said it happened all at once. What's *that* all about?'

Burke poured himself a cup of coffee. He'd just taken a sip when a plume of sensation shot through his chest. The federal courthouse in San Francisco was where Jack Wilson had been tried.

★ ★ ★

Later that day, Burke sat at a booth in the Cowboy Diner, drinking coffee from a thick mug and looking at his notebook. A television droned above the bar.

The authorities in San Francisco were leaning toward an explanation that involved a malfunction in the building's heating system. So far, no one had connected the event with Culpeper.

Burke flipped through the pages of his notebook, searching for leads that he might have overlooked. In the end, he found only one. A scribbled note that read

There was a telephone number next to it, and it took him a moment to remember how he'd come up with it. *The hotel clerk in Belgrade. For another twenty euros,* Burke thought, *I could probably have gotten a DNA sample.*

He went back to his room around eight, stopping to buy a phone card at a convenience store. God only knows how much it would cost to call Ukraine from a Holiday Inn.

Sitting on the bed with the phone, he punched in about twenty numbers and listened to the recorded message. Finally, he went for Option 5: talk to a representative.

Five minutes of Europop ensued, while Burke stared at the screen on the muted television. Stretchers and gurneys in the hallways of a hospital. Harried doctors coming out of a burn ward. Body bags and hapless officials.

He was tempted to hang up. Five minutes of Europop was a *lot,* especially when he didn't think anything was going to come of it. He was just basically crossing his *t*'s and dotting his *i*'s. He wasn't expecting the call to go anywhere.

Finally, a voice interrupted the music. 'Yes, hello? This is Olga Primakov.'

'Hi — '

'I am sorry to make you wait, but it is very late here.'

Burke hadn't even thought about that. 'I'm really sorry — '

'Is better the website, yes?' Olga said. 'You can see pictures of brides. But maybe . . . you don't have computer?'

'That's right,' Burke told her. 'I don't. Not where I am.'

'Perhaps the library — '

'Actually, I got your number from a friend. Jack Wilson?'

'Oh *yes*, I'm meeting him at Romantic Weekend. Of course.'

Burke sat up straight, and snapped off the television with the remote. 'He told me about that!'

'So Jack Wilson gives you this number. Wonderful! You are also looking for a pretty bride?'

Bride? Had Wilson *married* one of these women? Where did he find the time?

'The ring he's giving Irina — oooooh, is super-fantastic,' Olga gushed.

'Yeah,' Burke agreed, 'it's a great ring.' He pounced on the name. 'Irina's thrilled with it!'

'So big!'

'Well, that's Jack. He never does anything halfway. But that's why I'm calling. I wanted to give them a *present*, you know, and I was wondering where I should send it.'

Olga hesitated. 'But you can take it to the wedding,' she told him. 'Is soon, I think. Tomorrow or next day.'

'Ri-iighht,' Burke replied, 'but . . . where is it, anyway?'

There was a long silence, and then: 'You don't be . . . *invited*?'

'Oh, yeah, of course I was, but . . . I'm on the road, and I left the invitation at home, so — '

'I'm sorry,' Olga told him, 'I am not permitted to provide this . . . information. Only Madame Puletskaya can give this. And like you, she's traveling. But I know she calls Wednesday.' She paused. 'You're in U.S.?'

'Yes.'

'What is your time zone?' she asked crisply.

'Rocky Mountain.'

'Oh yes? Then I arrange she calls you — Rocky Mountain, eight to noon. Yes?'

'Yeah, sure, but — '

'Please? Your number? I am giving it to her on Wednesday.'

Burke recited the telephone number of the motel, and said, 'The problem is . . . that's a week! And — '

'Sorry. Is best I can do!' Then she thanked him. And hung up.

46

Seated at his desk, Ray Kovalenko shook his head and swore quietly to himself, then threw his hands in the air and half growled, half shouted, 'Shit!'

He'd turned his office upside down, and checked the clothes he'd been wearing. To no avail. The index card was nowhere to be found.

As for Burke, he was MIA. It wasn't just that he didn't answer his phone. The Garda was looking for him, and no one had seen the man for days.

The father-in-law, Aherne, was about as much help as a dose of the clap. *Feck off!*

Kovalenko had gone to the trouble of locating and contacting Burke's family in Virginia, but they seemed genuinely surprised to learn that their son wasn't in Dublin. (And that the FBI was looking for him.)

So he had racked his brain, trying to remember what Burke had said about d'Anconia — and who he was. He'd been to Belgrade. He'd been in Allenwood. He'd gone to UCLA. Or USC. One of those places. None of it was any help without a name, a *real* name, and Kovalenko didn't have a clue. *Sounds like . . .* It

497

was on the tip of his tongue, and then it was gone. *Williams* . . .

Meanwhile, Andrea Cabot called twice a day, once in the morning and again in the afternoon. He was dodging her.

In the end, it took a trip to Dublin and a large serving of crow before Tommy Aherne would even agree to see him. And then it was only to negotiate. He wanted the indictment dropped, the sanctions lifted, and a new passport for Burke.

'Done!' Kovalenko agreed.

'And there's the issue of compensation — '

'Compensation? Compensation for what?'

'Business lost,' Aherne told him.

'I can't — '

'Then I'll suppose you'll be on your way,' Aherne told him, taking the FBI agent by the elbow, and turning him toward the door.

Kovalenko froze. After a moment, he said, 'I can give you a letter.'

'And what would I do with a letter?' Aherne asked.

'As Legat, I'll acknowledge that a mistake was made. And that it was our fault.'

'You mean, *your* fault,' Aherne told him.

'Exactly. It was *my* fault. You can do what you want with the letter. I'm sure your solicitors will think of something.'

Aherne grunted his grudging assent, and went for pen and paper.

When the letter was written, and the ink blown dry, Aherne said, 'Michael's in the States, isn't he?'

498

'Where?'

'Nevada,' the old man told him.

'Where in Nevada? It's a big state!'

Aherne shrugged. 'Dunno,' he said. 'If he calls, I'll tell 'im you want a word.'

At first, Kovalenko thought the old man had tricked him, and that he was lying. But, eventually, he accepted the depressing truth. The old fart didn't know where his son-in-law was. And no, Burke hadn't said anything to him about d'Anconia's real identity.

'But didn't he tell you all about it?' Aherne asked. 'He said he went to London. Were you not in, man?'

★ ★ ★

It took only a day to confirm that Michael Burke had entered the United States from Ireland two days earlier, passing through immigration control at JFK. Credit card information revealed that Burke flew to Reno from New York, and rented a car from Alamo. A green Hyundai with California plates.

But that was it. Kovalenko contacted the FBI office in Las Vegas, and asked them to put out a BOL for Burke's rental car.

Then, seventy-six hours and seven phone calls after Andrea Cabot's initial call, Kovalenko persuaded his contacts in the Garda to visit Burke's apartment. 'We're getting information from a confidential, but very reliable source that Mr. Burke is a victim of foul play. If you could visit the apartment discreetly, just to see if he's

499

dead on the floor, we'd be very grateful. Oh! and while you're there, hopefully this morning, maybe you could make a copy of the hard drive on his computer and shoot it over to me . . . '

Eighteen hours later, he had the name of 'the American' Andrea was screaming about.

Wilson. Jack Wilson.

47

LAS VEGAS JUNE 16, 2005

Wilson was impatient — and worried that Irina had run into some kind of trouble at Immigration. Where was she? Her flight had landed half an hour ago. He stood with his double bouquet of red roses, looking for her in the parade of humanity streaming through Security.

He felt sorry for them. They were thrilled to be in Vegas — you could see it on their faces — but if they were here on June 22, they were going to be in for a rough time. The city was as artificial as that place in the Middle East, where they had the 'underwater restaurant.' A metropolis in the middle of nowhere, Vegas boasted nineteen out of twenty of the largest hotels in the world. And it was almost entirely dependent on the kindness of technology. The hotels would be uninhabitable in the absence of air-conditioning. (This June, temperatures were around a hundred degrees most days.) And what would they drink? The water supply depended on pumps that run on electricity, and even the dams allocating water around the state relied on state-of-the-art electrical systems using digital technologies. The water would be gone in a tick of the clock.

Forty miles away, Lake Mead would become a

mecca once everyone realized that the grid wouldn't be coming back 'up.' Not soon. Not ever. Maybe a few of them would think of Culpeper, and realize what was happening. But what they wouldn't know, and couldn't guess, was that this time they couldn't just walk to the next town. This time there was nowhere to go. This time the whole country was going down and, with it, the world.

Just getting to Lake Mead would be difficult for most of them. It was forty miles through high desert, so it wasn't as if they'd be able to carry much in the way of food and water. Eventually, the ones who survived would defend their access to water, build defensive perimeters, and retribalize. How long would that take? A month? Two, at the most.

Vulnerable people passed him. A woman in a wheelchair, a mother with an infant in a sling, a very obese man. They wouldn't have a chance. And neither, of course, would Mandy. He'd been tempted to bring her to the B-Lazy-B. But he'd resisted, hardening his heart to his purpose. Mandy was the past, and the past was something he could not risk revisiting.

The P.A. system was delivering its message about 'unattended luggage' when he finally saw Irina, a hesitant figure in blue, wheeling a black suitcase. She was scanning ahead, looking for him, a sweet furrow of concern in her forehead. He raised his hand and his voice: 'Irina!' And when she turned to see him, her face uncoiled into a child's unfettered delight. Her joy at seeing him bowled him over. He felt a rush of euphoria.

And then she was in his arms — sweet-smelling, real, a dream come true.

★ ★ ★

Showing Irina around Las Vegas was like taking a child to Disneyland. Wilson was more than indifferent to the pleasures the city offered, but her happiness gave him so much pleasure that, like an indulgent parent, he couldn't stop smiling.

She gaped at the casinos on the way from the airport, practically bouncing with excitement. She oohed and aahed at the lobby in the Mirage, and once they were in their suite, ran around like a little kid. 'Oh you are joking me! This is *our* room?!' She left no corner unexplored — delighted with the minibar, the toiletries, the television, the lavish bathroom, the gigantic bed. She threw herself on it, giggling and bouncing.

He joined her there and when they kissed, Wilson felt it in every molecule. Soon they were beginning to make love. She unbuttoned his shirt. She widened her eyes when she saw the tattoos. 'You have . . . pictures,' she said.

'Ummm-hmmmm.'

She traced the dragonfly with a finger, then ran her lips along the outline of the crescent moon. Raising her head, she saw the unfamiliar words emblazoned on his chest. 'And this? What is this meaning?'

Wilson smiled. 'It means, 'Don't be afraid.' '

As her lips moved to the words, he reached for

the buttons of her blouse, and she squirmed away.

'What?' he said, as he got up to turn out the lights, then climbed back into bed.

'I like the dark,' she whispered, and who was he to argue with her? Beyond the window, through the privacy sheer, the city glittered like a strange galaxy.

Afterward, she wrapped herself in a sheet and, blushing, closed herself into the bathroom to dress. When she came back, he opened a split of champagne. They drank a toast 'to us,' and went down to the casino. Wilson showed her how the games were played, and her glee at hitting a ten-quarter payoff at the slots was so endearing that even the most hardened gamblers smiled. Her wide-eyed apprehension as she sent the dice flying across the table, and her look of expectation and alarm as the roulette ball raced around the wheel, was pure gold.

It was the first time in a long time that Wilson had been happy. He'd been living on adrenaline the last few months, going from Allenwood to Washington, then Dublin, Belgrade, Bled, and Beirut. Odessa and Bunia, and places in between. Moving the money, buying the ranch, building the weapons. Then Culpeper and San Francisco, with Maddox as the filling.

It left him with a feeling of unreality, as if he'd been playing at being himself. It was a role of his own devising, that was true — he'd written the script. But the constant need to stay within himself and his emotions, to be on guard and always in the moment . . . it had taken a toll.

But now Irina was here and everything was different. There was something about her that made him feel solid and of a piece. Just being with her restored him to himself.

Later that evening, at the White Chapel, Irina's fantasy unfolded with the sweetness and precision of a sequel to *Shrek*. Las Vegas was a cluster of homages to the real thing: New York, Paris, Venice, and Cairo — the list went on and on. In the same way, a wedding in the White Chapel was a tricked-out version of the traditional ceremony. A chapel, yes, but not a church. Attendants and witnesses, of course, but strangers. 'Close strangers.' Flowers and scattered rose petals and wedding cake and photos — unplanned by the bride, but definitely a part of the package.

Getting married in Vegas was like hiring an interior decorator. It was a massive invasion of privacy, but that was okay, because they knew best. They really did.

Irina's elation at every detail transformed the ceremony. She emerged from the dressing room in an ankle-length satin sheath, hand-beaded with pearls by her mother, her cheeks rosy with excitement. 'My God, she's blushing,' one of the paid attendants whispered. 'We've actually got a blushing bride!' When they repeated their vows, Irina's voice shook with emotion. As Wilson slipped the ring on her finger, she beamed at him. Before the minister could grant permission, she threw herself into his arms. 'I am loving you, Jack Wilson!' she caroled. 'I am so lucky woman.'

He didn't know what to say. He didn't have a lot of experience making people happy.

'Now we go home?' she asked.

Wilson nodded. 'Yeah,' he said, 'now we go home. Let's go home.'

48

FALLON, NEVADA JUNE 21, 2005

A week can be a very long time. Long enough so that the woman who refilled the coffee urns and cereal dispensers in the breakfast room began to greet Burke with a friendly smile. 'How're *you* today?' she'd ask, realigning doughnuts and bagels between incursions of eaters.

He was ready to go back to Dublin. But he figured he might as well play the string out and wait for Madame Puletskaya's call. Then he could honestly say he'd done everything he could do. And there was a chance, a Super Lotto kind of chance, that Wilson himself would show up — at Mandy's, in Fallon. Maybe Burke would get lucky.

Meanwhile, he explored.

He went to Pyramid Lake, and then out to Grimes Point, where a millennium earlier Jack Wilson's ancestors had carved petroglyphs into the boulders. You could be standing there in the front of the glyphs, gazing into the past, while right behind you matte-black fighter jets — Tomcats and Hornets — took off and landed at the Naval Air Station.

Tuesday. June 21.

Would Madame Puletskaya even call? He sat in a chair beside the bed in his room, with a newspaper at his feet, silently rehearsing his friend-of-the-groom voice. *She says/I say* . . . It was almost ten when the phone rang. He lifted the receiver to his ear. 'Hullo?'

'This is Madame Puletskaya. Good morning!'

He introduced himself.

Olga must have briefed her because she got right to the point. 'You are friend of Jack's, you say? But how do I know this?'

'I'm a good friend of Jack's,' he told her. 'He gave me your number. Told me to call. To tell you the truth, he's so delighted with Irina, he thought I might have the same luck.'

He could almost hear Madame Puletskaya's crusty exterior cracking like packed ice. 'Beautiful girl,' she said. 'I am so happy for them. Very sweet, maybe shy — you like shy girl also?'

He didn't know what to say. 'Yeah! Shy girls are . . . something!'

'If you are signing up for our service,' she told him, her voice manifestly shrewd, 'for the Sweet Sixteen, you get sixteen pictures and e-mail contact is all. For the Great Eight, you get photos and complete biographies of eight girls, e-mail contact, one letter translated, and one delivery of flowers. This is better deal. Is more selective. And for friend of Jack, I'm especially picking only most beautiful girls. One hundred twenty-five euros. Maybe one hundred fifty dollars. You have computer? Is extra to send, but if you like, we can do FedEx.'

'About Jack — '

'We settle business first, okay? You prefer

508

Great Eight, yes? Is better deal. And you have computer?'

He got the picture. She might be willing to talk about Jack, but she wanted to make a sale first. 'Yes,' he said, 'I have a computer.'

'We take Visa and Master. Also PayPal, if you prefer.'

He pulled out his wallet, and read off the numbers from his Visa card. When she had finished giving him directions on how to access his 'Great Eight,' he asked her again. 'The thing is, about Jack and Irina — '

'You go to wedding?

He paused, realizing he didn't know if the wedding had occurred or not. 'I . . . *no*,' he said, 'but I'd really like to send a present.'

'Very nice, yes, for bride couple.'

'The thing is, Jack gave me his new address, but I don't have it with me.'

She hesitated, but she came through. 'Oh? Is beautiful place, my goodness! Irina shows me pictures. She is lucky lucky girl.' He heard typing on a keyboard, and then, as he held his breath, he listened as she read out the address.

'Post Office Box one-two-four, Juniper, Nevada.' She gave him the zip code.

'Thanks so much,' he said, thinking — *shit*, a post office box. 'Do you have a telephone number?' He was thinking that he might be able to pull up a street address using a reverse-lookup directory.

The Russian was quiet for a moment, then

said. 'This, I don't release. Privacy rules, yes?'

'It's just that sometimes FedEx wants a phone number, that's all.'

'There is possibility of UPS,' she told him. Then changed the subject. 'Such a couple!' she declared. 'This one, I can tell it works out. Sometimes, you can tell . . . no! It's . . . what do you say? A train wreck! But this one? This one is marriage made in heaven. And for Irina? I am so happy for this girl. If nothing else, God forbid, at least she gets good medical care.'

Burke thought he'd misheard. 'Medical care?'

'Sure! You have best medical care in America. I tell her this.'

'That's what they say.'

'In Ukraine, it's not so good. Doctors, they are all becoming taxi drivers and waiters. I can't blame them. It's more money. So . . . U.S.? It's better for my little Irina.'

'Is she . . . ill?'

'No-no-no-no-no-no-no. She's *perfectly* healthy, of course! Her condition, it's perfectly under control. Ukrainebrides guarantees this: healthy young women. Every girl can have children.'

'But she has a condition,' Burke said. 'If I'm going to hook up with someone — '

'Yes, but I'm telling you it's not serious.'

'I understand, but . . . ' He could sense her thinking on the other end of the line, worrying that she was about to lose a client.

'Okay,' she said, 'but maybe you don't mention this, okay? Irina, she's shy about this. You're promising?'

'Not a word. I just want to be sure — for myself.'

'Well,' Madame Puletskaya said with a sigh, 'it's like this . . . '

★ ★ ★

A post office box might not be the most useful address, but it was all Burke had. And when he looked up the location of Juniper, it seemed like it just might be enough. Juniper was a speck (Pop. 320) near the Idaho border, the kind of place where people would know about the new guy in town, especially if the new guy had a lot of money.

It was close to noon when he checked out. And he was beginning to worry. For the first time, the question arose in his mind: *What if I actually find the sonofabitch? Then what?* As he recalled, Francisco d'Anconia was kinda big. And, seemingly, pretty fit. Which wasn't surprising when you considered that he'd spent the last ten years doing push-ups, lifting weights, and jogging around his cage.

Fortunately, this was Nevada, and gun stores were about as common as Dunkin' Donuts shops in Massachusetts. On the way out of town, he passed a store with a rearing wooden Grizzly outside, and a sign that read 'Gun & Sun.' Making a U-turn, he parked in the lot and went inside. It was a gun store that doubled as a tanning salon.

The girl behind the counter couldn't have been more helpful. She would probably have

511

sold him an RPG, if he'd asked. But there was a problem. 'The phones are down,' she said.

'So what?' Burke asked, eyeing a sleek Beretta.

'We have to do an instant check with the state police before we can sell you a gun — to see if you have a criminal record. You don't have a criminal record, do you?' she teased.

'No,' Burke replied.

'Sometimes they're down for a minute — if there was a storm, or something? But sometimes it's an hour or more. You want to wait? I could put you in one of the pods at the back, get you some color.'

Burke shook his head. 'Not today. I'm kind of busy. How about a gun show? They don't have to do a check, do they?'

'No. And you can get anything you want at one of them. Only I don't think there *is* one until the weekend,' she told him. 'And we'll have our phones up before then. You sure you don't want to get a tan?'

'No, but . . . is that a cell phone?' He pointed to a glass case, which held an arsenal of handguns and miscellanea. A crossbow. Some kind of . . . wands. Cell phones.

'It *looks* like a cell phone,' she said. 'But it's a stun gun. One hundred eighty thousand volts.'

'What do you do with it?' Burke asked.

'Basically, you just touch someone and . . . he kinda loses it.' She paused. 'I could sell you that!' she said. 'Cuz it's nonlethal.'

★ ★ ★

He took I-95 to I-80 and followed it all the way to Elko. Eight hours later, he veered north in the direction of Jackpot. Soon, the pavement gave way to dirt and gravel. He drove on in a cloud of dust, locking headlights with a single car.

It was close to ten p.m. when the darkness brightened a few miles ahead. Juniper. The town consisted of two stick-built houses, facing each other across the road, and a cluster of trailers. 'Downtown' was a post office, a general store, and a bar with a sign that read BUCKET OF BLOOD.

The saloon reminded Burke of the nightmare bar in Quentin Tarantino's vampire film, but it was the only place that was open — and he was thirsty.

★ ★ ★

The Bucket of Blood had been decorated at the whim of its eccentric owner. Driven by a solar battery, a porcelain Hello Kitty sat on the bar, waving its paw unceasingly. A collection of dusty plastic horses marched along a ledge near a sign for the restroom. There was an entire wall covered with postcards, and a television set framed by a rack of elk antlers.

The Diamondbacks were at bat.

In a corner of the bar, a poker game was in progress. An old woman — her scalp visible beneath her thin red hair — pulled listlessly at one of the slots near the door. Burke bellied up to the bar, where a weedy man in a camouflage jumpsuit lifted his chin with a questioning look, as he dried a glass.

'Beer,' Burke said.

'Sierra Nevada's on draft. Coors Light, Bud, Bud Light — '

'Sierra Nevada would be grand.' He was so tired that he didn't really want to get into it. What he wanted was to go to bed. So he was halfway into his second beer before he got up the gumption to ask the question.

'You know a guy named Jack Wilson . . . lives around here?'

The bartender eyed him warily. 'Who wants to know?'

Burke was about to answer, when one of the poker players looked up and laughed. 'What do you care who wants to know, Denny? It's not like the guy's a friend of yours.'

'Maybe not, but what do you care if *I* care?' the bartender asked. 'Play the fuckin' game.'

'Yeah! Play the fuckin' game,' one of the other players said.

'You in or not?' asked a third.

Burke didn't know whether to laugh or cry.

The bartender put a glass of beer in front of him, and raised an eyebrow. 'So?'

Burke took a sip. 'Jesus, that's good.' After a moment, he added, 'Mike Burke.'

'Denny.' The bartender polished another glass.

Burke sighed. 'Wilson's foster mother is sick.'

'No shit,' the bartender replied, his voice thick with skepticism.

'No,' Burke said. 'Really, she's in a trailer, over in Fallon. The only address she had for him is a

514

P.O. box. I said I'd try to find him, but . . . '

'She ain't been up here?'

Burke shook his head. 'No. But he hasn't been up here all that long himself.'

The bartender thought about this for a moment. 'About three, four months is all,' he said.

'Building a plan-e-tar-i-um,' one of the poker players remarked.

'He's not building a *planetarium*,' the bartender corrected, 'he's just building a place for a telescope.'

'Big difference,' the poker player declared. 'He's still stargazin'.'

The bartender ignored everyone, his eyes on the television.

Burke wanted to get to the point, but he sensed that if he tried to rush it, he wouldn't get anything out of these men.

'I'll bet he's stargazin' right now,' said one of the players at the card table. 'You got your solstice tomorrow. Longest day of the year.'

'That concerns the *sun*,' the bartender told him.

'Uhhh, Denny?' the poker player said. 'The sun's *a star*?!' The other players at the table laughed.

The bartender turned to Burke. 'This foster mother,' he said, 'she doesn't have his telephone number?'

A shout rose up from around the card table. '*H-whoaa!* The Bat was bluffin'! The Bat was bluffin' your ass!'

The lady at the slot machine came over to the bar and pushed her glass toward Denny. She had the wistful eyes of a child, and a weather-beaten face. She was forty or sixty, Burke couldn't be sure. The bartender mixed her a 7 & 7, then turned to Burke and pointed west.

'It's about sixty miles,' he said. 'Nice place. National forest all around him.' He drew a tiny map on the back of a coaster, keeping up a running commentary as he made it. 'There's a blue trailer on your right, all beat to shit. Got some of them pink flamingo statues in the front. You see that, you hang a left, and it's about fifteen miles from there. You'll see the sign over the fence. B-Lazy-B. Can't miss it.'

'Bull*shit!*' someone exclaimed.

The bartender smiled. 'Well, yeah, I guess you could miss it, but . . . ' He handed the coaster to Burke. 'What are you drivin'?'

Burke shrugged, and laughed to himself. 'I forget. It's a rental.'

'Off-road?'

'No.'

The bartender leaned back. 'But it's an SUV, right?'

'No. It's just . . . a sedan.'

An incredulous wince. 'Well, that's gonna be exciting.'

The slot machine gushed, and a siren went off. A waterfall of coins crashed to the floor. The woman just stared.

'You want one for the road?' the bartender asked.

Before Burke could answer, one of the poker players corrected him. 'You mean one for the goat track!'

Everyone laughed.

Burke, too.

49

Burke rolled the trip counter in the dash to zero, and took it slow.

He had to. The road was so washboarded that twenty-five miles an hour amounted to reckless driving. He could taste the grit in his mouth, and he was thirsty. But there was nothing he could do about it. He'd forgotten to bring any water — not good planning if you think Armageddon is just around the corner. Or, more accurately, up ahead and to the left.

Somewhere around the thirtieth mile on the trip counter, he began to yawn. It was the beer, he told himself, a self-indulgent mistake. He turned on the radio. All he could get was a country-and-western station out of Boise. He turned it up, but it didn't help. A couple of times, he almost nodded off, but was jolted awake by a pothole. He rolled down the windows.

The effect was instantaneous. The freezing desert air hit him in the face like a bucket of ice water. Falling asleep was no longer a danger. What with the noise, the dust, and the cold, he was uncomfortable enough to stay awake without having to work at it. And the stars were amazing. Distinct and glittering, with the Milky Way draped across the night like a bridal veil.

He rolled up the windows, thinking he'd rather die in a crash than freeze to death. At least, it would be quicker.

Three hours later, he was hunched over the steering wheel, using his windshield wipers against the dust and bug spatter. He was looking for the blue trailer with the pink flamingos, and he was worried. Wilson's ranch was so isolated that surprise was out of the question. He'd see the headlights from a long way off, and even if Burke were to kill the lights (without somehow killing himself), the noise was inescapable. The car sounded like an avalanche of rebar tumbling down a mountainside.

If he saw the ranch soon enough, he could leave the car and walk in. But 'soon enough' was a big question mark in the wide-open spaces he was driving through. And if Mandy was right about this solstice thing, Wilson wouldn't be asleep at all. He'd be getting ready to dance.

He'd fire the transmitter at first light, Burke thought. And that would be the end of it.

Though, who knew what Wilson was planning to do. If he wanted, he could probably vaporize half the country, à la Tunguska. Just clear-cut the place, from sea to shining sea. *But he won't do that*, Burke told himself. *Wilson was about the Ghost Dance, and the Ghost Dance was all about the land. Loving the land.* So it wouldn't be Tunguska on a grander scale. It would probably be a reprise of Culpeper, but bigger. If Wilson could permanently disable the electrical and electronic infrastructure of the country, it would be a disaster of geological dimensions. Nearly every economy in the world would crash, and millions would die. People everywhere were

518

dependent on modern technology for everything from food and water to transportation, medicine, and lighting. It would be the end, if not of the world then of the last five hundred years of progress. It would be 1491, all over again.

The idea was so outrageous that Burke didn't want to take it seriously. It kept spinning away, like the radio signal out of Reno. The body count in San Francisco had 'stabilized' at 342. Police were looking for . . .

A new signal overrode the old. *Repent.*

Ten minutes later, a clusterfuck of pink flamingos materialized in the headlights in front of a darkened blue trailer, about fifty feet from the road. As Burke drove past, he saw that someone had sprayed the trailer with the words, 'Bad Dog!' written large.

Two miles farther along, Burke turned left as he'd been told to do, and immediately, the road got worse. The washboards were now so tall and deep and insistent that it seemed to Burke that the car's undercarriage wouldn't be able to take it. Then the road rose up, and the car began to climb the side of a mountain — a feature the bartender had sketched as an inverted V.

His ears popped as he maneuvered through a series of hairpin turns, his headlights strafing the mountainside on his right, then shining off into the abyss on his left. Suddenly, a jackrabbit sprang into the car's path and, reflexively, Burke slammed on the brakes.

Big mistake.

The car began to surf, riding the washboards, even as its rear wheels fishtailed out of control, spraying gravel. The sedan was moving on its own now, sliding over the road as if it were made of ice. Its relationship to the steering wheel and brakes was suddenly theoretical. In the end, the only thing that stopped the slide was the mountainside itself. The car slammed into a runoff beside the road. The chassis shrieked. There was a thud, a crunch, and the sideview mirror was airborne. Then the car came to a sudden and complete stop, one headlight shining toward the stars, the other in smithereens at the base of a wall of red rock.

Burke took a deep breath, and looked out the window, where the jackrabbit was contemplating with satisfaction his destruction of a once serviceable Nissan Sentra. Burke didn't know whether to laugh or cry, but was leaning toward the latter. *At least I wasn't going downhill,* he told himself. If he had been, the skid would have taken him over the edge.

He tried the ignition.

Again and again. But there was no way it was going to start, and even if it did, Burke doubted he'd be able to get the car out of the ditch. Not without a tow truck. And even then, it wouldn't be drivable.

He leaned in through the driver's window, and squinted at the trip counter: 51.2. That meant he had about nine miles to go before he got to the ranch. *About.*

Not that he had any choice. Reaching into the car, he grabbed his new 'cell phone,' and started walking.

It was harder than he'd expected, because he couldn't really see. The road itself was easy enough to distinguish because it was paler than the abyss to his left and the rocks to his right. But whenever he tried to pick up the pace, he stumbled over rocks or stepped into a pothole. Twice, he went sprawling, and turned his ankle badly enough that it hurt like hell. He was thirsty, but there wasn't anything he could do about it. A cloud of gnats hung in the air around him. They didn't bite, but they got in his eyes, forcing him to stop and knuckle one out every few minutes.

After an hour of this, he began to cramp up.

It seemed like forever since he'd left the saloon in Juniper, but when he looked at his watch, he saw that he'd been gone only about five hours. During that time, he'd thought a lot about what he was doing, and why. His obsession with finding Wilson, he decided, wasn't really about saving Tommy Aherne's business. That was just an excuse, and even Tommy didn't believe it. Eventually, the courts would resolve the matter, and that would be the end of it. No, Burke's interest in Wilson was deeper, and darker than that. It was . . . what? The good guy's version of 'suicide by cop.' Burke's pursuit of Wilson was suicide by terrorist, and it amounted to the same thing.

He hadn't wanted to live anymore. Not without Kate. Or so he'd thought. But somewhere along the line, this had begun to change. Slowly, and then all at once. He didn't know when it had happened. There wasn't *a moment* when everything changed. These stars . . .

So all of a sudden, he needed a plan about what to do when he got to the ranch. Because getting himself killed had suddenly lost its attraction. Trudging over the uneven ground, he thought about it long and hard; and slowly, a plan began to form. And it was pure genius: first, he'd get inside. And then he'd knock Wilson out.

★   ★   ★

It was five fifteen a.m. when he reached the entrance to the ranch, which announced itself with a sign on a lodgepole over the driveway. The sign read 'B-Lazy-B.' *Cute*, Burke thought.

About half a mile up the drive, a smattering of landscape lights glowed in the darkness. Over to the east, or what he guessed was the east, the sky was beginning to fade from black. One by one, the stars were winking out.

Burke crunched up the drive, alarmed by the noise his footsteps made. It wasn't really bright enough to see very well, but the house was something, a sprawling stone-and-timber affair set in a little mountain meadow. A rustic mansion that reminded Burke of something you'd see at an upscale ski resort. Jackson Hole, maybe, or Telluride.

Flagstone steps curved through a grove of pine trees to the front door. Burke avoided them, and went around to the back, where another door

522

opened onto the kitchen. He felt like a burglar, and worried that the snare drum in his chest would give him away. He tried the door, and it opened easily. *They're in bed*, he decided. Which didn't make sense, unless Burke was wrong about the solstice, or unless Wilson had changed his mind.

He stood in the kitchen with the phony cell phone in his hand, and waited for his eyes to adjust to the absence of stars. In the silence, he imagined the faint sound of music, as if there were a radio, way off in the woods. Then he moved quietly through the house, room by room, praying that Wilson didn't have a dog. Would a stun gun even work on a dog? Was fur *a conductor?*

Wilson's bedroom — number five, by Burke's count — was at the far end of the house. The bed was unmade, and a flowered bridal tiara rested, wilting, on a vanity crowded with little bottles of perfume. Beside the tiara was a photograph in a silver frame. Burke studied it in the moonlight.

It was a picture of Wilson in a tuxedo, with his arm around a blonde in a wedding dress. They were standing together in a gazebo, surrounded by flower arrangements, and Burke saw that she was wearing the tiara he'd found. Outsized gold and silver bows decorated the posts on either side, and a wall of candles burned in front of a stained-glass window. Burke couldn't tell if they were inside, posing on a kind of movie set, or if they were outdoors. But the affection they felt for each other was unmistakable. They were radiant. Beaming.

And somewhere else.

Burke sagged against the window frame. He didn't know whether to laugh or cry. He'd come all this way, and there was no one home.

He let himself out, and began to walk back the way he'd come. It was over now. Except . . . there was that music again, and the sound of laughter. It was a woman's laugh, he thought, but . . . where was it coming from? He turned in his tracks, this way and that, but it was gone now, muted by a breeze through the pines.

Then he saw it — a smudge of light in the treetops. A tall structure with crisscrossed timbers. It looked to be about half a mile away. It was a tower with a room at the top. Like Wardenclyffe.

On the horizon, the mountains were silhouetted against a pink seam that was just beginning to form. Burke turned toward the tower, and continued walking, certain that Wilson was there with his weapon and his woman.

As a bird began to sing, he picked up his pace, thinking, *Not good, not good.* He hurried on, but he was so tired that his progress was slow. Every once in a while he had to stop, hands on hips, his breath coming in ragged heaves. He was at a high altitude and he wasn't used to it.

And then he was there, at the base of the tower. He waited a minute until his breath came easier, listening to the muffled voices and music above his head.

Then he took to the winding staircase, and

began to climb. He was doing his best to be quiet, but the steps were metal and he might as well have been banging a drum.

'Jack?!' It was a woman's voice, and there was alarm in it.

Burke paused, and activated the stun gun. Then he resumed climbing, faster now, heading for the little cabin atop the superstructure. Access was through a hole in the floor above his head, a kind of trapdoor that was open. In the darkness on the stairs, it seemed to Burke that he was climbing toward the sun.

The music was gone now.

Two more flights of steps. He paused again to catch his breath, and stared at the door in the floor. The only way to enter the cab at the top was headfirst. If Wilson had a baseball bat, he could swing for the fences, and that would be the end of it.

Burke weighed his options. He could go up. Or he could go down. He went up, taking the stairs two at a time, arriving finally at the top — out of breath, and with a submachine gun staring him in the face.

The woman in the photograph was at Wilson's side, her mouth open, eyes wide with alarm. Behind Wilson, Burke could see what he guessed was the weapon. It looked like a telescope, mounted on a turret. It was aimed at the heavens, through what appeared to be an open skylight. A retractable roof, of sorts.

'Who the fuck are you?' Wilson asked. 'Get in here.' He gestured with the gun.

Burke came through the trapdoor, moving

525

slowly. Irina backed away.

He was halfway through when Wilson said, 'Hold it.'

Burke froze.

'What's that?' Wilson asked, and stepped on his hand.

'Cell phone,' Burke said.

Wilson reached down and took it away. Tossed it onto a chair in the corner. Beckoned Burke to come all the way into the cab. 'Who were you calling?'

Burke thought fast. 'Police. They're on their way.'

Wilson nodded. 'They'll never get here,' he said. Suddenly, he frowned. 'You're the guy from *Ireland.*' He laughed, incredulously. 'What are *you* doing here?'

Burke opened his mouth, but gave up. What was the point?

Wilson just shook his head. 'Irina,' he said, 'please sit down. Enjoy your wine.' He gestured to a pair of Adirondack chairs that flanked a small table. On the table were a candelabra, two champagne flutes, and a bucket of ice. A telephone sat on the floor.

The woman was in a panic, Burke saw. Her eyes flew between the two men. 'Is all right?' she asked, her voice trembling.

'Yeah,' Wilson said with a laugh. 'It's fine. This is Mr. Aherne — '

'Burke. Actually, it's — '

'Mr. Burke,' Wilson said with an apologetic nod. He turned toward Irina. 'Mr. Burke's a long way from home.'

'Like me,' she said, with a nervous smile.

'No,' Wilson said. 'Not like you. You *are* home. This is your home, sweetheart.'

She blushed. 'But why he is — ?'

Wilson cut her off with a gesture. 'I'm afraid we don't have a third glass,' he said. 'I wasn't expecting guests. It's kind of an old-fashioned celebration. Stay up till dawn. Greet the solstice. That kind of thing.'

Burke glanced around. He took in the candelabra, the only source of illumination in the cabin. It occurred to him that Wilson might have fired the transmitter already. It was almost light outside, and out here, how would you know if the world had ended? The landscape lights had been on, but . . . were they *still* on? 'Did you pull the trigger?'

'Not yet,' Wilson told him.

'Trigger?' This from Irina.

He's going to kill me, Burke thought. *But not in front of his bride.*

'Is that it?' Burke asked, gesturing at the transmitter.

Wilson nodded. 'You seem to know a lot. How'd you find us?'

'Ukrainebrides,' Burke replied.

Irina brightened. 'You know Madame Puletskaya?'

'Yeah,' Burke said. 'We're old friends.'

Wilson glanced outside. 'I think it's time,' he said. 'Why don't you sit over there?' He gestured toward the chair where he'd thrown the 'cell phone.'

Burke went over to it, and sat down.

'Do me a favor,' Wilson said.

'What's that?'

'Just stay off the phone.' With a look of warning to Burke, he laid his gun down on a table next to the transmitter, and began to attach a cable to a laptop on the floor.

Burke watched Wilson go about his business, and thought about the people he'd seen on television, their faces deranged by loss. Loss was something Burke understood, just as he understood what the people in the courthouse must have felt when the temperature began to soar inside their skin. Burke knew what it was like to be badly burned. It was a terrible way to die. A bullet would be better.

And he was going to get one, anyway. Sooner or later.

So he stopped thinking, and came out of the chair so fast that Wilson couldn't grab his gun quickly enough. Irina screamed, and a glass crashed to the floor as Burke plowed into the bigger man, driving him into the wall. The two men fell to the floor, wrestling. Burke had one arm around Wilson's neck, and was punching him with the hand that held the cell phone. But he was no match for the Indian. The guy was just too strong.

Though Wilson was on the bottom, he got a hand on Burke's neck and began to squeeze. Burke felt the air fly from his lungs, even as his thumb found the activator on the cell phone. He slammed the phone into Wilson's neck and, in an instant, there was a staticky crackle, and Wilson began to go limp. *Jesus Christ*, Burke thought, *it's working! It's actually —*

Lights out.

When he came to, about five minutes later, he was sitting in one of the Adirondack chairs, bleeding from his good ear, which Irina had clobbered with the candelabra.

Wilson stood next to the transmitter. Irina was pointing the submachine gun at Burke, crying softly to herself. 'Why is crazy man coming here?' she asked. 'What does he want? Jack!'

Wilson shook his head, typing on the laptop. 'He wants things to stay the way they are.'

'We call police, okay?' she asked.

'Well . . .'

'But he attacks you!'

'It doesn't matter,' Wilson told her. Then he turned to Burke. 'That was cute,' he said. 'A real surprise.'

'Thanks,' Burke replied. He brought his hand away from his ear and stared at the blood on it.

Wilson returned his attention to the computer.

Then they heard it — a *thwop thwop* sound, outside the tower. They turned and looked, and saw it right away: a helicopter hovering about a hundred yards from the ranch house.

Burke couldn't believe it. It could only be Kovalenko. Or someone sent by Kovalenko. He'd given the guy enough to figure it out. Once Culpeper and the courthouse got their attention, it wouldn't have been all that hard for the Bureau to find Wilson and the B-Lazy-B. They certainly had the resources. So the cavalry had arrived.

Too late.

'They friends of yours?' Wilson asked.

529

Burke shook his head. He would have laughed, but there was too much at stake and, besides, he hurt too much.

'I don't think the helicopter's going to be a problem,' Wilson said, typing furiously. 'In about a minute, it's going down. Everything is.' He looked out the window. 'Why are they at the house?'

'Because the guy who's running the operation is an idiot, that's why,' Burke explained.

Wilson nodded. 'I'm not surprised.'

'Why is there helicopter?' Irina asked.

'It's the police,' Wilson told her. 'They're coming to arrest Mr. Burke.'

'Good,' she said.

Wilson turned back to the laptop. In the distance, a bullhorn began to call his name. He shook his head.

'We should tell them where we are,' Irina said.

'In a minute,' Wilson replied.

'I thought you guys were in love,' Burke suggested.

Wilson paused, and turned to look at him.

'We are,' Irina insisted, proudly.

'What's that got to do with you?' Wilson asked.

'Nothing, I guess, but . . . you're gonna kill her with that thing,' Burke told him. 'Seems like a helluva way to end a honeymoon.'

'You don't know what you're talking about,' Wilson replied. 'It's not like a bomb.'

'I know,' Burke said. 'But . . . she's got a pacemaker.'

Wilson stared at him. Finally, he said, '*What?*'

'Irina. Has. A. Pacemaker.'

Wilson blinked a few times. Then he laughed. 'Good try,' he said. 'Full marks.'

But Irina started to cry. 'And how you are knowing this?' she demanded. 'This is my secret!' Her whimpers deepened into the soft sobs of a distraught child.

''Rina?' Wilson went to her side, his voice so soft it was barely audible.

'I don't want you to know,' she said, 'I am damage goods. Is why I make love with you in dark. No way you see scar. Is ugly.' She wailed. 'Now you're not wanting me!'

A strange smile came to Wilson's face. He gave an almost imperceptible shake of his head. Then he went to her, and crouched by her side. 'Show me,' he said, taking the submachine gun from her.

She complied, sobbing in the way little kids do, taking shuddery breaths. She fumbled at the buttons to her blouse, and finally pulled it aside, baring the scar. Wilson ran his finger along the ridgeline of skin, then pressed his lips to it.

Burke felt like a voyeur. He turned away.

'I love you,' Wilson told her, his voice thick with emotion.

'I — ' Her voice fell apart. The sobs came heavier.

'Shhhhh,' Wilson said. 'I love you. I'll always love you.'

In the corner of the room, a telephone rang. It was the last thing Burke expected to hear and the sound startled him.

Wilson kissed the top of Irina's head and tried

to dry her tears with his fingertips. Her weeping subsided. The phone continued to ring.

Finally, Wilson got to his feet. Burke couldn't read the expression on his face. 'It's an extension from the house,' he said as he moved toward the ringing phone. He picked up the receiver. Listened. With a smile, he put the palm of his hand over the phone and turned to Burke. 'Somebody named Kovalenko wants me to come out of the house with my hands in the air. He says he knows I'm in there.'

Burke didn't know what to tell him.

Wilson said into the phone: 'Give me a minute.' Then he hung up, and slowly crossed the room to the transmitter. Laying his fingertips on the laptop's keyboard, he took a deep breath. And hesitated.

For a moment, it seemed to Burke that Wilson was screwing up his courage to derail the world. But that wasn't it at all.

Wilson was sailing in a secret storm between one dream and another, tossed this way and that by the uncertainties of his own heart. Love and revenge waited in the darkness, sirens singing from the reefs surrounding his imagined Paradise. He'd risked everything, and it had come to this: Which reef would he wreck himself upon? Love . . . or Revenge?

Finally, he exhaled. Jerking the plug from the laptop, he closed the computer and gave it to Burke. 'Don't let them get this. It wouldn't be good.'

Burke nodded.

'Get Irina out of here,' Wilson said. 'Away

from here, and away from the house. There's a footpath behind the tower. It goes to the hot springs. She can show you the way.'

'No,' Irina cried. 'I stay with you.'

Both Burke and Wilson ignored her. 'And what do I do, once I'm there?' Burke asked.

'Get rid of the laptop,' Wilson said. 'There are caves, and the one that's farthest west has a cenote, about thirty feet inside the entrance.'

'A cenote?'

'A well. It's actually a mine shaft. They used to mine silver here. Anyway, the well is a couple of hundred feet deep. So be careful. Way down, it's filled with water. If you drop a rock in, and count to six, slowly, you'll hear the splash. So toss the laptop in, and forget about it.'

Burke nodded. In truth, he wasn't even sure he could walk. His ribs hurt, and his head was pounding. But he wasn't going to argue. If Wilson was going to make a last stand, Burke didn't want to be there for the finale.

'Irina, sweetheart. I want you to go with Mr. Burke,' Wilson said.

'No, no Jack,' she crooned. 'Nooooo. I stay with you. I want — '

Wilson smiled teasingly. 'Already? Just a week ago, you promised to obey. C'mon,' he cajoled, 'you promised. Remember?'

Burke had no idea what was going through Irina's mind, but suddenly, she stopped weeping. She nodded her head solemnly, and kissed Wilson on the lips. A long kiss that Wilson ended, drawing away, holding her face in his hands.

'Go on,' Wilson told her.

Irina turned. She was weeping again but she began to climb down. Burke was right behind her.

★　★　★

Wilson watched them descend from the tower, and begin running. Burke was practically dragging Irina, though Wilson could see that he was in pain. Irina kept her eyes turned toward the tower all the while. And then the two figures were gone, lost amid the trees.

The phone rang, and Wilson picked it up. A voice shouted at him over the *thwop thwop thwop* of a helicopter's rotors: 'I'm losing patience!'

'You'll be lucky if that's all you lose,' Wilson told him.

'*What?!* Let me explain something to you,' the voice screamed. 'You got one chance to walk out of that house alive. Either you come out, now — or I'm *taking* you out! Which way do you want it?'

Wilson nearly laughed. The uncertainties he'd felt a minute earlier were gone now, replaced with an unfamiliar clarity and calm. He was not going back to prison. He'd rather die. And would. Soon.

He could escape, of course — for a little while, anyway. He could lose himself in the trees, then make his way into the mountains. Like Geronimo. He could hide for a while, moving from place to place, scavenging food and shelter.

But what was the point? Better to die like a man than live like a dog.

And it was, as they say, a good day to die — the *right* day to die. The solstice.

'Wilson!' The FBI agent's voice crackled over the phone.

'I'm thinking . . . '

In fact, he'd made up his mind. But he had to get their attention before they turned their guns on the house and burned it to the ground. Irina would need the house. He could tell that she was going to love it here.

Grabbing the Ingram, he went to the window and smashed the glass. Without even bothering to aim, he fired a long burst in the direction of the helicopter — and then another. And another. The chopper swayed, jerked upwards, and turned toward the lookout tower.

Wilson laid the submachine gun on the floor. Straightening to his full height, he stripped to the waist, revealing the ghost shirt that was his flesh — the crudely etched crescent moon and dragonfly, the stars and birds, and the words in Paiute:

> *when the earth trembles,*
> *do not be afraid.*

Through the broken window, he saw the helicopter bearing down on the tower. Slowly, he began to dance, singing a song without words.

★ ★ ★

Running through the trees, Burke and Irina stumbled over the rocky ground, heading toward the hot springs. They were almost there when a burst of submachine-gun fire shattered the morning air. The volley of shots was answered a moment later by the distant *thwop* of the helicopter, growing louder and more urgent.

My God, Burke thought. *He's drawing them to the tower.* Irina was sobbing. Burke expected to hear a fusillade of gunfire, but what he heard instead was a zipper of noise, a sort of *whoosh*, followed by a blaze of light and a shock wave that threw the two of them to the ground.

Irina quaked in terror as a second explosion, and then a third, shook the trees around them. Looking up, they saw a pillar of black smoke churning into the sky. The tower was gone.

Irina screamed.

Burke grabbed her by the arm and pulled her toward the hot springs. 'Wait for me,' he told her and, getting to his feet, ran toward the caves. It took him a minute to find the one Wilson had told him about.

It was dark and damp, and he moved gingerly into the blackness, feeling his way with his hand on the wall, sliding his feet across the floor. When his right foot found the edge of something, he gave the laptop a little toss. And listened.

There was no sound. And then, just as Wilson promised, he heard a splash.

Returning the way he'd come, he called out to

Irina. But, of course, she wasn't there. She was on her way back to the tower, Burke thought, or to what was left of it. Looking for love. Or what was left of it.

It was something they had in common.

EPILOGUE

NAIROBI FEBRUARY 2006

Burke sat at a table outside the Giraffe Cafe, sipping strong, hot coffee. He was girding himself for a long day at the ministry, getting the necessary permissions for a convoy carrying food and medical supplies to southern Sudan. Dealing with the bureaucracy was like taking apart a set of matryoshka dolls. You had to keep going until you reached the innermost bureaucrat, whose magic stamp would provide passage through the checkpoints.

Ordinarily, he spent most of his time in remote villages or refugee camps, so he was enjoying the bustle of the city, the chance to pick up his mail, make phone calls, and read the papers.

He'd talked with Tommy the night before. 'Business is grand,' the old man reported. 'Maybe too good. Any chance of you coming back?'

Burke laughed.

'So when d'you come for a visit?'

Burke said he wasn't sure.

'Just like Katie. She'd never say.' Another pause, and then: 'Jay-sus, I almost forgot! Here's a bit o' news'll make you laugh. I got this off Billy Earnshaw — who's a mate of that Garda fella.'

'Doherty?' Burke asked.

'The very man!'

'So, what's up?'

'Remember that shite, Kovalenko? You won't believe it, but they're givin' the bleedin' eejit a medal! For meritorious service!'

'You're kiddin' me.'

'I couldn't make it up, Michael. That's a great country you've got!'

★   ★   ★

Most of his mail consisted of bills and junk, but he did have one real letter — in a lavender envelope. It was from Irina.

After the 'event,' Burke had stayed on in Nevada for a few days, more or less holding her hand, while keeping Kovalenko at bay.

He'd driven her to Fallon and introduced her to Mandy. The two of them got along like a house on fire, and Mandy took her under her wing. They organized a memorial service for Wilson, which was well attended by high school and college friends, a couple of teachers, and a tribal rep from Pyramid Lake. Eli Salzberg and Jill Apple made the trip from their respective coasts.

It was Mandy who got Irina a lawyer. The government was making noises about seizing Wilson's assets as 'ill-gotten gains.' But Wilson had been clever in covering his tracks, at least in so far as the money was concerned, and with the lawyer's help, his widow got to keep it all. She wrote:

Six members of my family, are joining me at the ranch. And we have plans! Uncle Viktor takes me to visit the tribal council in Pyramid Lake. We learn that 1847 treaty grants land of B-Lazy-B to tribe, then later, government takes land back, and sells it to religious people. Now, we find way to return this land to tribe. Then I think we open Internet gambling site with B-Lazy-B as home base! First one in U.S., I think. Very excitement! Money for tribe, money for us. And here is other thing — big big news — I am having baby! Soon. Little girl! Please to tell me you will be godfather!

I am thanking you always for your help to me.

Much kisses, Irina.

After he left the cafe, Burke spent the rest of the day at the ministry, shuffling from official to official to get the proper permits. Although traveling with the convoy was by far the most dangerous part of his work — you never knew when a kid at a checkpoint would go nova — it was the days at the ministry that he disliked the most. Each bureaucrat required an investment of time, a kind of toll: three hours for this stamp, two hours for that, eight hours for a laissez-passer.

Once on the road, if you happened to pick a route that passed through ground temporarily held by rebel forces, these hard-won documents were not just worthless but incriminating.

Burke shifted in his chair, stretched his legs.

He'd noticed that the time of the wait tended to increase with the rank of the bureaucrat, a measure of sorts. It was hard to be patient when you knew the situation: that people were suffering and dying while they waited for the supplies to arrive. But Burke had learned the hard way that protest or complaint only increased the time of the wait.

Finally, at eight in the evening, he had all the papers in order. He dined with three of his fellow aid workers. When dinner was done and the others adjourned to the bar, Burke went up to his room. Like many of the rooms he stayed in, the air in this one seemed to be filled with dust. But that was all right. He associated the gritty taste with Africa.

And he was happy to be back. He stripped off his clothes, brushed his teeth with some water tipped onto his brush from a bottle, then settled himself on the bed, pulling the mosquito netting around him. The ceiling fan ticking in its slow rotation might have irritated some, but for Burke it was a kind of lullaby.

Every night, whether he was sleeping on a cot, in a bed, or in the back of one of the convoy's trucks, he sank into sleep with gratitude.

Months earlier, he'd complained to Tommy that Kate never came to him, as she had come to her father. But as soon as Burke returned to Africa, she was there, each night, in his dreams. It was pure solace. She was alive and well, funny and smart and full of insights about the work that he was doing. At times, she spoke seriously about what was and might have been. 'We only live for a moment, Michael — the moment we call the present. But it lasts forever, and so will the love we had.'

Sometimes, she stayed all night, unless he tried to keep her there — in which case, she dissolved in the night. Eventually, he realized that the only way to keep her was to let her go.

And so he did.

ACKNOWLEDGMENTS

For more about the 1890 massacre at Wounded Knee, and the source of Kicking Bear's quotations of Wovoka, see: www.bgsu.edu/department/acs/1890s/woundedknee/WKmscr.html.

Hakim's hashish-packaging activity was inspired by Howard Marks' account of a similar operation, which he describes in his extraordinary autobiography, *Mr Nice* (Martin Secker & Warburg, Ltd., London, 1996).

A second autobiography, this one by a former CIA officer, tells of his 1965 plane crash in the Congo, and of the infestation of his injuries by bees and other bugs. See *The American Agent*, by Richard L. Holm (St. Ermin's Press, London, 2003).

Four books were essential sources for the Tesla material in *Ghost Dancer*. First and foremost, Margaret Cheney's *Man Out of Time* is a mesmerizing read. Many anecdotes about Tesla's life and exploits were drawn from its entertaining pages. John J. O'Neill's *Prodigal Genius: The Life of Nikola Tesla* was another key source, as were David Peat's *In Search of Nikola Tesla* and George Trinkhaus' *Tesla: The Lost Inventions*. In addition, on-line sources provided invaluable details about Tesla and his inventions. Colonel Tom

Bearden's various sites are intriguing and filled with information, as are sites associated with Rick Andersen. Recommended also are sites of the Tesla Society and the New Tesla Society, as well as 'Confessions of a Tesla Nerd', by Marc J. Seifer, Ph.D. Timothy Ventura's essay 'Tesla's Death Ray' was helpful in envisioning how such a weapon might work. 'Radiant Energy: Unraveling Tesla's Greatest Secret, Part 1' by Ken Adachi (June 1, 2001) (http:educate-yourself.org) offers insights into Tesla's explorations of electrical phenomena — and photographs of the inventor and some of his inventions and experiments. The website of the Nikola Tesla Museum (www.tesla-museum.org) provides a wealth of information about the inventor. No physics text could come close to the wonderfully clear explanation of how the voice of an opera singer breaks glass — and other examples of 'forced oscillation resonance' — at the website www.straightdope.com.

Legends abound about Tesla and the Tunguska incident, yet there is abdundant evidence that a devastating event did occur in Siberia at the same time Tesla was experimenting with the transmitter at Wardenclyffe. The notion that Tesla's experiment *caused* the disaster, while not invented by the author, remains speculative. Numerous stories alleging that Admiral Peary stood as Tesla's would-be witness to a promised arctic light show are clearly apocryphal; records show that Peary was not in the arctic at the time of the Tunguska incident. Windjammer Stevenson, an arctic explorer very famous in his time, lived for a long period above the arctic circle, much as described in the pages of *Ghost Dancer*. However, although Stevenson was in the arctic at the time of the Tunguska incident, the notion that he was Tesla's 'witness' is an invention of the author's.

Various Internet sources served to enhance the author's understanding of the electromagnetic pulse, including the explanation of the e-bomb as a possible terrorist weapon available at www.unitedstatesaction.com/emp-terror.htm. Although both authors have visited maximum-security facilities, for operational and architectural detail about the federal government's Supermax facilities, the authors thank the indispensable Wikipedia — which also contains an excellent essay on directed-energy weapons.

In September 2004, the *National Geographic* magazine published a piece on Native Americans. The magazine included a supplemental map of North America. One side of the map provides detail about the linguistic families of Native Americans and their dispersal through the continent. The reverse side displays current tribal areas and populations in the continental United States. At the base of the main map, a series of four smaller maps, dated from 1775 to 2004, shows in graphic and dramatic fashion the transfers of land from native populations to settlers. Entitled 'Long History of Losing Ground', this series of maps served as the inspiration for Jack Wilson's similarly titled high school project.

Various online sources, including the Berkeley Law Journal (www.law.berkeley.edu) provide further elucidation of the 1951 Invention Secrecy Act and its ongoing application.

The authors would like to thank Elaine Markson and Gary Johnson at the Elaine Markson Agency for their unflagging support. We are grateful also to Ronald Johnson and Ezra Sidran for answering technical questions. David Grove, a pilot, helped with queries about what would happen to an aircraft hit with an electromagnetic pulse.

Any errors, of course, belong to the authors and may not be attributed to their sources.

And finally, many thanks to everyone at Ballantine who helped bring this book to the shelves of bookstores and libraries.

May 4, 2006
Charlottesville, Virginia

We do hope that you have enjoyed reading this large print book.

Did you know that all of our titles are available for purchase?

We publish a wide range of high quality large print books including:
Romances, Mysteries, Classics
General Fiction
Non Fiction and Westerns

Special interest titles available in large print are:
The Little Oxford Dictionary
Music Book
Song Book
Hymn Book
Service Book

Also available from us courtesy of Oxford University Press:
Young Readers' Dictionary
(large print edition)
Young Readers' Thesaurus
(large print edition)

For further information or a free brochure, please contact us at:
Ulverscroft Large Print Books Ltd.,
The Green, Bradgate Road, Anstey,
Leicester, LE7 7FU, England.
Tel: (00 44) 0116 236 4325
Fax: (00 44) 0116 234 0205

Other titles published by
The House of Ulverscroft:

THE MURDER ARTIST

John Case

As a foreign correspondent, Alex Callahan has covered famine, plague and war and knows what it is to be afraid. But terror grabs him when, on a summer afternoon, he finds himself enmeshed in the dark side. Amid the hurly-burly of a countryside Renaissance Faire, his six-year-old twins vanish without a trace . . .Then the phone call comes: silence. A plaintive voice — 'Daddy?' — completes Alex's nightmare and sets in motion a juggernaut of frenzy and agony . . .The longer the police search, Alex's certainty grows that time is running out. And when telltale signs reveal a hidden pattern of bizarre abductions, Alex vows to use his investigative skills to rescue his children from the shadowy figure dubbed the Piper.

THE WATER'S LOVELY

Ruth Rendell

One summer's day, Ismay's stepfather, Guy, was found dead in the bath. Now, nine years on, she and her sister Heather still live in the same house in Clapham. But it has been divided into two self-contained flats. Their mother lives upstairs with her sister, Pamela. And the bathroom, where Guy had drowned, has disappeared . . . Ismay works in public relations, and Heather in catering. They get on well. They always have. They never discuss the changes to the house, still less what had happened that day in August . . . But even lives as private as these, where secrets hang in the air like dust, intertwine with other worlds and other individuals. And, with painful inevitability, the truth will emerge.

THE SECOND HORSEMAN

Kyle Mills

Brandon Vale is a career thief, the best there is. He's never been caught — until he is arrested for a crime he didn't commit. Then, one night, he is broken out of prison by Richard Scanlon, the former FBI agent who framed him in the first place. Scanlon has discovered that a Ukrainian crime organization is auctioning twelve nuclear warheads to the highest bidder, but he can't convince the government that the sale isn't a hoax. His solution: arrange for Brandon to steal the $200 million necessary and buy the warheads himself. As the day of the warhead sale approaches, though, their plan begins to break down, and Brandon starts to suspect that the deal has higher stakes than he could ever have imagined . . .

BUTCHER

Campbell Armstrong

Detective Sergeant Lou Perlman is an outcast from police HQ, doomed by the chief superintendent to a seemingly infinite 'sicklist'. He's barred from investigating the bloodbath that has rocked the foundations of the city's lower depths. A new man has powered his way to the top of Glasgow's gangster fraternity: Reuben Chuck is a villain who promotes cruelty and murder whilst he pursues an inscrutable religious awakening of his own. A gruesome discovery made in Perlman's own house launches him into an enquiry that becomes fraught with perplexities — the whereabouts of his missing love, Miriam; body parts; a seemingly haunted house; dubious part-time surgeons; a mob of dangerous hooded teenagers; and his own family's history — all leading, inexorably, to the deathly terrain of Reuben Chuck.

THE COLD MOON

Jeffery Deaver

On a freezing December night, with a full moon hovering in the black skies over New York City, two people are brutally murdered. Their prolonged deaths are marked by eerie calling cards: moon-faced clocks ticking away the victims' last minutes on earth. Lincoln Rhyme and his team have only hours to stop the icy-cold, brilliant Watchmaker, whose obsession with time drives him to plan his carnage with the precision of a fine timepiece. Amelia is not only Lincoln's eyes and ears on the Watchmaker investigation. She's now, for the first time, lead detective on a homicide — a case that sets into motion clockwork gears of its own. A case with consequences which will endanger many lives, as well as Lincoln and Amelia's future together . . .